Rock On:
The Greatest Hits of Science Fiction & Fantasy

OTHER BOOKS EDITED BY
PAULA GURAN

Embraces
Best New Paranormal Romance
Best New Romantic Fantasy
Zombies: The Recent Dead
The Year's Best Dark Fantasy & Horror: 2010
Vampires: The Recent Undead
The Year's Best Dark Fantasy & Horror: 2011
Halloween
New Cthulhu: The Recent Weird
Brave New Love
Witches: Wicked, Wild & Wonderful
Obsession: Tales of Irresistible Desire
The Year's Best Dark Fantasy & Horror: 2012
Extreme Zombies
Ghosts: Recent Hauntings

Rock On:
The Greatest Hits of Science Fiction & Fantasy

Edited by Paula Guran

PRIME BOOKS

ROCK ON: THE GREATEST HITS
OF SCIENCE FICTION & FANTASY

Prime Books
www.prime-books.com

For more information, contact Prime Books:
prime@prime-books.com

ISBN: 978-1-60701-315-0

This one was always supposed to be for you, Erik.
Damn it.

Erik John Guran
October 6, 1989 – June 9, 2012

If you never heard him sing
I guess you won't too soon.
—"Tonight's the Night,"
Neil Young

Contents

Introduction: Liner Notes
Paula Guran

TRACK 1: "IS ROCK AND ROLL STILL RELEVANT?"

"Of course it is," he said, twenty-two and immersed in popular music of all kinds, a singer, composing his own stuff, with an encyclopedic knowledge of pop music.

"But it is really different now. Music is fragmented," I replied. "You can download anything—new, old, obscure, whatever—plug it in your ears. For people my age, people who shared the experience of the Beatles or Jimi Hendrix as kids, it was a generational thing. Glue. Music brought us together. We found meaning in listening to the same stuff, it shaped our attitudes."

"For my generation, rap is probably our 'meaningful' music. But you hear what we listen to—the best of rock, pop, R&B, jazz, world music. What survives will survive. That's what *classic* means."

"So rock's not dead? It doesn't just belong in the Rock and Roll Hall of Fame up the road in Cleveland or in the hearts of old fogies like me?"

"Mom. This is *Akron*. It's not just Devo and Chrissie Hynde. Now it's The Black Keys."

"Hey hey, my my, rock and roll will never die?"

"Yeah, but Neil Young is Canadian."

"Ha. Akron connection! Who inspired 'Hey, Hey, My, My'? Mark Mothersbaugh. Devo."

"Why do you *know* these things?"

"Rust never sleeps?"

"That's the other thing."

"What?"

"*We* communicate through it. You get my allusions. I get yours."

"So, for the record . . . I mean I'm asking you this stuff for this anthology . . . you are saying rock brings the generations together?"

"No."

"Oh."

"I gotta go."

Track 2: "It's Only Rock and Roll"

Please. Don't try to define it. You can't. Paraphrasing Billy Joel: funk, punk, old junk, blues, stews, reggae, shred play, hip-hop, good pop, Motown, no town, next phase, new wave, dance craze, anyways . . . it's still rock and roll to me.

Track 3: "I Don't See the Connection Between Science Fiction/Fantasy and Rock"

Doesn't matter who sang that tune, but someone did when hearing of this anthology. They were dead wrong. Which words fill in the blanks below, "rock" or "science fiction"?

"[Blank] asks, and sometimes tries to answer, all manner of questions. And it reflects a broad spectrum of attitudes, yearnings, fulfillments, fantasies. [Blank] can be personal or collective, apolitical or polemical. It can be banal or piercingly evocative."

The correct answer is *rock* and the quote is from music critic Nat Hentoff. But it could just as easily be science fiction. Speculative fiction writers and rock musicians both make up lies that tell us something about the truth of being human.

Track 4: "Long Cuts"

Outside of these stories and many other short works, there is a long tradition of science fiction and fantasy novels with rock and roll connections (or close enough, be it blues, R&B, or pop). Here's a list of some of the more notable, if not always recommended, novels (alphabetically by author):

Lost Souls (1992), Poppy Z. Brite
War for the Oaks (1982), Emma Bull
Synners (1991), Pat Cadigan
Wrack and Roll (1986), Bradley Denton
Buddy Holly Is Alive and Well on Ganymede (1991), Bradley Denton
Joplin's Ghost (2005), Tananarive Due
My Soul to Take (2011), Tananarive Due
Jim Morrison's Adventures in the Afterlife (1999), Mick Farren
Idoru (1996), William Gibson

Illyria (2006), Elizabeth Hand

Heart-Shaped Box (2007), Joe Hill

Bold As Love series: *Bold As Love* (2001), *Castles Made of Sand* (2002), *Midnight Lamp* (2003), *Band of Gypsies* (2005), and *Rainbow Bridge* (2006), Gwyneth Jones

Planet Earth Rock and Roll Orchestra (2001), Paul Kantner

Silk (1998), Caitlín R. Kiernan

Big Rock Beat (2000), Greg Kihn

Mojo Hand (2002), Greg Kihn

The Five (2012), Robert McCammon

The Armageddon Rag (1983), George R. R. Martin

Flesh Guitar (1998), Geoff Nicholson

Soul Music: A Novel of Discworld (1994), Terry Pratchett

WVMP Series: *Wicked Game* (2008), *Bad to the Bone* (2009), and *Bring on the Night* (2010), Jeri Smith Ready

The Vampire Lestat (1991), Anne Rice

First two books of Persephone Alcmedi Series: *Wicked Circle* (2009) and *Hallowed Circle* (2009), Linda Robertson

The Kill Riff (1988), David J. Schow (Okay, it is not sf or fantasy, but it *is* horror)

Glimpses (1993), Lewis Shiner

Deserted Cities of the Heart (1998), Lewis Shiner

City Come-A-Walkin' (1980), John Shirley

Eclipse (1985), John Shirley

Echo and Narcissus (2003), Mark Siegel

The Scream (1988), John Skipp and Craig Spector

Vampire Junction (1984), *Valentine* (1992), and *Vanitas* (1995), S. P. Somtow

Little Heroes (1987), Norman Spinrad

Orbital Decay (1989), Allen Steele

The Armageddon Chord (2011), Jeremy Wagner

Elvissey (1993), Jack Womack

Elizabeth Hand's *Illyria* deals with performance, but her other novels are often permeated with rock; the characters tend to be part of the lifestyle rather than musicians. Still, her novels *Black Light*, *Generation Loss*, and *Available Dark* are close to being "rock novels" (although I'm stretching genre definition here to include the last.)

Musicians often play roles in the work of Charles de Lint, but most would not term them rockers. Still, some of the flavor is there, especially in *The Onion Girl*.

Stephen King—who obviously wanted to grow up to be a rock star—frequently makes references to rock in his novels and it's integral to at least one short story ("You Know They Have a Helluva Band"). He's yet to write a novel with music integral to the plot; *Christine*, however, comes close to having a beat you can dance to.

Author Michael Moorcock has been closely connected to rock through the band Hawkwind and, to a lesser extent Blue Öyster Cult—he wrote lyrics for both, performed with the former as well as other bands—his fiction is often informed by rock, but seldom about it. Even though his enduring character Elric is the epitome of a rock-and-roll nihilist anti-hero, he's not a rock star. Another Moorcock character, Jerry Cornelius, manages to get involved in the music business in a non-genre novel written based on the the Sex Pistols mockumentary movie *The Great Rock 'n' Roll Swindle*.

Another nongenre novel, *Spider Kiss* (originally *Rockabilly*), was one of the first (1961) fictional dissections of rock-and-roll's ruinous lifestyle; it tells of the rise and fall of a manufactured rocker. Written pre-Beatles when rock looked like a passing fad (Buddy Holly died in 1959, Little Richard sang gospel from 1957-1962, Elvis Presley was in the army between March 1958 and March 1960, Jerry Lee Lewis was in disgrace, Alan Freed's career was over due to a payola scandal . . .) it presents an interesting perspective.

The Bordertown series of anthologies, although not novels, should also be noted. [Will Shetterly's YA novels *Elsewhere* (1992) and *Nevernever* (1993) also take place in the invented world, as does Emma Bull's *Finder* (2003).] The stories are set in a world, created by Terri Windling, "where magic meets rock and roll." In this city bordering both the human and the faerie worlds, neither magic nor technology follow any rules. Bordertown is famous for its music, and you can find just about any kind, but rock of many varieties is an important part of the mix. After a thirteen-year hiatus since the previous volume, anthology *Welcome to Bordertown*, edited by Holly Black and Ellen Kushner, was published in 2011.

TRACK 5: "(DON'T EVEN) START ME UP"

Since this is an anthology of fiction, I'm not going to get into speculative fiction's influence on rock—trust me, there's plenty of it. Science fiction fed rock from Sheb Wooley's "Purple People Eater" to David Bowie's *The Rise and Fall of Ziggy Stardust and the Spiders from Mars* to Parliament's *Mothership*

Connection to Radiohead's *OK Computer* to Nine Inch Nails' *Year Zero* to Janelle Monáe's *The ArchAndroid* . . . and continues to do so.

The same with fantasy: prog rock could never have progged without it, Led Zeppelin must have smoked J. R. R. Tolkien, Robert E. Howard still lives in heavy metal, H. P. Lovecraft has inspired numerous bands, and Alice Cooper was only the first to personify dark fantasy on stage with a backbeat. Hell, the roots of rock are tangled in fantasy: Robert Johnson supposedly met the devil at a crossroads and worried about a hellhound on his trail.

And no, I will not discuss "wrock."

Track 6: "Don't Get Me Wrong"

There are minor aspects to some of the older stories herein that demonstrate that speculation is just that: speculating. Who needs sockets in a wireless world? Digitized recording, downloads, *Guitar Hero*, Garage Band, iPods, and smartphones that can hold 28,000 songs, do-it-yourself distribution—who knew? Ultimately, old tech doesn't affect the heart and soul of any of these stories and there's still tech-yet-to-come (maybe) in many, in others the speculation has been at least somewhat fulfilled. Of course there's supernatural doings in some stories—but rock itself is magical and transformative.

Track 7: "Are You Experienced?"

[Test . . . test . . . one, two, three . . . rock and rollll!]

Welcome to the first (and, so far, only) anthology ever of science fiction and fantasy stories about rock and roll . . . although *about* may not be the proper word. Some of the stories are certainly about rock, others are more *informed* by the music, but rock and roll is integral to them all. Like the music itself, some stories are nice and easy, but some of these go to eleven . . . or maybe twelve.

Horns up!

Paula Guran
June 2012

Flying Saucer Rock and Roll
Howard Waldrop

They could have been contenders.

Talk about Danny and the Juniors, talk about the Spaniels, the Contours, Sonny Till and the Orioles. They made it to the big time: records, tours, sock hops at $500 a night. Fame and glory.

But you never heard of the Kool-Tones, because they achieved their apotheosis and their apocalypse on the same night, and then they broke up. Some still talk about that night, but so much happened, the Kool-Tones get lost in the shuffle. And who's going to believe a bunch of kids, anyway? The cops didn't and their parents didn't. It was only two years after the president had been shot in Dallas, and people were still scared. This, then, is the Kool-Tones' story:

Leroy was smoking a cigar through a hole he'd cut in a pair of thick, red wax lips. Slim and Zoot were tooting away on Wowee whistles. It was a week after Halloween, and their pockets were still full of trick-or-treat candy they'd muscled off little kids in the projects. Ray, slim and nervous, was hanging back, "We shouldn't be here, you know? I mean, this ain't the Hellbenders' territory, you know? I don't know whose it is, but, like, Vinnie and the guys don't come this far." He looked around.

Zoot, who was white and had the beginnings of a mustache, took the yellow wax-candy kazoo from his mouth. He bit off and chewed up the big C pipe. "I mean, if you're scared, Ray, you can go back home, you know?"

"Nah!" said Leroy. "We need Ray for the middle parts." Leroy was twelve years old and about four feet tall. He was finishing his fourth cigar of the day. He looked like a small Stymie Beard from the old Our Gang comedies.

File still wore the cut-down coat he'd taken with him when he'd escaped from his foster home.

He was staying with his sister and her boyfriend. In each of his coat pockets he had a bottle: one Coke and one bourbon.

"We'll be all right," said Cornelius, who was big as a house and almost eighteen. He was shaped like a big ebony golf tee, narrow legs and waist blooming out to an A-bomb mushroom of arms and chest. He was a yard wide at the shoulders. He looked like he was always wearing football pads.

"That's right," said Leroy, taking out the wax lips and wedging the cigar back into the hole in them. "I mean, the kid who found this place didn't say anything about it being somebody's *spot*, man."

"What's that?" asked Ray.

They looked up. A small spot of light moved slowly across the sky. It was barely visible, along with a few stars, in the lights from the city.

"Maybe it's one of them UFOs you're always talking about, Leroy," said Zoot.

"Flying saucer, my left ball," said Cornelius. "That's Telstar. You ought to read the papers."

"Like your mama makes you?" asked Slim.

"Aww . . . " said Cornelius.

They walked on through the alleys and the dark streets. They all walked like a man.

"This place is Oz," said Leroy.

"Hey!" yelled Ray, and his voice filled the area, echoed back and forth in the darkness, rose in volume, died away.

"Wow."

They were on what had been the loading dock of an old freight and storage company. It must have been closed sometime during the Korean War or maybe in the unimaginable eons before World War II. The building took up most of the block but the loading area on the back was sunken and surrounded by the stone wall they had climbed. If you stood with your back against the one good loading door, the place was a natural amphitheater.

Leroy chugged some Coke, then poured bourbon into the half-empty bottle. They all took a drink, except Cornelius, whose mother was a Foursquare Baptist and could smell liquor on his breath three blocks away.

Cornelius drank only when he was away from home two or three days.

"Okay, Kool-Tones," said Leroy. "Let's hit sonic notes."

They stood in front of the door, Leroy to the fore, the others behind him in a semicircle: Cornelius, Ray, Slim, and Zoot.

"One, two, three," said Leroy quietly, his face toward the bright city beyond the surrounding buildings.

He had seen all the movies with Frankie Lymon and the Teenagers in them and knew the moves backwards. He jumped in the air and came down, and Cornelius hit it: "*Bah-doo, bah-doo, bah-doo-uhh.*"

It was a bass from the bottom of the ocean, from the Marianas Trench, a voice from Death Valley on a wet night, so far below sea level you could feel the absence of light in your mind. And then Zoot and Ray came in: *"Oooh-oooh, ooh-oooh,"* with Leroy humming under, and then Slim stepped out and began to lead the tenor part of "Sincerely," by the Crows. And they went through that one perfectly, flawlessly, the dark night and the dock walls throwing their voices out to the whole breathing city.

"Wow," said Ray, when they finished, but Leroy held up his hand, and Zoot leaned forward and took a deep breath and sang: *"Dee-dee-woo-oo, dee-eee-wooo-oo, dee-uhmm-doo-way."*

And Ray and Slim chanted: *"A-weem-wayy, a-wee,-wayyy."*

And then Leroy, who had a falsetto that could take hair off an opossum, hit the high notes from "The Lion Sleeps Tonight," and it was even better than the first song, and not even the Tokens on their number two hit had ever sounded greater.

Then they started clapping their hands, and at every clap the city seemed to jump with expectation, joining in their dance, and they went through a shaky-legged Skyliners-type routine and into: *"Hey-ahh-stah-huh, hey-ahh-stuh-uhh,"* of Maurice Williams and the Zodiacs' "Stay," and when Leroy soared his *"Hoh-wahh-yuh?"* over Zoot's singing, they all thought they would die.

And without pause, Ray and Slim started: *"Shoo-be-doop, shoo-doop-de-be-doop, shoo-doop-be-do-be-doop,"* and Cornelius was going, *"Ah-rem-em, ah-rem-em, ah-rememm bah."*

And they went through the Five Satins' "(I Remember) In the Still of the Night."

"Hey, wait," said Ray, as Slim *"woo-uh-wooo-uh-woo-ooo-ah-woo-ah"*-ed to a finish, "I thought I saw a guy out there."

"You're imagining things," said Zoot. But they all stared out into the dark anyway.

There didn't seem to be anything there.

"Hey, look," said Cornelius. "Why don't we try putting the bass part of 'Stormy Weather' with the high part of 'Crying in the Chapel'? I tried it the other night, but I can't—"

"Shit, man!" said Slim. "That ain't the way it is on the records. You gotta do it like on the records."

"Records are going to hell, anyway. I mean, you got Motown and some of that, but the rest of it's like the Beatles and Animals and Rolling Stones and Wayne shitty Fontana and the Mindbenders and . . . "

Leroy took the cigar from his mouth. "Fuck the Beatles," he said. He put the cigar back in his mouth.

"Yeah, you're right, I agree. But even the other music's not the—"

"Aren't you kids up past your bedtime?" asked a loud voice from the darkness.

They jerked erect. For a minute, they hoped it was only the cops.

Matches flared in the darkness, held up close to faces. The faces all had their eyes closed so they wouldn't be blinded and unable to see in case the Kool-Tones made a break for it. Blobs of faces and light floated in the night, five, ten, fifteen, more.

Part of a jacket was illuminated. It was the color reserved for the kings of Tyre.

"Oh shit!" said Slim. "Trouble. Looks like the Purple Monsters."

The Kool-Tones drew into a knot.

The matches went out and they were in a breathing darkness.

"You guys know this turf is reserved for friends of the local protective, athletic, and social club, viz., us?" asked the same voice. Chains clanked in the black night.

"We were just leaving," said Cornelius.

The noisy chains rattled closer.

You could hear knuckles being slapped into fists out there.

Slim hoped someone would hurry up and hit him so he could scream.

"Who are you guys with?" asked the voice, and a flashlight shone in their eyes, blinding them.

"Aww, they're just little kids," said another voice.

"Who you callin' little, turd?" asked Leroy, shouldering his way between Zoot and Cornelius's legs.

A *wooooooo*! went up from the dark, and the chains rattled again.

"For God's sake, shut up, Leroy!" said Ray.

"Who you people think you are, anyway?" asked another, meaner voice out there.

"We're the Kool-Tones," said Leroy. "We can sing it slow, and we can sing it low, and we can sing it loud, and we can make it go!"

"I hope you like that cigar, kid," said the mean voice, "because after we piss on it, you're going to have to eat it."

"Okay, okay, look," said Cornelius. "We didn't know it was your turf. We come from over in the projects and . . ."

"Hey, man, Hellbenders, Hellbenders!" The chains sounded like tambourines now.

"Naw, naw. We ain't Hellbenders. We ain't nobody but the Kool-Tones. We just heard about this place. We didn't know it was yours," said Cornelius.

"We only let Bobby and the Bombers sing here," said a voice.

"Bobby and the Bombers can't sing their way out of the men's room," said Leroy. Slim clamped Leroy's mouth, burning his hand on the cigar.

"You're gonna regret that," said the mean voice, which stepped into the flashlight beam, "because I'm Bobby, and four more of these guys out here are the Bombers."

"We didn't know you guys were part of the Purple Monsters!" said Zoot.

"There's lots of stuff you don't know," said Bobby. "And when we're through, there's not much you're gonna *remember*."

"I only know the Del Vikings are breaking up," said Zoot. He didn't know why he said it. Anything was better than waiting for the knuckle sandwiches.

Bobby's face changed. "No shit?" Then his face set in hard lines again. "Where'd a punk like you hear something like that?"

"My cousin," said Zoot. "He was in the Air Force with two of them. He writes to 'em. They're tight. One of them said the act was breaking up because nobody was listening to their stuff anymore."

"Well, that's rough," said Bobby. "It's tough out there on the road."

"Yeah," said Zoot. "It really is."

Some of the tension was gone, but certain delicate ethical questions remained to be settled.

"I'm Lucius," said a voice. "Warlord of the Purple Monsters." The flashlight came on him. He was huge. He was like Cornelius, only he was big all the way to the ground. His feet looked like blunt I-beams sticking out of the bottom of his jeans. His purple satin jacket was a bright fluorescent blot on the night. "I hate to break up this chitchat—" he glared at Bobby "—but the fact is you people are on Purple Monster territory, and some tribute needs to be exacted."

Ray was digging in his pocket for nickels and dimes.

"Not money. Something that will remind you not to do this again."

"Tell you what," said Leroy. He had worked himself away from Slim. "You think Bobby and the Bombers can sing?"

"Easy!" said Lucius to Bobby, who had started forward with the Bombers.

"Yeah, kid. They're the best damn group in the city."

"Well, *I* think we can outsing 'em," said Leroy, and smiled around his dead cigar.

"Oh, jeez," said Zoot. "They got a record, and they've—"

"I *said*, we can outsing Bobby and the Bombers, anytime, any place," said Leroy.

"And what if you can't?" asked Lucius.

"You guys like piss a lot, don't you?" There was a general movement toward the Kool-Tones. Lucius held up his hand. "Well," said Leroy, "how about all the members of the losing group drink a quart apiece?"

Hands of the Kool-Tones reached out to stifle Leroy. He danced away.

"I like that," said Lucius. "I really like that. That all right, Bobby?"

"I'm going to start saving it up now."

"Who's gonna judge?" asked one of the Bombers.

"Same as always," said Leroy. "The public. Invite 'em in."

"Who do we meet with to work this out?" asked Lucius.

"Vinnie of the Hellbenders. He'll work out the terms."

Slim was beginning to see he might not be killed that night. He looked on Leroy with something like worship.

"How we know you guys are gonna show up?" asked Bobby.

"I swear on Sam Cooke's grave," said Leroy.

"Let 'em pass," said Bobby.

They crossed out of the freight yard and headed back for the projects.

"Shit, man!"

"Now you've done it! I'm heading for Florida."

"What the hell, Leroy, are you crazy?"

Leroy was smiling. "We can take them, easy," he said, holding up his hand flat.

He began to sing "Chain Gang." The other Kool-Tones joined in, but their hearts weren't in it. Already there was a bad taste in the back of their throats.

Vinnie was mad.

The black outline of a mudpuppy on his white silk jacket seemed to swell as he hunched his shoulders toward Leroy.

"What the shit you mean, dragging the Hellbenders into this without asking us first? That just ain't done, Leroy."

"Who else could take the Purple Monsters in case they wasn't gentlemen?" asked Leroy.

Vinnie grinned. "You're gonna die before you're fifteen, kid."

"That's my hope."

"Creep. Okay, we'll take care of it."

"One thing," said Leroy. "No instruments. They gotta get us a mike and some amps, and no more than a quarter of the people can be from Monster territory. And it's gotta be at the freight dock."

"That's one thing?" asked Vinnie.

"A few. But that place is great, man. We can't lose there."

Vinnie smiled, and it was a prison-guard smile, a Nazi smile. "If you lose, kid, after the Monsters get through with you, the Hellbenders are gonna have a little party."

He pointed over his shoulder to where something resembling testicles floated in alcohol in a mason jar on a shelf. "We're putting five empty jars up there tomorrow. That's what happens to people who get the Hellbenders involved without asking and then don't come through when the pressure's on. You know what I mean?"

Leroy smiled. He left smiling. The smile was still frozen to his face as he walked down the street.

This whole thing was getting too grim.

Leroy lay on his cot listening to his sister and her boyfriend porking in the next room.

It was late at night. His mind was still working. Sounds beyond those in the bedroom came to him. Somebody staggered down the project hallway, bumping from one wall to another. Probably old man Jones. Chances are he wouldn't make it to his room all the way at the end of the corridor. His daughter or one of her kids would probably find him asleep in the hall in a pool of barf.

Leroy turned over on the rattly cot, flipped on his seven-transistor radio, and jammed it up to his ear. Faintly came the sounds of another Beatles song.

He thumbed the tuner, and the four creeps blurred into four or five other Englishmen singing some other stupid song about coming to places he would never see.

He went through the stations until he stopped on the third note of the Monotones' "Book of Love." He sang along in his mind.

Then the deejay came on, and everything turned sour again. "Another golden oldie, 'Book of Love,' by the Monotones. Now here's the WBKD pick of the week, the fabulous Beatles with 'I've Just Seen a Face.'" Leroy pushed the stations around the dial, then started back.

Weekdays were shit. On weekends you could hear good old stuff; but mostly the stations all played Top 40, and that was English invasion stuff, or if you were lucky, some Motown. It was Monday night. He gave up and turned to an all-night blues station, where the music usually meant something. But this was like, you know, the sharecropper hour or something, and all they were playing was whiny cotton-choppin' work blues from some damn Alabama singer who had died in 1932, for God's sake.

Disgusted, Leroy turned off the radio.

His sister and her boyfriend had quit for a while, so it was quieter in the place. Leroy lit a cigarette and thought of getting out of here as soon as he could.

I mean, Bobby and the Bombers had a record, a real big-hole forty-five on WhamJam. It wasn't selling worth shit from all Leroy heard, but that didn't matter. It was a record, and it was real, it wasn't just singing under some street lamp. Slim said they'd played it once on WABC, on the *Hit-or-Flop* show, and it was a flop, but people heard it. Rumor was the Bombers had gotten sixty-five dollars and a contract for the session. They'd had a couple of gigs at dances and such, when the regular band took a break. They sure as hell couldn't be making any money, or they wouldn't be singing against the Kool-Tones for free kicks.

But they had a record out, and they were working.

If only the Kool-Tones got work, got a record, went on tour. Leroy was just twelve, but he knew how hard they were working on their music. They'd practice on street corners, on the stoop, just walking, getting the notes down right—the moves, the facial expressions of all the groups they'd seen in movies and on Slim's mother's TV.

There were so many places to be out there. There was a real world with people in it who weren't punching somebody for berries, or stealing the welfare and stuff. Just someplace open, someplace away from everything else.

He flipped on the flashlight beside his cot, pulled it under the covers with him, and opened his favorite book. It was Edward J. Ruppelt's *Report on Unidentified Flying Objects*. His big brother John William, whom he had never seen, sent it to him from his Army post in California as soon as he found Leroy had run away and was living with his sister. John William also sent his sister part of his allotment every month.

Leroy had read the book again and again. He knew it by heart already. He couldn't get a library card under his own name because the state might trace him that way. (They'd already been around asking his sister about him. She lied. But she too had run away from a foster home as soon as she was old enough, so they hadn't believed her and would be back.) So he'd had to boost all his books. Sometimes it took days, and newsstand people got mighty suspicious when you were black and hung around for a long time, waiting for the chance to kipe stuff. Usually they gave you the hairy eyeball until you went away.

He owned twelve books on UFOs now, but the Ruppelt was still his favorite. Once he'd gotten a book by some guy named Truman or something who wrote poetry inspired by the people from Venus. It was a little sad, too, the things people believed sometimes. So Leroy hadn't read any more books by people who claimed they'd been inside the flying saucers or met the Neptunians or such. He read only the ones that gave histories of the sightings and asked questions, like why was the Air Force covering up? Those books never told you what was in the UFOs, and that was good because you could imagine it for yourself

He wondered if any of the Del Vikings had seen flying saucers when they were in the Air Force with Zoot's cousin. Probably not, or Zoot would have told him about it. Leroy always tried to get the rest of the Kool-Tones interested in UFOs, but they all said they had their own problems, like girls and cigarette money. They'd go with him to see *Invasion of the Saucermen* or *Earth vs. the Flying Saucers* at the movies, or watch *The Thing* on Slim's mother's TV on the *Creature Feature*, but that was about it.

Leroy's favorite flying-saucer sighting was the Mantell case, in which a P-51 fighter plane, which was called a Mustang, chased a UFO over Kentucky and then crashed after it went off the Air Force radar. Some say Captain Mantell died of asphyxiation because he went to 20,000 feet and didn't have on an oxygen mask, but other books said he saw "something metallic and of tremendous size" and was going after it. Ruppelt thought it was a Skyhook balloon, but he couldn't be sure. Others said it was a real UFO and that Mantell had been shot down with Z-rays.

It had made Leroy's skin crawl when he had first read it.

But his mind went back to the Del Vikings. What had caused them to break up? What was it really like out there on the road? Was music getting so bad that good groups couldn't make a living at it anymore?

Leroy turned off the flashlight and put the book away. He put out the cigarette, lit a cigar, went to the window, and looked up the airshaft. He leaned way back against the cool window and could barely see one star overhead. Just one star.

He scratched himself and lay back down on the bed.

For the first time, he was afraid about the contest tomorrow night.

We got to be good, he said to himself. *We got to be good*.

In the other room, the bed started squeaking again.

• • •

The Hellbenders arrived early to check out the turf. They'd been there ten minutes when the Purple Monsters showed up. There was handshaking all around, talk a little while, then they moved off into two separate groups. A few civilians came by to make sure this was the place they'd heard about.

"Park your cars out of sight, if you got 'em," said Lucius. "We don't want the cops to think anything's going on here."

Vinnie strut-walked over to Lucius.

"This crowd's gonna be bigger than I thought. I can tell."

"People come to see somebody drink some piss. You know, give the public what it wants." Lucius smiled.

"I guess so. I got this weird feelin', though. Like, you know, if your mother tells you she dreamed about her aunt, like right before she died and all?"

"I know what feelin' you mean, but I ain't got it," said Lucius.

"Who you got doing the electrics?"

"Guy named Sparks. He was the one lit up Choton Field."

At Choton Field the year before, two gangs wanted to fight under the lights. So they went to a high-school football stadium. Somebody got all the lights and the P.A. on without going into the control booth.

Cops drove by less than fifty feet away, thinking there was a practice scrimmage going on, while down on the field guys were turning one another into bloody strings. Somebody was on the P.A. giving a play-by-play. From the outside, it sounded cool. From the inside, it looked like a pizza with all the topping ripped off it.

"Oh," said Vinnie. "Good man."

He used to work for Con Ed, and he still had his ID card. Who was going to mess with Consolidated Edison? He drove an old, gray pickup with a smudge on the side that had once been a power-company emblem. The truck was filled to the brim with cables, wires, boots, wrenches, tape, torches, work lights, and rope.

"Light man's here!" said somebody.

Lucius shook hands with him and told him what they wanted. He nodded.

The crowd was getting larger, groups and clots of people drifting in, though the music wasn't supposed to start for another hour. Word traveled fast.

Sparks attached a transformer and breakers to a huge, thick cable.

Then he got out his climbing spikes and went up a pole like a monkey, the heavy *chunk-chunk* drifting down to the crowd every time he flexed his knees. His tool belt slapped against his sides.

He had one of the guys in the Purple Monsters throw him up the end of the inch-thick electrical cable.

The sun had just gone down, and Sparks was a silhouette against the purpling sky that poked between the buildings.

A few stars were showing in the eastern sky. Lights were on all through the autumn buildings. Thanksgiving was in a few weeks, then Christmas.

The shopping season was already in full swing, and the streets would be bathed in neon, in holiday colors. The city stood up like big, black fingers all around them.

Sparks did something to the breakdown box on the pole.

There was an immense blue scream of light that stopped everybody's heart.

New York City went dark.

"Fucking wow."

A raggedy-assed cheer of wonder ran through the crowd.

There were crashes, and car horns began to honk all over town.

"Uh, Lucius," Sparks yelled down the pole after a few minutes. "Have the guys go steal me about thirty automobile batteries."

The Purple Monsters ran off in twenty different directions.

"Ahhhyyyhhyyh," said Vinnie, spitting a toothpick out of his mouth. "The Monsters get to have all the fun."

It was 5:27 p.m. on November 9, 1965. At the Ossining changing station, a guy named Jim was talking to a guy named Jack.

Then the trouble phone rang. Jim checked all his dials before he picked it up.

He listened, then hung up.

"There's an outage all down the line. They're going to switch the two hundred K's over to the Buffalo net and reroute them back through here. Check all the load levels. Everything's out from Schenectady to Jersey City."

When everything looked ready, Jack signaled to Jim. Jim called headquarters, and they watched the needles jump on the dials.

Everything went black.

Almost everything.

Jack hit all the switches for backup relays, and nothing happened.

Almost nothing.

Jim hit the emergency battery work lights. They flickered and went out.

"What the hell?" asked Jack.

He looked out the window.

Something large and bright moved across a nearby reservoir and toward the changing station.

"Holy Mother of Christ!" he said.

Jim and Jack went outside.

The large bright thing moved along the lines toward the station. The power cables bulged toward the bottom of the thing, whipping up and down, making the stanchions sway. The station and the reservoir were bathed in a blue glow as the thing went over. Then it took off quickly toward Manhattan, down the straining lines, leaving them in complete darkness.

Jim and Jack went back into the plant and ate their lunches.

Not even the phone worked anymore.

It was really black by the time Sparks got his gear set up. Everybody in the crowd was talking about the darkness of the city and the sky. You could see stars all over the place, everywhere you looked.

There was very little noise from the city around the loading area.

Somebody had a radio on. There were a few Jersey and Pennsy stations on. One of them went off while they listened.

In the darkness, Sparks worked by the lights of his old truck. What he had in front of him resembled something from an alchemy or magnetism treatise written early in the eighteenth century. Twenty or so car batteries were hooked up in series with jumper cables. He'd tied those in with amps, mikes, transformers, a light board, and lights on the dock area.

"Stand clear!" he yelled. He bent down with the last set of cables and stuck an alligator clamp on a battery post.

There was a screeching blue jag of light and a frying noise. The lights flickered and came on, and the amps whined louder and louder.

The crowd, numbering around five hundred, gave out with prolonged huzzahs and applause.

"Test test test," said Lucius. Everybody held their hands over their ears.

"Turn that fucker down," said Vinnie. Sparks did. Then he waved to the crowd, got into his old truck, turned the lights off, and drove into the night.

"Ladies and gentlemen, the Purple Monsters . . . " said Lucius, to wild applause, and Vinnie leaned into the mike, "and the Hellbenders," more applause, then back to Lucius, "would like to welcome you to the first annual piss-off—I mean, singoff—between our own Bobby and the Bombers," cheers, "and the challengers," said Vinnie, "the Kool-Tones!" More applause.

"They'll do two sets, folks," said Lucius, "taking turns. And at the end, the unlucky group, gauged by your lack of applause, will win a prize!"

The crowd went wild.

The lights dimmed out. "And now," came Vinnie's voice from the still blackness of the loading dock, "for your listening pleasure, Bobby and the Bombers!"

"Yayyyyyyyyyy!"

The lights, virtually the only lights in the city except for those that were being run by emergency generators, came up, and there they were.

Imagine frosted, polished elegance being thrust on the unwilling shoulders of a sixteen-year-old.

They had on blue jackets, matching pants, ruffled shirts, black ties, cufflinks, tie tacks, shoes like obsidian mortar trowels. They were all black boys, and from the first note, you knew they were born to sing:

"*Bah bah,*" sang Letus the bassman, "*doo-doo dah-du doo-ahh, dah-doo—dee-doot,*" sang the two tenors, Lennie and Conk, and then Bobby and Fred began trading verses of the Drifters' "There Goes My Baby," while the tenors wailed and Letus carried the whole with his bass.

Then the lights went down and came up again as Lucius said, "Ladies and gentlemen, the Kool-Tones!"

It was magic of a grubby kind.

The Kool-Tones shuffled on, arms pumping in best Frankie Lymon and the Teenagers fashion, and they ran in place as the hand-clapping got louder and louder, and they leaned into the mikes.

They were dressed in waiters' red-cloth jackets the Hellbenders had stolen from a laundry service for them that morning. They wore narrow black ties, except Leroy, who had on a big, thick, red bow tie he'd copped from his sister's boyfriend.

Then Cornelius leaned over his mike and: "*Doook doook doook doookov,*" and Ray and Zoot joined with *dook dook dook dookov,* into Gene Chandler's "Duke of Earl," with Leroy smiling and doing all of Chandler's hand moves. Slim chugged away the *iiiiiiiyiyiyiiii*'s in the background in runs that made the crowd's blood run cold, and the lights went down.

Then the Bombers were back, and in contrast to the up tempo ending of "The Duke of Earl" they started with a sweet tenor a cappella line and then: "*woo-radad-da-dat, woo-radad—da-dat*" of Shep and the Limelites' "Daddy's Home."

The Kool-Tones jumped back into the light. This time Cornelius started off with "*Bom-a-pa-bomp, bomp-pa-pa-bomp, dang-a-dang-dang, ding-a-dong-ding,*" and into the Marcels' "Blue Moon," not just a mere hit but a monster back in 1961. And they ran through the song, Slim taking the lead, and the crowd began to yell like mad halfway through. And Leroy—smiling, singing, rocking back and forth, doing James Brown tantrum-steps in front of the mike—knew, could feel, that they had them; that no matter what, they were going to win. And he ended with his whining part and Cornelius went *"Bomp-ba-ba-bomp-ba-bom,"* and paused and then, deeper, *"booo mooo."*

The lights came up and Bobby and the Bombers hit the stage. At first Leroy, sweating, didn't realize what they were doing, because the Bombers, for the first few seconds, made this churning rinky-tink sound with the high voices. The bass, Letus, did this grindy sound with his throat. Then the Bombers did the only thing that could save them, a white boy's song, Bobby launching into Del Shannon's "Runaway," with both feet hitting the stage at once. Leroy thought he could taste that urine already.

The other Kool-Tones were transfixed by what was about to happen.

"They can't do that, man," said Leroy. "They're gonna cop out."

"That's impossible. Nobody can do it."

But when the Bombers got to the break, this guy Fred stepped out to the mike and went: *"Eee-de-ee-dee-eedle-eee-eee, eee-deee-eed le-deeee, eedle-dee-eed le-dee-dee-dee, eewheetle-eedle-dee-deedle-dee-eeeeee,"* in a splitting falsetto, half mechanical, half Martian cattle call—the organ break of "Runaway," done with the human voice.

The crowd was on its feet screaming, and the rest of the song was lost in stamping and cheers.

When the Kool-Tones jumped out for the last song of the first set, there were some boos and yells for the Bombers to come back, but then Zoot started talking about his girl putting him down because he couldn't shake 'em down, but how now he was back, to let her know . . . They all jumped in the air and came down on the first line of "Do You Love Me?" by the Contours, and they gained some of the crowd back. But they finished a little wimpy, and then the lights went down and an absolutely black night descended. The stars were shining over New York City for the first time since World War II, and Vinnie said, "Ten minutes, folks!" and guys went over to piss against the walls or add to the consolation-prize bottles.

It was like halftime in the locker room with the score *Green Bay 146, You 0.*

"A cheap trick," said Zoot. "We don't *do* shit like that."

Leroy sighed. "We're gonna have to," he said. He drank from a Coke bottle one of the Purple Monsters had given him. "We're gonna have to do something."

"We're gonna have to drink pee-pee, and then Vinnie's gonna denut us, is what's gonna happen."

"No, he's not," said Cornelius.

"Oh, yeah?" asked Zoot. "Then what's that in the bottle in the clubhouse?"

"Pig's balls," said Cornelius. "They got 'em from a slaughterhouse."

"How do you know?"

"I just know," said Cornelius, tiredly. "Now let's just get this over with so we can go vomit all night."

"I don't want to hear any talk like that," said Leroy. "We're gonna go through with this and give it our best, just like we planned, and if that ain't good enough, well, it just ain't good enough."

"No matter what we do, it just ain't good enough."

"Come on, Ray, man!"

"I'll do my best, but my heart ain't in it."

They lay against the loading dock. They heard laughter from the place where Bobby and the Bombers rested.

"Shit, it's dark!" said Slim.

"It ain't just us, just the city," said Zoot. "It's the whole goddamn U.S."

"It's just the whole East Coast," said Ray. "I heard on the radio. Part of Canada, too."

"What is it?"

"Nobody knows."

"Hey, Leroy," said Cornelius. "Maybe it's those Martians you're always talking about."

Leroy felt a chill up his spine.

"Nah," said Slim. "It was that guy Sparks. He shorted out the whole East Coast up that pole there."

"Do you really believe that?" asked Zoot.

"I don't know what I believe anymore."

"I believe," said Lucius, coming out of nowhere with an evil grin on his face, "that it's *show time*."

They came to the stage running, and the lights came up, and Cornelius leaned on his voice and: "*Rabbalabbalabba ging gong, rabbalabbalabba ging gong,*" and the others went "*wooooooooooo*" in the Edsels' "Rama Lama Ding Dong." They finished and the Bombers jumped into the lights and went into: "*Domm dom domm dom dobedoo dom domm dom dobedoobeedomm, wahwahwahwahhh,*" of the Del Vikings' "Come Go With Me."

The Kool-Tones came back with: "*Ahhhhhhhhanhhwoooowoooo, ow-ow-ow-owhwoo,*" of "Since I Don't Have You," by the Skyliners, with Slim singing in a clear, straight voice, better than he had ever sung that song before, and everybody else joined in, Leroy's voice fading into Slim's for the falsetto *weeeeooooow*'s so you couldn't tell where one ended and the other began.

Then Bobby and the Bombers were back, with Bobby telling you the first two lines and: *"Detooodwop, detooodwop, detooodwop,"* of the Flamingos' "I Only Have Eyes for You," calm, cool, collected, assured of victory, still running on the impetus of their first set's showstopper.

Then the Kool-Tones came back and Cornelius rared back and asked: *"Ahwunno wunno hooo? Be-do-be hoooo?"* Pause.

They slammed down into "Book of Love," by the Monotones, but even Cornelius was flagging, sweating now in the cool air, his lungs were husks. He saw one of the Bombers nod to another, smugly, and that made him mad. He came down on the last verse like there was no one else on the stage with him, and his bass roared so loud it seemed there wasn't a single person in the dark United States who didn't wonder who wrote that book.

And they were off, and Bobby and the Bombers were on now, and a low hum began to fill the air. Somebody checked the amp; it was okay. So the Bombers jumped into the air, and when they came down they were into the Cleftones' "Heart and Soul" and they *sang* that song, and while they were singing, the background humming got louder and louder.

Leroy leaned to the other Kool-Tones and whispered something. They shook their heads. He pointed to the Hellbenders and the Purple Monsters all around them. He asked a question they didn't want to hear. They nodded grudging approval, and then they were on again, for the last time.

"Dep dooomop dooomop doomop, doo ooo, ooowah oowah oooway ooowah," sang Leroy, and they all asked "Why Do Fools Fall in Love?" Leroy sang like he was Frankie Lymon—not just some kid from the projects who wanted to be him—and the Kool-Tones were the Teenagers, and they began to pull and heave that song like it was a dead whale. And soon they had it in the water, and then it was swimming a little, then it was moving, and then the sonofabitch started spouting water, and that was the place where Leroy went into the falsetto *"wyyyyyyyyyyyyyyyyyyyyyyyy,"* and instead of chopping it where it should have been, he kept on. The Kool-Tones went *ooom wahooomwah* softly behind him, and still he held that note, and the crowd began to applaud, and they began to yell, and Leroy held it longer, and they started stamping and screaming, and he held it until he knew he was going to cough up both his lungs, and he held it after that, and the Kool-Tones were coming up to meet him, and Leroy gave a tantrum-step, and his eyes were bugging, and

he felt his lungs tear out by the roots and come unglued, and he held the last syllable, and the crowd wet itself and—

The lights went out and the amp went dead. Part of the crowd had a subliminal glimpse of something large, blue, and cool looming over the freight yard, bathing the top of the building in a soft glow.

In the dead air the voices of the Kool-Tones dropped in pitch as if they were pulled upward at a thousand miles an hour, and then they rose in pitch as if they had somehow come back at that same thousand miles an hour.

The blue thing was a looming blur and then was gone.

The lights came back on. The Kool-Tones stood there blinking: Cornelius, Ray, Slim, and Zoot. The space in front of the center mike was empty.

The crowd had an orgasm.

The Bombers were being violently ill over next to the building.

"God, that was great!" said Vinnie. "Just great!"

All four of the Kool-Tones were shaking their heads.

They should be tired, but this looked worse than that, thought Vinnie. They should be ecstatic. They looked like they didn't know they had won.

"Where's Leroy?" asked Cornelius.

"How the hell should I know?" Vinnie said, sounding annoyed.

"I remember him smiling, like," said Zoot.

"And the blue thing. What about it?"

"What blue thing?" asked Lucius.

"I dunno. Something was blue."

"I saw was the lights go off and that kid ran away," said Lucius.

"Which way?"

"Well, I didn't exactly see him, but he must have run some way. Don't know how he got by us. Probably thought you were going to lose and took it on the lam. I don't see how you'd worry when you can make your voices do that stuff."

"Up," said Zoot, suddenly.

"What?"

"We went up, and we came down. Leroy didn't come down with us."

"Of course not. He was still holding the same note. I thought the little twerp's balls were gonna fly out his mouth."

"No. We . . . " Slim moved his hands up, around, gave up. "I don't know what happened, do you?"

Ray, Zoot, and Cornelius all looked like they had thirty-two-lane bowling alleys inside their heads and all the pin machines were down.

"Aw, shit," said Vinnie. "You won. Go get some sleep. You guys were really bitchin'."

The Kool-Tones stood there uncertainly for a minute.

"He was, like, smiling, you know?" said Zoot.

"He was always smiling," said Vinnie. "Crazy little kid."

The Kool-Tones left.

The sky overhead was black and spattered with stars. It looked to Vinnie as if it were deep and wide enough to hold anything. He shuddered.

"Hey!" he yelled. "Somebody bring me a beer!"

He caught himself humming. One of the Hellbenders brought him a beer.

• • •

As Eileen Gunn once wrote, **Howard Waldrop** is "a *legendary* unknown writer." He lives in Austin, Texas where he writes, fishes, and builds bookcases. He does not have a cellphone, a computer, or an email account. He's written a couple of novels and a bunch of short stories, most of which can be found in his eight collections. The winner of both a Nebula and a World Fantasy Award, both "Flying Saucer Rock and Roll" and "Heirs of the Perisphere," were nominated for the *same* Nebula award one year, placing hardcore Waldrop fans in a schizophrenia-inducing double-bind. Waldrop has garnered other honors as well, including a Nebula nomination for "Do Ya, Do Ya Wanna Dance," another rock-influenced story. Take the editor's advice: Darn near any of his stuff is worth seeking out.

• • • •

Bob Dylan, Troy Jonson, and the Speed Queen
F. Paul Wilson

Dylan walks in and I almost choke.

I've known all along it had to happen. I mean, it was inevitable. But still, finding yourself in the same room with a legend will tend to dry up your saliva no matter how well prepared you think you are.

My band's been doing weeknights at the Eighth Wonder for two months now, a Tuesday-Wednesday-Thursday gig, and I've made sure there's an electrified Dylan song in every set every night we play. Reactions have been mixed. At worst, hostile; at best, grudging acceptance. Electric music is a touchy thing here in Greenwich Village in 1964. All these folkies who think they're so hip and radical and grass-roots wise, they'll march in Selma, but they'll boo and walk out on a song by a black man named Chuck Berry. Yet if you play the same chord progression and damn near the same melody and say it's by Howlin' Wolf or Muddy Waters or Sonny Boy Williamson, they'll stay. So, although my band's electric, I've been showing my bona fides by limiting the sets to blues and an occasional protest song.

Slowly but surely, we've been building an audience of locals. That's what I want, figuring that the more people hear us, the sooner word will get around to Dylan that somebody's doing rocked-up versions of his songs. It has to. Greenwich Village is a tight, gossipy little community, and except maybe for the gays, the folkies are just about the tightest and most gossipy of the Village's various subcultures. I figured when he heard about us, he'd have to come and listen for himself. I've been luring him. It's all part of the plan.

And tonight he's taken the bait.

So here I am in the middle of Them's version of "Baby, Please Don't Go" and my voice goes hoarse and I fumble the riff when I see him, but I manage to get through the song without making a fool out of myself.

When I finish, I look up and panic for an instant because I can't find him. I search the dimness. The Eighth Wonder is your typical West Village dive, little more than a long, rectangular room with the band platform at one end, the bar right rear, and cocktail tables spread across the open floor. Then I catch his profile silhouetted against the bar lights. He's standing there talking to some gal with long, straight, dark hair who's even skinnier than he is—which isn't much of a description, because in 1964 it seems all the women in Greenwich Village are skinny with long, straight hair.

The band's ready to begin the next number on the set list, our Yardbirds-style "I'm a Man," but I turn and tell them we're doing "All I Really Want to Do." They nod and shrug. As long as they get paid, they don't give a damn what they play. They're not in on the plan.

I strap on the Rickenbacker twelve-string and start pickng out Jim McGuinn's opening. I've got this choice figured to be a pretty safe one since my wire tells me that the Byrds aren't even a group yet.

Dylan's taken a table at the rear with the skinny brunette. He's slouched down. He's got no idea this is his song. Then we start to sing and I see him straighten up in his chair. When we hit the chorus with the three-part harmony, I see him put down his drink. It's not a big move. He's trying to be cool. But I'm watching for it and I catch it.

Contact.

Research told me that he liked the Byrds' version when he first heard it, so I know he's got to like our version because ours is a carbon copy of the Byrds'. And naturally, he hasn't heard theirs yet because they haven't recorded it. I'd love to play their version of "Mr. Tambourine Man," but he hasn't written it yet.

There's some decent applause from the crowd when we finish the number and I run right into a Byrds version of "The Times They Are A-changin'." I remind myself not to use anything later than *Another Side of Bob Dylan*. We finish the set strong in full harmony on "Chimes of Freedom," and I look straight at Dylan's dim form and give him a smile and a nod. I don't see him smile or nod back, but he does join in the applause.

Got him.

We play our break number and then I head for the back of the room. But by the time I get there, his table's empty. I look around but Dylan's gone.

"Shit!" I say to myself. Missed him. I wanted a chance to talk to him.

I step over to the bar for a beer, and the girl who was sitting with Dylan sidles over. She's wearing jeans and three shirts. Hardly anybody in the Village wears a coat unless it's the dead of winter. If it's cool out, you put on another shirt over the one you're already wearing. And if it's even cooler, you throw an oversize work shirt over those.

"He sorta kinda liked your stuff," she says.

"Who?"

"Bob. He was impressed."

"Really?" I stay cool as the proverbial cucumber on the outside, but inside I want to grab her shoulders and shout, "Yeah? Yeah? What did he say?" Instead I ask, "What makes you think so?"

"Oh, I don't know. Maybe it's because as he was listening to you guys, he turned to me and said, 'I am impressed.'"

I laugh to keep from cheering. "Yeah. I guess that'd be a pretty good indication."

I like her. And now that she's close up, I recognize her. She's Sally something. I'm not sure anybody knows her last name. People around the Village just call her the Speed Queen. And by that, they don't mean she does laundry.

Sally is thin and twitchy, and she's got the sniffles. She's got big, dark eyes, too, and they're staring at me.

"I was pretty impressed with your stuff, too," she says, smiling at me. "I mean, I don't dig rock and roll at all, man, what with all the bop-shoo-boppin' and the shoo-be-dooin'. I mean, that stuff's nowhere, man. But I kinda like the Beatles. I mean, a bunch of us sat around and watched them when they were on Ed Sullivan and, you know, they were kinda cool. I mean, they just stood there and sang. No corny little dance steps or anything like that. If they'd done anything like that, we would've turned them right off. But no. Oh, they bounced a little to the beat, maybe, but mostly they just played and sang. Almost like folkies. Looked like they were having fun. We all kinda dug that."

I hold back from telling her that she and her folkie friends were watching the death of the folk music craze.

"I dig 'em, too," I say, dropping into the folkster patois of the period. "And I predict they're gonna be the biggest thing ever to hit the music business. Ten times bigger than Elvis and Sinatra and the Kingston Trio put together, man."

She laughs. "Sure! And I'm going to marry Bobby Dylan!"

I could tell her he's actually going to marry Sara Lowndes next year, but that would be stupid. And she wouldn't believe me, anyway.

"I like to think of what I play as 'folk rock,'" I tell her.

She nods and considers this. "Folk rock . . . that's cool. But I don't know if it'll fly around here."

"It'll fly," I tell her. "It'll fly high. I guarantee it."

She's looking at me, smiling and nodding, almost giggling.

"You're okay," she says. "Why don't we get together after your last set?"

"Meet you right here," I say.

• • •

It's Wednesday morning, three a.m., when we wind up back at my apartment on Perry Street.

"Nice pad," Sally says. "Two bedrooms. Wow."

"The second bedroom's my music room. That's where I work out all the band's material."

"Great! Can I use your bathroom?"

I show her where it. is and she takes her big shoulder bag in with her. I listen for a moment and hear the clink of glass on porcelain and have a pretty good idea of what she's up to.

"You shooting up in there?" I say.

She pulls open the door. She's sitting on the edge of the tub. There's a syringe in her hand and some rubber tubing tied around her arm.

"I'm tryin' to."

"What is it?"

"Meth."

Of course. They don't call her the Speed Queen for nothing.

"Want some?"

I shake my head. "Nah. Not my brand."

She smiles. "You're pretty cool, Troy. Some guys get grossed out by needles."

"Not me."

I don't tell her that we don't even have needles when I come from. Of course, I knew there'd be lots of shooting up in the business I was getting into, so before coming here I programmed all its myriad permutations into my wire.

"Well, then maybe you can help me. I seem to be running out of veins here. And this is good stuff. Super-potent. Two grams per cc."

I hide my revulsion and take it from her. Such a primitive-looking thing. Even though AIDS hasn't reared its ugly head yet, I find the needle point especially terrifying. I look at the barrel of the glass syringe.

"You've got half a cc there. A gram? You're popping a whole gram of speed?"

"The more I use, the more I need. Check for a vein, will you?"

I rub my fingertip over the inner surface of her arm until I feel a linear swelling below the skin. My wire tells me that's the place.

I say, "I think there's one here but I can't see it."

"Feeling's better than seeing any day," she says with a smile. "Do it."

I push the needle through the skin. She doesn't even flinch.

"Pull back on the plunger a little," she says.

I do, and see a tiny red plume swirl into the chamber.

"Oh, you're beautiful!" she says. "Hit it!"

I push the plunger home. As soon as the chamber is empty, the Speed Queen yanks off her tourniquet and sighs.

"Oh, man! Oh, baby!"

She grabs me and pulls me to the floor.

I lie in bed utterly exhausted while Sally runs around the apartment stark naked, picking up the clutter, chattering on at Mach two. She is painfully thin, Dachau thin. It almost hurts to look at her. I close my eyes.

For the first time since my arrival, I feel relaxed. I feel at peace. I don't have to worry about YD because I've had the routine immunizations against syphilis and the clap and even hepatitis B and C and AIDS. About the worst I can get is a case of crabs. I can just lie here and feel good.

It wasn't easy getting here, and it's been even harder staying. I thought I'd prepared myself for everything, but I never figured I'd be lonely. I didn't count on the loneliness. That's been the toughest to handle.

The music got me into this. I've been a fan of the old music ever since I can remember—ever since my ears started to work, probably. And I've got a good ear. Perfect pitch. You sit me down in front of a new piece of music, and guaranteed I'll be able to play it back to you note for note in less than half an hour—usually less than ten minutes for most things. I can sing, too, imitating most voices pretty closely.

Trouble is, I don't have a creative cell in my body. I can play anything that's already been played, but I can't make up anything of my own to play. That's the tragedy of my life. I should be a major musical talent of my time, but I'm an also-ran, a nothing.

To tell you the truth, I don't care to be a major musical talent of my time. And that's not sour grapes. I loathe what passes for music in my time. Push-button music—that's what I call it. Nobody actually gets their hands on the instruments and wrings the notes from them. Nobody gets together and cooks. It's all so cool, dispassionate. Leaves me cold.

So I came back here. I have a couple of relatives in the temporal sequencing lab. I gained their confidence, learned the ropes, and displaced myself to the 1960s.

Not an easy decision, I can assure you. Not only have I left behind everyone and everything I know, but I'm risking death. That's the penalty for altering the past. But I was so miserable that I figured it was worth the risk. Better to die trying to carve out a niche for myself here than to do a slow rot where I was.

Of course, there was a good chance I'd do a slow rot in the 1960s as well. I'm no fool. I had no illusions that dropping back a hundred years or so would make me any more creative than I already wasn't. I'd be an also-ran in the sixties, too.

Unless I prepared myself.

Which I did. I did my homework on the period. I studied the way they dressed, the way they spoke. I got myself wired with a wetchip encoding all the biographies and discographies of anyone who was anybody in music and the arts at this time. All I have to do is think of the name and suddenly I know all about him or her.

Too bad they can't do that with music. I had to bring the music with me. I wasn't stupid, though. I didn't bring a dot player with me. No technological anachronisms—that's a sure way to cause ripples in the time stream and tip your hand to the observation teams. Do that and a reclamation squad'll be knocking on your door. Not me. I spent a whole year hunting up these ancient vinyl discs—"LPs" they call them here. Paid antique prices for them, but it was worth it. Bought myself some antique money to spend here, too.

So here I am.

And I'm on my way. It's been hard, it's been slow, but I've only got one chance at this so I've got to do it right. I picked the other band members carefully and trained them to play what I want. They need work, so they go along with me, especially since they all think I'm a genius for writing such diverse songs as "Jumpin' Jack Flash," "Summer in the City," "Taxman," "Bad Moon Rising," "Rikki Don't Lose That Number," and so many others. People are starting to talk about me. And now Dylan has heard me. I'm hoping he'll bring John Hammond with him sometime soon. That way I've got a shot at a Columbia contract. And then Dylan will send the demo of "Mr. Tambourine Man" to me instead of Jim McGuinn.

After that, I won't need anyone. I'll be able to anticipate every trend in rock and I'll be at the forefront of all the ones that matter.

So far, everything's going according to plan. I've even got a naked woman running around my apartment. I'm finally beginning to feel at home.

"Where'd you get these?"

It's Sally's voice. I open my eyes and see her standing over me. I smile, then freeze.

She's holding up copies of the first two Byrds albums.

"Give me those!"

"Hey, really. Where'd—"

I leap out of bed. The expression on my face must be fierce because she jumps back. I snatch them from her.

"Don't ever touch my records!"

"Hey, sorreeeee! I just thought I'd spin something, okay? I wasn't going to steal your fucking records, man!"

I force myself to cool down. Quickly. It's my fault. I should have locked the music room. But I've been so wrapped up in getting the band going that I haven't had any company, so I've been careless about keeping my not-yet-recorded "antiques" locked away.

I laugh. "Sorry, Sally. It's just that these are rarities. I get touchy about them."

Holding the records behind me, I pull her close and give her a kiss. She kisses me back, then pulls away and tries to get another look at the records.

"I'll say they are," she says. "I never heard of these Byrds. I mean, like you'd think they were a jazz group, you know, like copping Charlie Parker or something, but the title on that blue album there is *Turn, Turn, Turn*, which I've like heard Pete Seeger sing. Are they new? I mean, they've gotta be new, but the album cover looks so old. And didn't I see 'Columbia' on the spine?"

"No," I say when I can finally get a word in. "They're imports."

"A new English group?"

"No. They're Swedish. And they're pretty bad."

"But that other album looked like it had a couple of Bobby's tunes on it."

"No chance," I say, feeling my gut coil inside me. "You need to come down."

I quickly put the albums back in the other room and lock the door.

"You're a real weird cat, Troy," she says to me.

"Why? Because I take care of my records?"

"They're only records. They're not gold." She laughs. "And besides that, you wear underwear. You must be the only guy in the Village who wears underwear."

I pull Sally back to the bed. We do it again and finally she falls asleep in my arms. But I can't sleep. I'm too shaken—even to close my eyes.

I like her. I really like her. But that was too close. I've got to be real careful about who I bring back to the apartment. I can't let anything screw up the plan, especially my own carelessness. My life is at stake.

No ripples, that's the key. I've got to sink into the timeline without making any ripples. Bob Dylan will go electric on his next album, just like he did before, but it will be my influence that nudged him to try it. "Mr. Tambourine Man" will be a big hit next summer, just as it's destined to be, but if things go according to plan, my band's name will be on the label instead of the Byrds. No ripples. Everything will remain much the same except that over the next few years, Troy Jonson will insinuate himself into the music scene and become a major force there. He will make millions, he will be considered a genius, the toast of both the public and his fellow artists.

Riding that thought, I drift off to sleep.

Dylan shows up at the Eighth Wonder the very next night in the middle of my note-perfect imitation of Duane Allman on "Statesboro Blues," perfect even down to the Coricidin bottle on my slide finger. There's already a good crowd in, the biggest crowd since we started playing. Word must be getting around that we're something worth listening to.

Dylan has about half a dozen scruffy types along with him. I recognize Allen Ginsberg and Gregory Corso in the entourage. Which gives me an idea.

"This one's for the poets in the audience," I say into the mike; then we jump into Paul Simon's "Richard Corey," only I use Van Morrison's phrasing, you know, with the snicker after the bullet-through-his-head line. I spend the rest of the set being political, interspersing Dylan numbers with "originals" such as "American Tune," "Won't Get Fooled Again," "Life During Wartime," and so on.

I can tell they're impressed. More than impressed. Their jaws are hanging open.

I figure now's the time to play cool. At the break, instead of heading for the bar, I slip backstage to the doorless, cinder-block-walled cubicle euphemistically known as the dressing room.

Eventually someone knocks on the doorjamb. It's a bearded guy I recognize as one of Dylan's entourage tonight.

"Great set, man," he says. "Where'd you get some of those songs?"

"Stole them," I say, hardly glancing at him.

He laughs. "No, seriously, man. They were great. I really like that 'Southern Man' number. I mean, like I've been makin' the marches and that says it all, man. You write them?"

I nod. "Most of them. Not the Dylan numbers."

He laughs again. From the glitter in his eyes and his extraordinarily receptive sense of humor, I gather that he's been smoking a little weed at that rear table.

"Right! And speaking of Dylan, Bobby wants to talk to you."

I decide to act a little paranoid.

"He's not pissed, is he? I mean, I know they're his songs and all, but I thought I'd try to do them a little different, you know. I don't want him takin' me to court or—"

"Hey, it's cool," he says. "Bobby digs the way you're doing his stuff. He just wants to buy you a drink and talk to you about it, that's all."

I resist the urge to pump my fist in the air.

"Okay," I say. "I can handle that."

"Sure, man. And he wants to talk to you about some rare records he hears you've got."

Suddenly I'm ice cold.

"Records?"

"Yeah, says he heard about some foreign platters you've got with some of his songs on 'em."

I force a laugh and say, "Oh, he must've been talking to Sally! You know how Sally gets. The Speed Queen was really flying when she was going through my records. That wasn't music she saw, that was a record from Ireland of Dylan *Thomas* reading his stuff. I think ol' Sally's brains are getting scrambled."

He nods. "Yeah, it was Sally, all right. She says you treat them things like gold, man. They must be some kinda valuable. But the thing that got to Dylan was, she mentioned a song with 'tambourine' in the title, and he says he's been doodling with something like that."

"No kidding?" My voice sounds like a croak.

"Yeah. So he really wants to talk to you."

I'm sure he does. But what am I going to say?

And then I remember that I left Sally back at my apartment. She was going to hang out there for a while, then come over for the late sets.

I'm ready to panic. Even though I know I locked the music room before I left, I've got this urge to run back to my place.

"Hey, I really want to talk to him, too. But I got some business to attend to here. My manager's stopping by in a minute and it's the only chance we'll have to talk before he heads for the West Coast, so tell Mr. Dylan I'll be over right after the next set. Tell him to make the next set—it'll be worth the wait."

The guy shrugs. "Okay. I'll tell him, but I don't know how happy he's gonna be."

"Sorry, man. I've got no choice."

As soon as he's gone, I dash out the back door and run for Perry Street. I've got to get Sally out of the apartment and never let her back in. Maybe I can even make it back to the Eighth Wonder in time to have that drink with Dylan. I can easily convince him that the so-called Dylan song on my foreign record is a product of amphetamine craziness—everybody in the Village knows how out of control Sally is with the stuff.

As I ram the key into my apartment door, I hear something I don't want to hear, something I can't be hearing. But when open up . . .

"Mr. Tambourine Man" is playing on the hi-fi.

I charge into the second bedroom, the music room. The door is open and Sally is dancing around the floor. She's startled to see me and goes into her little girl speedster act.

"Hiya, Troy, I found the key and I couldn't resist because I like really wanted to hear these weird records of yours and I love 'em, I really do, but I've never heard of these Byrds cats although one of them's named Crosby and he looks kinda like a singer I caught at a club last year only his hair was shorter then, and I never heard this 'Tambourine' song before, but it's definitely Dylan, although he's never sung it that I know of so I'll have to ask him about it. And I noticed something even weirder, I mean really weird, because I spotted some of these copyright dates on the records—you know, that little circle with the littler letter c inside them?—and like, man, some of them are in the future, man, isn't that wild? I mean, like there's circle-C 1965 on this one and a circle-C 1970 on that one over there, and it's like someone had a time machine and went into the future and brought 'em back or something. I mean, is this wild or what?"

Fury like I've never known blasts through me. It steals my voice. I want to throttle her. If she were in reach I'd do it, but lucky for her she's bouncing around the room. I stay put. I clench my fists at my sides and let my mind race over my options.

How do I get out of this? Sally had one look at a couple of my albums last night and then spent all day blabbing to the whole goddamn Village about them and how rare and unique they are. And after tonight I know exactly what she'll be talking about tomorrow: Dylan songs that haven't been written yet, groups that don't exist yet, and, worst of all, albums with copyright dates in the future!

Ripples . . . I was worried about ripples in the time stream giving me away. Sally's mouth is going to cause waves. Tsunamis!

The whole scenario plays out inside my head: Talk spreads, Dylan gets more curious, Columbia Records gets worried about possible bootlegs, lawyers get involved, an article appears in the *Voice*, and then the inevitable—a reclamation squad knocks on my door in the middle of the night, I'm tranqued, brought back to my own time, and then it's bye-bye musical career. Bye-bye Troy Jonson.

Sally's got to go.

The cold-bloodedness of the thought shocks me. But it's Sally or me. That's what it comes down to. Sally or me. What else can I do?

I choose me.

"Are you mad?" she says.

I shake my head. "A little annoyed, maybe, but I guess it's okay." I smile. "It's hard to say no to you."

She jumps into my arms and gives me a hug. My hands slide up to her throat, encircle it, then slip away. Can't do it.

"Hey, like what are you doing back, man? Aren't you playing?"

"I got . . . distracted."

"Well, Troy, honey, if you're flat, you've come to the right place. I know how to fix that."

In that instant, I know how I'll do it. No blood, no pain, no mess.

"Maybe you're right. Maybe I could use a little boost."

Her eyes light. "Groovy! I had my gear all set up in the bathroom but I couldn't find a vein. Let's go."

"But I want you to have some, too. It's no fun being up alone."

"Hey, I'm flyin' already. I popped a bunch of black beauties before you came."

"Yeah, but you're coming down. I can tell."

"You think so?" Her brow wrinkles with concern, then she smiles. "Okay. A little more'll be cool—especially if it's a direct hit."

"Never too much of a good thing, right?"

"Right. You'll shoot me up like last night?"

Just the words I want to hear.

"You bet."

While Sally's adjusting her tourniquet and humming along with "Mr. Tambourine Man," I take her biggest syringe and fill it all the way with the methedrine solution. I find the vein first try. She's too whacked-out to notice the size of the syringe until I've got most of it into her.

She tries to pull her arm away. "Hey, that's ten fucking cc's!"

I'm cool. I'm more than cool. I'm stone-cold dead inside.

"Yeah, but it wasn't full. I only put one cc in it." I pull her off the toilet seat. "Come on. Let's go."

"How about you, Troy? I thought you wanted—"

"Later. I'll do it at the club. I've got to get back."

As I pack up her paraphernalia, carefully wiping my prints off the syringe and bottles, she sags against the bathroom door.

"I don't feel so good, Troy. How much did you give me?"

"Not much. Come on, let's go."

Something's going to happen—twenty thousand milligrams of methamphetamine in a single dose has to have a catastrophic effect—and whatever it is, I don't want it happening in my apartment.

I hurry her out to the street. I'm glad my place is on the first floor; I'd hate to see her try a few flights of steps right now. We go half a block and she clutches her chest.

"Shit, that hurts! Troy, I think I'm having a heart attack!"

As she starts retching and shuddering, I pull her into an alley. A cat bolts from the shadows; the alley reeks of garbage. Sally shudders and sinks to her knees.

"Get me to a hospital, Troy," she says in a weak, raspy voice. "I think I overdid it this time."

I sink down beside her and fight the urge to carry her the few blocks to St. Vincent's emergency room. Instead, I hold her in my arms. She's trembling.

"I can't breathe!"

The shudders become more violent. She convulses, almost throwing me off her; then she lies still, barely breathing. Another convulsion, more violent than the last, choking sounds tearing from her throat. She's still again, but this time she's not breathing. A final shudder, and Sally the Speed Queen comes to a final, screeching halt.

As I crouch there beside her, still holding her, I begin to sob. This isn't the way I planned it, not at all the way it was supposed to be. It was all going to be peace and love and harmony, all Woodstock and no Altamont. Music, laughs, money. This isn't in the plan.

I lurch to my feet and vomit into the garbage can. I start walking. I don't look back at her. I can't. I stumble into the street and head for the Eighth Wonder, crying all the way.

The owner, the guys in the band, they all hassle me for delaying the next set. I look out into the audience and see Dylan's gone, but I don't care. Just as well. The next three sets are a mess, the worst of my life. The rest of the night is a blur. As soon as I'm done, I'm out of there, running.

I find Perry Street full of cops and flashing red lights. I don't have to ask why. The self-loathing wells up in me until I want to be sick again. I promise myself to get those records into a safety-deposit box first thing tomorrow so that something like this can never happen again.

I don't look at anybody as I pass the alley, afraid they'll see the guilt screaming in my eyes, but I'm surprised to find my landlord, Charlie, standing on the front steps to the apartment house.

"Hey, Jonson!" he says. "Where da hell ya been? Da cops is lookin' all ova for ya!"

I freeze on the bottom step.

"I've been working—all night."

"Sheesh, whatta night. First dat broad overdoses an' dies right downa street, and now dis! Anyway, da cops is in your place. Better go talk to 'em."

As much as I want to run, I don't. I can get out of this. Somebody probably saw us together, that's all. I can get out of this.

"I don't know anything about an overdose," I say. It's a form of practice. I figure I'm going to have to say it a lot of times before the cops leave.

"Not dat!" Charlie says. "About your apartment. You was broken into a few hours ago. I t'ought I heard glass break so's I come downstairs to check. Dey got in t'rough your back window, but I scared 'em off afore dey got much." He grins and slaps me on the shoulder. "You owe me one, kid. How many landlords is security guards, too?"

I'm starting to relax. I force a smile as I walk up the steps past him.

"You're the best, Charlie."

"Don't I know it. Dey did manage to make off wit your hi-fi an' your records but, hey, you can replace dose wit'out too much trouble."

I turn toward Charlie. I feel the whole world, all the weight of time itself crashing down on me. I can't help it. It comes unbidden, without warning. Charlie's eyes nearly bulge out of his head as I scream a laugh in his face.

• • •

F. Paul Wilson (www.repairmanjack.com) is the award-winning, *New York Times* bestselling author of forty-plus books and many short stories spanning horror, adventure, medical thrillers, science fiction, and virtually everything between. More than nine million copies of his books are in print in the U.S. and his work has been translated into twenty-four foreign languages. He also has written for the stage, screen, and interactive media. His latest thrillers, *Nightworld* and *Cold City*, feature his urban mercenary, Repairman Jack. The author resides at the REAL Jersey Shore. Wilson's referenced rock in other stories such as "Nyro Fiddles," "The Last Oldies Revival," and "The Years the Music Died." He even touches on disco in "When He Was Fab."

• • • •

Stone
Edward Bryant

1

Up above the burning city, a woman wails the blues. How she cries out, how she moans. Flames fed by tears rake fingers across the sky.

It is an old, old song:

Fill me like the mountains
Fill me like the sea

Writhing in the heat, she stands where there is no support.

The fire licks her body.

All of me

So finely drawn, and with the glitter of ice, the manipulating wires radiate outward. Taut bonds between her body and the flickering darkness, all wires lead to the intangible overshadowing figure behind her. Without expression, Atropos gazes down at the woman.

Face contorting, she looks into the hearts of a million fires and cries out.

All of me

As Atropos raises the terrible, cold-shining blades of the Nornshears and with only the barest hesitation cuts the wires. Limbs spread-eagled to the compass points, the woman plunges into the flames. She is instantly and utterly consumed.

The face of Atropos remains shrouded in shadows.

2

ALPERTRON PRESENTS
IN CONCERT
JAIN SNOW
with
MOOG INDIGO
Sixty-track stim by RobCal
June 23, 24
One show nightly at 2100

and there's been a lull in the usually boisterous flight conversation. Jain flips through a current Neiman-Marcus catalogue; exclusive mail order listings are her present passion.

I look up as she bursts into raucous laughter. "I'll be goddamned. Will you look at this?" She points at the open catalogue on her lap.

Hollis, Moog Indigo's color operator, is seated behind her. She leans forward and cranes her neck over Jain's shoulder. "Which?"

"That," she says. "The VTP."

"What's VTP?" says Stella.

Hollis says, "Video tape playback."

"Hey, everybody!" Jain raises her voice, cutting stridently trough everyone else's conversations. "Get this. For a small fee, these folks'll put a videotape gadget in my tombstone. It's got everything—stereo sound and color. All I've got to do is go in before I die and cut the tape."

"Terrific!" Hollis says. "You could leave an album of greatest hits. You know, for posterity. Free concerts on the grass every Sunday."

"That's really sick," Stella says.

"Free, hell." Jain grins. "Anybody who wants to catch the show can put a dollar in the slot."

Stella stares disgustedly out the window.

Hollis says, "Do you want one of those units for your birthday?"

"Nope." Jain shakes her head, "I'm not going to need one."

"Never?"

"Well . . . not for a long time." But I think her words sound unsure.

Then I only half listen as I look out from the plane across the scattered cloud banks and the Rockies looming to the west of us. Tomorrow night we play Denver. *"It's about as close to home as I'm gonna get," Jain had said in New Orleans when we found out Denver was booked.*

"A what?" Jain's voice is puzzled.

"A cenotaph," says Hollis.

"Shut up," Stella says. "Damn it."

5

We're in the Central Arena, the architectural pride of Denver District. This is the largest gathering place in all of Rocky Mountain, that heterogeneous, anachronistic strip-city clinging to the front ranges of the continental divide all the way from Billings down to the southern suburb of El Paso.

The dome stretches up beyond the range of the house lights, if it were rigid, there could never be a Rocky Mountain Central Arena. But it's made of a flexible plastic-variant and blowers funnel up heated air to keep it buoyant. We're on the inner skin of a giant balloon. When the arena's full, the body heat from the audience keeps the dome aloft, and the arena crew turns off the blowers.

I killed time earlier tonight reading the promo pamphlet on this place. As the designer says, the combination of arena and spectators turns the dome into one sustaining organism. At first I misread it as "orgasm."

I monitor crossflow conversations through plugs inserted in both ears as set-up people check out the lights, sound, color, and all the rest of the systems. Finally some nameless tech comes on circuit to give my stim console a run-through.

"Okay, Rob, I'm up in the booth above the east aisle. Give me just a tickle." *My nipples were sensitized to her tongue, rough as a cat's.*

I'm wired to a test set fully as powerful as the costume Jain'll wear later— just not as exotic. I slide a track control forward until it reaches the five-position on a scale calibrated to one hundred.

"Five?" the tech says.

"Reading's dead-on. Give me a few more tracks."

I comply. *She kisses me with lips and tongue, working down across my belly.*

"A little higher, please."

I push the tracks to fifteen.

"You're really in a mood, Rob."

"So what do you want me to think?" I say.

"Jesus," says the tech. "You ought to be performing. The crowd would love it."

"They pay Jain. She's the star." *I tried to get on top; she wouldn't let me. A moment later it didn't matter.*

"Did you just push the board to thirty?" The tech's voice sounds strange.

"No. Did you read that?"

"Negative, but for a moment it felt like it." He pauses. "You're not allowing your emotional life to get in the way of your work, are you?"

"Screw off," I answer. "None of your business."

"No threats," says the tech. "Just a suggestion."

"Stick it."

"Okay, okay. She's a lovely girl, Rob. And like you say, she's the star."

"I know."

"Fine. Feed me another five tracks, Rob; broad spectrum this time."

I do so and the tech is satisfied with the results. "That ought to do it," he says. "I'll get back to you later." He breaks off the circuit. All checks are done; there's nothing now on the circuits but a background scratch like insects climbing over old newspapers. *She will not allow me to be exhausted for long.*

Noisily, the crowd is starting to file into the Arena.

I wait for the concert.

6

There's never before been a stim star of the magnitude of Jain Snow. Yet somehow the concert tonight fails. Somewhere the chemistry goes wrong. The faces out there are as always—yet somehow they are not involved. They care, but not enough.

I don't think the fault's in Jain. I detect no significant difference from other concerts. Her skin still tantalizes the audience as nakedly, only occasionally obscured by the cloudy metal mesh that transforms her entire body into a single antenna. I've been there when she's performed a hell of a lot better, maybe, but I've also seen her perform worse and still come off the stage happy.

It isn't Moog Indigo; they're laying down the sound and light patterns behind Jain as expertly as always.

Maybe it's me, but I don't think I'm handling the stim console badly. If I were, the nameless tech would be on my ass over the com circuit.

Jain goes into her final number. It does not work. The audience is enthusiastic and they want an encore, but that's just it: they shouldn't want one. They shouldn't need one.

She comes off the stage crying. I touch her arm as she walks past my console. Jain stops and rubs her eyes and asks me if I'll go back to the hotel with her.

7

It seems like the first time I was in Jain Snow's bed. Jain keeps the room dark and says nothing as we go through the positions. Her breathing grows a little ragged; that is all. And yet she is more demanding of me than ever before.

When it's done, she holds me close and very tightly. Her rate of breathing slows and becomes regular. I wonder if she is asleep.

"Hey," I say.

"What?" She slurs the word sleepily.

"I'm sorry about tonight."

" . . . Not your fault."

"I love you very much."

She rolls to face me. "Huh?"

"I love you."

"No, babe. Don't say that."

"It's true," I say.

"Won't work."

"Doesn't matter," I say.

"It can't work."

I know I don't have any right to feel this, but I'm pissed, and so I move away in the bed. "I don't care." *The first time: "Such a goddamned adolescent, Rob."*

After a while, she says, "Robbie, I'm cold," and so I move back to her and hold her and say nothing. I realize, rubbing against her hip, that I'm hard again; she doesn't object as I pour back into her all the frustration she unloaded in me earlier.

Neither of us sleeps much the rest of the night. Sometime before dawn I doze briefly and awaken from a nightmare. I am disoriented and can't remember the entirety of the dream, but I do remember hard wires and soft flows of electrons. My eyes suddenly focus and I see her face inches away from mine. Somehow she knows what I am thinking. "Whose turn is it?" she says. *The antenna.*

8

At least a thousand hired kids are there setting up chairs in the arena this morning, but it's still hard to feel I'm not alone. The dome is that big. Voices get lost here. Even thoughts echo.

"It's gonna be a hell of a concert tonight. I know it." Jain had said that and smiled at me when she came through here about ten. She'd swept down the center aisle in a flurry of feathers and shimmering red strips, leaving all the civilians stunned and quivering.

God only knows why she was up this early; over the last eight months, I've never seen her get up before noon on a concert day. That kind of sleep-in routine would kill me. I was out of bed by eight this morning, partly because I've got to get this console modified by show-time, and partly because I didn't feel like being in the star's bed when she woke up.

"The gate's going to be a lot bigger than last night," Jain had said. "Can you handle it?"

"Sure. Can you?"

Jain had flashed me another brilliant smile and left. And so I sit here substituting circuit chips.

A couple kids climb on stage and pull breakfasts out of their backpacks. "You ever read this?" says one, pulling a tattered paperback from his hip pocket. His friend shakes her head. "You?" He turns the book in my direction; I recognize the cover.

It was two, maybe three months ago in Memphis, in a studio just before rehearsal. Jain had been sitting and reading. She reads quite a lot, though the promotional people downplay it—Alpertron, Ltd., likes to suck the country-girl image for all it's worth.

"What's that?" Stella says.

"A book." Jain holds up the book so she can see.

"I know that." Stella reads the title: *Receptacle.* "Isn't that the—"

"Yeah," says Jain.

Everybody knows about *Receptacle*—the best-seller of the year. It's all fact, about the guy who went to Prague to have a dozen artificial vaginas implanted all over his body. Nerve grafts, neural rerouting, the works. I'd seen him interviewed on some talk show where he'd worn a jumpsuit zipped to the neck.

"It's grotesque," Stella says.

Jain takes back the book and shrugs.

"Would you try something like this?"

"Maybe I'm way beyond it." *A receptacle works only one way.*

Stella goes white and bites off whatever it is she was about to say.

"Oh, baby, I'm sorry." Jain smiles and looks fourteen again. Then she stands and gives Stella a quick hug. She glances over at me and winks, and my face starts to flush. *One-way.*

Now, months later, I remember it and my skin again goes warm. "Get out of here," I say to the kids. "I'm trying to concentrate." They look irritated, but they leave.

I'm done with the circuit chips. Now the easy stuff. I wryly note the male and female plugs I'm connecting. *Jain* . . . The com circuit buzzes peremptorily and Jain's voice says, "Robbie? Can you meet me outside?"

I hesitate, then say, "Sure, I'm almost done with the board."

"I've got a car; we're going away."

"What?"

"Just for the afternoon."

"Listen, Jain—"

She says, "Hurry," and cuts off.

It's gonna be a hell of a concert.

• • •

9

Tonight's crowd strains even the capacity of the Rocky Mountain Central Arena. The gate people say there are more than nine hundred thousand people packed into the smoky recesses of the dome. It's not just hard to believe; it's scary. But computer ticket-totes don't lie.

I look out at the crowd and it's like staring at the Pacific after dark; the gray waves march out to the horizon until you can't tell one from the other. Here on the stage, the crowd-mutter even sounds like the sea, exactly as though I was on the beach trying to hear in an eighteen-foot surf. It all washes around me and I'm grateful for the twin earpieces, reassured to hear the usual check-down lists on the in-house com circuit.

I notice that the blowers have cut off. It's earlier than usual, but obviously there's enough body heat to keep the dome buoyed aloft. I imagine the Central Arena drifting away like that floating city they want to make out of Venice, California. There is something appealing about the thought of this dome floating away like dandelion fluff. But now the massive air-conditioning units hum on and the fantasy dies.

The house lights momentarily dim and the crowd noise raises a few decibels. I realize I can't see features or faces or even separate bodies. There are simply too many people to comprehend. The crowd has fused into one huge tectonic slab of flesh.

"Rob, are you ready?" The tech's soft voice in my earpiece.

"Ready."

"It's a big gate tonight. Can you do it?"

Sixty overlay tracks and one com board between Jain and maybe a cool million horny, sweating spectators? "Sure," I say. "Easy." But momentarily I'm not sure and I realize how tightly I'm gripping the ends of the console. I consciously will my fingers to loosen.

"Okay," the tech says. "But if anything goes wrong, cut it. Right? Damp it completely."

"Got it."

"Fine," he says. "About a minute, stand by. Ms. Snow wants to say hello."

"Hello, Robbie?"

"Yeah," I say. "Good luck."

Interference crackles and what she says is too soft to hear. I tell her, "Repeat, please."

"Stone don't break. At least not easy." She cuts off the circuit.

I've got ten seconds to stare out at that vast crowd. Where, I wonder, did the arena logistics people scrape up almost a million in/out headbands? I know I'm hallucinating, but for just a moment I see the scarlet webwork of broadcast power reaching out from my console to those million skulls. I don't know why; I find myself reaching for the shield that covers the emergency total cutoff. I stop my hand.

The house lights go all the way down; the only illumination comes from a thousand exit signs and the equipment lights. Then Moog Indigo troops onstage as the crowd begins to scream in anticipation. The group finds their instruments in the familiar darkness. The crowd is already going crazy.

Hollis strokes her color board and shoots concentric spheres of hard primaries expanding through the arena; red, yellow, blue. Start with the basics. Red.

Nagami's synthesizer spews a volcanic flow of notes like burning magma. And then Jain is there. Center stage.

"Damn it," says the tech in my ear. "Level's too low. Bring it up in back." I must have been dreaming. I am performing stupidly, like an amateur. Gently I bring up two stim balance slides.

"—love you. Every single one of you."

The crowd roars back. The filling begins. I cut in four more low-level tracks.

"—ready. How about you?"

They're ready. I cut in another dozen tracks, then mute two. Things are building just a little too fast. The fine mesh around Jain's body seems to glitter with more than reflected light. Her skin already gleams with moisture.

"—get started easy. And then things'll get hard. Yeah?"

"YEAH!" from thousands of throats simultaneously.

I see her stagger slightly. I don't think I am feeding her too much too fast, but mute another pair of tracks anyway. Moog Indigo takes their cue and begins to play. Hollis gives the dome the smoky pallor of slow-burning leaves, Then Jain Snow sings.

And I fill her with them. And give her back to them.

> space and time
> measured in my heart

10

In the afternoon:

Jain gestures in an expansive circle. "This is where I grew up."

The mountains awe me. "Right here?"

She shakes her head. "It was a lot like this. My pa ran sheep. Maybe a hundred miles north."

"But in the mountains?"

"Yeah. Really isolated. My pa convinced himself he was one of the original settlers. He was actually a laid-off aerospace engineer out of Seattle."

The wind flays us for a moment; Jain's hair whips and she shakes it back from her eyes. I pull her into the shelter of my arms, wrapping my coat around us both. "Do you want to go back down to the car?"

"Hell, no," she says. "A mountain zephyr can't scare me off."

I'm not used to this much open space; it scares me a little, though I'm not going to admit that to Jain. We're above timberline, and the mountainside is too stark for my taste. I suddenly miss the rounded, wooded hills of Pennsylvania. Jain surveys the rocky fields rubbed raw by wind and snow, and I have a quick feeling she's scared too. "Something wrong?"

"Nope. Just remembering."

"What's it like on a ranch?"

"Okay, if you don't like people," she says slowly, obviously recalling details. "My pa didn't."

"No neighbors?"

"Not a one in twenty miles."

"Brothers?" I say. "Sisters?"

She shakes her head. "Just my pa." I guess I look curious because she looks away and adds, "My mother died of tetanus right after I was born. It was a freak thing."

I try to change the subject. "Your father didn't come down to the first concert, did he? Is he coming tonight?"

"No way," she says. "He didn't and he won't. He doesn't like what I do." I can't think of anything to say now. After a while Jain rescues me. "It isn't your hassle, and it isn't mine anymore."

Something perverse doesn't let me drop it now. "So you grew up alone."

"You noticed," she says softly. "You've got a hell of a way with understatement."

I persist. "Then I don't understand why you still come up here. You must hate this."

"Ever see a claustrophobe deliberately walk into a closet and shut the door? If I don't fight it this way—" Her fingers dig into my arms. Her face is fierce. "This has got to be better than what I do on stage." She swings away from me. "Shit!" she says. "Damn it all to hell." She stands immovable, staring down the mountain for several minutes. When she turns back toward me, her eyes are softer and there's a fey tone in her voice. "If I die—" She laughs. "When I die. I want my ashes here."

"Ashes?" I say, unsure how to respond. *Humor her.* "Sure."

"You." She points at me. "Here." She indicates the rock face. The words are simple commands given to a child.

"Me." I manage a weak smile.

Her laugh is easy and unstrained now. "Kid games. Did you do the usual things when you were a kid, babe?"

"Most of them." *I hardly ever won, but then I liked to play games with outrageous risks.*

"Hammer, rock, and scissors?"

"Sure, when I was really young." I repeat by long-remembered rote: "Rock breaks scissors, scissors cut paper, paper covers rock."

"Okay," she says. "Let's play." I must look doubtful. "Rob," she says warningly.

"Okay." I hold out my right hand.

Jain says, "One, two, three." On "three," we each bring up our right hand. Hers is a clenched fist: stone. My first two fingers form the snipping blades of a pair of scissors. "I win!" she crows, delighted.

"What do you win?"

"You. Just for a little while." She pulls my hands close and lays them on her body.

"Right here on the mountain?" I say.

"I'm from pioneer stock. But you—" She shrugs. "Too delicate?"

I laugh and pull her close.

"Just—" She hesitates. "Not like the other times? Don't take this seriously, okay?"

In my want I forget the other occasions. "Okay."

Each of us adds to the other's pleasure, and it's better than the other times. But even when she comes, she stares through me, and I wonder whose face she's seeing—no, not even that: how many faces she's seeing. *Babe, no man can fill me like they do.*

And then I come also and—briefly—it doesn't matter.

My long coat is wrapped around the two of us, and we watch each other inches apart. "So much passion, Rob . . . It seems to build."

I remember the stricture and say, "You know why."

"You really like me so much?" *The little-girl persona.*

"I really do."

"What would you do for me, if I asked you?"

"Anything."

"Would you kill for me?"

I say, "Sure."

"Really?"

"Of course." I smile. I know how to play.

"This is no game."

My face must betray my confusion. I don't know how I should react.

Her expression mercurially alters to sadness. "You're scissors, Robbie. All shiny cold metal. How can you ever hope to cut stone?"

Would I want to?

11

Things get worse.

Is it simply that I'm screwing up on my own hook, or is it because we're exploring a place no performance has ever been? I don't have time to worry about it; I play the console like it was the keyboard on Nagami's synthesizer.

> *Take it*
> *When you can get it*
> *Where you can get it*

Jain sways and the crowd sways; she thrusts and the crowd thrusts. It is one gigantic act. It is as though a temblor shakes the Front Range.

Insect chittering in my earpiece: "What the hell's going on, Rob? I'm monitoring the stim feed. You're oscillating from hell to fade-out."

"I'm trying to balance." I juggle slides. "Any better?"

"At least it's no worse," says the tech. He pauses. "Can you manage the payoff?"

The payoff. The precision-engineered and carefully timed upslope leading to climax. The Big Number. I've kept the slim tracks plateaued for the past three sets. "Coming," I say. It's coming. There's time.

"You're in bad trouble with New York if there isn't," says the tech. "I want to register a jag. Now."

"Okay," I say.

> *Love me*
> *Eat me*
> *All of me*

"Better," the tech says. "But keep it rising. I'm still only registering a sixty percent."

Sure, bastard. It isn't your brain burning with the output of these million strangers. My violence surprises me. But I push the slim up to seventy. Then Nagami goes into a synthesizer riff, and Jain sags back against a vertical rank of amps.

"Robbie?" It comes into my left ear, on the in-house com circuit reserved for performer and me alone.

"I'm here, Jain."

"You're not trying, babe."

I stare across the stage and she's looking back at me. Her eyes flash emerald in the wave from Hollis's color generator. She subvocalizes so her lips don't move.

"I mean it."

"This is new territory," I answer. "We never had a million before." I know she thinks it's an excuse.

"This is it, babe," she says. "It's tonight. Will you help me?"

I've known the question would come, though I hadn't known who'd articulate it—her or me. My hesitation stretches much longer in my head than it does in realtime. *So much passion, Rob . . . It seems to build. Would you kill for me?*

"Yes," I say.

"Then I love you," and breaks off as the riff ends and she struts back out into the light. I reluctantly touch the console and push the stim to seventy-five. Fifty tracks are in. *Jain, will you love me if I don't?*

A bitter look

Eighty. I engage five more tracks. Five to go. The crowd's getting damn near all of her. And, of course, the opposite's true.

A flattering word

Since I first heard her in Washington, I've loved this song the best. I push more keys. Eighty-two. Eighty-five. I know the tech's happily watching the meters.

A kiss

The last tracks cut in. *Okay, you're getting everything from the decaying food in her gut to her deepest buried childhood fears of an empty echoing house.*

Ninety.

A sword

And the song ends, one last diminishing chord, but her body continues to move. For her there is still music.

On the com circuit the tech yells: "Idiot! I'm already reading ninety. Ninety, damn it. There's still one number to go."

"Yeah," I say. "Sorry. Just . . . trying to make up for previous lag-time."

He continues to shout and I don't answer. On the stage Nagarni and Hollis look at each other and at the rest of the group, and then Moog Indigo slides into the last number with scarcely a pause. Jain turns toward my side of the stage and gives me a soft smile. And then it's back to the audience and into the song she always tops her concerts with, the number that really made her.

Fill me like the mountains

Ninety-five. There's only a little travel left in the console slides.

The tech's voice is aghast. "Are you out of your mind, Rob? I've got a ninety-five here—damned needle's about to peg. Back off to ninety."

"Say again?" I say. "Interference. Repeat, please."

"I said back off! We don't want her higher than ninety."

Fill me like the sea

Jain soars to the climax. I shove the slides all the way forward. The crowd is on its feet; I have never been so frightened in my life.

"Rob! I swear to God you're canned, you—"

Somehow Stella's on the com line too: "You son of a bitch! You hurt her—"

Jain flings her arms wide. Her back arches impossibly.

All of me

One hundred.

I cannot rationalize electronically what happens. I cannot imagine the affection and hate and lust and fear cascading into her and pouring back out. But I see the antenna mesh around her naked body glowing suddenly whiter until it flares in an actinic flash and I shut my eyes.

When I open them again, Jain is a blackened husk tottering toward the front of the stage. Her body falls over the edge into the first rows of spectators.

The crowd still thinks this is part of the set, and they love it.

12

No good-byes. I know I'm canned. When I go into the Denver Alpertron office in another day and a half to pick up my final check, some subordinate I've never seen before gives me the envelope.

"Thanks," I say. He stares at me and says nothing.

I turn to leave and meet Stella in the hall. The top of her head comes only to my shoulders, and so she has to tilt her face up to glare at me. She says, "You're not going to be working for any promoter in the business. New York says so."

"Fine," I say. I walk past her.

Before I reach the door, she stops me by saying, "The initial report is in already."

I turn. "And?"

"The verdict will probably end up accidental death. Everybody's bonded.

Jain was insured for millions. Everything will turn out all right for everyone."
She stares at me for several seconds. "Except Jain. You bastard."

We have our congruencies.

The package comes later, along with a stiff legal letter from a firm of attorneys. The substance of the message is this: "Jain Snow wished you to have possession of this. She informed you prior to her demise of her desires; please carry them out accordingly." The package contains a chrome cylinder with a screw cap. The cylinder contains ashes; ashes and a few bone fragments. I check. Jain's ashes, unclaimed by father, friends, or employer.

I drive West, away from the soiled towers of the strip-city. I drive beyond the coal strip pits and into the mountains until the paved highway becomes narrow asphalt and then rutted earth and then only a trace, and the car can go no further. With the metal cylinder in one hand I flee on foot until I no longer hear sounds of city or human beings.

At last the trees end and I climb over bare mountain grades. I rest briefly when the pain in my lungs is too sharp. to ignore. At last I reach the summit.

I scatter Jain's ashes on the wind.

Then I hurl the empty cylinder down toward the timberline; it rolls and clatters and finally is only a distant glitter on the talus slope.

"Jain!" I scream at the sky until my voice is gone and vertigo destroys my balance. The echoes die. As Jain died.

I lie down unpeacefully—exhausted—and sleep, and my dreams are of weathered stone. And I awake empty.

• • •

Edward Bryant has had more than a dozen books published as well as numerous short stories. This story, "Stone," garnered Bryant a Hugo nomination and the first of his two Nebula Awards. Of it, and music, he writes: "Long, long ago, on a highway far away, I was roadtripping to the east and woke up in an Interstate rest area just outside Des Moines, Iowa. I rolled down the window to Midwestern mugginess and flipped on the radio. An AM station was playing a Janis Joplin set. I'd loved her from her albums and had seen her live at the Family Dog in Denver. Damn. 'Stone' pretty much came to me whole cloth. Me, I'm no musician. But I love to use music in my stories. If I weren't a writer, I'd love to be a musician—professional or amateur. At this moment I'm trying to compose a symphony, a giant retrospective of my short fiction for Arkham House."

• • • •

Mercenary
Lawrence C. Connolly

I got lost on my way home from a failed audition, took a bad turn near the East End, and wound up in a district of dark streets and derelict buildings. It was the last place you'd expect to find traffic, but suddenly there it was, closing in around me, streaming from all directions until I was bumper to bumper on a congested backstreet.

A biker roared past me, advanced a little ways ahead, then stopped to light a cigarette as the traffic crawled past her.

I rolled down my window, called to her. "Hey? Where's everyone headed?"

She had this black thing going: jacket, eyes, gages—all jet black. Only a streak of silver in her tied-back hair and the pale skin of her face broke the gloom. And there was something alluring about her, and something faintly familiar in her voice as she said: "What? You lost?"

"Yeah. Looks that way."

Ahead of us, the traffic inched forward. Behind, horns blared.

She ignored them. "So you're not here for the show?"

"What show?"

"Bobbie Quicksilver. Heard of him?"

"No."

"Well, now you have. Come on." She put the bike in gear. "There's a spot up ahead."

She swung into the space, then pulled onto the sidewalk to give me room. But it wasn't a parking zone. I saw that when I was halfway in.

"Come on!" She waved, urging me to take it. "Screw the hydrant! You won't be here long."

I angled in, turned off the car.

"Five minutes," she said. "Ten max. The traffic will clear out. You can turn around then. Be out of here in no time."

I got out of the car, turning to keep my left side toward her, the way I still do when I meet a woman I'm attracted to. It's not that I'm self-conscious. I just like making clean first impressions. "You said these people are here for a show?"

"Yeah. Curious?"

"You could say that."

"Want to come with me? I could give you a lift if you don't mind parking here." She took a last drag on her cigarette, then flicked it away. "Actually . . . truth is . . . if the cops come by, I don't think they'll be writing tickets."

A moment later I was sitting behind her, hugging her waist as she eased between the cars. She told me that her name was Ariana. She was a blogger, not a *Silverhead*.

"What's a Silverhead?"

"That's the obvious question, isn't it?"

A warehouse appeared at the end of the street, standing in a concrete lot that had crumbled into something resembling gravel. Cars were parked everywhere, wedged in tight around walls covered with boards, no-trespassing signs, and a fresh layer of graffiti reading:

BOBBIE QUICKSILVER JAMS TONIGHT

Ariana stopped her bike, got off, and looked around at the crowd. "What do you think? A thousand people?"

"Maybe."

"That's a lot for one of these, though the one in Allentown was supposedly bigger."

I considered the graffiti. "So Bobbie Quicksilver? He's some kind of performer?"

"Yeah. *Some* kind. Performs all over. Rust-belt towns mostly."

"He's on tour?"

"Not exactly. He only does guerilla shows. No advance notice, flash-media announcements only. The time and location for this gig went out less than two hours ago." She unzipped her jacket, took out a palm-size Nikon. "Stay close." She took my arm, pulling me in tight beside her. "Silverheads don't like having their events recorded." She held the camera between us, clicking the shutter. "Don't look at the camera. We're just two Silverheads hanging out before the show. Talk to me."

"Okay."

"Does that pass for talk where you come from?"

"No. Sorry. Uh . . . who do you write for?"

"I'm independent." She stopped snapping pictures, put the camera back in her pocket, took out a Sharpie. "Here." She wrote a URL on my palm. "Check this out when you get home." She folded my hand closed as if to keep me from dropping the address. "What about you? What do you do?"

There were two answers to that. I gave her the safe one. "I'm a musician." I was looking directly at her now, the right side of my face fully in view.

"Really?" She studied the scars running like train tracks along my neck and jaw. "You didn't get those playing 'Free Bird.'"

"No." I laughed. It was genuine. She had put me at ease. "The scars are from another life. It's behind me now." I had a few business cards in my wallet, printed out at home from a design template and featuring a photo taken with my iPhone. I'd made them special for my audition earlier that afternoon, had given one to the band manager, and was prepared to offer the rest to the other musicians if they'd seemed interested. They hadn't. I had plenty to spare. "This is what I do now."

She took it, tilting it toward the evening light. "Lorcan? What kind of name—"

"Irish."

"You Irish?"

"No, just Lorcan."

"You live on Spahr Street? I know that neighborhood." She put the card in her pocket. "Listen, would you want to maybe do an interview, give me a musician's assessment of Bobbie Quicksilver."

"What I think of his performance?"

"Yeah. I'm not really in a position to judge. I don't usually cover music."

"Sounds like you want me to catch the show."

"Sounds like you catch on fast, Lorcan." She put her camera away and started toward the building. "Coming?"

I followed, joined the crowd, and entered the warehouse. A portable stage stood at the far end, covered with instruments: guitars, keyboards, turntables, drums.

"How big's his band?"

"Not his. It's all Silverheads. Anyone who wants to play can. They jam. He sings. It's all improv. At least, that's what I've read. This is my first time too." She took my arm. "Stay close." She had her camera out again, cupping it in her palm, clicking the shutter while some audience members took the stage. Like the rest of the milling crowd, they were a mix of working-class types: a woman in grunge flannel shouldering a Fender bass, a kid in a black T and work boots dropping a needle to cue a track, and a man in bib-overalls sliding into position behind a drum kit, testing the pedals: *Whuuuump! Whuuuump!* All of them looked as if they would have been right at home working in the warehouse. Perhaps some of the older ones had.

"Which one's him?" I asked.

"Quicksilver? None of them. He doesn't show till everyone's playing."

"He's here somewhere?"

"Maybe. Maybe not. Everything I've read claims he simply appears. The band starts playing, finds a groove, and then—"

The guitarist tapped his microphone. "How y'all doing tonight?"

Cheers.

"Ready to bring on Bobbie?"

More cheers, louder.

The guitar player glanced behind himself at the rest of the stage. "Looks like we still have a few positions available. Anyone for congas?"

The crowd shifted. Someone called a name. Then a woman in a postal uniform stepped forward, taking the stage to friendly applause.

The guitar man stepped aside, making room. "Good to see you, Shauna."

"Good to be seen, Hank." She gave each skin an easy slap—*Thonk! Thunk!*—then set her hands in place, ready to go.

Hank turned back toward the mic. "Y'all know how this works. You want to play, you come up. No need to ask. There's room. Bobbie likes to keep it democratic." He shifted his guitar, resting the body on his hip. It was a raggedy looking Telecaster, a vintage hollow body that might have been worth a fortune if its finish hadn't been worn to bare wood around the pick guard. He tapped the strings, the contact registering as a crack from the amplifier. Then he swung his arm, brought it down hard on a power chord, and the band was off, thundering through the opening strains of something I knew but couldn't place, an easy slice of classic rock—primal and catchy—but infiltrated with turntable scratch and sampled loops. A wave rippled through the crowd. People danced. I would have joined them, but Ariana held me tight, apparently unmoved by the music. "I'm going to try some video." She still had the camera out, working it at her side. "Stay close." She turned with me, panning the crowd.

"This is amazing," I said.

"And it hasn't even started." She turned back toward the stage, angling closer, finding a vantage that offered a more-or-less unobstructed view. "Let's hold up here. I want to be—"

A new sound emerged, riding the band's rhythm as a figure appeared beside the guitar player. It crouched, hunkering low between the monitors. It looked small, disfigured, more troll than man. But that apparent trick of the light ended when he stood up and spread his arms. Spotlights converged, setting him aglow, his face like a flame in the crossing beams.

"That's him!" I shouted, knowing it had to be.

Ariana tensed.

"That's him, isn't it?"

She squeezed my arm, nails digging in as Quicksilver continued singing in a voice so close and clear that it seemed to come from somewhere inside me. I shivered, listening, hanging on words that didn't belong to anything the band was playing. Their music was predictable and familiar, wrapped around a three-chord jam that could have been "Johnny B. Goode" or "Going Up Country" or even "Spirit in the Sky"—but Quicksilver's vocals gave it something new, a wild counterpoint that transcended sound and meaning. And now I was dancing, unable to resist, feeling the music until Quicksilver suddenly dropped back into a crouch between the monitors.

I realized Ariana was no longer with me.

I looked around, didn't see her among the dancers, then turned back toward the stage where Quicksilver's glowing eyes seemed to be tracking something, focused on movement near the back of the warehouse.

Following his line of sight, I turned to see a door swing open on a wedge of twilight. Was it Ariana? Was she leaving?

The music faltered as I pushed through the crowd. A mic fell, landed with a pop, then squealed with feedback before someone turned it off. The players cut out one by one as I reached the door and looked into the blue-gray evening. The music had stopped. Lightning flashed bright against the face of an incoming storm. Ariana was twenty feet away, stumbling between parked cars, heading for her bike.

I went after her, moving faster as she paused, set her hand on the fender of a rusted Ford, and then dropped out of sight.

"Ariana!"

I rounded the car to find her doubled over, puking on the ground, splashing the tires. I came up behind her, set a hand on her back. A tremor went through her. "No!" She pushed me away.

"What happened?"

She wiped her mouth, then looked at me. Her eyes were wide, frightened. "You tell me, Lorcan. What did you see?"

"You mean Quicksilver?"

"Tell me!"

"Same thing you—"

"Don't bet on that, Lorcan. Tell me. What did he look like?"

I tried telling her, describing the glowing man with the silver voice.

She cut me off. "That's not what I saw. Jesus, Lorcan!" She shivered, hugged herself, then glanced toward the warehouse. "I need to get out of here."

People were leaving the building now, gathering along the graffitied wall, looking at us.

I tried walking her toward her bike.

"Hold on." She took out her camera, aimed it back at the crowd, hit record. "What do you see, Calder?" She angled the view screen toward me. I glanced at it. The people were small, pixilated. I had to look behind us to be sure what they were doing, and then I knew.

They were coming toward us.

"Maybe they just want to check on you," I said.

"Fat chance."

We hurried through the lot.

"They're after us, Lorcan." She put the camera away as we reached her bike. Then she climbed on, kicked the starter. "Get on if you want. If not, you're on your own."

The crowd was coming faster now.

I climbed on behind her, holding tight as she sped out of the lot and down the street. My car came into view, still wedged tight beside the hydrant. She braked hard. I climbed off, expecting to follow her in my car, but she gunned the bike as soon as I was clear of the saddle, roaring away, leaving me in a cloud of exhaust.

The crowd sounded nearer, out of sight but still advancing. I got into my car, pulled from the curb, and burned rubber till I reached the cross street. She wasn't in sight when I rounded the corner . . . nor when I rounded the next.

By the third street, I realized I was only a block from Smallman, the main artery leading through the Strip District and toward Fort Pitt Boulevard.

No longer lost, I steered toward home.

An hour later, dressed in a robe and still damp from a shower that had cleaned everything but the permanent marker on my palm, I went to my computer and logged on to Ariana's blog. It was pretty barebones, no bio or graphics, but plenty of posts about politics, fringe science, weird news.

Her most recent screed bore the heading:

THE SECRET WORLD OF SILVERHEADS
THE MUSIC SCENE YOU'VE NEVER SEEN

It gave an overview of Bobbie Quicksilver, purporting to be based on information gained after hacking a private Quicksilver site.

Apparently, the first place anyone had encountered Bobbie Quicksilver had been on a community discussion board, on a thread devoted to the doubts and aspirations of bottom-feeding musicians. It was there that someone with the username Hg80 had posted a link to a private forum, one that he claimed might be of interest to likeminded dreamers.

People going to the site confronted a string of apparently random images, each accompanied with the same question: *What do you see?* Those who made it to the next level were asked to respond to a list of personal and philosophical prompts. After that, selected applicants received access to a private discussion board where they found a posted manifesto by Hg80, in which he revealed that the forum would serve as a place for planning private gatherings to be held in free spaces throughout the rustbelt region of Pennsylvania, West Virginia, and Ohio:

We'll focus on towns where security is minimal, where police forces are bankrupt and understaffed, where the industries and businesses that once provided our nonmusical livelihoods sit empty and forgotten. Fittingly, our venues will be abandoned warehouses, wharfs, rooftops, lots, depots, and mills—places abandoned by the world at large.

I have set up this discussion in hopes of attracting the attention of the creative and adventurous souls needed to make our dream a reality, people who can play music, paint signs, highjack power lines, rig locations for light and sound. At each event, we will move in fast, spend a couple hours celebrating who we are, and clear out before the Powers That Be realize we were ever there.

Anyone who wishes to jam at these events is free to do so, and if all goes well I will join in. My name is Bobbie Quicksilver. I may not be one of you, but I share your dreams. Together, we can make things happen.

The first concert was in a derelict depot near Pittsburgh, where Quicksilver sang for an hour in front of a hundred stunned spectators before vanishing (some claimed literally) just ahead of the cops.

A week later, Silverheads commandeered a vacant lot in McKeesport, withheld announcement of the event until ninety minutes before the show, and got Quicksilver for nearly two sets. Some said he would have played longer if a television crew hadn't arrived with satellite van and cameras.

"We're not about publicity," Quicksilver wrote in a post the next day. "When people are ready, we will reveal our agenda. Until then, we'll play in the shadows."

Soon fans were staging five to six shows a month, with Silverheads commandeering locations as far west as Indiana. But not everyone who discovered the concerts became a true believer, and some of the skeptics posted blogs warning of hidden threats, secret agendas. Inexplicably, such comments soon disappeared, and their sources never posted on the subject again.

Ariana's preliminary survey of the Quicksilver scene ended with her announcing she was one such skeptic. Unlike the others, however, she claimed to possess the journalistic acumen to expose the mystery. She wrote: "This screed has been timed to go live while I'm attending Quicksilver's most recent show. Later tonight, I intend to report what I see. Check back. All will be revealed."

It was nearly midnight. I refreshed my screen, hoping Ariana had posted her update. But instead of getting a new blog entry, I was soon staring at *404 Error: Page Not Found*. Her site had vanished. I hit the browser's reload; the error message reappeared.

I was in the process of reentering the URL from my palm when a sudden buzzing broke my concentration.

Someone was downstairs, ringing to be let in.

I crossed the room, pressed the talk button. "Yeah?"

"Lorcan!" It was Ariana, sounding even more unhinged than when we'd been running from the Silverheads. "Lorcan! Help me!"

I put my finger on the unlock switch, hesitated, then hit the talk button once more. "Hold on. I'm coming down."

"Lorcan!" Her voice echoed in the hall outside my apartment, rising up the stairwell. With it came a frantic pounding, as if she were slapping her hands against the glass. "Help me!"

I hurried down, bare feet slipping on the nappy carpet, trying to get to her before she broke the window. But when I reached the front hall, I stopped cold.

"Lorcan! Help me!"

Handprints covered the pane, smeared and streaked, almost hiding her face behind a haze of blood.

Quicksilver had ambushed her as she rode away. But it wasn't the Quicksilver I had seen in the warehouse. That image had been a lie.

"You didn't see the truth, Lorcan." She lay in my bathtub, cleaning her wounds, her clothes a bloody heap on the bathroom floor. "What you saw tonight—what you and all those other people saw, it wasn't the real Quicksilver." She had three gashes running from her left temple to the corner of her mouth. One gash just missed her eye, but another had snagged her ear and ripped out the gage. Her lobe dangled, split in two.

"I should take you to the hospital."

"No, Lorcan. No way."

"I don't think I can patch you up myself."

"You're going to try." She sat up, sloshing in the bloody water. In spite of her wounds, she was beautiful. I shouldn't have noticed that, considering her condition. But there it was, and she must have sensed what I was thinking because she said: "We could get it on if I wasn't so messed up, Lorcan."

"That's okay, Ariana."

"What? That I'm messed up?"

"Not that."

"That we can't get it on?"

"You know what I mean."

She reached for me, pushing back the collar of my robe, seeing how the worst of my scars extended to my chest. "Tell me about this."

"It's from another life, Ariana."

"You said that before. Now tell me the rest." She shifted again, wincing deeper this time. "Come on. I'm in a pretty good position to sympathize. Tell me."

I turned away, thinking it through, deciding where to begin, how much to tell. "I was in Afghanistan," I said at last. "I'd gotten into some trouble. I was lost."

"Like tonight?"

"Yeah, but that's not typical. I almost never get lost, even in unfamiliar terrain. I have an intuitive sense of direction, but that night I'd been injured." I raised my robe enough for her to see the scars on my thigh. "I was on foot, night falling fast, then along came an old Jeep full of Afghans, all impeccably dressed, going to a wedding."

"A wedding party in the middle of Afghanistan?"

"Not the middle. The boarder area near Pakistan. And they weren't the wedding party, just the musicians. They offered to take me to the village, get someone to patch me up, send word to my people."

"The military?"

"No. My people weren't the military."

"Journalists?"

"Listen, here's the part you need to know. I was bleeding and dirty, but they made room and drove me to the village where the locals found me a bed for the night." I stared at the wall, reliving it now, seeing it all as if it were happening again. "It was a small bed, made for a child. I couldn't lie flat, and I was sitting up, listening to the wedding music playing across the way. The sound lessened my pain, put me at ease. That's the thing about music, it changes us, alters our perceptions. At least, it's always been that way with me. So I was sitting there, no longer hurting . . . and then suddenly everything exploded. It was a drone attack . . . direct hit on the celebration." I paused, swallowed. "Score one for the insurgents."

"The insurgents had drones?"

"No. The American forces had drones, but insurgents had information. They provided the coordinates, claimed the place was a Taliban safe house. That's the way they like to do it. They get others to settle their differences. Keeps them from having to take out their own kind."

I had a pretty well stocked first-aid kit, and after she'd soaked for a while I used it to patch her up. Then I went downstairs and cleaned her blood from the door. When I got back she was lying on my couch, staring at the ceiling. "Got any beer, Lorcan?"

"I don't think that's a good idea."

"I need to talk, Lorcan. Trust me. Drinking will make it easier."

I got us each a bottle, then sat beside her as she described the Quicksilver she had seen, a creature only vaguely human. "He uses the music as a shield. Somehow, in the lights, performing for the right people, he hides what he really is."

"The *right* people."

"Yeah. People like you. Like you said, music alters moods, changes perspective—"

"Changes a monster to a man?"

"I know. Sounds crazy. But it explains why he started singing before stepping into the lights, and why he left the stage so quickly when the music stopped."

"I really don't think—"

"You were there, Lorcan. You saw—"

"A charismatic performer—"

"But that's not what I saw, and that's why Quicksilver came for me, would have killed me if I hadn't gotten away."

There was no denying her wounds, but I needed more proof. "You took pictures, right? There's no music on a still image. We should look—"

"We can't." She sat up, wincing the way she had when sitting in the tub. "Quicksilver took my jacket, pulled it off me when I tried getting away. My camera and wallet were in the pockets."

"We should call the police."

"And tell them what?"

I had been sitting on the floor beside the couch. Now I got up and paced, thinking.

"My wallet, Lorcan! You know what that means? It knows who I am, where I live!"

"Maybe not. You said it pulled the jacket off you. Are you sure it kept it, took those things from your pockets?"

"No, but—"

"Will you be okay on your own for a while?"

"You leaving me?"

"I need to check on some things."

"Where?"

"I'll tell you. Hang on."

I went into my bedroom. My guitar case leaned against the cabinet, right where I had put it after returning home. It was the same Stratocaster I'd been playing since high school, the same one I'd come back to off-and-on ever since, trying to become the musician I knew I really didn't have the chance of being. I had a decent ear, but my marketable skills lay elsewhere.

I picked up the case, tossed it onto the bed, then opened the closet and got out my field clothes, vest, knife, pistol—tools of my other trade.

She called from down the hall, voice weak and frightened. "What're you doing?"

I dressed and hurried back to her, the weapons secured under the vest. "You remember where Quicksilver ambushed you? The street name, any landmarks?"

"No."

"Was it far from the warehouse?"

"It was close. Within a couple blocks."

"A couple meaning two?"

She paused, thinking. "Maybe three."

"You were riding, right? Did Quicksilver step in front of you? Force you to stop?"

"Yes."

"Did you brake hard? Leave a skid?"

"Yes. I lost control, crashed to the pavement."

I picked up the apartment's landline, dialed my cell phone number, and hung up. "Hit redial if you need me," I said. "I'm going to go look for your jacket. Then I'll drop by the warehouse, see if there's anyone there who'll talk to me."

"Why?"

"They might be able to help. I'm thinking that might have been all they were trying to do when you ran away. If Quicksilver's hiding behind their music, there's a good chance they're no more complicit than I am."

"But what if they are?"

"Then maybe they'll give that away when I talk to them, and that'll be all right too. It'll tell us a little more about where we stand, what we're dealing with." I started toward the door, paused, looked back at her. "It's not that I don't believe you, Ariana. It's just . . . I need to do this."

She stared at me. "All right." Her voice was thin and full of pain, but something in her eyes told me she approved. We couldn't just huddle together in my apartment. We had to take action, even if it was only revisiting the scene, gathering information, assessing our losses.

The rain that had been threatening earlier in the evening had come and gone, leaving behind a heavy fog that muted the streetlights, stilled the air. I felt alone, uncommonly afraid, and more willing than ever to believe Ariana's crazy stories. Yet one thing gnawed at me. If Quicksilver was a monster, what was the agenda? What harm could Quicksilver possibly do by helping musicians find one another, celebrate their talents, and bring joy to an increasingly joyless world? It seemed more like the work of an angel than a demon.

I drove east on Smallman until I reached the now-familiar side street. From there I headed back to the dark, boarded-up warehouse. The cars and people were gone, only the graffiti announcing Quicksilver's performance remained. I did a U-turn and drove the route again, making two circuits before noticing a streak of burned rubber on the pavement two blocks from the warehouse. I parked and got out, studied the concrete and found some shards of broken taillight. Nearby, an alley ran deep and shadowed between close-set walls. About fifty feet back, something lay sprawled beside a sewer grate. I walked to it, picked it up, studied it in the glare of my flashlight. It was a jacket, or had been. It was now a mass of shredded leather and ripped lining. Only one of the pockets remained. Nothing in it. I knelt beside the sewer, shined my light through the grate . . .

Something moved beside me. I swung the beam to my left.

There it was, twenty feet away, looking at first like a large dog. But then it stood, raising its arms in a gesture that recalled Quicksilver's appearance on the warehouse stage. This time it didn't sing. It just stared with eyes the color of mucus set in skin so pale it revealed the tendons and veins of its tapered face.

I drew my pistol, braced it on my flashlight hand, took aim.

"Easy now." Its voice was low and rough, like the growl of an animal. No music in it now. "I'm not threatening you. Just watching." It lowered its arms. They were muscular and long, extending nearly to its knees. "I saw you shining that light, figured you were looking for something. Did she send you?"

I kept the light centered on the creature, drawing down on its chest. Hideous as it was, its basic physiology seemed human. No doubt it had a heart. If necessary, I was prepared to find out.

"I want her things."

"Things?" Its long mouth seemed to chew the word. "Is this one of them?" It opened a hand, revealing Ariana's driver's license, her face smiling through the glare on the plastic.

"Where's the rest of it?" I said.

"Don't have it on me."

"Let's go get it then."

"No. I can't take you there. Not yet. But look. I have this too." It opened its other hand, revealing my business card, the edges slightly bent. "See? I know both of you—who you are, where you live."

"Put them on the ground and back away."

"I don't think so." It balled its fists, hiding the cards again. "How about I bring them to you . . . not now, though. At your place, sometime late, maybe when you're sleeping. I could sing for you."

"I want them now."

"Was nice meeting you, Lorcan."

"On the ground! Now!"

It stood there a second longer, staring at me. Then it vanished, but not into thin air. It was too corporeal for that. Instead it leaped backward, moving so quickly that an unskilled observer might have claimed it disappeared. But I heard the slap of its taloned feet scrabbling away in the darkness. I panned my light, caught the streak of its second leap, and then it was gone.

I stayed up all night, standing watch in my living room while Ariana slept on the couch. She got up late the next morning, alert but looking worse:

the side of her face clearly infected. I changed the dressing, then crashed on the couch while she monitored the Quicksilver forum for word of a second weekend event.

I wasn't sure I could sleep, but I did, falling into dreams that swirled with images of ordinary people dancing and singing, forgetting the bad luck and wrong turns that had stifled their lives. But the people in my dreams were not Silverheads. At first they were the disenfranchised youth at Golden Gate Park in 1966, drawn together by The Grateful Dead and a desire to end the war in Viet Nam. They were the people of Czechoslovakia in 1989, defying Soviet oppression by attending Prague's first appearance by The Rolling Stones. They were Hindu kids in 2008, rocking to the power chords of a Pakistani band that defied decades of blood-feuding politics to play live in Kashmir. I knew of these events. I was a student of music and politics, of rock and war. My life may have gravitated toward the latter, but I had not forgotten my roots . . . nor my disillusioned hope that rock 'n' roll might one day save the world from the politics of hate and division. I had believed that once. But I was older now, too disillusioned not to wonder what might happen when the music stopped and the thing called Quicksilver revealed its true agenda.

"Lorcan!"

I woke. Afternoon light spilled through my windows, illuminating a hovering silhouette. A bandaged hand grabbed my shoulder, shook me hard.

"Lorcan. It's in central West Virginia!"

I sat up.

Ariana turned, her face catching the light. She looked tired, but there was no pain in her eyes. "I mapped it, Lorcan. It's a hundred fifty miles south, show goes live in two hours."

"Too far," I said. "Not enough time. We'll have to wait for the next—"

"No! If we leave now—"

"We'll have to speed the whole way, do eighty . . . eighty-five through those mountains."

"Right. Like I said. We *can* do it!"

I packed my gear.

The site was a derelict foundry, dead smokestacks and yard houses standing dark behind chain-links, razor wire, and no-trespassing signs. The Silverheads had cut the fence. Inside, the mill's yard had filled with cars.

I parked on an access road outside the lot, then got out and started toward the crowd as it made its way toward a cavern of concrete and iron beams.

Ariana waited in the car. This was a one-man mission.

I didn't enter the building with the Silverheads, but made my way to a rusted ladder that led to a catwalk one hundred feet back from the band's stage. Here I unpacked my rifle, assembled the pieces, plugged my ears, and watched the crowd converge.

There was no sign of Quicksilver. *But he's here!* I felt his presence in the air, in the pulse of the people, the shadows they cast in the spotlight as they took the stage.

Electricity came from a line running in through a broken window. It connected to a box on a wooden pole. The setup looked improvised, a patchwork of spliced wires. I could only imagine what the other end looked like, the side that connected to a power company box somewhere beyond the derelict site. But from what I could see the work looked functional—the improvisations of skilled tradesmen who had learned to make do with what they had. It made me wonder again, as I had while dreaming on the couch, at the things such people could accomplish when they set their sights on bigger goals, when music shifted to political action. But such concerns weren't my reason for being here. My motivations were personal. I couldn't spend my life waiting for the thing that called itself Bobbie Quicksilver to come for me. I needed to be preemptive, stop the monster before it stopped me. If my actions served a larger good, so be it—all the better to justify the deed.

Tonight the stage featured an even more eclectic mix of instruments than it had the night before. Here, amid the drum kit, keyboards, turntables, bass, and guitars were a fiddle, dulcimer, Dobro, and a washtub bass—all affixed with pickups and jacked in to the main system. The musicians were mostly men, but it was a dreadlocked woman at the turntables who addressed the crowd through an ear-clip microphone. "How we feeling tonight?"

The crowd answered: cheers, clapping, a whistle from somewhere in the back. I heard it all clearly through my earplugs. The little foam cones were designed to suppress high-powered ballistics. They did not block sound. The woman's voice came through clear but muted.

"You ready to bring out Bobbie?"

More cheers.

"All right, then! Let's do it with this." The LED lamp on her headband cut a streak in the air as she looked around. Then she dropped a needle onto a rhythm track, a slice of vintage rock 'n' roll with a driving backbeat. One bar, and the band joined in, laying the foundation for Quicksilver's arrival.

Holding my position, I felt the bass in the trembling catwalk. And there was something else, fainter but undeniable. I felt Quicksilver. He was close.

I braced myself, resisted the music's power, trying not to get caught up in the pulsing mix. I admired it but remained detached, locked in position, focused on my craft until a new sound welled beneath the rhythm.

It came on first as a swirling chant beneath the music, rising between the punching riffs. Suddenly he was crouching in the lights, grinning at the crowd. He wore the same silver-white clothes he'd had on the night before, spotless and glowing, cutting tracers in the air as he leaped into a dervish spin. And all the while he sang, improvising over the band's foundation, taking the jam to a place so perfect that I couldn't believe it hadn't been planned.

The crowed danced, and in my mind—despite my efforts to remain aloof—I danced with them. My body remained as before, but my emotions soared.

Unlike the roar of the band, Quicksilver's words passed undimmed through my earplugs . . . or maybe they weren't passing through my ears at all. Maybe they were from someplace deeper, from inside me—as if his thoughts were singing directly into mine. The words were simple, but within them lay a coded story—an allegory of opposing entities: one intent on bringing people together, the other set on driving them apart. They weren't metaphysical forces, though they were often depicted that way. Instead, they were physical—living things that hid in plain sight. One worked by twisting perceptions through the power of sound. The other was a shape shifter, constantly altering its form but never its intentions.

Quicksilver looked up, eyes catching the light. For a moment I thought he was looking at me, but then his focus veered back to the crowd.

Shape shifter!

My mind flashed to the previous night, to details that hadn't quite fit together. But they did now. Now I understood.

I knew what I had to do.

I fired.

The music stopped.

I ran.

She stood outside the car, first looking toward the mill and the growing murmmer of the crowd, then toward me as I raced along the access road. "You did it!" Her voice sounded stronger than before. "I feel safer already."

I opened the trunk, tore down the rifle, closed the case.

She took my arm. Her touch felt warm, somehow alluring. Suddenly, in the valley below us, the music started again.

She turned, momentarily confused.

I could imagine what she was thinking. If I had shot Quicksilver, stopped his song, and left his true form lying in the spotlight—why would the band be playing again, picking up right where it had left off?

"Lorcan?"

I froze, suddenly certain I had made the wrong choice. But then Quicksilver's voice came welling from the valley, filling me with the conviction I had felt while lying on the catwalk.

"The power line," I said, watching her face. "I shot the power line."

Her face paled in the moonlight.

"I cut their power, but those people . . . they're good with their hands. They must have spliced it back together."

The color bled from her face, and with it went the wounds and swelling. Something new emerged, sharp and pale. Her grip moved from my shoulder to my neck, but my hand was already on my knife. I pulled it out and brought it up hard, driving it under her ribs, into the heart that I hoped lay slightly to the left of center.

She gasped.

The moonlight shifted, giving way to clouds, darkening her face. Her wounds returned, and with them her dark and frightened eyes. "Lorcan?" She stared, accusingly, and then her color changed again, becoming almost luminescent. "Lorcan!" She grabbed my hand, squeezing until my fingers felt ready to break against the knife's handle. Then she pulled the blade free and shoved me away, leaving me holding the weapon, its edge bright with silver blood. "Lorcan!" She growled my name, the sound deep in her throat, bubbling through the wound in her chest. "He got to you!"

"No. The choice was mine."

"Really?" And then she leaped away, but more slowly than last night when she had followed me from my apartment to reveal herself in the alley. She had planted that tire skid on the street, placed those bits of taillight on the pavement, and left the shredded jacket by the sewer. Then she had waited for me to find her . . . just as she had waited for me to find her in that line of traffic before the Quicksilver show. Each time, she had lured me, manipulated me, drawn me into position. I wasn't sure how she had done it the first time, but one fact remained: "I never get lost!" I shouted as she vanished into the darkness. "Never!"

But I wasn't convinced.

Even then, after all that I had seen and heard, doubts lingered.

I drove until Quicksilver's song gave way to the rush of traffic and the access road's darkness became the ebb and flow of passing headlights.

I came to a bridge, drove partway across, then parked in the emergency lane and got out to stand against the rail. I was shaking, too unmanned to drive.

The river below me caught the lights from the bridge, drawing them into long shimmers against the black water, and not for the first time in my life I felt caught between things vast and unknowable.

Or maybe they were not completely unknowable, for on one level the creatures that had called themselves Quicksilver and Ariana had one distinctly human trait.

They get others to settle their differences. Keeps them from having to take out their own kind.

I got back into my car, dialed in a classic rock station, and for a long time I just drove, going nowhere, riding the rhythms, trying to lose myself in the pulsing darkness.

• • •

Lawrence C. Connolly's music projects include *Veins: The Soundtrack*, an ambient-rock CD featuring soundscapes inspired by his novel *Veins* (2008); and *Songs of the Horror Writer*, a one man show that he performed for Reggie Oliver's Gaslight Music Hall at World Horror in 2010. His collections *Visions* (2009), *This Way to Egress* (2010), and *Voices* (2011) collect his best stories from *Amazing, Borderlands, Cemetery Dance, F&SF, Twilight Zone, Year's Best Horror*, and other sf/f/h magazines and anthologies. *Voices* was nominated for a 2011 Bram Stoker Award. Connolly blogs about storytelling, performance, and music at LawrenceCConnolly.com.

• • • •

The Erl-King
Elizabeth Hand

The kinkajou had been missing for two days now. Haley feared it was dead, killed by one of the neighborhood dogs or by a fox or wildcat in the woods. Linette was certain it was alive; she even knew where it was.

"Kingdom Come," she announced, pointing a long lazy hand in the direction of the neighboring estate. She dropped her hand and sipped at a mug of tepid tea, twisting so she wouldn't spill it as she rocked back and forth. It was Linette's turn to lie in the hammock. She did so with feckless grace, legs tangled in her long peasant skin, dark hair spilled across the faded canvas. She had more practice at it than Haley, this being Linette's house and Linette's overgrown yard bordering the woods of spindly young pines and birches that separated them from Kingdom Come. Haley frowned, leaned against the oak tree, and pushed her friend desultorily with one foot.

"Then why doesn't your mother call them or something?" Haley loved the kinkajou and justifiably feared the worst. With her friend exotic pets came and went, just as did odd visitors to the tumbledown cottage where Linette lived with her mother, Aurora. Most of the animals were presents from Linette's father, an elderly Broadway producer whose successes paid for the rented cottage and Linette's occasional artistic endeavors (flute lessons, sitar lessons, an incomplete course in airbrushing) as well as the bottles of Tanqueray that lined Aurora's bedroom. And, of course, the animals. An iguana whose skin peeled like mildewed wallpaper, finally lost (and never found) in the drafty dark basement where the girls held annual Hallowe'en seances. An intimidatingly large Moluccan cockatoo that escaped into the trees, terrorizing Kingdom Come's previous owner and his garden-party guests by shrieking at them in Gaelic from the wisteria. Finches and fire weavers small enough to hold in your fist. A quartet of tiny goats, Haley's favorites until the kinkajou.

The cockatoo started to smell worse and worse, until one day it flopped to the bottom of its wrought-iron cage and died. The finches escaped when Linette left the door to their bamboo cage open. The goats ran off into the woods surrounding Lake Muscanth. They were rumored to be living there still. But this summer Haley had come over every day to make certain the kinkajou had enough to eat, that Linette's cats weren't terrorizing it; that Aurora didn't try to feed it crème de menthe as she had the capuchin monkey that had fleetingly resided in her room.

"I don't know," Linette said. She shut her eyes, balancing her mug on her stomach. A drop of tea spilled onto her cotton blouse, another faint petal among faded ink stains and the ghostly impression of eyes left by an abortive attempt at batik. "I think Mom knows the guy who lives there now, she doesn't like him or something. I'll ask my father next time."

Haley prodded the hammock with the toe of her sneaker. "It's almost my turn. Then we should go over there. It'll die if it gets cold at night."

Linette smiled without opening her eyes. "Nah. It's still summer," she said, and yawned.

Haley frowned. She moved her back up and down against the bole of the oak tree, scratching where a scab had formed after their outing to Mandrake Island to look for the goats. It was early August, nearing the end of their last summer before starting high school, the time Aurora had named "the summer before the dark."

"My poor little girls," Aurora had mourned a few months earlier. It had been only June then, the days still cool enough that the City's wealthy fled each weekend to Kamensic Village to hide among the woods and wetlands in their Victorian follies. Aurora was perched with Haley and Linette on an ivied slope above the road, watching the southbound Sunday exodus of limousines and Porsches and Mercedes. "Soon you'll be gone."

"Jeez, Mom," laughed Linette. A plume of ivy tethered her long hair back from her face. Aurora reached to tug it with one unsteady hand. The other clasped a plastic cup full of gin. "No one's going anywhere, I'm going to Fox Lane,"—that was the public high school—"you heard what Dad said. Right, Haley?"

Haley had nodded and stroked the kinkajou sleeping in her lap. It never did anything but sleep, or open its golden eyes to half-wakefulness oh so briefly before finding another lap or cushion to curl into. It reminded her of Linette in that, her friend's heavy lazy eyes always ready to shut, her legs quick to curl around pillows or hammock cushions or Haley's own battle-scarred knees. "Right," said Haley, and she had cupped her palm around the soft warm globe of the kinkajou's head.

Now the hammock creaked noisily as Linette turned onto her stomach, dropping her mug into the long grass. Haley started, looked down to see her hands hollowed as though holding something. If the kinkajou died she'd never speak to Linette again. Her heart beat faster at the thought.

"I think we should go over. If you think it's there. *And*—" Haley grabbed the ropes restraining the hammock, yanked them back and forth so that Linette shrieked, her hair caught between hempen braids—"it's—*my*—turn—*now*."

They snuck out that night. The sky had turned pale green, the same shade as the crystal globe wherein three ivory-bellied frogs floated, atop a crippled table. To keep the table from falling Haley had propped a broom handle beneath it for a fourth leg—although she hated the frogs, bloated things with prescient yellow eyes. Some nights when she slept over they broke her sleep with their song, high-pitched trilling that disturbed neither Linette snoring in the other bed nor Aurora drinking broodingly in her tiny shed-roofed wing of the cottage. It was uncanny, almost frightening sometimes, how nothing ever disturbed them: not dying pets nor utilities cut off for lack of payment nor unexpected visits from Aurora's small circle of friends, People from the Factory Days she called them. Rejuvenated junkies or pop stars with new careers, or wasted beauties like Aurora Dawn herself. All of them seemingly forever banned from the real world, the adult world Haley's parents and family inhabited, magically free as Linette herself was to sample odd-tasting liqueurs and curious religious notions and lost arts in their dank corners of the City or the shelter of some wealthier friend's up-county retreat. Sleepy-eyed from dope or taut from amphetamines, they lay around the cottage with Haley and Linette, offering sips of their drinks, advice about popular musicians and contraceptives. Their hair was streaked with gray now, or dyed garish mauve or blue or green. They wore high leather boots and clothes inlaid with feathers or mirrors, and had names that sounded like the names of expensive perfumes: Liatris, Coppelia, Electric Velvet. Sometimes Haley felt that she had wandered into a fairy tale, or a movie. *Beauty and the Beast* perhaps, or *The Dark Crystal*. Of course it would be one of Linette's favorites; Linette had more imagination and sensitivity than Haley. The kind of movie Haley would choose to wander into would have fast cars and gunshots in the distance, not aging refugees from another decade passed out next to the fireplace.

She thought of that now, passing the globe of frogs. They went from the eerie interior dusk of the cottage into the strangely aqueous air outside. Despite the warmth of the late summer evening Haley shivered as she gazed back at the cottage. The tiny bungalow might have stood there unchanged for five hundred years, for a thousand. No warm yellow light spilled from the windows as it did at her own house. There was no smell of dinner cooking, no television chattering. Aurora seldom cooked, Linette never. There was no TV. Only the frogs hovering in their silver world, and the faintest cusp of a new moon like a leaf cast upon the surface of the sky.

The main house of the neighboring estate stood upon a broad slope of lawn overlooking the woods. Massive oaks and sycamores studded the grounds, and formal gardens that had been more carefully tended by the mansion's previous owner, a New York fashion designer recently dead. At the foot of the long drive a post bore the placard on which was writ in spidery silver letters: KINGDOM COME.

In an upstairs room Lie Vagal perched upon a windowsill. He stared out at the same young moon that watched Haley and Linette as they made their way through the woods. Had Lie known where to look he might have seen them as well; but he was watching the kinkajou sleeping in his lap.

It had appeared at breakfast two days earlier. Lie sat with his grandmother on the south terrace, eating Froot Loops and reading the morning mail, *The Wall Street Journal* and a quarterly royalty statement from BMI. His grandmother stared balefully into a bowl of bran flakes, as though discerning there unpleasant intimations of the future.

"Did you take your medicine, Gram?" asked Lie. A leaf fell from an overhanging branch into his coffee cup. He fished it out before Gram could see it as another dire portent.

"Did you take yours, Elijah?" snapped Gram. She finished the bran flakes and reached for her own coffee, black and laced with chicory. She was eighty-four years old and had outlived all of her other relatives and many of Lie's friends. "I know you didn't yesterday."

Lie shrugged. Another leaf dropped to the table, followed by a hail of bark and twigs. He peered up into the greenery, then pointed.

"Look," he said. "A squirrel or cat or something."

His grandmother squinted, shaking her head peevishly. "I can't see a thing."

The shaking branches parted to show something brown attached to a slender limb. Honey-colored, too big for a squirrel, it clung to a branch that dipped lower and lower, spattering them with more debris. Lie moved his coffee cup and had started to his feet when it fell, landing on top of the latest issue of *New Musical Express*.

For a moment he thought the fall had killed it. It just lay there, legs and long tail curled as though it had been a doodlebug playing dead. Then slowly it opened its eyes, regarded him with a muzzy golden gaze, and yawned, unfurling a tongue so brightly pink it might have been lipsticked. Lie laughed.

"It fell asleep in the tree! It's a—a what-you-call-it, a sloth."

His grandmother shook her head, pushing her glasses onto her nose. "That's not a sloth. They have grass growing on them."

Lie stretched a finger and tentatively stroked its tail. The animal ignored him, closing its eyes once more and folding its paws upon its glossy breast. Around its neck someone had placed a collar, the sort of leather-and-rhinestone ornament old ladies deployed on poodles. Gingerly Lie turned it, until he found a small heart-shaped tab of metal.

KINKAJOU
My name is Valentine
764-0007

"Huh," he said. "I'll be damned. I bet it belongs to those girls next door." Gram sniffed and collected the plates. Next to Lie's coffee mug, the compartmented container holding a week's worth of his medication was still full.

The animal did nothing but sleep and eat. Lie called a pet store in the City and learned that kinkajous ate insects and honey and bananas. He fed it Froot Loops, yogurt and granola, a moth he caught one evening in the bedroom. Tonight it slept once more, and he stroked it, murmuring to himself. He still hadn't called the number on the collar.

From here he could just make out the cottage, a white blur through dark leaves and tangled brush. It was his cottage, really; a long time ago the estate gardener had lived there. The fashion designer had been friends with the present tenant in the City long ago. For the last fourteen years the place had been leased to Aurora Dawn. When he'd learned that, Lie Vagal had given a short laugh, one that the realtor had mistaken for displeasure.

"We could evict her," she'd said anxiously. "Really, she's no trouble, just the town drunk, but once you'd taken possession—"

"I wouldn't *dream* of it." Lie laughed again, shaking his head but not explaining. "Imagine, having Aurora Dawn for a neighbor again . . ."

His accountant had suggested selling the cottage, it would be worth a small fortune now, or else turning it into a studio or guest house. But Lie knew that the truth was, his accountant didn't want Lie to start hanging around with Aurora again. Trouble; all the survivors from those days were trouble.

That might have been why Lie didn't call the number on the collar. He hadn't seen Aurora in fifteen years, although he had often glimpsed the girls playing in the woods. More than once he'd started to go meet them, introduce himself, bring them back to the house. He was lonely here. The visitors who still showed up at Aurora's door at four a.m. used to bang around Lie's place in the City. But that was long ago, before what Lie thought of as The Crash and what *Rolling Stone* had termed "the long tragic slide into madness of the onetime *force majeur* of underground rock and roll." And his agent and his lawyer wouldn't think much of him luring children to his woodland lair.

He sighed. Sensing some shift in the summer air, his melancholy perhaps, the sleeping kinkajou sighed as well, and trembled where it lay curled between his thighs. Lie lifted his head to gaze out the open window.

Outside the night lay still and deep over woods and lawns and the little dreaming cottage. A Maxfield Parrish scene, stars spangled across an ultramarine sky, twinkling bit of moon, there at the edge of the grass a trio of cottontails feeding peacefully amidst the dandelions. He had first been drawn to the place because it looked like this, like one of the paintings he collected. "Kiddie stuff," his agent sniffed; "fairy tale porn." Parrish and Rackham and Nielsen and Clarke. Tenniel prints of Alice's trial. The DuFevre painting of the Erl-King that had been the cover of Lie Vagal's second, phenomenally successful album. For the first two weeks after moving he had done nothing but pace the labyrinthine hallways, planning where they all would hang, this picture by this window, that one near another. All day, all night he paced; and always alone.

Because he was afraid his agent or Gram or one of the doctors would find out the truth about Kingdom Come, the reason he had really bought the place. He had noticed it the first time the realtor had shown the house. She'd commented on the number of windows there were—

"South-facing, too, the place is a hundred years old but it really functions as passive solar with all these windows. That flagstone floor in the green room acts as a heat sink—"

She nattered on, but Lie said nothing. He couldn't believe that she didn't notice. No one did, not Gram or his agent or the small legion of people brought in from Stamford who cleaned the place before he moved in.

It was the windows, of course. They always came to the windows first.

The first time he'd seen them had been in Marrakech, nearly sixteen years ago. A window shaped like a downturned heart, looking out onto a sky so blue it seemed to drip; and outside, framed within the window's heavy white curves, Lie saw the crouching figure of a young man, bent over some object that caught the sun and flared so that he'd had to look away. When he'd turned back the young man was staring up in amazement as reddish smoke like dust roiled from the shining object. As Lie watched, the smoke began to take the shape of an immense man. At that point the joint he held burned Lie's fingers and he shouted, as much from panic as pain. When he looked out again the figures were gone.

Since then he'd seen them many times. Different figures, but always familiar, always fleeting, and brightly colored as the tiny people inside a marzipan egg. Sinbad and the Roc; the little mermaid and her sisters; a brave little figure carrying a belt engraved with the words SEVEN AT A BLOW. The steadfast tin soldier and a Christmas tree soon gone to cinders; dogs with eyes as big as teacups, as big as soup plates, as big as millstones. On tour in Paris, London, Munich, L.A., they were always there, as likely (or unlikely) to appear in a hotel room overlooking a dingy alley as within the crystal mullions of some heiress's bedroom. He had never questioned their presence, not after that first shout of surprise. They were the people, *his* people; the only ones he could trust in what was fast becoming a harsh and bewildering world.

It was just a few weeks after the first vision in Marrakech that he went to that fateful party; and a few months after that came the staggering success of *The Erl-King*. And then The Crash, and all the rest of it. He had a confused memory of those years. Even now, when he recalled that time it was as a movie with too much crosscutting and no dialogue. An endless series of women (and men) rolling from his bed; dark glimpses of himself in the studio cutting *Baba Yaga* and *The Singing Bone*; a few overlit sequences with surging crowds screaming soundlessly beneath a narrow stage. During those years his visions of the people changed. At first his psychiatrist was very interested in hearing about them. And so for a few months that was all he'd talk about, until he could see her growing impatient. That was the last time he brought them up to anyone.

But he wished he'd been able to talk to someone about them; about how different they were since The Crash. In the beginning he'd always noticed only how beautiful they were, how like his memories of all those stories from his childhood. The little mermaid gazing adoringly up at her prince; the two children in the cottage made of gingerbread and gumdrops; the girl in her glass coffin awakened by a kiss. It was only after The Crash that he remembered the *other* parts of the tales, the parts that in childhood had made it impossible for him to sleep some nights and which now, perversely, returned to haunt his dreams. The witch shrieking inside the stove as she was burned to death. The wicked queen forced to dance in the red-hot iron shoes until she died. The little mermaid's prince turning from her to marry another, and the mermaid changed to sea foam as punishment for his indifference.

But since he'd been at Kingdom Come these unnerving glimpses of the people had diminished. They were still there, but all was as it had been at the very first, the myriad lovely creatures flitting through the garden like moths at twilight. He thought that maybe it was going off his medication that did it; and so the full prescription bottles were hoarded in a box in his room, hidden from Gram's eyes.

That was how he made sure the people remained at Kingdom Come. Just like in Marrakech: they were in the windows. Each one opened onto a different spectral scene, visual echoes of the fantastic paintings that graced the walls. The bathroom overlooked a twilit ballroom; the kitchen a black dwarf's cave. The dining room's high casements opened onto the Glass Hill. From a tiny window in the third-floor linen closet he could see a juniper tree, and once a flute of pale bone sent its eerie song pulsing through the library.

"You hear that, Gram?" he had gasped. But of course she heard nothing; she was practically deaf.

Lately it seemed that they came more easily, more often. He would feel an itching at the corner of his eyes, Tinkerbell's pixie dust, the Sandman's seed. Then he would turn, and the placid expanse of new-mown lawn would suddenly be transformed into gnarled spooky trees beneath a grinning moon, rabbits holding hands, the grass frosted with dew that held the impressions of many dancing feet. He knew there were others he didn't see, wolves and witches and bones that danced. And the most terrible one of all—the Erl-King, the one he'd met at the party; the one who somehow had set all this in motion and then disappeared. It was Lie's worst fear that someday he would come back.

Now suddenly the view in front of him changed. Lie started forward. The kinkajou slid from his lap like a bolt of silk to lie at his feet, still drowsing. From the trees waltzed a girl, pale in the misty light. She wore a skirt that fetched just above her bare feet, a white blouse that set off a tangle of long dark hair. Stepping onto the lawn she paused, turned back and called into the woods. He could hear her voice but not her words. A child's voice, although the skirt billowed about long legs and he could see where her breasts swelled within the white blouse.

Ah, he thought, and tried to name her. Jorinda, Gretel, Ashputtel?

But then someone else crashed through the brake of saplings. Another girl, taller and wearing jeans and a halter top, swatting at her bare arms. He could hear what *she* was saying; she was swearing loudly while the first girl tried to hush her. He laughed, nudged the kinkajou on the floor. When it didn't respond he bent to pick it up and went downstairs.

• • •

"I don't think anyone's home," Haley said. She stood a few feet from the haven of the birch grove, feeling very conspicuous surrounded by all this open lawn. She killed another mosquito and scratched her arm. "Maybe we should just call, or ask your mother. If she knows this guy."

"She doesn't like him," Linette replied dreamily. A faint mist rose in little eddies about them. She lifted her skirts and did a pirouette, her bare feet leaving darker impressions on the gray lawn. "And it would be even cooler if no one was there, we could go in and find Valentine and look around. Like a haunted house."

"Like breaking and entering," Haley said darkly, but she followed her friend tiptoeing up the slope. The dewy grass was cool, the air warm and smelling of something sweet, oranges or maybe some kind of incense wafting down from the immense stone house.

They walked up the lawn, Linette leading the way. Dew soaked the hem of her skirt and the cuffs of Haley's jeans. At the top of the slope stood the great main house, a mock-Tudor fantasy of stone and stucco and oak beams. Waves of ivy and cream-colored roses spilled from the upper eaves; toppling ramparts of hollyhocks grew against the lower story. From here Haley could see only a single light downstairs, a dim green glow from behind curtains of ivy. Upstairs, diamond-paned windows had been pushed open, forcing the vegetation to give way and hang in limp streamers, some of them almost to the ground. The scent of turned earth mingled with that of smoke and oranges.

"Should we go to the front door?" Haley asked. Seeing the back of the house close up like this unnerved her, the smell of things decaying and the darkened mansion's *dishabille*. Like seeing her grandmother once without her false teeth: she wanted to turn away and give the house a chance to pull itself together.

Linette stopped to scratch her foot. "Nah. It'll be easier to just walk in if we go this way. If nobody's home." She straightened and peered back in the direction they'd come. Haley turned with her. The breeze felt good in her face. She could smell the distant dampness of Lake Muscanth, hear the croak of frogs and the rustling of leaves where deer stepped to water's edge to drink. When the girls turned back to the big house each took a step forward. Then they gasped, Linette pawing at the air for Haley's hand.

"Someone's there!"

Haley nodded. She squeezed Linette's fingers and then drew forward.

They had only looked away for an instant. But it had been long enough for lights to go on inside and out, so that now the girls blinked in the glare of spotlights. Someone had thrown open a set of French doors opening onto a sort of patio decorated with tubs of geraniums and very old wicker porch furniture, the wicker sprung in threatening and dangerous patterns. Against the brilliance the hollyhocks loomed black and crimson. A trailing length of white curtain blew from the French doors onto the patio. Haley giggled nervously, and heard Linette breathing hard behind her.

Someone stepped outside, a small figure not much taller than Haley. He held something in his arms, and cocked his head in a way that was, if not exactly welcoming, at least neutral enough to indicate that they should come closer.

Haley swallowed and looked away. She wondered if it would be too stupid just to run back to the cottage. But behind her Linette had frozen. On her face was the same look she had when caught passing notes in class, a look that meant it would be up to Haley, as usual, to get them out of this.

"Hum," Haley said, clearing her throat. The man didn't move. She shrugged, trying to think of something to say.

"Come on up," a voice rang out; a rather high voice with the twangy undercurrent of a Texas accent. It was such a cheerful voice, as though they were expected guests, that for a moment she didn't associate it with the stranger on the patio. "It's okay, you're looking for your pet, right?"

Behind her Linette gasped again, in relief. Then Haley was left behind as her friend raced up the hill, holding up her skirts and glancing back, laughing.

"Come on! He's got Valentine—"

Haley followed her, walking deliberately slowly. Of a sudden she felt odd. The too-bright lights on a patio smelling of earth and mandarin oranges; the white curtain blowing in and out; the welcoming stranger holding Valentine. It all made her dizzy, fairly breathless with anticipation; but frightened, too. For a long moment she stood there, trying to catch her breath. Then she hurried after her friend.

When she got to the top Linette was holding the kinkajou, crooning over it the way Haley usually did. Linette herself hadn't given it this much attention since its arrival last spring. Haley stopped, panting, next to a wicker chair, and bent to scratch her ankle. When she looked up again the stranger was staring at her.

"Hello," he said. Haley smiled shyly and shrugged, then glanced at Linette.

"Hey! You got him back! I told you he was here—"

Linette smiled, settled onto a wicker loveseat with Valentine curled among the folds of her skirt. "Thanks," she said softly, glancing up at the man. "He found him two days ago, he said. This is Haley—"

The man said hello again, still smiling. He was short, and wore a black T-shirt and loose white trousers, like hospital pants only cut from some fancy cloth. He had long black hair, thinning back from his forehead but still thick enough to pull into a ponytail. He reminded her of someone; she couldn't think who. His hands were crossed on his chest and he nodded at Haley, as though he knew what she was thinking.

"You're sisters," he said; then when Linette giggled shook his head, laughing. "No, of course, that's dumb: you're just friends, right? Best friends, I see you all the time together."

Haley couldn't think of anything to say, so she stepped closer to Linette and stroked the kinkajou's head. She wondered what happened now: if they stayed here on the porch with the stranger, or took Valentine and went home, or—

But what happened next was that a very old lady appeared in the French doors that led inside. She moved quickly, as though if she slowed down even for an instant she would be overtaken by one of the things that overtake old people, arthritis maybe, or sleep; and she swatted impatiently at the white curtains blowing in and out.

"Elijah," she said accusingly. She wore a green polyester blouse and pants patterned with enormous orange poppies, and fashionable eyeglasses with very large green frames. Her white hair was carefully styled. As she stood in the doorway her gaze flicked from Linette and the kinkajou to the stranger, then back to Linette. And Haley saw something cross the old woman's face as she looked at her friend, and then at the man again: an expression of pure alarm, terror almost. Then the woman turned and looked at Haley for the first time. She shook her head earnestly and continued to stare at Haley with very bright eyes, as though they knew each other from somewhere, or as though she had quickly sized up the situation and decided Haley was the only other person here with any common sense, which seemed precisely the kind of thing this old lady might think. "I'm Elijah's grandmother," she said at last, and very quickly crossed the patio to stand beside the stranger.

"Hi," said Linette, looking up from beneath waves of dark hair. The man smiled, glancing at the old lady. His hand moved very slightly toward Linette's head, as though he might stroke her hair. Haley desperately wanted to scratch her ankle again, but was suddenly embarrassed lest anyone see her. The old lady continued to stare at her, and Haley finally coughed.

"I'm Haley," she said, then added, "Linette's friend." As though the lady knew who Linette was.

But maybe she did, because she nodded very slightly, glancing again at Linette and then at the man she had said was her grandson. "Well," she said. Her voice was strong and a little shrill, and she too had a Texas accent. "Come on in, girls. *Elijah*. I put some water on for tea."

Now this is too weird, thought Haley. The old lady strode back across the patio and held aside the white curtains, waiting for them to follow her indoors. Linette stood, cradling the kinkajou and murmuring to it. She caught Haley's eye and smiled triumphantly. Then she followed the old lady, her skirt rustling about her legs. That left Haley and the man still standing by the wicker furniture.

"Come on in, Haley," he said to her softly. He extended one hand toward the door, a very long slender hand for such a short man. Around his wrist he wore a number of thin silver- and gold-colored bracelets. There came again that overpowering scent of oranges and fresh earth, and something else too, a smoky musk like incense. Haley blinked and steadied herself by touching the edge of one wicker chair. "It's okay, Haley—"

Is it? she wondered. She looked behind her, down the hill to where the cottage lay sleeping. If she yelled would Aurora hear her? Would anyone? Because she was certain now that something was happening, maybe had already happened and it was just taking a while (as usual) to catch up with Haley. From the woods edging Lake Muscanth came the yapping of the fox again, and the wind brought her the smell of water. For a moment she shut her eyes and pretended she was there, safe with the frogs and foxes.

But even with her eyes closed she could feel the man staring at her with that intent dark gaze. It occurred to Haley then that the only reason he wanted her to come was that he was afraid Linette would go if Haley left. A wave of desolation swept over her, to think she was unwanted, that even here and now it was as it always was: Linette chosen first for teams, for dances, for secrets, and Haley waiting, waiting.

"Haley."

The man touched her hand, a gesture so tentative that for a moment she wasn't even sure it was him: it might have been the breeze, or a leaf falling against her wrist. She looked up and his eyes were pleading, but also apologetic; as though he really believed it wouldn't be the same without her. And she knew that expression—now who stared at her just like that, who was it he looked like?

It was only after she had followed him across the patio, stooping to brush the grass from her bare feet as she stepped over the threshold into Kingdom Come, that she realized he reminded her of Linette.

The tea was Earl Grey, the same kind they drank in Linette's kitchen. But this kitchen was huge: the whole cottage could practically have fit inside it. For all that it was a reassuring place, with all the normal kitchen things where they should be—microwave, refrigerator, ticking cat clock with its tail slicing back and forth, back and forth.

"Cream and sugar?"

The old lady's hands shook as she put the little bowl on the table. Behind her Lie Vagal grinned, opened a cabinet and took out a golden jar.

"I bet she likes *honey*," he pronounced, setting the jar in front of Linette.

She giggled delightedly. "How did you know?"

"Yeah, how did you know?" echoed Haley, frowning a little. In Linette's lap the kinkajou uncurled and yawned, and Linette dropped a spoonful of honey into its mouth. The old lady watched tight-lipped. Behind her glasses her eyes sought Haley's, but the girl looked away, shy and uneasy.

"Just a feeling I had, just a lucky guess," Lie Vagal sang. He took a steaming mug from the table, ignored his grandmother when she pointed meaningfully at the pill bottle beside it. "Now, would you girls like to tour the rest of the house?"

It was an amazing place. There were chairs of brass and ebony, chairs of antlers, chairs of neon tubes. Incense burners shaped like snakes and elephants sent up wisps of sweet smoke. From the living room wall gaped demonic masks, and a hideous stick figure that looked like something that Haley, shuddering, recalled from *Uncle Wiggly*. There was a glass ball that sent out runners of light when you touched it, and a jukebox that played a song about the Sandman.

And everywhere were the paintings. Not exactly what you would expect to find in a place like this: paintings that illustrated fairy tales. Puss in Boots and the Three Billy Goats Gruff. Aladdin and the Monkey King and the Moon saying goodnight. Famous paintings, some of them—Haley recognized scenes from books she'd loved as a child, and framed animation cells from *Pinocchio* and *Snow White* and *Cinderella*.

These were parceled out among the other wonders. A man-high tank seething with piranhas. A room filled with nothing but old record albums, thousands of them. A wall of gold and platinum records and framed clippings from *Rolling Stone* and *NME* and *New York Rocker*. And in the library a series of Andy Warhol silk-screens of a young man with very long hair, alternately colored green and blue, dated 1972.

Linette was entranced by the fairy-tale paintings. She walked right past the Warhol prints to peruse a watercolor of a tiny child and a sparrow, and dreamily traced the edge of its frame. Lie Vagal stared after her, curling a lock of his hair around one finger. Haley lingered in front of the Warhol prints and chewed her thumb thoughtfully.

After a long moment she turned to him and said, "I know who you are. You're, like, this old rock star. Lie Vagal. You had some album that my babysitter liked when I was little."

He smiled and turned from watching Linette. "Yeah, that's me."

Haley rubbed her lower lip, staring at the Warhol prints. "You must've been really famous, to get him to do those paintings. What was that album called? The Mountain King?"

"*The Erl-King.*" He stepped to an ornate ormolu desk adrift with papers. He shuffled through them, finally withdrew a glossy pamphlet. "Let's see—"

He turned back to Haley and handed it to her. A CD catalog, opened to a page headed ROCK AND ROLL ARCHIVES and filled with reproductions of album cover art. He pointed to one, reduced like the others to the size of a postage stamp. The illustration was of a midnight landscape speared by lightning. In the foreground loomed a hooded figure, in the background tiny specks that might have been other figures or trees or merely errors in the printing process. *The Erl-King*, read the legend that ran beneath the picture.

"Huh," said Haley. She glanced up to call Linette, but her friend had wandered into the adjoining room. She could glimpse her standing at the shadowed foot of a set of stairs winding up to the next story. "Awesome," Haley murmured, turning toward Lie Vagal. When he said nothing she awkwardly dropped the catalog onto a chair.

"Let's go upstairs," he said, already heading after Linette. Haley shrugged and followed him, glancing back once at the faces staring from the library wall.

Up here it was more like someone had just moved in. Their footsteps sounded louder, and the air smelled of fresh paint. There were boxes and bags piled against the walls. Amplifiers and speakers and other sound equipment loomed from corners, trailing cables and coils of wire. Only the paintings had been attended to, neatly hung in the corridors and beside windows. Haley thought it was weird, the way they were beside all the windows: not where you usually hung pictures. There were mirrors like that too, beside or between windows, so that sometimes the darkness threw back the night, sometimes her own pale and surprised face.

They found Linette at the end of the long hallway. There was a door there, closed, an ornate antique door that had obviously come from somewhere else. It was of dark wood, carved with hundreds of tiny figures, animals and people and trees, and inlaid with tiny mirrors and bits of glass. Linette stood staring at it, her back to them. From her tangled hair peeked the kinkajou, blinking sleepily as Haley came up behind her.

"Hey," she began. Beside her Lie Vagal smiled and rubbed his forehead.

Without turning Linette asked, "Where does it go?"

"My bedroom," said Lie as he slipped between them. "Would you like to come in?"

No, thought Haley.

"Sure," said Linette. Lie Vagal nodded and opened the door. They followed him inside, blinking as they strove to see in the dimness.

"This is my inner sanctum." He stood there grinning, his long hair falling into his face. "You're the only people who've ever been in it, really, except for me. My grandmother won't come inside."

At first she thought the room was merely dark, and waited for him to switch a light on. But after a moment Haley realized there *were* lights on. And she understood why the grandmother didn't like it. The entire room was painted black, a glossy black like marble. It wasn't a very big room, surely not the one originally intended to be the master bedroom. There were no windows. An oriental carpet covered the floor with purple and blue and scarlet blooms. Against one wall a narrow bed was pushed—such a small bed, a child's bed almost—and on the floor stood something like a tall brass lamp, with snaky tubes running from it.

"Wow," breathed Linette. "A hookah."

"A what?" demanded Haley; but no one paid any attention. Linette walked around, examining the hookah, the paintings on the walls, a bookshelf filled with volumes in old leather bindings. In a corner Lie Vagal rustled with something. After a moment the ceiling became spangled with lights, tiny white Christmas-tree lights strung from corner to corner like stars.

"There!" he said proudly. "Isn't that nice?"

Linette looked up and laughed, then returned to poring over a very old book with a red cover. Haley sidled up beside her. She had to squint to see what Linette was looking at—a garishly tinted illustration in faded red and blue and yellow. The colors oozed from between the lines, and there was a crushed silverfish at the bottom of the page. The picture showed a little boy screaming while a long-legged man armed with a pair of enormous scissors snipped off his thumbs.

"Yuck!" Haley stared open-mouthed, then abruptly walked away. She drew up in front of a carved wooden statue of a troll, child-sized. Its wooden eyes were painted white, with neither pupil nor iris. "Man, this is kind of a creepy bedroom."

From across the room Lie Vagal regarded her, amused. "That's what Gram says." He pointed at the volume in Linette's hands. "I collect old children's books. That's *Struwwelpeter*. German. It means Slovenly Peter."

Linette turned the page. "I love all these pictures and stuff. But isn't it kind of dark in here?" She closed the book and wandered to the far end of the room where Haley stared at a large painting. "I mean, there's no windows or anything."

He shrugged. "I don't know. Maybe. I like it like this."

Linette crossed the room to stand beside Haley in front of the painting. It was a huge canvas, very old, in an elaborate gilt frame. Thousands of fine cracks ran through it. Haley was amazed it hadn't fallen to pieces years ago. A lamp on top of the frame illuminated it, a little too well for Haley's taste. It took her a moment to realize that she had seen it before.

"That's the cover of your album—"

He had come up behind them and stood there, reaching to chuck the kinkajou under the chin. "That's right," he said softly. "The Erl-King."

It scared her. The hooded figure in the foreground hunched towards a tiny form in the distance, its outstretched arms ending in hands like claws. There was a smear of white to indicate its face, and two dark smudges for eyes, as though someone had gouged the paint with his thumbs. In the background the smaller figure seemed to be fleeing on horseback. A bolt of lightning shot the whole scene with splinters of blue light, so that she could just barely make out that the rider held a smaller figure in his lap. Black clouds scudded across the sky, and on the horizon reared a great house with windows glowing yellow and red. Somehow Haley knew the rider would not reach the house in time.

Linette grimaced. On her shoulder the kinkajou had fallen asleep again. She untangled its paws from her hair and asked, "The Erl-King? What's that?"

Lie Vagal took a step closer to her.

"—'Oh father! My father! And dost thou not see?
The Erl-King and his daughter are waiting for me?'
—'Now shame thee, my dearest! Tis fear makes thee blind
Thou seest the dark willows which wave in the wind.'"

He stopped. Linette shivered, glanced aside at Haley. "Wow. That's creepy—you really like all this creepy stuff . . . "

Haley swallowed and tried to look unimpressed. "That was a *song?*"

He shook his head. "It's a poem, actually. I just ripped off the words, that's all." He hummed softly. Haley vaguely recognized the tune and guessed it must be from his album.

"'Oh father, my father,'" he sang, and reached to take Linette's hand. She joined him shyly, and the kinkajou drooped from her shoulder across her back.

"Lie!"

The voice made the girls jump. Linette clutched at Lie. The kinkajou squealed unhappily.

"Gram." Lie's voice sounded somewhere between reproach and disappointment as he turned to face her. She stood in the doorway, weaving a little and with one hand on the doorframe to steady herself.

"It's late. I think those girls should go home now."

Linette giggled, embarrassed, and said, "Oh, we don't have—"

"Yeah, I guess so," Haley broke in, and sidled toward the door. Lie Vagal stared after her, then turned to Linette.

"Why don't you come back tomorrow, if you want to see more of the house? Then it won't get too late." He winked at Haley. "And Gram is here, so your parents shouldn't have to worry."

Haley reddened. "They don't care," she lied. "It's just, it's kind of late and all."

"Right, that's right," said the old lady. She waited for them all to pass out of the room, Lie pausing to unplug the Christmas-tree lights, and then followed them downstairs.

On the outside patio the girls halted, unsure how to say goodbye.

"Thank you," Haley said at last. She looked at the old lady. "For the tea."

"Yeah, thanks," echoed Linette. She looked over at Lie Vagal standing in the doorway. The backlight made of him a black shadow, the edges of his hair touched with gold. He nodded to her, said nothing. But as they made their way back down the moonlit hill his voice called after them with soft urgency.

"Come back," he said.

It was two more days before Haley returned to Linette's. After dinner she rode her bike up the long rutted dirt drive, dodging cabbage butterflies and locusts and looking sideways at Kingdom Come perched upon its emerald hill. Even before she reached the cottage she knew Linette wasn't there.

"Haley. Come on in."

Aurora stood in the doorway, her cigarette leaving a long blue arabesque in the still air as she beckoned Haley. The girl leaned her bike against the broken stalks of sunflowers and delphiniums pushing against the house and followed Aurora.

Inside was cool and dark, the flagstones' chill biting through the soles of Haley's sneakers. She wondered how Aurora could stand to walk barefoot, but she did: her feet small and dirty, toenails buffed bright pink. She wore a short black cotton tunic that hitched up around her narrow hips. Some days it doubled as nightgown and daywear; Haley guessed this was one of those days.

"Tea?"

Haley nodded, perching on an old ladderback chair in the kitchen and pretending interest in an ancient issue of *Dairy Goat* magazine. Aurora walked a little unsteadily from counter to sink to stove, finally handing Haley her cup and then sinking into an overstuffed armchair near the window. From Aurora's mug the smell of juniper cut through the bergamot-scented kitchen. She sipped her gin and regarded Haley with slitted eyes.

"So. You met Lie Vagal."

Haley shrugged and stared out the window. "He had Valentine," she said at last.

"He still does—the damn thing ran back over yesterday. Linette went after it last night and didn't come back."

Haley felt a stab of betrayal. She hid her face behind her steaming mug. "Oh," was all she said.

"You'll have to go get her, Haley. She won't come back for me, so it's up to you." Aurora tried to make her voice light, but Haley recognized the strained desperate note in it. She looked at Aurora and frowned.

You're her mother, you bring her back, she thought, but said, "She'll be back. I'll go over there."

Aurora shook her head. She still wore her hair past her shoulders and straight as a needle; no longer blond, it fell in streaked gray and black lines across her face. "She won't," she said, and took a long sip at her mug. "He's got her now and he won't want to give her back." Her voice trembled and tears blurred the kohl around her eyelids.

Haley bit her lip. She was used to this. Sometimes when Aurora was drunk, she and Linette carried her to bed, covering her with the worn flannel comforter and making sure her cigarettes and matches were out of sight. Linette acted embarrassed, but Haley didn't mind, just as she didn't mind doing the dishes sometimes or making grilled cheese sandwiches or French toast for them all, or riding her bike down to Schelling's Market to get more ice when they ran out. She reached across to the counter and dipped another golden thread of honey into her tea.

"Haley. I want to show you something."

The girl waited as Aurora weaved down the narrow passage into her bedroom. She could hear drawers being thrown open and shut, and finally the heavy thud of the trunk by the bed being opened. In a few minutes Aurora returned, carrying an oversized book.

"Did I ever show you this?"

She padded into the umber darkness of the living room, with its frayed kilims and cracked sitar like some huge shattered gourd leaning against the stuccoed wall. Haley followed, settling beside her. By the door the frogs hung with splayed feet in their sullen globe, their pale bellies turned to amber by the setting sun. On the floor in front of Haley glowed a rhomboid of yellow light. Aurora set the book within that space and turned to Haley. "Have I shown you this?" she asked again, a little anxiously.

"No," Haley lied. She had in fact seen the scrapbook about a dozen times over the years—the pink plastic cover with its peeling Day-Glo flowers hiding newspaper clippings and magazine pages soft as fur beneath her fingers as Aurora pushed it towards her.

"He's in there," Aurora said thickly. Haley glanced up and saw that the woman's eyes were bright red behind their smeared rings of kohl. Tangled in her thin fine hair were hoop earrings that reached nearly to her shoulder, and on one side of her neck, where a love bite might be, a tattoo no bigger than a thumbprint showed an Egyptian Eye of Horus. "Lie Vagal—him and all the rest of them—"

Aurora started flipping through the stiff plastic pages, too fast for Haley to catch more than a glimpse of the photos and articles spilling out. Once she paused, fumbling in the pocket of her tunic until she found her cigarettes.

YOUTHQUAKER! the caption read. Beside it was a black-and-white picture of a girl with long white-blond hair and enormous, heavily kohled eyes. She was standing with her back arched, wearing a sort of bikini made of playing cards. MODEL AURORA DAWN, BRIGHTEST NEW LIGHT IN POP ARTIST'S SUPERSTAR HEAVEN.

"Wow," Haley breathed. She never got tired of the scrapbooks: it was like watching a silent movie, with Aurora's husky voice intoning the perils that befell the feckless heroine.

"That's not it," Aurora said, almost to herself, and began skipping pages again. More photos of herself, and then others—men with hair long and lush as Aurora's; heavy women smoking cigars; twin girls no older than Haley and Linette, leaning on a naked man's back while another man in a doctor's white coat jabbed them with an absurdly long hypodermic needle. Aurora at an art gallery. Aurora on the cover of *Interview* magazine. Aurora and a radiant woman with shuttered eyes and long, long fishnet-clad legs—the woman was really a man, a transvestite Aurora said; but there was no way you could tell by looking at him. As she flashed through the pictures Aurora began to name them, bursts of cigarette smoke hovering above the pages.

"Fairy Pagan. She's dead.

"Joey Face. He's dead.

"Marletta. She's dead.

"Precious Bane. She's dead.

"The Wanton Hussy. She's dead."

And so on, for pages and pages, dozens of fading images, boys in leather and ostrich plumes, girls in miniskirts prancing across the backs of stuffed elephants at F.A.O. Schwartz or screaming deliriously as fountains of champagne spewed from tables in the back rooms of bars.

"Miss Clancy de Wolff. She's dead.

"Dianthus Queen. She's dead.

"Markey French. He's dead."

Until finally the clippings grew smaller and narrower, the pictures smudged and hard to make out beneath curls of disintegrating newsprint— banks of flowers, mostly, and stiff faces with eyes closed beneath poised coffin lids, and one photo Haley wished she'd never seen (but yet again she didn't close her eyes in time) of a woman jackknifed across the top of a convertible in front of the Chelsea Hotel, her head thrown back so that you could see where it had been sheared from her neck neatly as with a razor blade.

"Dead. Dead. Dead," Aurora sang, her finger stabbing at them until flecks of paper flew up into the smoke like ashes; and then suddenly the book ended and Aurora closed it with a soft heavy sound.

"They're all dead," she said thickly; just in case Haley hadn't gotten the point.

The girl leaned back, coughing into the sleeve of her T-shirt. "What happened?" she asked, her voice hoarse. She knew the answers, of course: drugs, mostly, or suicide. One had been recent enough that she could recall reading about it in the *Daily News*.

"What *happened*?" Aurora's eyes glittered. Her hands rested on the scrapbook as on a Ouija board, fingers writhing as though tracing someone's name. "They sold their souls. Every one of them. And they're all dead now. Edie, Candy, Nico, Jackie, Andrea, even Andy. Every single one. They thought it was a joke, but look at it—"

A tiny cloud of dust as she pounded the scrapbook. Haley stared at it and then at Aurora. She wondered unhappily if Linette would be back soon; wondered, somewhat shamefully because for the first time, exactly what had happened last night at Kingdom Come.

"Do you see what I mean, Haley? Do you understand now?" Aurora brushed the girl's face with her finger. Her touch was ice cold and stank of nicotine.

Haley swallowed. "N-no," she said, trying not to flinch. "I mean, I thought they all, like, OD'd or something."

Aurora nodded excitedly. "They did! *Of course* they did—but that was afterward—that was how they *paid*—"

Paid. Selling souls. Aurora and her weird friends talked like that sometimes. Haley bit her lip and tried to look thoughtful. "So they, like, sold their souls to the devil?"

"Of course!" Aurora croaked triumphantly. "How else would they have ever got where they did? Superstars! Rich and famous! And for what reason? None of them had any talent—*none* of them—but they ended up on TV, and in *Vogue*, and in the movies—how else could they have done it?"

She leaned forward until Haley could smell her sickly berry-scented lipstick mingled with the gin. "They all thought they were getting such a great deal, but look how it ended—famous for fifteen minutes, then *pffftttt!*"

"Wow," Haley said again. She had no idea, really, what Aurora was talking about. Some of these people she'd heard of, in magazines or from Aurora and her friends, but mostly their names were meaningless. A bunch of nobodies that nobody but Aurora had ever even cared about.

She glanced down at the scrapbook and felt a small sharp chill beneath her breast. Quickly she glanced up again at Aurora: her ruined face, her eyes; that tattoo like a faded brand upon her neck. A sudden insight made her go *hmm* beneath her breath—

Because maybe that was the point; maybe Aurora wasn't so crazy, and these people really *had* been famous once. But now for some strange reason no one remembered any of them at all; and now they were all dead. Maybe they really were all under some sort of curse. When she looked up Aurora nodded, slowly, as though she could read her thoughts.

"It was at a party. At the Factory," she began in her scorched voice. "We were celebrating the opening of *Scag*—that was the first movie to get real national distribution, it won the Silver Palm at Cannes that year. It was a fabulous party, I remember there was this huge Lalique bowl filled with cocaine and in the bathroom Doctor Bob was giving everyone a pop—

"About three a.m. most of the press hounds had left, and a lot of the neophytes were just too wasted and had passed out or gone on to Max's. But Candy was still there, and Liatris, and Jackie and Lie Vagal—all the core people—and I was sitting by the door, I really was in better shape than most of them, or I thought I was, but then I looked up and there is this *guy* there I've never seen before. And, like, people wandered in and out of there all the time, that was no big deal, but I was sitting right by the door with Jackie,

I mean it was sort of a joke, we'd been asking to see people's invitations, turning away the offal, but I swear I never saw this guy come in. Later Jackie said *she'd* seen him come in through the fire escape; but I think she was lying. Anyway, it was weird.

"And so I must have nodded out for a while, because all of a sudden I jerk up and look around and here's this guy with everyone huddled around him, bending over and laughing like he's telling fortunes or something. He kind of looked like that, too, like a gypsy—not that everyone didn't look like that in those days, but with him it wasn't so much like an act. I mean, he had this long curly black hair and these gold earrings, and high suede boots and velvet pants, all black and red and purple, but with him it was like maybe he had *always* dressed like that. He was handsome, but in a creepy sort of way. His eyes were set very close together and his eyebrows grew together over his nose—that's the mark of a warlock, eyebrows like that—and he had this very neat British accent. They always went crazy over anyone with a British accent.

"So obviously I had been missing something, passed out by the door, and so I got up and staggered over to see what was going on. At first I thought he was collecting autographs. He had this very nice leather-bound book, like an autograph book, and everyone was writing in it. And I thought, God, how tacky. But then it struck me as being weird, because a lot of those people—not Candy, she'd sign *anything*—but a lot of the others, they wouldn't be caught dead doing anything so bourgeois as signing autographs. But here just about everybody was passing this pen around—a nice gold Cross pen, I remember that—even Andy, and I thought, Well this I got to see.

"So I edged my way in, and that's when I saw they *were* signing their names. But it wasn't an autograph book at all. It wasn't like anything I'd ever seen before. There was something printed on every page, in this fabulous gold and green lettering, but very official-looking, like when you see an old-fashioned decree of some sort. And they were all signing their names on every page. Just like in a cartoon, you know, 'Sign here!' And, I mean, everyone had done it—Lie Vagal had just finished and when the man saw me coming over he held the book up and flipped through it real fast, so I could see their signatures . . . "

Haley leaned forward on her knees, heedless now of the smoke and Aurora's huge eyes staring fixedly at the empty air.

"What was it?" the girl breathed. "Was it—?"

"It was *their souls.*" Aurora hissed the last word, stubbing out her cigarette in her empty mug. "Most of them, anyway—because, *get it*, who would ever want *their* souls? It was a standard contract—souls, sanity, first-born children.

They all thought it was a joke—but look what happened." She pointed at the scrapbook as though the irrefutable proof lay there.

Haley swallowed. "Did you—did *you* sign?"

Aurora shook her head and laughed bitterly. "Are you crazy? Would I be here now if I had? No, I didn't, and a few others didn't—Viva, Liatris and Coppelia, David Watts. We're about all that's left, now—except for one or two who haven't paid up . . . "

And she turned and gazed out the window, to where the overgrown apple trees leaned heavily and spilled their burden of green fruit onto the stone wall that separated them from Kingdom Come.

"Lie Vagal," Haley said at last. Her voice sounded hoarse as Aurora's own. "So he signed it, too."

Aurora said nothing, only sat there staring, her yellow hands clutching the thin fabric of her tunic. Haley was about to repeat herself, when the woman began to hum, softly and out of key. Haley had heard that song before—just days ago, where was it? and then the words spilled out in Aurora's throaty contralto:

> "—'Why trembles my darling? Why shrinks she with fear?'
> —'Oh father! My father! The Erl-King is near!
> The Erl-King, with his crown and his hands long and white!'
> —'Thine eyes are deceived by the vapors of night.'"

"That song!" exclaimed Haley. "He was singing it—"

Aurora nodded without looking at her. "'The Erl-King,'" she said. "He recorded it just a few months later . . . "

Her gaze dropped abruptly to the book at her knees. She ran her fingers along its edge, then as though with long practice opened it to a page towards the back. "There he is," she murmured, and traced the outlines of a black-and-white photo, neatly pressed beneath its sheath of yellowing plastic.

It was Lie Vagal. His hair was longer, and black as a cat's. He wore high leather boots, and the picture had been posed in a way to make him look taller than he really was. But what made Haley feel sick and frightened was that he was wearing makeup—his face powdered dead white, his eyes livid behind pools of mascara and kohl, his mouth a scarlet blossom. And it wasn't that it made him look like a woman (though it did).

It was that he looked exactly like Linette.

Shaking her head, she turned towards Aurora, talking so fast her teeth chattered. "You—does she—does he—does he know?"

Aurora stared down at the photograph and shook her head. "I don't think so. No one does. I mean, people might have suspected, I'm sure they talked, but—it was so long ago, they all forgot. Except for *him*, of course—"

In the air between them loomed suddenly the image of the man in black and red and purple, heavy gold rings winking from his ears. Haley's head pounded and she felt as though the floor reeled beneath her. In the hazy air the shining figure bowed its head, light gleaming from the unbroken ebony line that ran above its eyes. She seemed to hear a voice hissing to her, and feel cold sharp nails pressing tiny half-moons into the flesh of her arm. But before she could cry out the image was gone. There was only the still dank room, and Aurora saying,

" . . . for a long time thought he would die, for sure—all those drugs—and then of course he went crazy; but then I realized he wouldn't have made that kind of deal. Lie was sharp, you see; he *did have* some talent, he didn't need this sort of—of *thing* to make him happen. And Lie sure wasn't a fool. Even if he thought it was a joke, he was terrified of dying, terrified of losing his mind—he'd already had that incident in Marrakech—and so that left the other option; and since he never knew, I never told him; well it must have seemed a safe deal to make . . . "

A deal. Haley's stomach tumbled as Aurora's words came back to her—*A standard contract—souls, sanity, first-born children.* "But how—" she stammered.

"It's time." Aurora's hollow voice echoed through the chilly room. "It's time, is all. Whatever it was that Lie wanted, he got; and now it's time to pay up."

Suddenly she stood, her foot knocking the photo album so that it skidded across the flagstones, and tottered back into the kitchen. Haley could hear the clatter of glassware as she poured herself more gin. Silently the girl crept across the floor and stared for another moment at the photo of Lie Vagal. Then she went outside.

She thought of riding her bike to Kingdom Come, but absurd fears—she had visions of bony hands snaking out of the earth and snatching the wheels as she passed—made her walk instead. She clambered over the stone wall, grimacing at the smell of rotting apples. The unnatural chill of Linette's house had made her forget the relentless late-August heat and breathless air out here, no cooler for all that the sun had set and left a sky colored like the inside of a mussel shell. From the distant lake came the desultory thump of bullfrogs. When she jumped from the wall to the ground a windfall popped beneath her foot, spattering her with vinegary muck. Haley swore to herself and hurried up the hill.

Beneath the ultramarine sky the trees stood absolutely still, each moored to its small circle of shadow. Walking between them made Haley's eyes hurt, going from that eerie dusk to sudden darkness and then back into the twilight. She felt sick, from the heat and from what she had heard. It was crazy, of course, Aurora was always crazy; but Linette *hadn't* come back, and it had been such a creepy place, all those pictures, and the old lady, and Lie Vagal himself skittering through the halls and laughing . . .

Haley took a deep breath, balled up her T-shirt to wipe the sweat from between her breasts. It was crazy, that's all; but still she'd find Linette and bring her home.

On one side of the narrow bed Linette lay fast asleep, snoring quietly, her hair spun across her cheeks in a shadowy lace. She still wore the pale blue peasant's dress she'd had on the night before, its hem now spattered with candle wax and wine. Lie leaned over her until he could smell it, the faint unwashed musk of sweat and cotton and some cheap drugstore perfume, and over all of it the scent of marijuana. The sticky end of a joint was on the edge of the bedside table, beside an empty bottle of wine. Lie grinned, remembering the girl's awkwardness in smoking the joint. She'd had little enough trouble managing the wine. Aurora's daughter, no doubt about that.

They'd spent most of the day in bed, stoned and asleep; most of the last evening as well, though there were patches of time he couldn't recall. He remembered his grandmother's fury when midnight rolled around and she'd come into the bedroom to discover the girl still with him, and all around them smoke and empty bottles. There'd been some kind of argument then with Gram, Linette shrinking into a corner with her kinkajou; and after that more of their laughing and creeping down hallways. Lie showed her all his paintings. He tried to show her the people, but for some reason they weren't there, not even the three bears drowsing in the little eyebrow window in the attic half-bath. Finally, long after midnight, they'd fallen asleep, Lie's fingers tangled in Linette's long hair, chaste as kittens. His medication had long since leached away most sexual desire. Even before The Crash, he'd always been uncomfortable with the young girls who waited backstage for him after a show, or somehow found their way into the recording studio. That was why Gram's accusations had infuriated him—

"She's a friend, she's just a *friend*—can't I have any friends at all? Can't I?" he'd raged, but of course Gram hadn't understood, she never had. Afterwards had come that long silent night, with the lovely flushed girl asleep in his arms, and outside the hot hollow wind beating at the walls.

Now the girl beside him stirred. Gently Lie ran a finger along her cheekbone and smiled as she frowned in her sleep. She had her mother's huge eyes, her mother's fine bones and milky skin, but none of that hardness he associated with Aurora Dawn. It was so strange, to think that a few days ago he had never met this child; might never have raised the courage to meet her, and now he didn't want to let her go home. Probably it was just his loneliness; that and her beauty, her resemblance to all those shining creatures who had peopled his dreams and visions for so long. He leaned down until his lips grazed hers, then slipped from the bed.

He crossed the room slowly, reluctant to let himself come fully awake. But in the doorway he started.

"Shit!"

Across the walls and ceiling of the hall huge shadows flapped and dove. A buzzing filled the air, the sound of tiny feet pounding against the floor. Something grazed his cheek and he cried out, slapping his face and drawing his hand away sticky and damp. When he gazed at his palm he saw a smear of yellow and the powdery shards of wing.

The hall was full of insects. June bugs and katydids, beetles and lacewings and a Prometheus moth as big as his two hands, all of them flying crazily around the lights blooming on the ceiling and along the walls. Someone had opened all the windows; he had never bothered to put the screens in. He swatted furiously at the air, wiped his hand against the wall and frowned, trying to remember if he'd opened them; then thought of Gram. The heat bothered her more than it did him—odd, considering her seventy-odd years in Port Arthur—but she'd refused his offers to have air conditioning installed. He walked down the corridor, batting at clouds of tiny white moths like flies. He wondered idly where Gram had been all day. It was strange that she wouldn't have looked in on him; but then he couldn't remember much of their argument. Maybe she'd been so mad she took to her own room out of spite. It wouldn't be the first time.

He paused in front of a Kay Nielsen etching from *Snow White*. Inside its simple white frame the picture showed the wicked queen, her face a crimson O as she staggered across a ballroom floor, her feet encased in red-hot iron slippers. He averted his eyes and stared out the window. The sun had set in a wash of green and deep blue; in the east the sky glowed pale gold where the moon was rising. It was ungodly hot, so hot that on the lawn the crickets and katydids cried out only every minute or so, as though in pain. Sighing, he raised his arms, pulling his long hair back from his bare shoulders so that the breath of breeze from the window might cool his neck.

It was too hot to do anything; too hot even to lie in bed, unless sleep had claimed you. For the first time he wished the estate had a pool; then remembered the Jacuzzi. He'd never used it, but there was a skylight in there where he'd once glimpsed a horse like a meteor skimming across the midnight sky. They could take a cool bath, fill the tub with ice cubes. Maybe Gram could be prevailed upon to make some lemonade, or he thought there was still a bottle of champagne in the fridge, a housewarming gift from the realtor. Grinning, he turned and paced back down the hall, lacewings forming an iridescent halo about his head. He didn't turn to see the small figure framed within one of the windows, a fair-haired girl in jeans and T-shirt scuffing determinedly up the hill towards his home; nor did he notice the shadow that darkened another casement, as though someone had hung a heavy curtain there to blot out the sight of the moon.

Outside the evening had deepened. The first stars appeared, not shining so much as glowing through the hazy air, tiny buds of silver showing between the unmoving branches above Haley's head. Where the trees ended Haley hesitated, her hand upon the smooth trunk of a young birch. She felt suddenly and strangely reluctant to go further. Before her, atop its sweep of deep green, Kingdom Come glittered like some spectral toy: spotlights streaming onto the patio, orange and yellow and white gleaming from the window casements, spangled nets of silver and gold spilling from some of the upstairs windows, where presumably Lie Vagal had strung more of his Christmas lights. On the patio the French doors had been flung open. The white curtains hung like loose rope to the ground. In spite of her fears Haley's neck prickled at the sight: it needed only people there moving in the golden light, people and music . . .

As though in answer to her thought a sudden shriek echoed down the hill, so loud and sudden in the twilight that she started and turned to bolt. But almost immediately the shriek grew softer, resolved itself into music— someone had turned on a stereo too loudly and then adjusted the volume. Haley slapped the birch tree, embarrassed at her reaction, and started across the lawn.

As she walked slowly up the hill she recognized the music. Of course, that song again, the one Aurora had been singing a little earlier. She couldn't make out any words, only the wail of synthesizers and a man's voice, surprisingly deep. Beneath her feet the lawn felt brittle, the grass breaking at her steps and releasing an acrid dusty smell. For some reason it felt cooler here away from the trees. Her T-shirt hung heavy and damp against her skin, her jeans chafed against her bare ankles. Once she stopped and looked back, to see if she could make out Linette's cottage behind its scrim of greenery; but it was gone. There were only the trees, still and ominous beneath a sky blurred with stars.

She turned and went on up the hill. She was close enough now that she could smell that odd odor that pervaded Kingdom Come, oranges and freshly turned earth. The music pealed clear and sweet, an insidious melody that ran counterpoint to the singer's ominous phrasing. She *could* hear the words now, although the singer's voice had dropped to a childish whisper—

> "—'Oh Father! My father! And dost thou not hear
> What words the Erl-King whispers low in mine ear?'
> —'Now hush thee, my darling, thy terrors appease.
> Thou hearest the branches where murmurs the breeze.'"

A few yards in front of her the patio began. She was hurrying across this last stretch of lawn when something made her stop. She waited, trying to figure out if she'd heard some warning sound—a cry from Linette, Aurora shrieking for more ice. Then very slowly she raised her head and gazed up at the house.

There was someone there. In one of the upstairs windows, gazing down upon the lawn and watching her. He was absolutely unmoving, like a cardboard dummy propped against the sill. It looked like he had been watching her forever. With a dull sense of dread she wondered why she hadn't noticed him before. It wasn't Lie Vagal, she knew that; nor could it have been Linette or Gram. So tall it seemed that he must stoop to gaze out at her, his face enormous, perhaps twice the size of a normal man's and a deathly yellow color. Two huge pale eyes stared fixedly at her. His mouth was slightly ajar. That face hung as though in a fog of black, and drawn up against his breast were his hands, knotted together like an old man's—huge hands like a clutch of parsnips, waxy and swollen. Even from here she could see the soft glint of the spangled lights upon his fingernails, and the triangular point of his tongue like an adder's head darting between his lips.

For an instant she fell into a crouch, thinking to flee to the cottage. But the thought of turning her back upon that figure was too much for her. Instead Haley began to run towards the patio. Once she glanced up: and yes, it was still there, it had not moved, its eyes had not wavered from watching her; only it seemed its mouth might have opened a little more, as though it was panting.

Gasping, she nearly fell onto the flagstone patio. On the glass tables the remains of this morning's breakfast sat in congealed pools on bright blue plates. A skein of insects rose and trailed her as she ran through the doors.

"Linette!"

She clapped her hand to her mouth. Of course it would have seen where she entered; but this place was enormous, surely she could find Linette and they could run, or hide—

But the room was so full of the echo of that insistent music that no one could have heard her call out. She waited for several heartbeats, then went on.

She passed all the rooms they had toured just days before. In the corridors the incense burners were dead and cold. The piranhas roiled frantically in their tank, and the neon sculptures hissed like something burning. In one room hung dozens of framed covers of *Interview* magazine, empty-eyed faces staring down at her. It seemed now that she recognized them, could almost have named them if Aurora had been there to prompt her—

Fairy Pagan, Dianthus Queen, Markey French . . .

As her feet whispered across the heavy carpet she could hear them breathing behind her, *dead, dead, dead.*

She ended up in the kitchen. On the wall the cat-clock ticked loudly. There was a smell of scorched coffee. Without thinking she crossed the room and switched off the automatic coffee maker, its glass carafe burned black and empty. A loaf of bread lay open on a counter, and a half-empty bottle of wine. Haley swallowed: her mouth tasted foul. She grabbed the wine bottle and gulped a mouthful, warm and sour; then coughing, found the way upstairs.

Lie pranced back to the bedroom, singing to himself. He felt giddy, the way he did sometimes after a long while without his medication. By the door he turned and flicked at several buttons on the stereo, grimacing when the music howled and quickly turning the levels down. No way she could have slept through *that.* He pulled his hair back and did a few little dance steps, the rush of pure feeling coming over him like speed.

> *" 'If you will, oh my darling, then with me go away,*
> *My daughter shall tend you so fair and so gay . . . ' "*

He twirled so that the cuffs of his loose trousers ballooned about his ankles. "Come, darling, rise and shine, time for little kinkajous to have their milk and honey—" he sang. And stopped.

The bed was empty. On the side table a cigarette—she had taken to cadging cigarettes from him—burned in a little brass tray, a scant half-inch of ash at its head.

"Linette?"

He whirled and went to the door, looked up and down the hall. He would have seen her if she'd gone out, but where could she have gone? Quickly he paced to the bathroom, pushing the door open as he called her name. She would have had to pass him to get there; but the room was empty.

"Linette!"

He hurried back to the room, this time flinging the door wide as he entered. Nothing. The room was too small to hide anyone. There wasn't even a closet. He walked inside, kicking at empty cigarette packs and clothes, one of Linette's sandals, a dangling silver earring. "Linette! Come on, let's go downstairs—"

At the far wall he stopped, staring at the huge canvas that hung there. From the speakers behind him the music swelled, his own voice echoing his shouts.

> "*My father! My father! Oh hold me now fast!*
> *He pulls me, he hurts, and will have me at last—*'"

Lie's hands began to shake. He swayed a little to one side, swiping at the air as though something had brushed his cheek.

The Erl-King was gone. The painting still hung in its accustomed place in its heavy gilt frame. But instead of the menacing figure in the foreground and the tiny fleeing horse behind it, there was nothing. The yellow lights within the darkly silhouetted house had been extinguished. And where the hooded figure had reared with its extended claws, the canvas was blackened and charred. A hawkmoth was trapped there, its furled antennae broken, its wings shivered to fragments of mica and dust.

"Linette."

From the hallway came a dull crash, as though something had fallen down the stairs. He fled the room while the fairy music ground on behind him.

In the hall he stopped, panting. The insects moved slowly through the air, brushing against his face with their cool wings. He could still hear the music, although now it seemed another voice had joined his own, chanting words he couldn't understand. As he listened he realized this voice did not come from the speakers behind him but from somewhere else—from down the corridor, where he could now see a dark shape moving within one of the windows overlooking the lawn.

"Linette," he whispered.

He began to walk, heedless of the tiny things that writhed beneath his bare feet. For some reason he still couldn't make out the figure waiting at the end of the hallway: the closer he came to it the more insubstantial it seemed, the more difficult it was to see through the cloud of winged creatures that surrounded his face. Then his foot brushed against something heavy and soft. Dazed, he shook his head and glanced down. After a moment he stooped to see what lay there.

It was the kinkajou. Curled to form a perfect circle, its paws drawn protectively about its elfin face. When he stroked it he could feel the tightness beneath the soft fur, the small legs and long tail already stiff.

"Linette," he said again; but this time the name was cut off as Lie staggered to his feet. The kinkajou slid with a gentle thump to the floor.

At the end of the hallway he could see it, quite clearly now, its huge head weaving back and forth as it chanted a wordless monotone. Behind it a slender figure crouched in a pool of pale blue cloth and moaned softly.

"Leave her," Lie choked; but he knew it couldn't hear him. He started to turn, to run the other way back to his bedroom. He tripped once and with a cry kicked aside the kinkajou. Behind him the low moaning had stopped, although he could still hear that glottal voice humming to itself. He stumbled on for another few feet; and then he made the mistake of looking back.

The curved staircase was darker than Haley remembered. Halfway up she nearly fell when she stepped on a glass. It shattered beneath her foot; she felt a soft prick where a shard cut her ankle. Kicking it aside, she went more carefully, holding her breath as she tried to hear anything above that music. Surely the grandmother at least would be about? She paused where the staircase turned, reaching to wipe the blood from her ankle, then with one hand on the paneled wall crept up the next few steps.

That was where she found Gram. At the curve in the stairwell light spilled from the top of the hallway. Something was sprawled across the steps, a filigree of white etched across her face. Beneath Haley's foot something cracked. When she put her hand down she felt the rounded corner of a pair of eyeglasses, the jagged spar where she had broken them.

"Gram," the girl whispered.

She had never seen anyone dead before. One arm flung up and backwards, as though it had stuck to the wall as she fell; her dress raked above her knees so that Haley could see where the blood had pooled onto the next riser, like a shadowy footstep. Her eyes were closed but her mouth was half-open, so that the girl could see how her false teeth had come loose and hung above her lower lip. In the breathless air of the passageway she had a heavy sickly odor, like dead carnations. Haley gagged and leaned back against the wall, closing her eyes and moaning softly.

But she couldn't stay like that. And she couldn't leave, not with Linette up there somewhere; even if that horrible figure was waiting for her. It was crazy: through her mind raced all the movies she had ever seen that were just like this, some idiot kid going up a dark stairway or into the basement where the killer waited, and the audience shrieking *No!* but still she couldn't go back.

The hardest part was stepping over the corpse, trying not to actually *touch* it. She had to stretch across three steps, and then she almost fell but scrabbled frantically at the wall until she caught her balance. After that she ran the rest of the way until she reached the top.

Before her stretched the hallway. It seemed to be lit by some kind of moving light, like a strobe or mirror ball; but then she realized that was because of all the moths bashing against the myriad lamps strung across the ceiling. She took a step, her heart thudding so hard she thought she might faint. There was the doorway to Lie Vagal's bedroom; there all the open windows, and beside them the paintings.

She walked on tiptoe, her sneakers melting into the thick carpeting. At the open doorway she stopped, her breath catching in her throat. But when she looked inside there was no one there. A cigarette burned in an ashtray next to the bed. By the door Lie Vagal's stereo blinked with tiny red and green lights. The music went on, a ringing music like a calliope or glass harp. She continued down the hall.

She passed the first window, then a painting; then another window and another painting. She didn't know what made her stop to look at this one; but when she did her hands grew icy despite the cloying heat.

The picture was empty. A little brass plate at the bottom of the frame read *The Snow Queen;* but the soft wash of watercolors showed only pale blue ice, a sickle moon like a tear on the heavy paper. Stumbling, she turned to look at the frame behind her. *La Belle et La Bête*, it read: an old photograph, a film still, but where two figures had stood beneath an ornate candelabra there was only a whitish blur, as though the negative had been damaged.

She went to the next picture, and the next. They were all the same. Each landscape was empty, as though waiting for the artist to carefully place the principals between glass mountain and glass coffin, silver slippers and seven-league boots. From one to the other Haley paced, never stopping except to pause momentarily before those skeletal frames.

And now she saw that she was coming to the end of the corridor. There on the right was the window where she had seen that ghastly figure; and there beneath it, crouched on the floor like some immense animal or fallen beam, was a hulking shadow. Its head and shoulders were bent as though it fed upon something. She could hear it, a sound like a kitten lapping, so loud that it drowned out even the muted wail of Lie Vagal's music.

She stopped, one hand touching the windowsill beside her. A few yards ahead of her the creature grunted and hissed; and now she could see that there was something pinned beneath it. At first she thought it was the kinkajou. She was stepping backwards, starting to turn to run, when very slowly the great creature lifted its head to gaze at her.

It was the same tallowy face she had glimpsed in the window. Its mouth was open so that she could see its teeth, pointed and dulled like a dog's, and the damp smear across its chin. It seemed to have no eyes, only huge ruined holes where they once had been; and above them stretched an unbroken ridge of black where its eyebrows grew straight and thick as quills. As she stared it moved its hands, huge clumsy hands like a clutch of rotting fruit. Beneath it she could glimpse a white face, and dark hair like a scarf fluttering above where her throat had been torn out.

"Linette!"

Haley heard her own voice screaming. Even much later after the ambulances came she could still hear her friend's name; and another sound that drowned out the sirens: a man singing, wailing almost, crying for his daughter.

Haley started school several weeks late. Her parents decided not to send her to Fox Lane after all, but to a parochial school in Goldens Bridge. She didn't know anyone there and at first didn't care to, but her status as a sort-of celebrity was hard to shake. Her parents had refused to allow Haley to appear on television, but Aurora Dawn had shown up nightly for a good three weeks, pathetically eager to talk about her daughter's murder and Lie Vagal's apparent suicide. She mentioned Haley's name every time.

The nuns and lay people who taught at the high school were gentle and understanding. Counselors had coached the other students in how to behave with someone who had undergone a trauma like that, seeing her best friend murdered and horribly mutilated by the man who turned out to be her father. There was the usual talk about satanic influences in rock music, and Lie Vagal's posthumous career actually was quite promising. Haley herself gradually grew to like her new place in the adolescent scheme of things, half-martyr and half witch. She even tried out for the school play, and got a small part in it; but that wasn't until spring.

• • •

Elizabeth Hand fell in love with rock and roll when she was six years old and first heard the Beatles' "She Loves You" on a NYC AM radio station. As a teenager in the 1970s, she was a participant observer in the nascent punk scenes in New York and Washington, D.C. Her award-winning novels and short stories have featured characters and bands inspired by Syd Barrett, Joey Ramone, Richard Thompson, the Velvet Underground, Mayhem, Gorgoroth, Brian Wilson, Elvis Presley, and Amy Winehouse, among others. She divides her time between the Maine coast and North London, and still owns every vinyl single and LP she ever bought. Her most recent books are *Available Dark*, *Radiant Days*, a newly revised edition of her 1997 novel *Glimmering*, and the collection *Errantry: Strange Stories*, all published in 2012.

• • • •

We Love Lydia Love
Bradley Denton

She knows me, and she's happy, and she's not asking how or why. She's clutching me so tight that I can't keep my balance, and my shoulder collides with the open door. The door is heavy, dark wood with a circular stained-glass eye set into it. The eye, as blue as the spring sky, is staring at me as if it knows I'm a fraud.

From down the hill comes the sound of the car that brought me, winding its way back through the live oaks and cedars to Texas 27. Daniels didn't even stay long enough to say hello to his number-one recording artist. He said he'd leave the greetings up to me and the Christopher chip.

Stroke her neck. She likes that.

Yes. She's burying her face in my shoulder, biting, crying. Her skin is warm, and she tastes salty. She says something, but her mouth is full of my shirt. Her hair smells of cinnamon.

"Lydia," I say. My voice isn't exactly like Christopher's, but CCA has fixed me so that it's close enough. She shouldn't notice, but if she does, I'm to say that the plane crash injured my throat. "I tried to get a message to you, but the village was cut off, and I was burned, and my leg was broken—"

Not so much. We're the stoic type.

The whisper sounds like it's coming from my back teeth. I've been listening to it for two weeks, but that wasn't long enough for me to get used to it. I still flinch. I told Daniels that I needed more time, but he said Lydia would be so glad to see me that she wouldn't notice any tics or twitches. And by the time she settles back into a routine life with me—with Christopher—I'll be so used to the chip that it'll be as if it's the voice of my own conscience. So says Daniels. I'm not convinced, but I'll do my best. Not just for my sake, but for Lydia's. She needs to finish her affair with Christopher so she can move on. The world is waiting for her new songs.

And as a bonus, they'll get mine. Willie Todd's, I mean. Not Christopher Jennings'. Christopher Jennings is dead.

You are Christopher.

Right. I know.

She's looking at our eyes. She thinks we're distracted, and she wants our attention. Her lips are moist. Kiss her.

You bet. I'll concentrate on being Christopher.

Being Christopher means that Lydia and I have been apart for ten months. She has thought me dead, but here I am. She kisses me hard enough to make my mouth hurt. Her face is wet from crying, and she breathes in sobs. The videos make her look seven feet tall, but she's no more than five-four. Otherwise, she is as she appears on the tube. Her hair is long, thick, and red. Her eyes are green. Her skin is the color of ivory. Her lips are so full that she always seems to be pouting. I would think she was beautiful even if I hadn't admired her for so long.

I meaning me. Willie.

You are Christopher.

To Lydia I'll be Christopher. But to myself I can be Willie.

You are Christopher.

"I didn't believe it when Daniels called," Lydia says. She's still sobbing. "I thought he was mindfucking me like he usually does."

Say "That son of a bitch." We hate Danny Daniels.

"That son of a bitch." It seems ungrateful, considering that Daniels has just now returned us to her.

She's trembling. Hold her tighter.

A moment ago she was crushing me, but now she seems so fragile that I'm afraid I'll hurt her. It's as if she's two different women.

And why not? I'm two different men.

Carry her to the bedroom. When she gets all soft and girly like this, she wants us to take charge. You'll know when she's tired of it.

She weighs nothing. I carry her into the big limestone house, leaving the June heat for cool air that makes me shiver. When I kick the door shut I see that the stained-glass eye is staring at me on this side too. I turn away from it and go through the tiled foyer into the huge front room with the twenty-foot ceiling, the picture windows, the fireplace, the expensive AV components, and the plush couches.

No. Not in here. When she was a child, she went to her bedroom to feel safe. So take her to the bedroom. It's down the long hall, third door on the right.

I know where it is, and I've already changed direction. But the chip's yammering makes me stumble, and Lydia's head bumps against the wall. She yelps.

"Jesus, I'm sorry," I say, and think of an excuse. "My leg's still not right."

"I know," Lydia says. "I know they hurt you."

Who are "they," I wonder? There was a plane crash, and—in this new version of Christopher's life—a village. A war was being fought in the ice and snow around the village, but all of my injuries were from the crash. The villagers did their best for me, but there was no way to get me out until I'd healed, and no communication with the rest of the world. The soldiers had cut the telecom lines and confiscated the radios, but had then become too busy fighting each other to do anything more to the village. So if the soldiers didn't hurt me, and the villagers didn't hurt me, who are "they"?

There is a "they" in Willie's story, but while what they did to me was painful, they did it with my consent. Getting my album recorded and released is worth some pain. It's also worth being Christopher for a while. And it's for damn sure worth having Lydia Love in my arms.

On the bed. Pin her wrists over her head.

That seems a little rough for a tender homecoming, but I remember that the Christopher chip is my conscience. I let my conscience be my guide.

I still worry that she'll know I'm not him, but it turns out all right. If there's a difference between the new Christopher and the old one, she doesn't seem to be aware of it. The chip tells me a few things that she likes, but most of the time it's silent. I guess that at some point, sex takes control away from its participants—even from Lydia Love and a computer chip—and instructions aren't necessary.

She's sweet.

And here I am deceiving her.

But this pang is undeserved. In any respect that matters to Lydia, I *am* Christopher. I will live with her, recharge her soul, and give her what she needs before she sends me away. And then, at last, she'll rise again from the ashes of her life to resume her work. Willie can be proud of that.

You are Christopher.

Lydia and I have spent most of the past six days in bed. It's been a repeating cycle: Tears, sex, a little sleep, more sex, and food. Then back to the tears. According to what Daniels and the Christopher chip have told me, everything with Lydia goes in cycles.

But this particular cycle has to be interrupted, because we've run out of food. Despite her huge house, Lydia has no hired help; and since no one will deliver groceries this far out in the Hill Country, one or both of us will have to make a trip to Kerrville. But Lydia isn't supposed to leave the estate alone without calling CCA-Austin for a bodyguard . . . and if she were to go out with me, the hassle from the videorazzi would be even worse than usual. The headlines would be something like "Lydia Performs Satanic Ritual to Bring Boy-Toy Back from Beyond the Grave." I don't think she can handle that just yet.

But if I slip out by myself, I tell her, I'll be inconspicuous. Christopher Jennings is an ordinary guy. Put him in his old jeans and pickup truck, and no one would suspect that he's the man living with Lydia Love. I have the jeans, and the pickup's still in Lydia's garage. So I can hit the Kerrville H.E.B. supermarket and be back before the sweat from our last round of lovemaking has dried. It makes perfect sense.

But Lydia shoves me away and gets out of bed. She stands over me wild-eyed, her neck and arm muscles popped out hard as marble.

"You just got back, and now you want to leave?" Her voice is like the cry of a hawk. She is enraged, and I'm stunned. This has come on like storm clouds on fast-forward.

She's waiting for an answer, so I listen for a prompt from the Christopher chip. But there isn't one.

"Just for groceries," I say. My voice is limp.

Lydia spins away. She goes to her mahogany dresser, pulls it out from the wall, and shoves it over. The crash makes me jump. Then she flings a crystal vase against the wall. Her hair whips like fire in a tornado. All the while she rants, "I thought you were dead, and you're going out to die again. I thought you were dead, and you're going out to die again. I thought—"

I start up from the bed. I want to grab her and hold her before she hurts herself. She's naked, and there are slivers of crystal sticking up from the thick gray carpet.

Stay put. We never try to stop her.

But she already has a cut on her arm. It's small, but there's some blood—

She always quits before she does serious damage. So let her throw her tantrum. It's a turn-on for her. She expects it to have the same effect on us.

Lydia looks down and sees herself in the dresser mirror on the floor. She screams and stamps her feet on it. The mirror doesn't crack, but she's still stamping, and when it breaks she'll gash her feet. I have to stop her.

No.

This isn't right. But if Christopher would let her rage, then I must do likewise if I want her to believe I'm him. Even now, as she attacks the mirror, she's looking at me with suspicion inside her fury.

She expects arousal.

Having trouble getting aroused in the presence of a naked Lydia Love was not a problem I anticipated.

She stops screaming and stamping as if a switch in her brain has been flipped to OFF. The mirror has cracked, but it hasn't cut her feet. She leaves it and comes toward me, moving with tentative steps, avoiding the broken pieces of crystal. Except for the nick on her arm, she seems to be all right. The rage has drained from her eyes, and what's left is a puzzled fear.

"Christopher?" she says. Her voice quavers. Her ribs strain against her skin as she breathes.

She is looking at my crotch.

What did I tell you?

This was the one area I hoped the surgeons wouldn't touch, and to my relief they decided that it was close enough as it was. Christopher had an average body with average parts, and so do I. So they didn't change much besides my face and voice.

But the surgeons couldn't see me with Lydia's eyes. And now she's looking close for the first time. She's realizing that I'm someone else.

No. She's only confused because we're not excited.

Lydia stops at the foot of the bed and shifts her weight from one hip to the other. Her tangled hair is draped over her left shoulder. Her lips are even more swollen than usual.

"I'm sorry," she whispers.

Oh. Well.

Maybe I'm more like Christopher than I thought.

You are Christopher.

Shut up. I can do this myself now. Whoever I am.

Later I take Christopher's beat-up white Chevy pickup truck and head for the H.E.B. in Kerrville. Lydia worries over me as I leave the house, but she doesn't pitch another fit. She gives me a cash card with ten thousand bucks on it, kisses me, and tells me to come home safe, goddamn it. As I let the truck coast down the switchbacked driveway, I glance into the rearview mirror and see that both Lydia and the stained-glass eye are watching me. Then the trees obscure them, but I know they're still there.

As I reach Texas 27, a guy in a lawn chair under the trees on the far side of the highway points a camcorder at me. He's probably only a tabloid 'razzi, but I wait until the driveway's automatic gate closes behind me before I turn toward Kerrville. After all, Lydia Love has more than her share of obsessive fans. That hasn't changed even though she hasn't recorded and has hardly performed in the three years since Christopher Jennings came into her life. But I guess her fans know as well as I do that the phoenix will rise again.

And it will rise thanks to me. To Willie.

You are Christopher.

Thanks to both of us, then.

The pickup doesn't have air-conditioning, which says something about Christopher's economic situation before he met Lydia. I roll down both windows and let the hot breeze blast me as I follow the twisting highway eastward alongside the Guadalupe River. Kerrville, a small town with a big reputation, is just a few miles away.

Its big reputation is the result of its annual folk-music festival, but I stopped going to the festival two years ago. It seemed as if almost everyone was using amplifiers and distortion, trying to be Lydia Love. She's my favorite singer too, but some of these kids can't get it through their heads that if Lydia didn't make it big by trying to look and sound like someone else, they shouldn't try to look and sound like someone else either.

Like I've got room to talk. It's only now that I *do* look and sound like someone else that I have a shot at a future in the music business.

The supermarket's the first thing on my left as I come into town. After parking the truck, I find a pay phone on the store's outside wall, run the cash card through it, and punch up Danny Daniels' number in Dallas. Daniels is an L.A. boy, but he says he'll be working at CCA-Dallas until he can get a new Lydia Love album in the can. If he wants to stay close to her, he'd do better to relocate to CCA-Austin—but when I pointed that out, he gave a theatrical shudder and said, "Hippies." I guess Dallas is closer to being his kind of scene.

He comes on the line before it rings. "Yo, Christopher," he says. "Except for that minor bout of impotence this morning, you're doing peachy-keen. Keep it up. And I mean that."

Unlike the original Christopher, I know that I'm being observed while I'm with Lydia. But there ought to be limits.

"You don't have to watch us screw," I say. "Sex is just sex. It's the other stuff that'll break us up."

"But sex is part of 'the other stuff,' Chris," Daniels says. "So just pretend you're alone with her. Besides, if everything continues going peachy-keen, I'm the only one who'll see it. And it's not like I'm enjoying it."

How could anyone not enjoy seeing Lydia Love naked? I wonder.

Or is that Christopher?

You are Christopher.

Not when I'm on the phone with Danny Daniels.

You are Christopher.

Let me think.

You are Christopher.

"The chip's talking too much," I tell Daniels. "It's getting in my face, and Lydia's going to notice that something's not right."

Daniels sighs. "We put everything we know about the Christopher-Lydia relationship into that chip, so of course it's gonna have a lot to say. I've already told you, just think of it as your conscience."

"My conscience doesn't speak from my back teeth."

"It does now," Daniels says. "But it won't last long. The shrinks say that Lydia would have given Christopher the heave-ho in another six weeks if he hadn't been killed, and now they tell me that she won't stay with the resurrected version for more than another three months. Then you'll be out on your butt, she'll do her thing, and everybody'll be happy. Including Willie Todd."

What about me?

You'll be happy too, because I'm you. Isn't that what you keep telling me? Now back off. Daniels sounds like he might be pissed-off, and I don't want him pissed-off. Not at me, anyway.

Why? You scared of him?

No. But I know where my bread's buttered.

"Thanks, Danny," I say. "We just had a bad morning, that's all. Sorry I griped."

The phone is voice-only, but I can sense his grin. "No problem. You need a pep talk, I'm your guy. And if you feel like chewing my ass, that's cool too. After all, you're Christopher now, and Christopher once told me that he wanted to rip off my head and shit down my neck."

"Why'd he—I mean why'd I—"

We.

"—do that?"

"Because I told him he was fucking up Lydia's creative process," Daniels says. "Which he was. But I shouldn't have told him so. She was going to dump you anyway."

Or maybe I would have dumped her. Smug asshole never considers that.

I remember Lydia's rage this morning. No matter how beautiful and talented she is, that sort of thing can wear a man down. "I think she might be about half-crazy," I say.

Daniels laughs. "The bitch is a genius. What do you expect?"

Well, I guess I expect her to dump me, have her usual creative burst, and for the world to be in my debt. And for my first album, *Willie Todd*, to be released on datacard, digital audio tape, and compact disc.

You are Christopher.

Yeah, yeah.

"Guess that's all, Danny," I say. "Just figured I should check in."

Why? He's watching us all the time anyway.

"Glad you did, Chris," Daniels says, and the line goes dead.

I head into the ice-cold store, and now that I'm off the phone, I have a moment in which all of this—my new voice, my new face, my new name, my place in the bed of Lydia Love—seems like a lunatic scam that can't work and can't be justified.

But CCA has the psychological profiles, the gizmos, and the money, so CCA knows best. If it makes sense to them, it makes sense to me too. And what makes sense to CCA is that Lydia Love's creative process has followed a repeating cycle for the past eleven years:

At seventeen, after graduating from high school in Lubbock, Lydia had a violent breakup with her first serious boyfriend, a skate-punk Nintendo freak. Immediately following that breakup, she went without sleep for six days, writing songs and playing guitar until her fingers bled. Then she slept for three days. When she awoke she drained her mother's savings account, hopped a bus to Austin, and bought twelve hours of studio time. She mailed a digital tape of the results to Creative Communications of America and went to bed with the engineer who'd recorded it.

The recording engineer became her manager, and he lasted in both his personal and professional capacities for a little over a year—long enough for Lydia to start gigging, to land a contract with CCA, and to buy a house in a rich Austin suburb. Then her new neighbors were awakened one night by the sounds of screaming and breaking glass, and some of them saw the manager/boyfriend running down the street, naked except for a bandanna. The sound of breaking glass stopped then, but the screaming continued, accompanied by electric guitar.

The next day, Lydia's debut album, *First Love*, was released at a party held in the special-events arena on the University of Texas campus. The party was supposed to include a concert, but Lydia didn't show up. She was in the throes of her second creative burst.

The music that emanated from her house over the next three weeks was loud, distorted, disruptive, and Just Not Done in that suburb. The neighbors called the cops every night, and at the end of Lydia's songwriting frenzy, one of the cops moved in with her.

The cop suggested that Lydia take the advance money for her second album and build a home and studio out in the Hill Country west of the city, where she could crank her amplifiers as high as she liked. He supervised the construction while Lydia toured for a year, and when she came home they went inside together and stayed there for a year and a half. Lydia's career might have ended then had it not been for the fact that both her tour and her second album had grossed more money than the rest of CCA's acts combined. So between CCA, the tabloid papers and TV shows ("Lydia Love Pregnant with Elvis's Siamese Twins"), and the continuing popularity of her music, Lydia's name and image remained in the public eye even if Lydia didn't.

Then the ex-cop showed up at an emergency room in Kerrville with a few pellets of birdshot in his buttocks, and the county sheriff found the alleged shooter making loud noises in her basement studio. CCA rejoiced, and the third album sold even better than the first two.

Lydia's next boyfriend lasted almost as long as the ex-cop had. He was your basic Texas bubba (Lydia seems to go for us common-man types), and he and Lydia settled into a happy routine that could have ruined her. But then he went to a rodeo and was seduced by two barrel racers. The photos and videos hit the stands and the tube before the bubba even got out of bed. When he tried to go back to Lydia's, he found the driveway blocked by a pile of his possessions. They were on fire.

Creative Burst #4 followed, and that resulted in the twenty-three songs of *Love in Flames*, my favorite album by anybody, ever. Lydia followed that with a world tour that took two years of her life and made CCA enough money to buy Canada, if they'd wanted it. And it was while Lydia was on that tour, Daniels says, that CCA bugged her house. The corporation wanted to be sure that they could send help fast if she hurt herself in one of her rages.

When Lydia came home from the tour, she discovered that a hailstorm had beaten up her roof. She hired an Austin company to repair it, and Christopher Jennings, a twenty-four-year-old laborer and semi-professional guitarist, was on the crew. When the job was finished and the rest of the crew went back to the city, he stayed.

Christopher and Lydia had been together for almost eighteen months when Lydia agreed to do a free concert in India. They went together, but Christopher took a side trip to Nepal. On the way back to New Delhi, his plane detoured to avoid a storm, hit a worse one, and went down in a mountainous wasteland claimed by both India and Pakistan. The mountains, frequent storms, and constant skirmishes between the opposing armies made the area inaccessible, and all aboard the airplane were presumed dead.

Lydia remained in India for two months before coming back to Texas, and then CCA rubbed their collective hands. They figured that with Christopher now a corpse on a mountainside, they'd soon have more Lydia Love songs to sell to the world.

But six more months passed, and the studio in Lydia's basement remained silent. Death and grief couldn't substitute for betrayal and anger. CCA, and the world, had lost her.

Then one night a scruffy day laborer and aspiring singer-songwriter named Willie Todd was playing acoustic guitar for tips in a South Austin bar, and a man wearing a leather necktie approached him.

"Son," the necktied man said, "my name is Danny Daniels, and I sign new artists for CCA. How would you like to record your songs for us?"

To a guy who grew up in a Fort Worth trailer park with six brothers and sisters, no father, and no money, Daniels looked and sounded like Jesus Christ Himself. I'd been trying to break into the money strata of the Austin music scene for five years, and I was still lugging junkyard scrap by day and playing for tips at night. But with just a few words from Danny Daniels, all of that was over. He took me into a studio and paid for my demo, then flew me to Los Angeles to meet some producers.

It was only then that I found out what I'd have to do before CCA would give Willie Todd his shot. And although it sounded weird, I was willing. I still am. As Daniels explained, this thing should have no down side. After the breakup, I get my old face and voice back, Lydia's muse gets busy again, and CCA releases great albums from both of us.

So here I am in the Kerrville H.E.B., buying tortillas and rice for Lydia Love, the biggest Texas rock 'n' roll star since Buddy Holly . . . and for her most recent boyfriend, a dead man named Christopher.

You are Christopher.

But I'm not dead. Dead men don't buy groceries.

Dead men don't sleep with Lydia Love.

It's my seventh week with Lydia, and something I didn't expect is happening. As I've settled back into life with her, I've begun to see her as something other than the singer, the sex symbol, the video goddess: I have begun to see her as a dull pain in the ass.

Her rage before my first grocery run hasn't repeated itself, and I wish that it would. She's gone zombie on me. Sometimes when she's lying on the floor with a bowl of bean dip on her stomach, watching the tube through half-closed eyes, I wonder if she was the one who decided to end her previous relationships. I wonder if maybe one or two of the men made the decision themselves.

Why do you think I took that side trip to Nepal?

She has a gym full of exercise equipment, but she hasn't gone in there since I've come back. So I've been working out by myself to take the edge off my frustration, and I'm heading there now while she watches a tape of a lousy old movie called *A Star Is Born*. A run on the treadmill sounds appropriate.

Even the sex has started going downhill.

We could look elsewhere. I was starting to, before the plane crash.

No. Forget I said anything. Lydia's just moody; that's part of what makes her who she is. It would be stupid of me to mess up a good thing.

Isn't that what you're supposed to be doing?

I don't know. Are we talking about Willie or Christopher? According to CCA, Willie is here to give Lydia someone to break up with, but Christopher ought to be here because he cares about her. So which one am I?

You are Christopher.

All right, then. We can't just let things go on like this, so let's try something. Lydia hasn't picked up a guitar since I came back, and neither have I. Maybe if she and I played together—

She's too critical of other guitar players. We don't like being humiliated.

In front of whom?

Ourselves. And the people behind the walls.

But CCA's already agreed to put out my album. They already know I'm good. What difference will it make if Lydia and I play a few tunes together?

CCA is putting out an album by Willie Todd. You are Christopher.

I don't care.

So I hop off the treadmill, and as I start to leave the gym, Lydia appears in the doorway. She's wearing the same gray sweats she wore yesterday and the day before. Her skin is blotchy, and she looks strung-out. It occurs to me that she might be taking drugs.

Of course she is. When things don't go her way, she takes something. Or breaks something.

"I'm going to kill myself," Lydia says. Her voice is a monotone.

Oh shit.

Don't worry. This is old news. She craves drama, and if she doesn't get it, she invents it. Ignore her.

She's threatening suicide. I'm not going to ignore that.

I would.

Well, Willie wouldn't.

Sure he would. CCA wouldn't pick a new Christopher who didn't have the same basic character traits as the old Christopher.

Shut up. I've got to concentrate on Lydia.

But she's already disappeared from the doorway. I zoned out, and she's gone to kill herself.

No, she's gone to eat or get wasted. Or both.

Fuck off. Just fuck off.

That's no way to talk to yourself.

I run down the hallway, yelling for her. She's not in any of the bedrooms, the kitchen, the dining room, the front room, or the garage. Not out on the deck or in the back yard. But she could be hidden among the trees, hanging herself. She could already be dead, and it would be me that killed her. Just because I wanted a break, just because I made a deal with CCA, just because I flew off and died on a mountainside, leaving her alone and unable to write or sing.

And at that thought I know where she is. She's where her music has lain as if dead all these months. She's gone to join it.

So I find her down in the studio, sitting cross-legged on the floor. She's plinking on a Guild acoustic, but the notes are random. She's staring at the carpet, paying no attention to what she's playing. I sit down facing her. *She looks like a toad.*

No, she's beautiful. Look at her fingers. They're slender, but strong. Dangerous. Can't you see that?

Sure. But seeing it isn't enough.

She's still alive. That's enough for me.

"I don't think you should kill yourself," I tell her. The gray egg-crate foam on the walls and ceiling makes my voice sound flat and unconvincing.

"Why not?" she asks without looking at me. Her hair is tied back, but some of it has come loose and is hanging against her cheek, curling up to touch her nose. I'm close enough to smell the sweat on her neck, and I want to kiss it away.

If you touch her now, she'll go ballistic.

"Why not?" Lydia asks again.

"Because you wouldn't like being dead," I say. "It's boring."

"So's being alive."

She has a point there.

Quiet. "It doesn't have to be."

Lydia's shoulders hunch, as if she's trying to shrink into herself. "Yes, it does," she says. "Life and death are really the same thing, except that life is more work."

She's still plinking on the Guild, but I notice that the notes aren't random anymore. They're starting to punctuate and echo her words. They sound familiar.

It's the progression for "Love in Flames," but she's playing it a lot bluesier than on the album.

It sounds good, though. It gives me an idea.

"I think you should do some gigs," I say.

Lydia looks up at me now. Her eyes are like stones. "I don't have anything new."

And except for the India concert, she's always refused to perform unless she has new material.

Well, there's a first time for everything. "So play your old stuff," I say, "only do something different with it, like you are now. Play it like it was the blues. See if it gets your juices flowing—"

I'm just able to duck out of the way as she swings the Guild at my head. Then she stands up and smashes the guitar against the floor over and over again.

I could have told you that she doesn't like being given advice.

So why didn't you?

Because I thought it was good advice.

Thanks, Christopher.

You are Christopher.

Whatever.

When the guitar is little more than splinters and strings, Lydia flings the neck away and glares down at me.

"I'll call Danny Daniels and have him schedule some dates," she says. "Small clubs, I think. And then I'm going to bed. See you there." She goes out, and the studio's padded steel door swings shut behind her with a solid click.

Now you've done it. When this doesn't work out, it'll be our fault. She likes it when it's our fault.

I thought you said it was good advice.

But good advice isn't enough. Nothing is. Not for Lydia Love.

Apparently not for you either, Christopher.

You are Christopher.

We're at a blues club on Guadalupe Street in Austin on a Wednesday night, and it's jam-packed even though there's been no advertising. Word spreads fast. I'm in the backstage lounge with Lydia, and it's jam-packed back here too. The cigarette smoke is thick. We're sitting on the old vinyl couch under the Muddy Waters poster, and I'm trying not to be afraid of being crushed by the mob. CCA has sent a dozen beefy dudes to provide security, and I can tell that they're itching for someone to try something.

But Lydia, dressed in faded jeans and a black T-shirt, doesn't seem to be aware that anyone else is in the room. She's picking away on a pale green Telecaster, eyes focused on the frets. The guitar isn't plugged in, so in all of this cacophony she can't possibly hear what she's playing. But she plays anyway. She hears it in her head.

A spot between my eyes gets hot, as if a laser-beam gunsight has focused on me, and I look across the room and see Danny Daniels in the doorway. He's giving me a glare like the Wicked Witch gave Dorothy. When he jerks his head backward, I know it's a signal to me to get over there.

He's got our career in his pocket. Better see what he wants.

Why? You scared of him?

Up yours.

That's no way to talk to yourself.

I lean close to Lydia and yell that I'm going to the john. She nods but doesn't look up. Her music matters to her again, so screw CCA and their shrinks.

I squeeze through the throng to Daniels, and he yanks me toward the fire exit. My new black-and-white cowboy hat gets knocked askew.

Out in the alley behind the club, I pull away and straighten my hat. "You grab some guys like that," I say, "and you'd get your ass kicked."

Daniels' face is pale in the white glow of the mercury lamp on the back wall. "You haven't been doing your job," he says.

I take a deep breath of the humid night air. "How do you figure?"

As if we didn't know.

I'll handle this. "I'm supposed to be Lydia Love's boyfriend, right? Well, that's what I'm doing."

Daniels tugs at his leather necktie. "You're supposed to behave as Christopher would behave so that she'll go berserk and kick you out. But you're obviously ignoring the Christopher chip's instructions."

I can't help chuckling. "The chip hasn't been handing out many instructions lately. It's been making comments, but not giving orders. So I must be behaving as Christopher would. After all, I'm him, right?"

Daniels shakes his balding head. "Not according to CCA's psychs. Christopher wouldn't reason with Lydia when she goes wacko. He gave up on reasoning with her a long time ago."

Never really tried.

Guess you should have.

Guess so.

"If the chip's lying down on the job," I say, "that's not my fault. I'm holding up my end of the contract."

Daniels grins.

Watch out when the son of a bitch does that.

"Our contract," Daniels says, "is with Willie Todd. But if you were Willie, you'd be behaving more like Christopher even without the chip. That's why we picked Willie in the first place. You, however, seem to be a third party with whom CCA has no arrangement whatsoever." He sighs. "And if Willie has disappeared, there's no point in releasing his album."

This is bullshit.

"This is bullshit."

Daniels shrugs. "Maybe so, Willie-Chris, Chris-Willie, or whoever you are. But it's legal bullshit, the most potent kind."

My back teeth are aching. "So if I have to be Willie for you to honor his contract," I say, "how can I be Christopher?"

You can beat his ugly face into sausage, that's how.

"Chris and Willie are interchangeable," Daniels says. "Both are working-class dullards who think they deserve better because they know a few chords. Any superficial differences can be wiped out by the chip. So I say again: Listen to the chip as if it were your conscience."

If I listened to the chip, Danny, you'd have blood running out your nose.

If he was lucky.

"I know you're getting attached to Lydia," Daniels continues, his tone now one of false sympathy, "but sooner or later she'll dump you. That's just what she does. It wasn't until Christopher's death that we realized she trashes her boyfriends for inspiration, but then it became obvious. So we brought Christopher back to life so she could get on with it. The only variable is how long it takes, and that's up to you. If you drag things out until CCA loses patience, Willie's songs will never be heard. And he won't get his own face back, either, because we won't throw good money after bad. He might not even be able to regain his legal identity. He'll have lost his very existence."

There are worse things.

"Willie's existence wasn't much to begin with," I say.

Daniels puts a hand on my shoulder, and I resist the urge to break his fingers. "Something is always better than nothing, Christopher. And if you go on the way you've been going, nothing is what you'll be."

Big deal.

"So what do you want me to do?" I ask.

"Only what the chip and I tell you," Daniels says. "If you don't like my conscience metaphor, then think of CCA, me, and the chip as the Father, Son, and Holy Ghost. Mess with any one of us, and you get slapped down with heavenly wrath. Mess with all of us, and you go straight to hell." He gestures at the club's back wall. "See, this kind of crap can't continue. Neither Lydia nor CCA makes real money from a gig like this. So your current directive from the Son of God is as follows: Go and spend thee the night in a motel. You still have that cash card?"

"Yeah, but—"

Daniels gives me a shove. "You, whoever you are, talked her into doing this gig. So she'll expect you to be here for it. But you won't be. So saith the Son."

No. We can't leave now. Not with Lydia about to go on stage for the first time since India. She'd hate me. Us.

Yeah. But that might be what she wants. She thrives on being treated like dirt. That's why she goes for guys like us. But we've been too nice lately, and it's screwed her up.

That's sick.

That's Lydia.

"All right," I tell Daniels. "I'm going. But I don't like it."

Daniels grins again. "Shit, neither do I. But it's for her own good, and yours too. If you weren't fucked in the head right now, you'd know that."

Come on. Let's get out of here.

I turn away from Daniels and walk off down the dark alley, abandoning Lydia to herself. My boots crunch on the broken asphalt. A bat flies past my—our—face, coming so close that we feel a puff of air from its wings.

Is Daniels right? Am I fucked in the head?

In the soul, Christopher. In the soul.

The stained-glass eye has become an open mouth surrounded by jagged teeth. Blue shards cover the front step, and they make snapping sounds as I come up to the door. I smell something burning. The stereo in the front room is blaring an old thrash-metal number about a murder-suicide. My back teeth begin to ache again.

As I cross the foyer into the front room, I see what Lydia has done. The picture windows have been broken, and the walls are pockmarked with holes. Some of the holes seem to be the results of shotgun blasts, and some have been punched with free-weight bars from the gym. The bars are still sticking out of some of these.

All of the furniture has been torn to pieces. The only things left intact are the AV components, which are stacked on the floor in front of the fireplace. But the cabinet that housed them is with everything else from the room—with everything else from the entire house, I think. Everything has been broken, shredded, crumpled, melted, or twisted, and then piled in the center of the room. A misshapen pyramid reaches three-quarters of the way up to the ceiling.

Lydia, wearing the jeans and T-shirt from last night's gig, is sitting atop the pyramid and using a fireplace-lighter to burn holes into white cloth that used to be drapes. She doesn't notice me until I cross the room and turn off the stereo.

"Christopher," she says, glancing at me with a distracted expression. "You're back." Her voice is thick. I wonder if she's taken pills.

No. Her eyes are clear. She knows what she's doing. If the shotgun's handy, she might kill us now.

"I'm sorry I left last night," I say, trying to think of a lie to explain myself. "Daniels told me it was my fault that you were playing a joint instead of an arena, and I was afraid that if I stuck around I was gonna pop him. So I went for a walk, but when I got back, you and the truck were gone. I tried to call, but my card wouldn't work. And I couldn't find a cab that would bring me out here at night. So I stayed in a motel."

Too much. She won't buy it.

"I thought your card didn't work," Lydia says.

We're meat.

Not if you back off and let me deal with this.

"It didn't work in the phone," I say. "But the motel took it."

"So why didn't you call from the motel?"

Told you.

Piss on it, then. I'm going to tell her the truth, including who I am.

Who's that?

"Don't answer," Lydia says. "Just turn on the VCR and watch the monitor."

So I do as she says. The monitor flashes on as the tape starts, and there I am, doing it with a brown-haired girl I've never seen before.

Yee-oww. Where was I when this was going on?

This never went on. I know that's the motel room we stayed in last night, because I recognize the bent corner on the picture frame over the bed. But I don't know that girl. So that can't be me.

Looks like us.

So it must be you. It's Christopher before the crash.

You are Christopher.

Yeah, but I'm Christopher after the crash.

Check out the hat on the floor. We were wearing it last night. We're wearing it right now. And it didn't belong to Christopher before the crash. It's brand new.

But I don't have a chance to figure out what that means, because Lydia has succeeded in setting the white drapery on fire. She waves it like a flag, bringing its flames close to her hair, so I move to yank it away from her. But she tosses it away before I can reach for it, and it snags on a chair leg sticking out of the pyramid. To my relief, the flames start to die down.

Lydia is staring at me now. "Tell me what happened last night," she says. "Tell me where you found that girl while I was sweating in front of all those people. Tell me whether you started with her while I was singing, or whether you waited until you knew I'd be on my way home. Tell me whether she can suck the chrome off a trailer hitch." She points the fireplace-lighter at me. "Tell me the truth, Christopher."

I look at the video monitor. The brown-haired girl and I are still going at it. The clothes on the floor are the ones I'm wearing now. The stamp on my left hand is the one that was put on at the club last night, the one that's still here on my skin. But that man is not me. I didn't do those things. We're watching an imaginary past with false faces and artificial voices.

Whoa. Sounds familiar.

Danny Daniels. CCA.

"Where'd the tape come from?" I ask, turning back toward Lydia. But if there's an answer I don't hear it, because the fire, instead of dying, has jumped to some paper and plastic in the pyramid. I can still smother it with the drapery if I hurry.

But Lydia jumps down partway and jabs her lighter at my face, stopping me. The yellow flame at the end of the barrel is two inches from my nose. The brim of my hat scorches.

"Tell me the truth," Lydia says.

A wisp of black smoke rises to the ceiling.

All right, then. The truth. Or as close as I can get.

"I've never seen that girl before," I say. "Daniels faked that tape to split us up."

Just doing his job.

Right. This is the way things are supposed to be, and I'm supposed to help them along.

But I don't want to anymore, and I don't care if it costs me my album or my face or my name. Looking at her now, I realize that I only care about one thing: I love Lydia Love.

I know. So do I. But loving her isn't enough.

Lydia's upper lip pulls back from her teeth. "Why should Danny care who I'm with? He doesn't have a thing for me." The flame waves before my eyes.

"No," I say, "but CCA does."

"What—" Lydia begins, and then a deafening buzz buries her words.

It's the smoke alarm. The pyramid shudders with the sound, and Lydia loses her balance and pitches forward. My hat gets knocked off, and Lydia's flame burns across my cheek as I catch her and fall backward. We hit the floor as pieces of the pyramid crash down around us.

The video monitor is right before our eyes. The brown-haired girl's lips are forming a name over and over again.

Christopher, she says. Christopher, Christopher.

But that's not my name.

No. You are Willie.

But we are Christopher.

Sprinkler nozzles pop out of the ceiling hissing and begin drenching us. The fireplace-lighter sputters out, and Lydia drops it. Then she pushes away from us, snatches up a pump shotgun from behind the AV components, and runs from the room. The fire in the pyramid dies, but the alarm keeps buzzing and the sprinklers keep spraying.

We struggle up and go after her. The door to the studio slams shut as we come down the stairs. A glimpse before it closes shows us that the sprinklers aren't on in there. We try the door but it won't open, so we pound on it and try to shout through the noise of the alarm. The door isn't padded on this side, and the steel is cold and hard. We tell Lydia our names and the truth of why we put on this face and came back to her. We tell her about CCA wanting to get its money's worth, about the surgery and the chip, about everything we can think of. The burn on our cheek stings as the water hits it.

She wouldn't believe anything we said now. Even if she could hear us.

But we have to try. She has the shotgun. And last week she said she was going to kill herself—

The alarm stops, and we shout Lydia's name as loud as we can.

There are two quick explosions, and circular patterns of bumps appear in the door's metal skin. From the other side, Lydia's muffled voice tells us to go back to the dead where we belong.

Then comes the sound of an electric guitar, and of a scream fueled by betrayal and anger.

Lydia Love is writing songs again.

And we know what that means. It means that our name, or whether we even have a name, doesn't matter anymore.

We are—

Shut up. It doesn't matter.

No. We guess not.

We sit down to soak in the artificial rain.

On the day after our return to Austin, Danny Daniels called us at the motel and asked when we wanted to have the surgery to remove the chip and to return Willie's face and voice to their pre-Christopher states. We'd had a night to calm down, so we didn't accuse him of using the sex video to give our relationship with Lydia a shove over a cliff. Of course he had done it. But his job, and ours, was to get Lydia Love to start producing again. We had a contract, and all he did was help it along.

And he lived up to his end of the bargain. We got Willie's face and voice back, more or less, and the chip was removed from our jaw. The doctors made a point of showing it to us after the operation.

As if a conscience could be removed so easily.

Quiet. Willie can't shake hands, think, and listen to Christopher all at the same time.

So let Christopher take over the social duties. Crush a few knuckle-bones.

Deal.

Today our album, *Willie Todd*, has been released on datacard, DAT, and compact disc. Just in time for Christmas. And thanks to Daniels, three of its tracks are already in heavy rotation on the audio and video networks. He even arranged for this release party at the Austin Hyatt Regency with a whole shitload of CCA bigshots and performers in attendance.

We asked Daniels if one performer in particular would be here, and he winked. But we don't see her anywhere.

The son of a bitch can lie without opening his mouth.

Daniels has done a lot for us, but we still don't like him.

Wait. There she is, by the waterfall, talking to a couple of CCA execs.

She might not want to see us.

Sure she will. We don't look like Christopher anymore.

There's a touch on our arm. It's Daniels. Our well-wishers melt away until we're alone with him beside the fake creek burbling through the atrium.

"Your hat's crooked, Willie," he says, giving us that alligator grin of his. "You want to make a good impression on her, don't you?"

"It's all right if I meet her?" we ask.

Daniels raises his eyebrows. "None of my business."

What a load. It's exactly his business.

"You've finished her sessions?" we ask.

He straightens his necktie. "Yup. Got the last four tracks in the can yesterday. She wants to call the album *Go Back to the Dead*, but we're trying to talk her into something more upbeat. My co-producers like *Once More With Love*, but I'm partial to *What Goes Around Comes Around*. We've gotta decide soon, because it has to be out by Valentine's Day."

"Valentine's Day?"

Cute.

"Yeah, her tour kicks off in New York on February 14," Daniels says. He nudges our shoulder. "How'd you like to be the opening act?"

Opening act. Right. You know what kind of act he wants us to be.

Should we refuse?

Like we could.

We turn away from Daniels and start toward her.

"Attaboy," Daniels says behind us.

The CCA honchos move away from her as we approach. Her hair is even longer now, and her skin is smooth and healthy. Her eyes are a bright green, like sunlight shining through emeralds.

"You're Willie Todd," she says, extending her right hand. "I'm Lydia Love. Congratulations on the album. It's good work."

Our fingers touch hers with a snap of electricity. We jump, then laugh.

"Danny Daniels played me some songs from your own new album," we say. "They sound okay too."

She smiles at the understatement. "Gee, thanks." She tilts her head, and her hair falls over one eye. "Did he mention that I'd like you to open for me on the tour? Your music makes you sound like a guy I could get along with."

For a while, maybe.

But a while is better than never. A while is all anyone ever has.

"Maybe we could talk about it after the party," we say.

"Maybe we could," Lydia says.

And so the cycle comes back to its beginning. But now Lydia isn't the only one who can play the phoenix game.

Across the atrium, Daniels raises his glass to us.

Like the man said: What goes around comes around.

Or "Once more with Love."

So we might as well plan ahead. What name shall we go under next time?

One we can use for both of us. It'll avoid confusion.

If you want to avoid confusion, you're in love with the wrong woman, Christopher.

My name is Willie.

Whatever. She's looking at our eyes. Her lips are moist. Kiss her.

We let our conscience be our guide.

• • •

Bradley Denton's first professional sf story, "The Music of the Spheres," appeared in *The Magazine of Fantasy & Science Fiction* in 1984. Some of his subsequent stories have been collected in the World Fantasy Award-winning collections *A Conflagration Artist* and *The Calvin Coolidge Home for Dead Comedians*. His 2004 novella "Sergeant Chip" won the Theodore Sturgeon Memorial Award, and his novels include *Wrack & Roll*, *Blackburn*, *Laughin' Boy*, *Lunatics*, and the John W. Campbell Memorial Award-winning *Buddy Holly Is Alive and Well On Ganymede* (soon to be a motion picture starring Jon "Napoleon Dynamite" Heder). Brad played drums in the Austin-based blues band Ax Nelson for over ten years, and now he plays guitar and harmonica in his own act, Bland Lemon Denton.

• • • •

Last Rising Sun
Graham Joyce

That number came on the radio today. I wanted to knock it off but the guy in the next bed said he liked it, so I let it play. Just another dose of déjà vu. I lie here thinking of what happened to Colleen, and how it all could have been different. I think of that old bastard her father. And lying here in bed like this reminds me of when I was a kid.

I used to lie awake at nights and hear that number ghosting from the All-Nite Milk Bar, wondering exactly what those folk were putting in their milk. I couldn't really understand it. I'd drunk milk. I knew its best effects. Let me tell you there's nothing about milk would make me want to stay up talking until 3:00 a.m.

We lived close enough to the milk bar so that, if the wind was right, the music from that huge Wurlitzer could hitch a ride on a swelling breeze and jump off in a clatter right outside my bedroom window. My old man was always complaining about it. I never minded at all. I'd seen those bikes chopped and winking with chrome, blazing with DayGlo decals, leaning in regimental order outside the milk bar, and I could lie awake wondering what it was they used to lace the shakes. When you're twelve, the mind sails free.

There is a house in New Orleans
They call The Rising Sun.

Now I can hardly stand to hear that tune any more. Ever since I got my first ax (Ax? Do I date? Natch, it's in the pressing of things—a hand-me-down Hohener with wires strung so high above the fretboard they made my fingers bleed) I mastered those blues chords and every desperate jam I can remember eventually degenerated into "House." And still does. Hold down a chord. It's why I couldn't run away.

And then I got old enough myself to hang out at the All-Nite Milk Bar. But times had changed. When I was a kid lying in bed at night, kept awake by a rising chord, the young blades in the milk bar were switched on to FAST. That was it. Tip it in your milk; stir it round; drink it down: FAST. But like I said, times change. Now we were on SLOW, and we put something other in the milk. Tip it in; stir it round; drink it down: SLOW. That's all it is, this youth culture thing. Everyone talks about semiotics and style and the endless rebellion. But all it is is cranking the lever back from FAST to SLOW, and then in a few years some younger kids come along and throw it back on FAST. That's what being young is about. You want to take time and speed it up or slow it down. No, it doesn't matter what they wear. They still powder the milk. They're still cranking the lever.

What can I say about getting older? You're more prepared to listen to the B-sides of old singles than the A-sides of new ones. That's about all.

But let me tell you this: they never took "House" off the Wurlitzer in all that time, whatever changed, whatever the kids were listening to next. And that must count for something.

And it's been the ruin of many a poor boy.

Though I'll be the first to admit it might have been because of the legend. I mean a lot of solid, gutbucket blues got spun on that Wurlitzer before going the way of all pressed vinyl. But the legend . . . someone must have decided to keep "House" up there on the rack, and whoever it was knew about the legend.

That Wurlitzer. Now it's lasers and CDs and circuits so small they're only just this side of theoretical, but the Wurlitzer offered a real, emotional interface. It was a Model 1800, built to last forever in 1955 and it did what jukeboxes are supposed to do: it radiated presence. When you plugged in, electro-blue and rhinestone-red lights sparkled across a humped frame the size of a piano; silver-colored columns on the front grille featured rocket starbursts in red, while blue light splashed across the speaker screen. The effect was one of rockets bursting against a nightblue sky.

It was visual entertainment. A chrome-and-glass canopy sloped across the carousel, over the selection-strip and right down to the button bank. It let you see what was happening inside, there was no shame, you could stare right into its guts. At its head, neon tubes spelled out the word WURLITZER in worms of white light. Below, a green badge-light winked on, inviting you to MAKE SELECTION.

You dropped your coin in a chrome mouth, hit those huge white Bakelite buttons and stood back to take the pause. Then you felt a tension in the machine, before it kicked. Yes, kicked. And clicked. And whirred. And then paused again, before you'd hear the hum of the carousel turning, a chuck as your disc flipped on to the turntable, and finally five-and-a-half seconds of empty vinyl hiss before it delivered. Jangling chords. Growling vocals. The mood. You were buying a mood.

And sometimes the Wurlitzer would kick into action on its own. No coins. No selection. No one would be standing near it, everyone hard up and what little money in their jean pocket, and off it would go.

Kick. Click; whirr. Pause. Chuck, hiss . . .

There is a house in New Orleans.

This is electro-mechanical technology, remember. Overplayed discs stuck, selections sometimes got confused in an overloaded memory, your coin might go down the tube and you'd get nothing. Old Wurlitzers are only human after all. But that kicking into gear unprompted, and under its own steam, that spooked everyone. Every time. It's how the legend got started.

I was there the night Dermott was telling everyone.

"The last time it did that, and played that same number," Dermott pushed my elbows off the counter so he could wipe up spilled sugar with a dirty rag, "was the night Fox went from here and did you-know-what."

It was a quiet night. Nothing had been going in the milk, and no one was in a mood to feed the jukebox. Dermott, lecherous but generous, long-suffering owner of the All-Nite Milk Bar, had been in a shit mood all evening and I was ready to go home. Then for no reason the Wurlitzer had kicked into action and played "House."

There was Tony and Colleen and Francis and me, all too young to remember this guy Fox. Only Sleaze, himself timestuck in the era of the Teds, knew what Dermott was talking about.

"What's you-know-what?" I asked.

"What you kids ought to do," said Dermott. "Now all of you go, please; I'm closing early tonight."

"I don't know why you call this an all-nite bar," Tony tried weakly. Dermott's answer was to upend stools on to tables. Eric Burdon belted it out to an otherwise empty bar.

She sold my new blue jeans.

"Fox went from here, down the path and strung himself up from a tree branch," said Sleaze. "The paper boy comes to deliver the Sundays next mornin' and this winkle-picker taps him in the eye. He looks up and attached to this winkle-picker is Fox, hanging from a noose with his plonker out."

"You're making it up!" Colleen looked at Dermott for confirmation.

He shrugged. "It's about right. And all I know is that," jabbing a finger at the Wurlitzer, "did that, and played that. Now piss off."

"Sure. When the song finishes."

Outside, neon lights of the bar flickering out over his shoulder, Sleaze kickstarted his Norton. We were still talking about Fox hanging himself.

was fucked up," said Sleaze. "Dressed like a biker, full regalia, everything, but drove a Lambretta. A Lambretta with a dozen mirrors. Is that or is that fucked up?"

Sleaze tried to get Colleen to climb on behind him, even though he knew she was with me. She declined and put her arm around me; I loved her for that. Sleaze gave it hard throttle and tried to impress us with a wheelie, front of his bike rearing three feet in the air, back wheel leaving a deposit of hot tire in the middle of the road as he screeched off into the night.

Next evening we had a few beers and weighed in at the All-Nite after pub closing time. The place was heaving, and we had to stand near the bar.

"Hear about Sleaze?" asked Dermott, serving up coffee the color of engine grease.

"What about him?"

"Accident. Ran his bike off the bridge up Tuttle Hill last night."

"Hey Col; good thing you didn't go with him."

Colleen shivered. "Did he hurt himself?"

"I'll say." Dermott laid plastic spoons on each of our four saucers. "They had to scrape him off the road with a shovel. Cremation Tuesday."

Someone went and put a coin in the Wurlitzer.

The legend got embroidered after Sleaze died. Unprompted, the Wurlitzer would kick into gear from time to time, and though I never knew anyone involved, someone always knew someone who knew someone who died a few days later. People would stand in the bar and enumerate: *then there was Fox, then there was Sleaze, then there was Mike Sutton who went for a midnight swim in the quarry pool, and then* . . . And so on. And always the same number on the Wurlitzer, "House of the Rising Sun." The milk bar jinx. Bad luck even to talk about it.

Then a band called Frijid Pink produced a cover version, and it wasn't a bad cover either; but some arsehole from the jukebox servicing company substituted it for the old Animals rendition. West Coast psychedelics imitate an English Geordie imitating a New Yorker imitating a Mississippi sharecropper: did they think we wouldn't notice? Naw, we all said to Dermott, get the old one back. Dermott, to his credit, the old buffer—he'd fought over the years to keep the ancient Wurlitzer—got the villain to come down, and as a kind of compromise the two versions were left on adjacent selections.

Being a pair of smart-arses, me and Tony went around for a while challenging everyone to name who originally recorded "House": none of the bastards had even heard of Josh White, so we collected every time. We even hunted down the original in seven-inch vinyl and persuaded Dermott to stick it alongside the other two.

"What the fuck for?" Dermott had no interest in history.

"It'll make a tasty timeslip."

"A what?"

"A timeslip," said Tony, waving the Josh White in the air. "It'll give people a nice confusion about what era they're in."

Dermott looked at us with unmitigated contempt. "Half these kids don't know what fucking day it is, and you want to confuse 'em about the era?"

"Just put it on, Dermott."

Truth is, it appealed to our sense of déjà vu. Naturally, déjà vu came out of the milk we drank, and we liked to replicate this by stacking the Wurlitzer with cover versions. That been-here-before feeling. It led to a lot of prototype adolescent destiny discussions. Fate. Reincarnation. Predestination. The Next World. All that.

Colleen was the worst. She was a fatalist down to her long, pinkpainted fingernails. Blinking from another milk-induced dose of déjà vu, she first came out with the pressed-vinyl model of the universe. "Yeh, and what it is, this is all a spinning disc, right, 'cos you're just on another play, right? Another incarnation. Just another stroll down the same old spiral track right?" Colleen could stretch out this sort of thing for hours. "And death, see, that's the hole in the middle, right, right, and you go tumbling through, waiting for your number to get punched again on the Great Big Wurlitzer."

I know what you're thinking. But this sort of stuff can seem meaningful when you've been powdering the milk.

Just then something playing on the Wurlitzer—the real one—decided to stick. Dermott, who happened to be passing, showed it the heel of his boot.

Tony, milkless and bored, yawned and said, "So what's it mean when the record sticks?"

"That," said Colleen, "that's your déjà vu, right?"

"And when it jumps?" I chipped in.

"Premonitions. Seeing the future. Travel in time."

"Scratches?"

"Moral mistakes."

And so on. She made it all fit. Tony wished he hadn't encouraged her.

"But the thing is," Colleen became serious, "once you're on, you know, your spiral path, there's no changing it. You can't steer it in another direction. It's a set groove." She looked hard into her milk.

"Bollocks," said Tony after a pause. Then he went home.

• • •

But I was there on the night it all came to an end. It was mid-week and Dermott was talking about closing early because business was so slack. It wasn't even ten o'clock when he wanted us to go. He didn't look too good at all. His face was the color of putty and he was dribbling perspiration. Two huge oval sweat stains darkened his denim shirt around his armpits. We tried to give him a lot of stick and the usual banter, but he was in no mood for it. Colleen and Francis helped him collect a few coffee cups, and he seemed unusually grateful.

We were just about to leave when the Wurlitzer did its old trick.

Kick, click, whirr. Pause. Play.

Sure enough, "House" came on. Dermott marched over and crashed his boot into the jukebox before snatching out the plug wire. We all giggled nervously and ran outside. The last I saw of Dermott, he was bolting the doors behind us. And wiping perspiration from his face with a white teatowel.

The All-Nite Milk Bar never opened the next evening; nor any other evening. Dermott had had a stroke in the night. He was dead at the age of forty.

"You realize what was playing before we left?" Colleen looked searchingly at me with her brown eyes.

"Don't," I said. "Don't."

The milk bar got closed up. A few windows got poked out by kids before they boarded it over. There was some talk of it re-opening or being converted, but nothing ever happened. Its location was useless as a commercial proposition, and Dermott had only ever kept it on because he didn't know what else to do.

The weeks went by, and Colleen and I began to spend more and more time with each other. It was going to be our last summer together, as I was preparing to go off to college. We avoided talking about it. Then her folks found some stuff in her bedroom drawer. It all got blamed on me, which was ridiculous since Colleen was always first over the edge in anything we did, and I was banned from seeing her. Her old man belted her black and blue, and threatened to bury me. Then her folks told my folks, and there was a lot of hysteria and squawking, but that was the deal, to keep the police out of it.

Of course we didn't stop seeing each other. We just couldn't phone or meet in any obvious place. Ironically, she was powdering the milk more than ever before, and, well, I sort of went along with anything she did. Then one night I got a phone call from a friend of hers. It was quite late, but Colleen needed to see me urgently. We had a meeting place, a tryst-hole, the wooden kissing-gate at the entrance to the woods, up near the old All-Nite Milk Bar.

I walked there, shivering in my T-shirt. My hands were shaking, because I knew what she was going to tell me. I couldn't think straight. She was waiting by the kissing-gate, staring into the dark woods. She wouldn't look me in the eye.

"Jesus," I said.

"That's what Mum said. Jesus, Mary and Joseph."

"You told her? Has she told your old man?" I shook her. She was crying.

"Not yet. But she will. I can't go back there! I can't!"

"What do you mean?"

"I can't! I can't!"

But I knew what she meant. The bruises from her last round with the old bastard had only just faded. I needed to think but nothing was coming into my head.

I slumped down on the grass and tried to light up a snout, but I couldn't get the match to come into contact with the cigarette. I had this notion that life ended as soon as you became a parent. I wasn't even eighteen. This wasn't the spiral path. There was my college. There was all of life. I wasn't ready.

"You'll have to get rid of it."

"Bastard," she said. Only two weeks earlier I'd told her I'd love her forever, we were locked in the same spiral, the same pressing, might as well accept it beginning to end.

"What else can we do? I've got my life to live. You've got yours. What do you expect?"

It was as if I'd plunged a knife into her breast. She collapsed on to the grass, gasping and wailing and hugging herself so hard I thought she might crack a rib. I'd never in my life seen such a ferocious fit of sobbing. "I'm a Catholic," she kept crying, "I'm a Catholic."

I told her I took back everything I'd said, and that I'd do anything she wanted if only she'd stop crying like that. I seriously thought she was in danger. After a long while the fit subsided, and I held her. I couldn't take her to her own house, and I couldn't take her to mine: Colleen's parents were probably at my house even at that moment, creating hysterical scenes. I had an idea.

Colleen let me lead her around the back of the milk bar. It was all nailed up tight but I managed to prise open a board and lever it from the window frame. There was an almighty cracking sound as it came away, but no one else was around. We climbed in.

It was dark. There was a musty, earthy smell to the property. I did my best to replace the board behind us.

It had been only a couple of months since Dermott died, yet the place smelled like it had been shut up for years. Everything was draped in ghostly white dust-sheets. I tried a light switch, but the juice was off. Anyway, the lights would have been seen from the road, and I had an idea we might even be able to spend a few days there. I found a couple of candle stubs behind the counter and they gave us enough light to get comfortable. I pulled some dust-sheets off the stacked stools and the Wurlitzer, and did my best to make a bed out of them.

I was still making a thousand unkeepable promises to Colleen. She snuffled and looked at me without saying anything. Her nose was sore from wiping. I hunted round for something to eat or drink, anything to comfort her, but all the stock had been cleared. The candlelight danced over the settled white dust. I snuggled down beside Colleen, putting my arm around her, wondering what the hell we were going to do and staring into the darkness of the milk bar for an answer that never came.

We heard someone's steps outside, and I snuffed out the candle. We sat in complete darkness until long after they'd gone. It was way after midnight. Maybe it was just someone walking their dog, but the thought of prowlers had us spooked.

We tried to get some sleep but the place was full of creaks. The wind moaned outside, rattling the wood-built milk bar and slapping the loose board where we'd forced an entry.

"I'm scared," said Colleen.

"Don't be. We're safe here."

"Not for this. For everything."

I was about to light the candle again when it happened.

The Wurlitzer lit up.

The juice was switched off; I'd already checked. Yet the Wurlitzer was lighting up in the dark like a firework display.

First a starburst of red illuminated the milk bar, followed by a wash of blue light. Pools of color rippled across the floor. Then the soft amber lights under the canopy flickered on, neon worms fizzing as they spelled out WURLITZER in crazy, dislocated style. I heard Colleen gasp. We stared at the machine, huddled together, seeming to shrink in size as the Wurlitzer floated before us in the dark like some massive spaceship.

There was a moment of suffocating tension. Then the Wurlitzer kicked. I knew every sound that was coming. It clicked; it whirred; it chucked. It was like machinery working in my guts. I heard the carousel move. Then there was another click, and a loud hissing. Freezing wings brushed my neck. At that moment I did indeed feel like my whole life was a pressed disc, and that I'd been down this way many, many times before, and that every new time was nothing more than a cover version of the same experience: same beginning, same ending, and the same inscrutable, terrifying hole at the end of the spiraling groove. There it was, doom-laden, echoing in chambers of the mind, the old whorehouse lament.

And it's been the ruin of many a poor boy
And God I know I'm one.

Colleen and I stared in horrible, frozen awe at the pulsating Wurlitzer. Its sound swamped the empty milk bar, loud enough to vibrate the glass windows, loud enough to shake Dermott in his grave. I remembered when I was a kid again, listening to music carried on the back of spirits.

Then it stopped. The colored lights died. We were in darkness again.

We got out quick, same way as we'd got in. "But who's it for?" Colleen said. "You or me?"

Then we spent three dreadful hours sitting in a bus shelter until the dawn chorus started. Colleen had a couple of friends with a bedsit in town, and she decided to see if they'd let her stay until she could find somewhere. I didn't want to let her, but she insisted on going alone.

I eventually found the address and went up there myself. A girl with a towel around her head came to the door and told me Colleen wasn't in, but I knew she was lying. I could feel her presence behind the door.

I was walking up by the kissing-gate one evening when I saw Tony and Francis.

"She won't see me. She won't have anything to do with me."

"I wish she would," said Francis.

"How is she?"

"Doing far too much powder these days. I don't like it."

"Tell her, will you, Francis?"

"Tell her what?"

"Just tell her."

Then I heard. I heard before that stupid story got into the papers. She thought she was an orange and tried to peel herself. That was the garbage that got written up in the *Evening Post*. They didn't have to write it like that. They could have just said it as it was.

Colleen was too clever to believe any of my promises. She saw only one way out, and she took it. My God she didn't have to die. It was that fucking banshee jukebox. I should have told her it had already had its victim with Dermott. He just hadn't let it play out the night before he died. It wasn't in the pressing. She didn't have to do it.

Her folks wouldn't even let me go to the funeral. They blamed it on me. I watched it all from a distance; I didn't need to go and eat a pickle sandwich with people like that. I could do my own crying.

The night of her funeral I went back to the milk bar with a can of petrol. I climbed in the same way as before. I doused the Wurlitzer, and the petrol ran down the glass canopy and between the button bank. Something touched on. A green light winked, inviting me to MAKE SELECTION. I could almost have smiled.

I flung the rest of the petrol around the milk bar. I wanted the whole lot to go up, but first I had one last thing to do. I tapped out the buttons I knew by heart. Kick. Click; whirr. Pause. Chuck; hiss. Jangling chords. Growling vocals. Just like it had always been.

They call The Rising Sun.

Then I lit up. The Wurlitzer exploded into flame six feet high. The fire raced around the floor and up the walls of the wooden shack milk bar. It went up like tinder. I must have spilled petrol on myself, because I felt my jeans and my jacket burning, before I felt my hair on fire. I remember writhing around the floor, frantically trying to tear myself out of my clothes, but rolling into more flame. The Wurlitzer was still belting out those moondog lyrics at high volume, loud over the crackle and roar of the flame.

So Mother tell your children
Not to do what I have done

I kicked at the boarded doors of the bar, splintering wood and smashing glass, finally flinging myself outside and away from the scorching heat and smoke. I could still hear "House" ringing in my ears as I blacked out. I don't remember anything after that.

They took off some of the bandages yesterday. I made them hold a mirror up to my face. One eye looks something like a charred walnut, but I can still see through the other one. They said I was lucky.

I have to ask myself if I called up my own misfortune by that perverse act of playing "House" one last time. Perhaps that wasn't in the pressing. Maybe next time I won't get fried to a crisp. Maybe Colleen doesn't have to die. Maybe we can make a new cover version where none of that happens. Whatever, I can wait for the next play.

• • •

As a schoolboy in a mining village on the western side of Coventry, **Graham Joyce**'s first efforts as a writer were reports of Coventry City FC football games. He later found inspiration in rock and roll lyrics. Before he became an acclaimed, award-winning novelist, he was a youth worker who believed "you can talk about sex and drugs and rock 'n' roll to young people because they're immediately interested in those things. In those three issues there are as many moral questions to be addressed as you can find anywhere in the world. So that was the agenda: to find a way through the moral maze of sex and drugs and rock 'n' roll. I don't know what I gave the kids, but I'm still stuck in the maze myself, trying to write my way out." "Last Rising Sun" was, in 1992, his first published short story. His twentieth novel, *Some Kind of Fairy Tale* was published earlier this year. See www.grahamjoyce.co.uk for more information.

• • • •

Freezone
John Shirley

Freezone floated in the Atlantic Ocean, a city afloat in the wash of international cultural confluence.

The city was anchored about a hundred miles north of Sidi Ifni, a drowsy city on the coast of Morocco in a warm, gentle current, and in a sector of the sea only rarely troubled by large storms. What storms arose here spent their fury on the maze of concrete wave-baffles Freezone Admin had spent years building up around the artificial island.

But the affluent could feel the crumbling of their kingdom. They didn't feel safe in the States. They needed someplace outside, somewhere controlled. Europe was out now; Central and South America, too risky. The Pacific theater was another war zone.

So that's where Freezone came in.

The community was now seventeen square miles of urban raft protected with one of the meanest security forces in the world. Freezone dealt in pleasant distractions for the rich in the exclusive section and—in the second-string places around the edge—for technickis from the drill rigs. And the second-string places sheltered a few thousand semi-illicit hangers-on, and a few hundred performers.

Like Rickenharp.

Rick Rickenharp stood against the south wall of the Semiconductor, letting the club's glare and blare wash over him, and mentally writing a song. The song went something like, "Glaring blare, lightning stare/Nostalgia for the electric chair."

Then he thought, Fucking drivel.

All the while he was doing his best to look cool but vulnerable, hoping one of the girls flashing through the crowd would remember having seen him in the band the night before, would try to chat him up, play groupie. But they were mostly into wifi dancers.

And *no fucking way* Rickenharp was going to wire into minimono.

Rickenharp was a rock classicist; he was retro. He wore a black leather motorcycle jacket that was some seventy-some years old, said to have been worn by John Cale when he was still in the Velvet Underground. The seams were beginning to pop for the third time; three studs were missing from the chrome trimming. The elbows and collar edges were worn through the black dye to the brown animal the leather had come from. But the leather was second skin to Rickenharp. He wore nothing under it. His bony, hairless chest showed translucent-bluewhite between the broken zippers. He wore blue jeans that were only ten years old but looked older than the coat; he wore genuine Harley Davidson boots. Earrings clustered up and down his long, slightly too prominent ears, and his rusty brown hair looked like a cannon-shell explosion.

And he wore dark glasses.

And he did all this because it was gratingly unfashionable.

His band hassled him about it. They wanted their lead-git and frontman minimono.

"If we're gonna go minimono, we oughta just sell the fucking guitars and go wires," Rickenharp had told them.

And the drummer had been stupid and tactless enough to say, "Well, fuck, man, maybe we *should* go to wires."

Rickenharp had said, "Maybe we should get a fucking drum machine, too, you fucking Neanderthal!" and kicked the drum seat over, sending Murch into the cymbals with a fine crashing, so that Rickenharp added, "you should get that good a sound outta those cymbals on stage. Now we know how to do it."

Murch had started to throw his sticks at him, but then he'd remembered how you had to have them lathed up special because they didn't make them anymore, so he'd said, "Suck my ass, big shot," and got up and walked out, not the first time. But that was the first time it meant anything, and only some heavy ambassadorial action on the part of Ponce had kept Murch from leaving the band.

The call from their agent had set the whole thing off. That's what it really was. Agency was streamlining its clientele. The band was out. The last two albums hadn't sold, and in fact the engineers claimed that live drums didn't digitize well onto the miniaturized soundcaps that passed for CDs now. Rickenharp's holovid and the videos weren't getting much airplay.

Anyway, Vid-Co was probably going out of business. Another business sucked into the black hole of the depression. "So it ain't our fault the stuff's not selling," Rickenharp said. "We got fans but we can't get the distribution to reach 'em."

Mose had said, "Bullshit, we're out of the Grid, and you know it. All that was carrying us was the nostalgia wave anyway. You can't get more'n two bits out of a revival, man."

Julio the bassist had said something in technicki which Rickenharp hadn't bothered to translate because it was probably stupid and when Rickenharp had ignored him he'd gotten pissed and it was his turn to walk out. Fucking touchy technickis anyway.

And now the band was in abeyance. Their train was stopped between the stations. They had one gig, just one: opening for a wifi act. And Rickenharp didn't want to do it. But they had a contract and there were a lot of rock nostalgia freaks on Freezone, so maybe that was their audience anyway and he owed it to them. Blow the goddamn wires off the stage.

He looked around the Semiconductor and wished the Retro-Club was still open. There'd been a strong retro presence at the RC, even some rockabillies, and some of the rockabillies actually knew what rockabilly sounded like. The Semiconductor was a minimono scene.

The minimono crowd wore their hair long, fanned out between the shoulders and narrowing to a point at the crown of the head, and straight, absolutely straight, stiff, so from the back each head had a black or gray or red or white teepee-shape. Those, in monochrome, were the only acceptable colors. Flat tones and no streaks. Their clothes were stylistic extensions of their hairstyles. Minimono was a reaction to Flare—and to the chaos of the war, and the war economy, and the amorphous shifting of the Grid. The Flare style was going, dying.

Rickenharp had always been contemptuous of the trendy Flares, but he preferred them to minimono. Flare had energy, anyway.

A flare was expected to wear his hair up, as far over the top of his head as possible, and that promontory was supposed to *express*. The more colors the better. In that scene, you weren't an individual unless you had an expressive flare. Screwshapes, hooks, aureola shapes, layered multicolor snarls. Fortunes were made in flare hair-shaping shops, and lost when it began to go out of fashion. But it had lasted longer than most fashions; it had endless variation and the appeal of its energy to sustain it. A lot of people copped out of the necessity of inventing individual expression by adopting a politically standard flare. Shape your hair like the insignia for your favorite downtrodden third world country (back when they were downtrodden, before the new marketing axis). Flares were so much trouble most people took to having flare wigs. And their drugs were styled to fit the fashion. Excitative neurotransmitters; drugs that made you seem to glow. The wealthier flares had nimbus belts, creating artificial auroras. The hipper flares considered this to be tastelessly narcissistic, which was a joke to nonflares, since all flares were floridly vain.

Rickenharp had never colored or shaped his hair, except to encourage its punk spikiness.

But Rickenharp wasn't a punkrocker. He identified with prepunk, late 1950s, mid-1960s, early 1970s. Rickenharp was a proud anachronism. He was simply a hard-core rocker, as out of place in the Semiconductor as bebop would have been in the 1980s dance clubs.

Rickenharp looked around at the flat-back, flat-gray, monochrome tunics and jumpsuits, the black wristfones, the cookie-cutter sameness of JAS's; at the uniform tans and ubiquitous FirStep Colony-shaped earrings (only one, always in the left ear). The high-tech-fetishist minimonos were said to aspire toward a place in the Colony the way Rastas had dreamed of a return to Ethiopia. Rickenharp thought it was funny that the Russians had blockaded the Colony. Funny to see the normally dronelike, antiflamboyant minimonos quietly simmering on ampheticool, standing in tense groups, hissing about the Russian blockade of FirStep, in why-doesn't-someone-do-something outrage.

The stultifying regularity of their canned music banged from the walls and pulsed from the floor. Lean against the wall and you felt a drill-bit vibration of it in your spine.

There were a few hardy, defiant flares here, and flares were Rickenharp's best hope for getting laid. They tended to respect old rock.

The music ceased; a voice boomed, "Joel NewHope!" and spots hit the stage. The first wifi act had come on. Rickenharp glanced at his watch. It was ten. He was due to open for the headline act at 11:30. Rickenharp pictured the club emptying as he hit the stage. He wasn't long for this club.

NewHope hit the stage. He was anorexic and surgically sexless: radical minimono. A fact advertised by his nudity: he wore only gray and black spray-on sheathing, his dick in a drag queen's tuck. How did the guy piss? Rickenharp, wondered. Maybe it was out of that faint crease at his crotch. A dancing mannequin. His sexuality was clipped to the back of his head: a single chrome electrode that activated the pleasure center of the brain during the weekly legally controlled catharsis. But he was so skinny—hey, who knows, maybe he went to a black-market cerebrostim to interface with the pulser. Though minimonos were supposed to be into stringent law and order.

The neural transmitters jacked into NewHope's arms and legs and torso transmitted to pickups on the stage floor. The long, funereal wails pealing from hidden speakers were triggered by the muscular contractions of his arms and legs and torso. He wasn't bad, for a minimono, Rickenharp thought. You can make out the melody, the tune shaped by his dancing, and it had a shade more complexity than the M'n'Ms usually had . . . The M'n'M crowd moved into their geometrical dance configurations, somewhere between disco dancing and square dance, Busby Berkley kaleidoscopings worked out according to formulas you were simply expected to know, if you had the nerve to participate. Try to dance freestyle in their interlocking choreography, and sheer social rejection, on the wings of body language, would hit you like an arctic wind.

Sometimes Rickenharp did an acid dance in the midst of the minimono configuration, just for the hell of it, just to revel in their rejection. But his band had made him stop that. Don't alienate the audience at our only gig, man. Probably our *last* fucking gig . . .

The wiredancer rippled out bagpipelike riffs over the digitalized rhythm section. The walls came alive.

A good rock club—in 1965 or 1975 or 1985 or 1995 or 2012 or 2039 should be narrow, dark, close, claustrophobic. The walls should be either starkly monochrome—all black or mirrored, say—or deliberately garish. Camp, layered with whatever was the contemporary avant-garde or gaudy graffiti.

The Semiconductor showed both sides. It started out butch, its walls glassy black; during the concert it went in gaudy drag as the sound-sensitive walls reacted to the music with color streaking, wavelengthing in oscilloscope patterns, shades of blue-white for high end, red and purple for bass and percussion, reacting vividly, hypnotically to each note. The minimonos disliked reactive walls. They called it kitschy.

The dance spazzed the stage, and Rickenharp grudgingly watched, trying to be fair to it. Thinking, It's another kind of rock 'n' roll, is all. Like a Christian watching a Buddhist ceremony, telling himself, "Oh, well, it's all manifestations of the One God in the end." Rickenharp thinking: But real rock is better. *Real rock is coming back,* he'd tell almost anyone who'd listen. Almost no one would.

A chaotichick came in, and he watched her, feeling less alone. Chaotics were much closer to real rockers. She was a skinhead, with the sides of her head painted. The Gridfriend insignia was tattooed on her right shoulder. She wore a skirt made of at least two hundred rags of synthetic material sewn to her leather belt—a sort of grass skirt of bright rags. The nipples of her bare breasts were pierced with thin screws. The minimonos looked at her in disgust; they were prudish, and calling attention to one's breasts was decidedly gauche with the M'n'Ms. She smiled sunnily back at them. Her handsome Semitic features were slashed randomly with paint. Her makeup looked like a spinpainting. Her teeth were filed.

Rickenharp swallowed hard, looking at her. Damn. She was *his type*.

Only . . . she wore a blue-mesc sniffer. The sniffer's inverted question mark ran from its hook at her right ear to just under her right nostril. Now and then she tilted her head to it, and sniffed a little blue powder.

Rickenharp had to look away. Silently cursing.

He'd just written a song called "Stay Clean."

Blue mesc. Or syncoke. Or heroin. Or amphetamorphine. Or XTZ. But mostly he went for blue mesc. And blue mesc was addictive.

Blue mesc, also called boss blue. It offered some of the effects of mescaline and cocaine together, framed in the gelatinous sweetness of methaqualone. Only . . . stop taking it after a period of steady use and the world drained of meaning for you. There was no actual withdrawal sickness. There was only a deeply resonant depression, a sense of worthlessness that seemed to settle like dust and maggot dung into each individual cell of the user's body.

Some people called blue mesc "the suicide ticket." It could make you feel like a coal miner when the mineshaft caved in, only you were buried in yourself.

Rickenharp had squandered the money from his only major microdisc hit on boss blue and synthmorph. He'd just barely made it clean. And lately, at least before the band squabbles, he'd begun feeling like life was worth living again.

Watching the girl with the sniffer walk past, watching her use, Rickenharp felt stricken, lost, as if he'd seen something to remind him of a lost lover. An ex-user's syndrome. Pain from guilt of having jilted your drug.

And he could imagine the sweet burn of the stuff in his nostrils, the backward-sweet pharmaceutical taste of it in the back of his palate; the rush; the autoerotic feedback loop of blue mesc. Imagining it, he had a shadow of the sensation, a tantalizing ghost of the rush. In memory he could taste it, smell it, feel it . . . Seeing her *use* brought back a hundred iridescent memories and with them came an almost irrepressible longing. (While some small voice in the back of his head tried to get his attention, tried to warn him, *Hey, remember the shit makes you want to kill yourself when you run out; remember it makes you stupidly overconfident and boorish; remember it eats your internal organs* . . . a small, dwindling voice . . .)

The girl was looking at him. There was a flicker of invitation in her eyes.

He wavered.

The small voice got louder.

Rickenharp, if you go to her, go with her, you'll end up using.

He turned away with an anguished internal wrenching. Stumbled through the wash of sounds and lights and monochrome people to the dressing room; to guitar and earphones and the safer sonic world.

Rickenharp was listening to a collector's item Velvet Underground tape, from 1968. It was capped into his Earmite. The song was "White Light/White Heat." The guitarists were doing things that would make Baron Frankenstein say, "There are some things man was not meant to know." He screwed the Earmite a little deeper so that the vibrations would shiver the bone around his ear, give him chills, chills that lapped through him in harmony with the guitar chords. He'd picked a visorclip to go with the music: a muted documentary on expressionist painters. Listening to the Velvets and looking at Edvard Munch. Man!

And then Julio dug a finger into his shoulder.

"Happiness is fleeting," Rickenharp muttered, as he flipped the visorclip back. Some visors came with camera eye and fieldstim. The fieldstim you wore snugged to the skin, as if it were a sheer corset. The camera picked up an image of the street you were walking down and routed it to the fieldstim, which tickled your back in the pattern of whatever the camera saw. Some part of your mind assembled a rough image of the street out of that. Developed for blind people in the 1980s. Now used by viddy addicts who walked or drove the streets wearing visors, watching TV, reflexively navigating by using the fieldstim, their eyes blocked off by the screen but never quite bumping into anyone. But Rickenharp didn't use a fieldstim.

So he had to look at Julio with his own eyes. "What do YOU want?"

"N'ten," Julio said. Julio the technicki bassist. They went on in ten minutes.

Mose, Ponce, Julio, Murch. Rhythm guitar backup vocals. Keyboards. Bass. Drums.

Rickenharp nodded and reached up to flip the visor back in place, but Ponce flicked the switch on the visor's headset. The visor image shrank like a landscape vanishing down a tunnel behind a train, and Rickenharp felt like his stomach was shrinking inside him at the same rate. He knew what was coming down. "Okay," he said, turning to look at them. "*What?*"

They were in the dressing room. The walls were black with graffiti. All rock club dressing rooms will always be black with graffiti; flayed with it, scourged with it. Like the flat declaration THE PARASITES RULE, the cheerful petulance of symbiosis THE SCREAMIN' GEEZERS GOT

FUCKING BORED HERE, the oblique existentialism of THE ALKOLOID BROTHERS LOVE YOU ALL BUT THINK YOU WOULD BE BETTER OFF DEAD, and the enigmatic ones like SYNC 66 CLICKS NOW. It looked like the patterning of badly wrinkled wallpaper. It was in layers; it was a palimpsest. Hallucinatory stylization as if tracing the electron firings of the visual cortex.

The walls, in the few places they were visible under the graffiti, were a gray-painted pressboard. There was just enough room for Rickenharp's band, sitting around on broken-backed kitchen chairs and one desk chair with three legs. Crowded between the chairs were instruments in their cases. The edges of the cases were false leather peeling away. Half the snaps broken.

Rickenharp looked at the band, looked clockwise one face to the next, taking a poll from their expressions: Mose on his left, a bruised look to his eyes; his hair a triple-Mohawk, the center spine red, the outer two white and blue; a smoky crystal ring on his left index finger that matched—he knew it matched—his smoky crystal amber eyes. Rickenharp and Mose had been close. Each looked at the other a little accusingly. There was a lover's sulkiness between them, though they'd never been lovers. Mose was hurt because Rickenharp didn't want to make the transition: Rickenharp was putting his own taste in music before the survival of the band. Rickenharp was hurt because Mose wanted to go minimono wifi act, a betrayal of the spiritual ethos of the band; and because Mose was willing to sacrifice Rickenharp. Replace him with a wire dancer. They both knew it, though it had never been said. Most of what passed between them was semiotically transmitted with the studied indirection of the terminally cool.

Tonight, Mose looked like serious bad news. His head was tilted as if his neck were broken, his eyes lusterless.

Ponce had gone minimono, at least in his look, and they'd had a ferocious fight over that. Ponce was slender—like everyone in the band—and fox-faced, and now he was sprayed battleship gray from head to toe, including hair and skin. In the smoky atmosphere of the clubs he sometimes vanished completely.

He wore silver contact lenses. Flat-out glum, he stared at a ten-slivered funhouse reflection in his mirrored fingernails.

Julio, yeah, he liked to give Rickenharp shit, and he wanted the change-up. Sure, he was loyal to Rickenharp, up to a point. But he was also a conformist. He'd argue for Rickenharp maybe, but he'd go with the consensus. Julio had lush curly black Puerto Rican hair piled prowlike over his head. He had a woman's profile and a woman's long-lashed eyes. He had a silver-stud earring, and wore classic retro-rock black leather like Rickenharp. He twisted the skull-ring on his thumb, returning a scowl for its grin, staring at it as if deeply worried that one of its ruby-red glass eyes was about to come out.

Murch was a thick slug of a guy with a glass crew cut. He was a mediocre drummer, but he was a drummer, with a trap set and everything, a species of musician almost extinct. "Murch's rare as a dodo," Rickenharp said once, "and that's not all he's got in common with a dodo." Murch wore horn-rimmed dark glasses, and he was holding a bottle of Jack Daniels on his knee. The Jack Daniels was a part of his outfit. It went with his cowboy boots, or so he thought.

Murch was looking at Rickenharp in open contempt. He didn't have the brains to dissemble.

"Fuck you, Murch," Rickenharp said.

"Whuh? I didn't say nothing."

"You don't have to. I can smell your thoughts. Enough to gag a faggot maggot." Rickenharp stood and looked at the others. "I know what's on your mind. Give me this: one last good gig. After that you can have it how you want."

Tension lifted its wings and flew away.

Another bird settled over the room. Rickenharp saw it in his mind's eye: a thunderbird. Half made of an Indian teepee painting of a thunderbird, and half of chrome T-Bird car parts. When it spread its wings the pinfeathers glistened like polished bumpers. There were two headlights on its chest, and when the band picked up their instruments to go out to the stage, the headlights switched on.

Rickenharp carried his Stratocaster in its black case. The case was bandaged with duct tape and peeling with faded stickers. But the Strat was spotless. It was transparent. Its lines curved hot like a sports car.

They walked down a white plastibrick corridor toward the stage. The corridor narrowed after the first turn, so they had to walk sideways, holding the instruments out in front of them. Space was precious on Freezone.

The stagehand saw Murch go out first, and he signaled the DJ, who cut the canned music and announced the band through the PA. Old-fashioned, like Rickenharp requested: "Please welcome . . . *Rickenharp*."

There was no answering roar from the crowd. There were a few catcalls and a smattering of applause.

Good, you bitch, fight me, Rickenharp thought, waiting for the band to take up their positions. He'd go on stage last, after they'd set up the spot for him. Always.

Rickenharp squinted from the wings to see past the glare of lights into the dark snakepit of the audience. Only about half minimono now. That was good, that gave him a chance to put this one over.

The band took its place, pressed their automatic tuners, fiddled with dials.

Rickenharp was pleasantly surprised to see that the stage was lit with soft red floods, which is what he'd requested. Maybe the lighting director was one of his fans. Maybe the band wouldn't fuck this one up. Maybe everything would fall into place. Maybe the lock on the cage door would tumble into the right combination, the cage door would open, the T-Bird would fly.

He could hear some of the audience whispering about Murch. Most of them had never seen a live drummer before, except for salsa. Rickenharp caught a scrap of technicki: "*Whuzziemackzut?*" What's he making with that, meaning: What are those things he's adjusting? The drums.

Rickenharp took the Strat out of its case and strapped it on. He adjusted the strap, pressed the tuner. When he walked onto the stage, the amp's reception field would trigger, transmit the Strat's signals to the stack of Marshalls behind the drummer. A shame, in a way, about miniaturization of electronics: the amps were small, though just as loud as twentieth century amps and speakers. But they looked less imposing. The audience was muttering about the Marshalls, too. Most of them hadn't seen old-fashioned amps. "What's those for?" Murch looked at Rickenharp. Rickenharp nodded.

Murch thudded 4/4, alone for a moment. Then the bass took it up, laid down a sonic strata that was kind of off-center strutting. And the keyboards laid down sheets of infinity.

Now he could walk on stage. It was like there'd been an abyss between Rickenharp and the stage, and the bass and drum and keyboards working together made a bridge to cross the abyss. He walked over the bridge and into the warmth of the floods. He could feel the heat of the lights on his skin. It was like stepping from an air-conditioned room into the tropics. The music suffered deliciously in a tropical lushness. The pure white spotlight caught and held him, focusing on his guitar, as per his directions, and he thought, Good, the lighting guy really is with me.

He felt as if he could feel what the guitar felt. The guitar ached to be touched.

Without consciously knowing it, Rickenharp was moving to the music. Not too much. Not in the pushy, look-at-me way that some performers had. The way they had of trying to *force* enthusiasm from the audience, every move looking artificial.

No, Rickenharp was a natural. The music flowed through him physically, unimpeded by anxieties or ego knots. His ego was there: it was the fuel for his personal Olympics torch. But it was also as immaculate as a pontiff's robes.

The band sensed it: Rickenharp was in rare form tonight. Maybe it was because he was freed. The tensions were gone because he knew this was the end of the line: the band had received its death sentence: Now, Rickenharp was as unafraid as a true suicide. He had the courage of despair.

The band sensed it and let it happen. The chemistry was there, this time, when Ponce and Mose came into the verse section. Mose with a sinuous riffing picked low, almost on the chrome-plate that clamped the strings; Ponce with a magnificently redundant theme washed through the brass mode of the synthesizer. The whole band felt the chemistry like a pleasing electric shock, the pleasurable shock of individual egos becoming a group ego.

The audience was listening, but they were also resisting. They didn't want to like it. Still, the place was crowded—because of the club's rep, not because of Rickenharp—and all those packed-in bodies make a kind of sensitive atmospheric exo-skeleton, and he knew that made them vulnerable. He knew what to touch.

Feeling the Good Thing begin to happen, Rickenharp looked confident but not quite arrogant—he was too arrogant to show arrogance.

The audience looked at Rickenharp as a man will look at a smug adversary just before a hand-to-hand fight and wonder, "Why's he so smug, what does he know?"

He knew about timing. And he knew there were feelings even the most aloof among them couldn't control, once those feelings were released: and he knew how to release them.

Rickenharp hit a chord. He let it shimmer through the room and he looked out at them. He made eye contact.

He liked seeing the defiant stares, because that was going to make his victory more complete.

Because he *knew*. He'd played five gigs with the band in the last two weeks, and for all five gigs the atmosphere had been strained, the electricity hadn't been there; like a Jacob's ladder where the two poles aren't properly lined up for the sparks to jump.

And like sexual energy, it had built up in them, dammed behind their private resentments; and now it was pouring through the dam, and the band shook with the release of it as Rickenharp thundered into his progression and began to sing . . .

Strumming over the vocals, he sang,

And for me, yeah for me
PAIN IS EVERYTHING!
Pain is all there is
Babe take some of mine
or lick some of his
PAIN IS EVERYTHING!
Pain is all there is
Babe take some of mine . . .

Singing it insolently, half shouting, half warbling at the end of each note, with that fuck-you tone, performing that magic act: shouting a melody. He could see doors opening in their faces, even the minimonos, even the neutrals, all the flares, the rebs, the chaotics, the preps, the retros. Forgetting their subcultural classifications in the unification of the music. He was basted in sweat under the lights, he was squeezing sounds with his fingers and it was as if he could feel the sounds taking shape in his hands the way a sculptor feels clay under his fingers, and it was like there was no gap between his hearing the sound in his head and its coming out of the speakers. His brain, his body, his fingers had closed the gap, was one supercooled circuit breaker fused shut.

Some part of him was looking through the crowd for the chaotichick he'd spotted earlier. He was faintly disappointed when he didn't see her. He told himself, *You ought to be happy, you had a narrow escape, she would've got you back into boss blue.*

But when he saw her press to the front and nod at him ever so slightly in that smug insider's way, he was simply glad, and he wondered what his subconscious was planning for him . . . All those thoughts were flickers. Most of the time his conscious mind was completely focused on the sound, and the business of acting out the sound for the audience. He was playing out of sorrow, the sorrow of loss. His family was going to die, and he played tunes that touched the chord of loss, in everyone . . .

And the band was supernaturally tight. The gestalt was there, uniting them, and he thought: The band feels good, but it's not going to help when the gig's over.

It was like a divorced couple having a good time in bed but knowing that wouldn't make the marriage right again; the good time was a function of having given up.

But in the meantime there were fireworks.

By the last tune in the set the electricity was so thick in the club that—as Mose had said once, with a rocker's melodrama—"If you could cut it, it would bleed." The dope and smashweed and tobacco smoke moiling the air seemed to conspire with the stage lights to create an atmosphere of magical apartness. With each song-keyed shift in the light, red to blue to white to sulfurous yellow, a corresponding emotional wavelength rippled through the room. The energy built, and Rickenharp discharged it, his Strat the lightning rod.

And then the set ended.

Rickenharp bashed out the last five notes alone, nailing a climax onto the air. Then he walked offstage, hardly hearing the roar from the crowd. He found himself half running down the white, grimy plastibrick corridor, and then he was in the dressing room and didn't remember coming there. The graffiti seemed to writhe on the walls as if he'd taken a psychedelic. Everything felt more real than usual. His ears were ringing like Quasimodo's belfry.

He heard footsteps and turned, working up what he was going to say to the band. But it was the chaotichick and someone else, and then a third dude coming in after the someone else.

The someone else was a skinny guy with brown hair that was naturally messy, not messy as part of one of the cultural subcurrents. His mouth hung a little ajar, and one of his incisors was decayed black. His nose was windburned and the back of his bony hands were gnarled with veins. The third dude was Japanese; small, brown-eyed, nondescript, his expression was mild, just a shade more friendly than neutral. The skinny Caucasian guy wore an army jacket sans insignia, shiny jeans, and rotting tennis shoes. His hands were nervous, like there was something he was used to holding in them that wasn't there now. An instrument? Maybe.

The Japanese guy wore a Japanese Action Suit—surprise, surprise—sky-blue and neat as a pin. There was a lump on his hip—something he could reach by putting his right arm across his body and through the open zipper down the front of the suit—and Rickenharp was pretty sure it was a gun.

There was one thing all three of them had in common: they looked half-starved.

Rickenharp shivered—his gloss of sweat cooling on him, but he forced himself to say, "Whusappnin'?" It was wooden in his mouth. He was looking past them, waiting for the band.

"Band's in the wings," the chaotichick said. "The bass player said to tell you . . . well, it was *Telm zassouter.*"

Rickenharp had to smile at her mock of Julio's technicki. Tell him, get his ass out here.

Then some of the druggy feeling washed away and he heard the shouts from the audience and he realized they wanted an encore.

"Jeez, an encore," he said without thinking. "Been so fucking long."

"'Ey mate," the skinny guy said, pronouncing mate like *mite*. Brit or Aussie. "I saw you at Stone'enge five years ago when you 'ad yer second 'it."

Rickenharp winced a little when the guy said *your second hit*, inadvertently underlining the fact that Rickenharp had had only two, and everyone knew he wasn't likely to have any more.

"I'm Carmen," the chaotichick said. "This is Willow and Yukio." Yukio was standing sideways from the others, and something about the way he did it told Rickenharp he was watching down the corridor without seeming to.

Carmen saw Rickenharp looking at Yukio and said, "Cops are coming down."

"Why?" Rickenharp asked. "The club's licensed."

"Not for you or the club. For us."

He looked at her and said, "Hey, I don't need to get busted . . . " He picked up his guitar and went into the hall. "I got to do my encore before they lose interest."

She followed along, into the hall and the echo of the encore stomps, and asked, "Can we hang out in the dressing room for a while?"

"Yeah, but it ain't sacrosanct. You come back here, the cops can, too." They were in the wings now. Rickenharp signaled to Murch and the band started playing.

Standing beside him, she said, "These aren't exactly cops. They probably don't know these kind of places, they'd look for us in the crowd, not the dressing room."

"You're an optimist. I'll tell the bouncer to stand here, and if he sees anyone else start to come back, he'll tell 'em it's empty back here 'cause he just checked. Might work, might not."

"Thanks." She went back to the dressing room. He spoke to the bouncer and went on stage. Feeling drained, the guitar heavy on him. But he picked up on the energy level in the room and it carried him through two encores. He left them wanting more—and, sticky with sweat, walked back to his dressing room.

They were still there. Carmen, Yukio, Willow.

"Is there a stage door?" Yukio asked. "Into alley?"

Rickenharp nodded. "Wait in the hall; I'll come out and show you in a minute."

Yukio nodded, and they went into the hall. The band came in, filed past Carmen and Yukio and the Brit without much noticing them, assuming they were backstage hangout flotsam, except Murch stared at Carmen's tits and swaggered a bit, twirling his drumsticks.

The band sat around laughing in the dressing room, slapping palms, lighting several kinds of smokes. They didn't offer Rickenharp any; they knew he didn't use it.

Rickenharp was packing his guitar away, when Mose said, "You blew good."

"You mean he gave you a good head?" Murch said, and Julio snickered.

"Yeah," Ponce said, "the guy gives a good head, good collarbone, good kidneys—"

"Good kidneys? Rick sucks on your kidneys? I think I'm gonna puke."

And the usual puerile band banter because they were still high from a good set and putting off what they knew had to come, till Rickenharp said, "What you want to talk about, Mose?"

Mose looked at him, and the others shut up.

"I know there's something on your mind," Rickenharp said softly. "Something you haven't come out with yet."

Mose said, "Well, it's like—there's an agent Ponce knows, and this guy could take us on. He's a technicki agent and we'd be taking on a technicki circuit, but we'd work our way back from there, that's a good base. But this guy says we have to get a wire act in."

"You guys been busy," Rickenharp said, shutting the guitar case.

Mose shrugged, "Hey, we ain't been doing it behind your back; we didn't hear from the guy till yesterday night. We didn't have a real chance to talk to you till now, so, uh, we have the same personnel but we change costumes, change the band's name, write new tunes."

"We'd lose it," Rickenharp said. Feeling caved-in. "We'd lose the thing we got, doing that shit, because it's all superimposed."

"Rickenharp—rock 'n' roll is not a fucking religion," Mose said.

"No, it's not a religion, it's a way of life. Now, here's *my* proposal: we write new songs in the same style as always. We did good tonight. It could be the beginning of a turnaround for us. We stay here, build on the base audience we established tonight."

It was like throwing coins into the Grand Canyon. You couldn't even hear them hit bottom.

The band just looked back at him.

"Okay," Rickenharp said. "Okay. We've been through this ten fucking times. Okay. That's all." He'd had an exit speech worked out for this moment, but it caught in his throat. He turned to Murch and said, "You think they're going to keep you on, they tell you that? Bullshit! They'll be doing it without a drummer, man. You better learn to program computers, fast." Then he looked at Mose. "Fuck you, Mose." He said it quietly.

He turned to Julio, who was looking at the far wall as if to decipher some particularly cryptic piece of graffiti. "Julio, you can have my amp, I'll be traveling light."

He turned and, carrying his guitar, walked out, leaving silence behind him.

He nodded at Yukio and his friends and they followed him to the stage door. At the door, Carmen said, "Any chance you could help us find a little cover?"

Rickenharp needed company, bad. He nodded and said, "Yeah, if you'll gimme a hit of that blue boss."

She said, "Sure." And they went into the alley.

Rickenharp put on his dark glasses, because of the way the Walk tugged at him.

The Walk wound through the interlinked Freezone outfloats for a half-mile, looping up and back, a hairpin canyon of arcades crusted with neon and glowflake, holos and screens. It was involuted, intensified by layering and a blaze of colored light.

Stoned, very stoned: Rickenharp and Carmen walked together through the sticky-warm night, almost in step. Yukio walked behind, Willow ahead, and Rickenharp felt like part of a jungle patrol formation. And he had another feeling: that they were being followed, or watched. Maybe it was suggestion, from seeing Yukio and Willow glance over their shoulders now and then . . .

Rickenharp felt a ripple of kinetic force under his feet, an arc of wallow moving in languid whiplash through the flexible streetstuff, telling him that the breakers were up today, the baffles around the artificial island feeling the strain.

The arcades ran three levels above the narrow street; each level had its own sidewalk balcony; people stood at the railing to look down at the segmented snake of street traffic. The stack of arcades funneled a rich wash of scents to Rickenharp: the french-fry toastiness of the fast food; the sweet harshness of smashweed smoke, gyno-smoke, tobacco smoke—the cloy of perfumes; the mixed odors of fish-ka-bob stands, urine, rancid beer, popcorn, sea air; and the faint ozone smell of the small, eerily quiet electric cars jockeying on the street. His first time here, Rickenharp had thought the place smelled wrong for a red light cluster. "It's wimpy," he'd said. Then he'd realized he was missing the bass-bottom of carbon monoxides. There were no combustion cars on Freezone. Some parts of America still permitted pollutive, resource-greedy gasoline cars, and Rickenharp, being a retro, had preferred those places.

The sounds splashed over Rickenharp in a warm wave of cultural fecundity; pop tunes from thudders and wrist-boxes swelled in volume as they passed, the guys exuding the music insignificant in comparison to the noise they carried, the skanky tripping of protosalsa or the calculatedly redundant pulse of minimono.

Rickenharp and Carmen walked beneath a fiberglass arch—so covered with graffiti its original commemorative meaning was lost—and ambled down the milky walkway under the second-story arcade boardwalk. The multinational crowd thickened as they approached the heart of the Walk. The soft lights glowing upward from beneath the polystyrene walkway gave the crowd a 1940s-horror-movie look; even through the dark glasses the place tugged at Rickenharp with a thousand subliminal come-hithers.

Rickenharp was still riding the blue mesc surf, but the wave was beginning to break; he could feel it crumbling under him. He looked at Carmen. She glanced back at him, and they understood one another. She looked around, then nodded toward the darkened doorway of a defunct movie theater, a trash-cluttered recess twenty feet off the street. They went into the doorway; Yukio and Willow stood with their backs to the door, blocking the view from the street, so that Rickenharp and Carmen could each do a double hit of blue mesc. There was a kind of little-kid pleasure in stepping into seclusion to do drugs, a rush of outlaw in-crowd romance to it. On the second sniff the graffiti on the pad-locked, fiberglass doors seemed to writhe with significance. "I'm running low," Carmen said, checking her mesc bottle.

"Running low on drugs? Whoever heard of *that* happening?" Rickenharp said and they both burst in peals of laughter. His mind was racing now, and he felt himself click into the boss blue verbal mode. "You see that graffiti? *You're gonna die young because the ITE took the second half of your life.* You know what that is? I didn't know what ITE was till yesterday, I used to see those things and wonder and then somebody said—"

"Immortality something or other," she said, licking blue mesc off her sniffer.

"Immortality Treatment Elite. Supposedly some people keeping an immortality treatment to themselves because the government doesn't want the public to live too long and overpopulate the place. Another bullshit conspiracy theory."

"You don't believe in conspiracies?"

"I don't know—some. Nothing that far-fetched. But—I think people are being manipulated all the time. Even here . . . this place tugs at you, you know. Like—"

Willow said, "Right, we'll 'ave our sociology class later children, you gotter? Where's this place with the bloke can get us off the fooking island?"

"Yeah, okay, come on," Rickenharp said, leading them back into the flow of the crowd—but seamlessly picking up his blue mesc rap. "I mean, this place is a Times Square, right? You ever read the old novels about that place? That was the archetype. Or some places in Bangkok. I mean, these places are carefully arranged. Maybe subconsciously. But arranged as carefully as Japanese florals, only with the inverse esthetic. Sure, every whining, self-righteous tightassed evangelist who ever preached the diabolic seductiveness of places like this was right—in a way—was fully justified 'cause, yeah, the places titillate and they seduce and they vampirize people. Yeah, they're Venus's-flytraps. Architectural Svengalis. Yes to all the clichés about the bad part of town. All the reverend preachers—Reverend who, Reverend—what's his name?—Rick Crandall . . . "

She looked sharply at him. He wondered why but the mesc swept him on.

"All the preachers are right, but the reason they're right is why they're wrong, too. Everything here is trying to sell you something. Lots of lights and whirligig suction to seduce you into throwing your energy into it—in the form of money. People mostly come here to buy or to be titillated up to the verge of buying. The tension between wanting to buy and the resistance to buying can give you a charge. That's what I get into: I let it tickle my glands, but I hold back from paying into it. You know? Just constant titillation but no orgasm, because you waste your money or you get a social disease or mugged or sold bad drugs or something . . . I mean, anything sold here is pointless bullshit. But it's harder for me to resist tonight . . . " *Because I'm stoned.* "Makes you susceptible. Receptive to subliminals worked into the design of the signs, that gaudy kinetics, those fucking on/off bulbs—makes you flash on the old computer-thinking models, binomial thinking, on-off, on-off, blink blink—all those neon tubes, pulling you like the hypnotist's spiral pendant in the old movies . . . And the kinds of colors they use, the energy of the signs, the rate of pulse, the rate of on/offing in the bulbs, all of it's engineered according to principles of psychology the people who make them don't even know they're using, colors that hint about, you know, glandular discharges and tingly chemical flows to the pleasure center . . . like obscenities you pay for in the painted mouth of a whore . . . like video games . . . I mean—"

"I know what you mean," she said, in desperation buying a waxpaper cup of beer. "You must be thirsty after that monologue. Here." She shoved the foaming cup under his nose.

"Talking too much. Sorry." He drank off half the beer in three gulps, took a breath, finished it, and it was paradise for a moment. A wave of quietude soothed him—and then evaporated mesc burned through again. Yeah, he was wired.

"I don't mind listening to you talk," she said, "except you might say too much, and I'm not sure if we're being scanned."

Rickenharp nodded sheepishly, and they walked on. He crushed the cup in his hand, began methodically to shred it as they went.

Rickenharp luxuriated in the colors of the place, colors that mixed and washed over the crowd, making the stream of hats and heads into a living swatch of iridescent gingham; shining the cars into multicolored lumps of mobile ice.

You take the word *lurid*, Rickenharp thought, and you put it raw in a vat filled with the juice of the word *appeal*. You leave it and let the acids of appeal leach the colors out of *lurid*, so that you get a kind of gasoline rainbow on the surface of the vat. You extract the petro-rainbow on the surface of the vat with cheesecloth and strain it into a glass tube, dilute heavily with oil of cartoon innocence and extract of pure subjectivity. Now run a current through the glass tube and all the other tubes of the neon signs interlacing Freezone's Walk.

The Walk, stretching ahead of them, was itself almost a tube of colored lights, converging in a kaleidoscope; the concave fronts of the buildings to either side were flashing with a dozen varieties of signs. The sensual flow of neon data in primary colors was broken at cunningly irregular intervals by stark trademark signs: SYNTHLIFE SYSTEMS and MICROSOFT-APPLE and NIKE and COCA-COLA and WARNER AMEX and NASA CHEMCO and BRAZILIAN EXPORTS INTL and EXXON ELECTRICS and NESSIO. In all of that only one hint of the war: two unlit signs, FABRIZZIO and ALLINNE—an Italian and a French company, killed by the Russian blockades. The signs were unlit, dead.

They passed a TV-shirt shop; tourists walked out with their shirts flashing video imagery, fiberoptics woven into the shirtfront playing the moving sequence of your choice.

Sidewalk hawkers of every race sold beta candy spiked with endorphins; sold shellfish from Freezone's own beds, tempura'd and skewered; sold holocube pornography key rings; sold instapix of you and your wife, oh that's your boyfriend . . . Despite the nearness of Africa, black Africans were few here: Freezone Admin considered them a security risk and few on the contiguous coast could afford the trip. The tourists were mostly Japanese, Canadian, Brazilians—riding the crest of the Brazilian boom—South Koreans, Chinese, Arabs, Israelis, and a smattering of Americans; damned few Americans anymore, with the depression. Screens scanned them, one of them caught Rickenharp with a facial recognition program and on it a sexy animated Asian woman cooed, *"Rick Rickenharp—try Wilcox Subsensors and walk in a glow of excitement . . . "*

As they got deeper into the Walk the atmosphere became even more hot-house. It was a multicolored steam bath. The air was sultry, the various smokes of the place warping the neon glow, filtering and smearing the colors of signs and TV shirts and DayGlo jewelry. High up, between the not-quite-fitted jigsaw parts of signs and lights, were blue-black slices of night sky. At street level the jumble was given shape and borders by the doors opening on either side: by people using the doors to check out malls and stimsmoke parlors and memento shops and cubey theaters and, especially, tingler galleries. Dealers drifted up like reef fish, nibbling and moving on, pausing to offer, "DH, gotcher good Dee Ech": Direct Hookup, illegal cerebral pleasure center stimulation. And drugs: synth-cocaine and smokeable herbs; stims, and downs. About half of the dealers were burn artists, selling baking soda or pseudostims. The dealers tended to hang on to Rickenharp and Carmen because they looked like users, and Carmen was wearing a sniffer. Blue mesc and sniffers were illegal, but so were lots of things the Freezone cops ignored. You could wear a sniffer, carry the stuff, but the understanding was, you don't use it openly, you step into someplace discreet.

And whores of both sexes cruised the street, flagrantly soliciting. Freezone Admin was supposed to regulate all prostitution, but black-market pros were tolerated as long as somebody paid off the beat security and as long as they didn't get too numerous.

The crowd streaming past was a perpetually unfolding revelation of human variety. It unfolded again and a specialty pimp appeared, pushing a man and woman ahead of him; they had to hobble because they were straitjacket-packaged in black-rubber bondage gear. Their faces were ciphers in blank black-rubber masks; aluminum racks held their mouths wide-open, intended to be inviting, but to Rickenharp whispered to Carmen, "Victims of a mad orthodontist!" and she laughed.

Studded down the streets were Freezone security guards in bullet-proofed uniforms that made Rickenharp think of baseball umpires, faces caged in helmets. Their guns were locked by combination into their holsters; they were trained to open the four-digit combination in one second.

Mostly they stood around, gossiped on their helmet radios. Now two of them hassled a sidewalk three-card-monte artist—a withered little black guy who couldn't afford the baksheesh—pushing him back and forth between them, bantering one another through helmet amplifiers, their voices booming over the discothud from the speakers on the download shops:

"WHAT THE FUCK YOU DOING ON MY BEAT SCUMBAG. HEY BILL YOU KNOW WHAT THIS GUY'S DOING ON MY BEAT."

"FUCK NO I DUNNO WHAT'S HE DOING ON YOUR BEAT."

"HE'S MAKING ME SICK WITH THIS RIP-OFF MONTE BULLSHIT IS WHAT HE'S DOING."

One of them hit the guy too hard with the waldo-enhanced arm of his riot suit and the monte dealer spun to the ground like a top running out of momentum, out cold.

"LOITERING ON THE ZONE'S WALKS, YOU SEE THAT BILL."

"I SEE AND IT MAKES ME SICK JIM."

The bulls dragged the little guy by the ankle to a lozenge-shaped kiosk in the street and pushed him into a man-capsule. They sealed the capsule, scribbled out a report, pasted it onto the capsule's hard plastic hull. Then they shoved the man-capsule into the kiosk's chute. The capsule was sucked by mail-tube principle to Freezone Lockup.

"Looks like they're using some kind of garbage disposal to get rid of people here," Carmen said when they were past the cops.

Rickenharp looked at her. "You weren't nervous walking by the cops. So it's not them we're avoiding, huh?"

"Nope."

"You wanna tell me who it is we're supposed to be avoiding?"

"Uh-uh, I do not."

"How do you know these out-of-town cops you're worried about haven't gone to the locals and recruited some help?"

"Yukio says they won't, they don't want anybody to scan what they're doing here because the Freezone admin don't like 'em."

Rickenharp guessed: the *who* they were avoiding was the Second Alliance. Freezone's chairman was Jewish. The Second Alliance could *meet* in Freezone—the idea was, the place was open to anyone for meetings, or recreation; anyone, even people the Freezone boss would like to see gassed—but the SA couldn't *operate* here, except covertly.

The fucking SA bulls! Shit! . . . The blue mesc worked with his paranoia. Adrenaline spurted, making his heart bang. He began to feel claustrophobic in the crowd; began to see patterns in the movement around him, patterns charged with meaning superimposed by his own fear-galvanized mind. Patterns that taunted him with, *The SA's close behind*. He felt a stomach-churning combination of horror and elation.

All night he'd worked hard at suppressing thoughts of the band. And of his failure to make the band work. *He'd lost the band*. And it was almost impossible to make anyone understand why that was, to him, like a man losing his wife and children. And there was the career. All those years of pushing for that band, struggling to program a place for it in the Grid. Shot to hell now, his identity along with it. He knew, somehow, that it would be futile to try to put together another band. The Grid just didn't want him; and he didn't want the fucking Grid. And the elation was this: that ugly pit of displacement inside him closed up, was just gone, when he thought about the SA bulls. The bulls threatened his life, and the threat caught him up in something that made it possible to forget about the band. *He'd found a way out.*

But the horror was there, too. If he got caught up in this . . . if the SA bulls got hold of him . . .

Fuck it. What else did he have?

He grinned at Carmen, and she looked blankly back at him, wondering what the grin meant.

So now what? he asked himself. *Get to the OmeGaity. Find Frankie.* Frankie was the doorway.

But it was taking so long to get there. Thinking. The drug's fucking with your sense of duration. Heightened perception makes it seem to take longer.

The crowd seemed to get thicker, the air hotter, the music louder, the lights brighter. It was getting to Rickenharp. He began to lose the ability to make the distinction between things in his mind and things around him. He began to see himself as an enzyme molecule floating in some macrocosmic bloodstream—the sort of things that always OD'd him when he did an energizing drug in a sensory-overflow environment.

What am I?

Sizzling orange-neon arrows on the marquee overhead seemed to crawl off the marquee, slither down the wall, down into the sidewalk, snaking to twine around his ankles, to try to tug him into a tingler emporium. He stopped and stared. The emporium's display holos writhed with fleshy intertwinings; breasts and buttocks jutted out at him, and he responded against his will, like all the clichés, getting hard in his pants: visual stimuli; monkey see, monkey respond. He thought: *Bell rings and dog salivates.*

He looked over his shoulder. Who was that guy with the sunglasses back there? Why was he wearing sunglasses at night? Maybe he's SA—

Noooo, man. *I'm* wearing sunglasses at night. Means nothing.

He tried to shrug off the paranoia, but somehow it was twined into the undercurrent of sexual excitement. Every time he saw a whore or a pornographic video sign, the paranoia hooked into him as a kind of scorpion stinger on the tail of his adolescent surge of arousal. And he could feel his nerve ends begin to extrude from his skin. After having been clean so long, his-blue mesc tolerance was low.

Who am I? Am I the crowd?

He saw Carmen look at something in the street, then whisper urgently to Yukio.

"What's the matter?" Rickenharp asked.

She whispered, "You see that silver thing? Kind of a silvery fluttering? There—over the cab . . . Just look, I don't wanna point."

He looked into the street. A cab was pulling up at the curb. Its electric motor whined as it nosed through a heap of refuse. Its windows were dialed to mercuric opacity. Above and a little behind it a chrome bird hovered, its wings a hummingbird blur. It was about thrush-sized, and it had a camera-lens instead of a head. "I see it. Hard to say whose it is."

"I think it's run from inside that cab. That's like them. They'll send it after us from there. Come on." She ducked into a tingler gallery; Willow and Yukio and Rickenharp followed her. They had to buy a swipe card to get in. A bald, jowly old dude 'it the counter took the cards, swiped them without looking, his eyes locked on a wrist-TV screen. On his wrist a miniature newscaster was saying in a small tinny voice, " . . . attempted assassination of SA director Crandall today . . . " Something mumbled, distorted. " . . . Crandall is in serious condition and heavily guarded at Freezone Medicenter . . . "

The turnstile spun for them and they went into the gallery. Rickenharp heard Willow mutter to Yukio, "The bastard's still alive."

Rickenharp put two and two together.

The tingler gallery was predominantly fleshtone, every available vertical surface taken up by emulsified nude humanity. As you passed from one photo or holo to the next, you saw the people in them were inverted or splayed or toyed with, turned in a thousand variations on coupling, as if a child had been playing with unclothed dolls and left them scattered. A sodden red light hummed in each booth: the light snagged you, a wavelength calculated to produce sexual curiosity. In each "privacy booth" was a screen and a tingler. An oxygen mask that dropped from a ceiling trap pumped out a combination of amyl nitrite and pheromones. The tingler looked like a twentieth-century vacuum cleaner hose with an oversized salt-shaker top on one end: You watched the pictures, listened to the sounds, and ran the tingler over your erogenous zones; the tingler stimulated the appropriate nerve ends with a subcutaneously penetrative electric field, very precisely attenuated. You could pick out the guys in the health-club showers who'd used a tingler too long: use it more than the "recommended thirty-five-minute limit" and it made your skin look sunburned. One time Rickenharp's drummer had asked him if he had any lotion: "I got 'tingler dick,' man."

"To phrase it in the classic manner," Yukio said abruptly, "is there another way out of here?"

Rickenharp nodded. "Yeah . . . Uh—somewhere."

Willow was staring at a teaser blurb under a still-image of two men, a woman and a goat. He took a step closer, squinting at the goat.

"You looking for a family resemblance, Willow?" Rickenharp said.

"Shut your 'ole, ya retro greaser."

The booth sensed his nearness: the images on the sample placard began to move, bending, licking, penetrating, reshaping themselves with a weirdly formalized awkwardness; the booth's light increased its red glow, puffed out a tease of pheromone and amyl nitrite, trying to seduce him.

"Well, where *is* the other door?" Carmen hissed.

"Huh?" Rickenharp looked at her. "Oh! I'm sorry, I'm so—uh I'm not sure." He glanced over his shoulder, lowered his voice. "The bird didn't follow us in."

Yukio murmured, "The electric fields on the tinglers confuse the bird's guidance system. But we must keep a step ahead."

Rickenharp looked around—but he was still stoned: the maze of black booths and fleshtones seemed to twist back on itself, to turn ponderously, as if going down some cubistic drain . . .

"I will find the other door," Yukio said. Rickenharp followed him gratefully. He wanted out.

They hurried through the narrow hall between tingler booths. The customers moved pensively—or strolled with excessive nonchalance—from one booth to another, reading the blurbs, scanning the imagery, sorting through fetishistic indexings for their personal libido codes, not looking at one another except peripherally, carefully avoiding the margins of personal-space.

Chuffing, sighing music played from somewhere; the red lights were like the glow of blood in a hand held over a bright light. But the place was rigorously Calvinistic in its obstacle course of tacit regulations. And here and there, at the turns in the hot, narrow passageways between rows of booths, bored security guards rocked on their heels and told the browsers, *No loitering, please, you can purchase more time at the front desk.*

Rickenharp flashed that the place wanted to drain his sexuality, as if the vacuum-cleaner hoses in the booths were going to vacuum his orgone energy, leave him chilled as a gelding.

Get the fuck out of here.

Then he saw EXIT, and they rushed for it, through it.

They were in an alley. They looked up, around, half expecting to see the metal bird. No bird. Only the gray intersection of styroconcrete planes, stunningly monochrome after the hungry chromatics of the tingler gallery.

They walked out to the end of the alley, stood for a moment watching the crowd. It was like standing on the bank of a torrent. Then they stepped into it, Rickenharp, blue mesc'd, fantasizing that he was getting wet with the liquefied flesh of the rush of humanity as he steered by sheer instinct to his original objective: the OmeGaity.

They pushed through the peeling black chessboard doors into the dark mustiness of the OmeGaity's entrance hall, and Rickenharp gave Carmen his coat to hide her bare breasts. "Men only, in here," he said, "but if you don't shove your femaleness into their line of sight, they might let us slide."

Carmen pulled the jacket on, zipped it up—very carefully—and Rickenharp gave her his dark glasses.

Rickenharp banged on the window of the screening kiosk beside the locked door that led into the cruising rooms. Beyond the glass, someone looked up from a fat-screen TV. "Hey, Carter," Rickenharp said.

"Hey." Carter grinned at him. Carter was, by his own admission, "a trendy faggot." He was flexicoated battleship gray with white trim, a minimono style. But the real M'n'Ms would have spurned him for wearing a luminous earring—it blinked through a series of words in tiny green letters— *Fuck . . . you . . . if . . . you . . . don't . . . like . . . it . . . Fuck . . . you . . . if*—and they'd have considered that unforgivably "Griddy." And anyway Carter's wide, froggish face didn't fit the svelte minimono look. He looked at Carmen. "No girls, Harpie."

"Drag queen," Rickenharp said. He slipped a folded twenty newbux note through the slot in the window. "Okay?"

"Okay, but she takes her chances in there," Carter said, shrugging. He tucked the twenty in his charcoal bikini briefs.

"Sure."

"You hear about Geary?"

"Nope."

"Snuffed hisself with China White 'cause he got green pissed."

"Oh, shit." Rickenharp's skin crawled. His paranoia flared up again, and to soothe it he said, "Well, I'm not gonna be licking anybody's anything. I'm looking for Frankie."

"That asshole. He's there, holding court or something. But you still got to pay admission, honey."

"Sure," Rickenharp said.

He took another twenty newbux out of his pocket, but Carmen put a hand on his arm and said, "We'll cover this one." She slapped a twenty down.

Carter took it, chuckling. "Man, that queen got some real nice larynx work." Knowing damn well she was a girl. "Hey, Rick, you still playing at the—"

"I blew the gig off," Rickenharp cut in, trying to head off the pain. The boss blue had peaked and left him feeling like he was made out of cardboard inside, like any pressure might make him buckle. His muscles twitched now and then, fretful as restive children scuffing feet. He was crashing. He needed another hit. When you were up, he thought, things showed you their frontsides, their upsides; when you peaked, things showed you their hideous insides. When you were down, things showed you their backsides, their downsides. File it away for lyrics.

Carter pressed the buzzer that unlocked the door. It razzed them as they walked through.

Inside it was dim, hot, humid.

"I think your blue was cut with coke or meth or something," Rickenharp told Carmen as they walked past the dented lockers. "Cause I'm crashing harder than I should be."

"Yeah, probably . . . What'd he mean 'he got green pissed'?"

"Positive test for AIDS-three. The HIV that kills you in three weeks. You drop this testing pill in your urine and if the urine turns green you got AIDS. There's no cure for the new HIV yet, won't be in three weeks, so the guy . . . " He shrugged.

"What the 'ell is this place?" Willow asked.

In a low voice Rickenharp told him, "It's a kind of bathless gay baths, man. Cruising places for 'mos. But about a lotta the people are straights who ran out of bux at the casinos, use it for a cheap place to sleep, you know?"

"Yeah? And 'ow come you know all about it, 'ey?"

Rickenharp smirked. "You saying I'm gay? The horror, the horror."

Someone in a darkened alcove to one side laughed at that.

Willow was arguing with Yukio in an undertone. "Oi don't like it, that's all, fucking faggots got a million fucking diseases. Some side o' beef with a tan going to wank on me leg."

"We just walk through, we don't touch," Yukio said. "Rickenharp knows what to do."

Rickenharp thought, *Hope so.*

Maybe Frankie could get them safely off Freezone, maybe not.

The walls were black pressboard. It was a maze like a tingler gallery but in the negative. There was a more ordinary red light; there was the peculiar scent that lots of skin on skin generates and the accretion of various smokes, aftershaves, cheap soap, and an ingrained stink of sweat and semen gone rancid. The walls stopped at ten feet up and the shadows gathered the ceiling into themselves, far overhead. It was a converted warehouse space, with a strange vibe of stratification: claustrophobia layered under agoraphobia. They passed mossy dark cruising warrens. Faces blurred by anonymity turned to monitor them as they passed, expressions cool as video cameras.

They strolled through the game room with its stained pool tables and stammering holo-games, its prized-open vending machines. Peeling from the walls between the machines were posters of men—caricatures with oversized genitals and muscles that seemed themselves a kind of sexual organ, faces like California surfers. Carmen bit her finger to keep from laughing at them, marveling at the idiosyncratic narcissism of the place.

They passed through a cruising room designed to look like a barn. Two men ministered to one another on a wooden bench inside a "horse stall" with wet fleshy noises. Willow and Yukio looked away. Carmen stared at the gay sex in fascination. Rickenharp walked past without reacting, led the way through other midnight nests of pawing men; past men sleeping on benches and couches, sleepily slapping unwanted hands away.

And found Frankie in the TV lounge.

The TV lounge was bright, well-lit, the walls cheerful yellow. The OmeGaity was cheap—there were no holo cubes. There were motel-standard living-room lamps on end tables; a couch; a regular color screen showing a rock video channel; and a bank of monitors on the wall. It was like emerging from the underworld. Frankie was sitting on the couch, waiting for customers.

Frankie dealt on a porta-terminal he'd plugged into a Grid-socket. The buyer gave him an account number or credit card; Frankie checked the account, transferred the funds into his own (registered as consultancy fees), and handed over the packets.

The walls of the lounge were inset with video monitors; one showed the orgy room, another a porn vid, another ran a Grid network satellite channel. On that one a newscaster was yammering about the attempted assassination, this time in technicki, and Rickenharp hoped Frankie wouldn't notice it and make the connection. Frankie the Mirror was into taking profit from whatever came along, and the SA paid for information.

Frankie sat on the torn blue vinyl couch, hunched over the pocket-sized terminal on the coffee table. Frankie's customer was a disco 'mo with a blue sharkfin flare, steroid muscles, and a white karate robe; the guy was standing to one side, staring at the little black canvas bag of blue packets on the coffee table as Frankie completed the transaction.

Frankie was black. His bald scalp had been painted with reflective chrome; his head was a mirror, reflecting the TV screens in fish-eye miniature. He wore a pinstriped three-piece gray suit. A real one, but rumpled and stained like he'd slept in it, maybe fucked in it. He was smoking a Nat Sherman cigarette, down to the gold filter. His synthcoke eyes were demonically red. He flashed a yellow grin at Rickenharp. He looked at Willow, Yukio, and Carmen, made a mocking scowl. "Fucking narcs—get more fancy with their setups every day. Now they got four agents in here, one of 'em looks like my man Rickenharp, other three took like refugees and a computer designer. But that Jap hasn't got a camera. Gives him away."

"What's this 'ere about—" Willow began.

Rickenharp made a dismissive gesture that said, *He isn't serious, dumbshit.* "I got two purchases to make," he announced and looked at Frankie's buyer. The buyer took his packet and melted back into the warrens.

"First off," Rickenharp said, taking his card from his wallet, "I need some blue blow, three grams."

"You got it, homeboy." Frankie ran a lightpen over the card, then punched a request for data on that account. The terminal asked for the private code number. Frankie handed the terminal to Rickenharp, who punched in his code, then erased it from visual. Then he punched to transfer funds to Frankie's account. Frankie took the terminal and double-checked the transfer. The terminal showed Rickenharp's adjusted balance and Frankie's gain.

"That's gonna eat up half your account, Harpie," Frankie said.

"I got some prospects."

"I heard you and Mose parted company."

"How'd you get that so fast?"

"Ponce was here buying."

"Yeah, well—now I've dumped the dead weight, my prospects are even better." But as he said it he felt dead weight in his gut.

"'S your bux, man." Frankie reached into the canvas carry-on, took out three pre-weighed bags of blue powder. He looked faintly amused. Rickenharp didn't like the look. It seemed to say, *I knew you'd come back, you sorry little wimp.*

"Fuck off, Frankie," Rickenharp said, taking the packets.

"What's this sudden squall of discontent, my child?"

"None of your business, you smug bastard."

Frankie's smugness tripled. He glanced speculatively at Carmen and Yukio and Willow. "There's something more, right?"

"Yeah. We got a problem. My friends here—they're getting off the raft. They need to slip out the back way so Tom and Huck don't see 'em."

"Mmm. What kind of net's out for them?"

"It's a private outfit. They'll be watching the copter port, everything legit . . . "

"We had another way off," Carmen said suddenly. "But it was blown—"

Yukio silenced her with a look. She shrugged.

"Verr-rry mysterious," Frankie said. "But there are safety limits to curiosity. Okay. Three grand gets you three berths on my next boat out. My boss's sending a team to pick up a shipment. I can probably get 'em on there. That's going *east*, though. You know? Not west or south or north. One direction and one only."

"That's what we need," Yukio said, nodding, smiling. Like he was talking to a travel agent. "East. Someplace Mediterranean."

"Malta," Frankie said. "Island of Malta. Best I can do." Yukio nodded. Willow shrugged. Carmen assented by her silence.

Rickenharp was sampling the goods. In the nose, to the brain, and right to work. Frankie watched him placidly. Frankie was a connoisseur of the changes drugs made in people. He watched the change of expression on Rickenharp's face. He watched Rickenharp's visible shift into ego drive.

"We're gonna need four berths, Frankie," Rickenharp said.

Frankie raised an eyebrow. "You better decide after that shit wears off."

"I decided before I took it," Rickenharp said, not sure if it was true.

Carmen was staring at him. He took her by the arm and said, "Talk to you a minute?" He led her out of the lounge, into the dark hallway. The skin of her arm was electrically sweet under his fingers. He wanted more. But he dropped his hand from her and said, "Can you get the bux?"

She nodded. "I got a fake card, dips into—well, it'll get it for us. I mean, for me and Yukio and Willow. I'd have to get authorization to bring you. And I can't do that."

"Know what? I won't help you get out otherwise."

"You don't know—"

"Yeah, I do. I'm ready to go. I just go back and get my guitar."

"The guitar'll be a burden where we're going. We're going into occupied territory, to get where we want to be. You'd have to leave the guitar."

He almost wavered at that. "I'll check it into a locker. Pick it up someday. Thing is—if they watched us with that bird, they saw me with you. They'll assume I'm part of it. Look, I know what you're doing. The SA's looking for you. Right? So that means you're—"

"Okay, hold it, shit; keep your voice down. Look—I can see where maybe they marked you, so you got to get off the raft, too. Okay, you go with us to Malta. But then you—"

"I got to stay with you. The SA's everywhere. They marked me."

She took a deep breath and let it out in a soft whistle through her teeth. She stared at the floor. "You can't do it." She looked at him. "You're not the type. You're a fucking *artist*."

He laughed. "You say that like it's the lowest insult you can come up with. Look—I can do it. I'm going to do it. The band is dead. I need to . . . " He shrugged helplessly. Then he reached up and took her sunglasses off, looked at her shadowed eyes. "And when I get you alone I'm going to batter your cervix into jelly."

She punched him hard in the shoulder. It hurt. But she was smiling. "You think that kind of talk turns me on? Well, it does. But it's not going to get you into my pants. And as for going with us—What you think this is? You've seen too many movies."

"The SA's marked me, remember? What else can I do?"

"That's not a good enough reason to . . . to become part of this thing. You got to really believe in it, because *it's hard*. This is not a celebrity game show."

"Jesus. Give me a break. I know what I'm doing."

That was bullshit. He was trashed. He was blown. *My computer's experiencing a power surge. Motherboard fried. Hell, then burn out the rest.*

He was living a fantasy. But he wasn't going to admit it. He repeated, "I know what I'm doing."

She snorted. She stared at him. "Okay," she said.

And after that everything was different.

Besides having written numerous stories and books, being seminal to cyberpunk sf, and termed a "post-modern Poe," **John Shirley** was lead singer of the punk band Sado-Nation, the post-punk band Obsession (Celluloid Records), and was later in the band Panther Moderns. He currently records with The Screaming Geezers. He's also written eighteen song lyrics recorded by Blue Öyster Cult. His latest novel is *Everything Is Broken* and his classic cyberpunk trilogy, *A Song Called Youth*, was recently released as an omnibus. ("Freezone" and Rickenharp became part of the first volume, *Eclipse*.) A compilation double album with selections of his music, *Broken Mirror Glass: Recordings by John Shirley 1978-2012*, will be released by Black October Records in December 2012. Other music by John can be heard at reverbnation.com/johnshirley. His website is john-shirley.com.

• • • •

Hobnoblin Blues
Elizabeth Bear

Tracks: How do you define yourself?
Loki: I don't. (laughter) Fuck, why do you people always ask me that?[1]

There's always a secret history, stories that remain unreported, tales too ticklish to tell. No matter how many soul-and-skin-baring biographies are writ, no matter how many groupies sell their stories to *The Midnight Sun*.

It's a source of intense frustration to the press that more—don't.

Something about Loki makes people keep secrets. Not just his lovers (the ephemeral ones or the few that linger over more than breakfast). Even the interviewers do it, as if they need to hoard clandestine fragments to gloat over.

You do it, too.

But you have more to work with. You know his real name isn't that stupid collection of nonsense syllables. And you know he doesn't come from here.

When he fell, you fell with him.

Not for rebellion, but for love.

Monster Bones, the second album by controversial British songwriter Loki, looks to be a major breakout. The nine tracks, unified by themes of loss and catastrophe, range from "Golden Apples," a meditation on mortality—the apples hold the secret of eternal life, but like Sleeping Beauty's are poisoned—to the epic, Zeppelinesque crunch of "Bad Water," while the title track—a transparent commentary on the likely eventual legacy of the Vietnam conflict—uses crisp guitar and a killer bassline to underscore the point of view of a giant-killer revisiting the resting place of the adversary that crippled him: *Prone under a forked white sky / I stare up a roof of bones / Bake under a crucified sun.*

---

[1]   Henry Morrisseau, "Diamonds & Diesel: A Candid Interview With Loki," *Tracks*, August 1972.

For a rock-and-roll singer, Loki demonstrates an astonishing vocal range. It's surprising to learn that he has no classical training, because the overall impression of his soaring performance is something like a Carole King with balls. With *Monster Bones*, Loki takes a hard look at the blues, and dumps it on its ass to take up with rock 'n' roll. A brilliant departure.[2]

Loki says, laughing, "Look at this nonsense, Hob. They can't even get their own fairy tales right."

You pull the flimsy magazine from his hand, already folded to the important page. Loki is paying more attention to the pretty redheaded boy nuzzling his neck.

Later, on the title track of a 1983 release, Loki will revisit those lyrics, in a song that most people will assume is about cocaine addiction.

People, you will both have learned by then, will almost always assume.

The cancer, he'll sing, in the wailing apocalyptic style that's just a crippled echo of his true voice, *speaks with a forked white tongue. The cancer croons with a forked white tongue.*

He was born Martin Trevor Blandsford in Manchester, UK, in 1950, where he attended grammar and vocational schools. In 1966, he dropped out, ran off to London, and in the company of three other young men took a famously squalid two-room flat in Soho.

There was nothing to indicate that within six years, Martin Blandsford would be transformed into a rock-and-roll avatar.

He craved shock, but for years it must have seemed he was born just a little too late. His mid-seventies revelations of drug abuse, bisexuality, and financial mismanagement failed to adequately galvanize a press already inured to the excesses of performers such as Led Zeppelin, Jimi Hendrix, David Bowie, Janis Joplin, and the Rolling Stones.

The fulfillment of Loki's desire to set the music establishment on its heels—or on its ear—would have to wait until 1980. When he'd do just that, in the most spectacular manner possible.[3]

---

[2]   Frank Randall, album reviews, *Bontemps Magazine*, April 1972.

[3]   Eric Greg, *Playing with Fire: The Unauthorized Biography of Loki*, London, Plasma Publishing Ltd., 1998.

Robbin Howard "Hobnoblin" Just:

7 July 1950 –

Instruments: saxophone, mandolin, keyboards, rhythm guitar. Backing vocals.

A respected and steady-handed session musician, most noted for his work with **Loki**. Just was one of two members of the legendary 1970's touring band to continue performing with the singer after his 1980-1981 transformation (the other was bassist **Ramona Henkman**). He continued to record and travel with Loki until 2004, when the androgynous rocker put himself, Just—and the entire music industry—out of a job.[4]

Loki purses his lips, sips Irish coffee, and lifts the back-folded newspaper in his left hand. He reads over the tops of his sunglasses. "Seven months ago, when Loki toured in support of *Monster Bones*, he and his five-man backing band shattered attendance records—and possibly a few eardrums. Ranting, charismatic, with an indefatigable stage presence, the tall black-haired rock God bestrode the stage—and the microphone stand—like a modern titan."

But the flesh around his lips is taut. Fine furrows lead from his nose to the corners of his mouth. You wince in anticipation.

He doesn't disappoint. The paper crumples in his hand, ink smearing under his thumb. "Titan. *Titan*. Wankers. Can't even tell the difference between a giant's son and a goddamned pansy titan. Do you believe this rubbish?"

"At least they're not making any misinformed cracks about fire gods," you say, eyes on your eggs.

It's unwise to provoke him. But sometimes irresistible.

He snorts, and hunches down to the paper again. His hair falls over his eyes. He shoves it back with a gaunt hand, sniffling. He sniffles constantly.

It's the cocaine. The gauntness is that, plus amphetamines. He takes them when he works, in heroic quantities, as if they could replace the forbidden mead of poetry.

Loki never knew when to shut up. Which is both why he's here, and why you followed him down.

He drinks more coffee and continues reading. "But the tour for the follow-up album *Barbed Hearts* is little more than bloated indulgence, the raw edges of the rock and roll buried under a stage show whose self-

---

4   *The Last Ultimate Encyclopedia of Rock & Roll*, New York, New American Library, 2009.

importance might give pause to Blue Öyster Cult. Dear Mr. Loki, a message from your loyal fans: lasers and lipstick are not the markers of a brilliant career. Bah!"

He smacks the paper down on the table, splashing your tea, and finishes his whiskey-laced coffee. One of the staff is at his elbow in a moment with the pot, and—always polite—he remembers to thank her. It's as reflexive as the thanks he offers when you pass him the silver flask kept warm inside your gaudy velvet waistcoat.

You could refuse. But that wouldn't stop him drinking, and he'd be even worse in a rage. You pass him the whipped cream too.

At least it's calories.

"Fuck 'em," you say. The reek of alcohol from his coffee stings your nostrils. You pick a flake of skin beside your nail.

These bodies. There's always something going wrong. Exile is a kind word for *death sentence*. Nobody likes spilling the blood of a god if they can help it.

Bad precedent.

"You should see what they say about your sax, sweetheart." He finger-flicks the paper away. "Gods *rot* it, Hobnoblin. I want to go home."

He doesn't mean England. You don't mean England either when you say, softly, "Yeah," and reach over and pat his hand.

He shakes it off, though, and jerks his head side to side, sniffing. "Well, as long as we're stuck here, maybe we can bust things up a little. Let in some damned light and air."

It never worked on the Aesir, but you don't say that. It won't help either of you to remind him that he provoked the exile he mourns. Loki has never been any good at all at keeping his head down.

You're a little too good at it. That's one of the reasons why you love him: when the Aesir came, Loki was the one who would not be silenced, who forced them to treat with him as an equal.

For a time.

But that's a second thing you can't say. And the third one you don't tell him is that, despite the coffee mug, his fingers are chill.

Tracks: Would you rather talk about the music? How much of the process is collaborative?

Loki: Oh, let's. And—frankly—a lot! I mean, the songs are mine, but the arrangements, that's all of us. And that's most of what makes it work. The Hobnoblin [*Robbin "Hobnoblin" Just is Loki's saxophone* *player—Ed.*] has a great ear for layering sounds. (Loki laughs and takes a drag on his cigarette, holding the smoke while he finishes the thought.) And a good bass player, that holds the whole thing together. We hired this chick you're gonna love. (Smirking.) Oh, it's all collaboration. I'm pretending modesty this week. I just write the pretty words and play a little lousy guitar.[5]

He drifts on the music sometimes. The sound system in the estate in Kent is extraordinary, and sometimes you'll walk out on the patio and find Loki in jeans and a T-shirt, arms spread wide, head lolled back, letting the music lift him like a thermal lifts a hawk.

It's not his own stuff he plays to go there. As often as not, it's not even rock. Beethoven; Mozart; Charlie Parker; Thelonious Monk; Bessie Smith; Big Mama Thornton; Joni Mitchell; Crosby, Stills, and Nash.

You won't disturb him while he's listening.

But sometimes you'll sit at the breakfast table and watch.

Word gets around.

I knew when I arranged the interview that Martin Blandsford—Loki, to his young fans—would rather be interviewed at home. He doesn't go out much. He's been assaulted by feral packs of adolescent maenads one time too many, and says self-deprecatingly that it's in the interest of everyone's safety if he stays home with his slippers on.

Not that he was wearing slippers when I arrived. His bare knobby feet looked cold on the tile floor of his half-furnished house, and his white summer-weight pants were rolled up to show equally knobby ankles. He wore no shirt over his sinewy, hairless chest. His shaggy black hair stuck to itself in streaks of blue and goldenrod.

He'd been painting the upstairs bedroom, he explained.

To this reporter, accustomed to his commanding stage presence—the black leather and platform boots and smeared eyeliner—he seemed younger in person, slight, polite, dangerously thin. But the lack of costume bulk did make him appear even taller. He offered me a glass of wine and a cup of coffee, took one of each himself, and showed me into his den.

The actual interview did not go as smoothly.[6]

---

5   Henry Morrisseau, "Diamonds & Diesel: A Candid Interview With Loki," *Tracks*, August 1972.

6   Henry Morrisseau, "Diamonds & Diesel: A Candid Interview With Loki," *Tracks*, August 1972.

Melody Monitor: Do you categorize yourself as feminine?
Loki: Oh, no. I'm très butch. Don't you think?[7]

The rest of the *Barbed Hearts* tour is a kind of hell, though you manage to tempt him sometimes with chocolate milk and yellow apples dipped in honey. Everybody in and around the band—the road manager, the guys from the record companies—assumes you are Loki's loyal and long-suffering lover, and you are treated with equal parts pity and disdain.

They expect you to play his keeper.

So you do.

He's worse at home, where it's just the two of you and whatever girl or boy (or girls, or boys) he's collected.

He doesn't eat for days. He hates the human food, the life-or-death choice. You're not immortal anymore, not without Iduna's stolen apples, and you're prey to all the needs and ills the flesh is heir to. Feed yourself, and live, and with it acknowledge that you are bound unto death in this mortal realm.

Well, that, and cocaine kills your appetite.

He stays up for four days writing songs for an album that never does get cut, because he pitches the whole lot into the woodstove one night when you're out by the pasture, feeding perfectly unmagicked apples to the perfectly unmagical horses, four bays and duns and chestnuts and grays with a leg at each corner, whose hides do not shine like faceted jewels, like beaten gold and steel and silver.

He never rides. You think perhaps he keeps them around to make himself sad.

Before the next tour, he wants to reinvent himself.

You sit behind him and chat and hand him the comb and scissors while he cuts his hair in front of the mirror. You help him bleach it white-blond, and once he's rinsed off the searing chemicals, the pair of you drink champagne and eat peaches and watch this month's crop of girls splash in the pool.

You kid yourself it might keep getting better.

But by month's end, you've packed for the new tour, painfully titled *Ragnarock-and-Roll*. It's soon apparent that the "fresh start" has been only a moment of reprieve.

Loki has always been thin, but the drugs and anorexia whittle him to bone and wire. He suffers hallucinations and fits of cocaine paranoia. He has

---

[7]   Hugh Carter, "Loki, Unplugged," *Melody Monitor*, May 1982.

a houngan brought in to exorcise the drum kit, because you can't trust those damned Norns.

Okay, that one is almost reasonable.

At his worst, he weighs one hundred and seven pounds at six foot two, and won't wear his earplugs on stage because he feels them squirming. He keeps singing, though, even if nobody can hear him. Because what he has to say is important, even if it's doomed to go unheard. What worries you most is what will happen if he forgets himself enough to raise his voice—because he could make people listen. He *could*.

If he were willing to pay the price.

He's a dying man clutching a microphone, and it's an ugly thing.

> **Melody Monitor:** Seriously, your sexuality's been an open question for years—
>
> **Loki:** My sexuality is an answered question. But apparently nobody likes the answer. I am what I am. Musically, personally. I don't like categories. I'm not going to assign myself to one.
>
> It's boring to repeat myself.

"Wankers," he says, with that polite measured quietness. He drops a copy of *Rolling Stone* on the floor and kicks it under the table. It skitters, pages fluttering, and fetches against the leg of your chair. You butter a scone. "Loki hasn't got a damned thing to do with fire. That's Surtr, for fuck's sake. I swear they do it just to piss me off. It's a goddamned conspiracy."

You break the scone and lay the larger portion on Loki's empty plate.

He sniffles and ignores it. "They called me 'a Ziggy Stardust-influenced Elvis impersonator.' Bunch of ignorant fuckers in the press."

"Yeah," you say.

He's not even drinking the coffee anymore.

SINGER COLLAPSES ON STAGE

British pop idol Loki collapsed during a concert last night at the Tingley Coliseum in Albuquerque, NM. The performer, 26, has been hospitalized for exhaustion. Presbyterian Hospital reports that he is in stable condition, receiving intravenous fluids, and in no immediate danger.

Band member Robbin "Hob" Just issued a public statement early this morning, blaming Loki's illness on fatigue and "dieting prior to a photo shoot."

He also said, "[The weather] is never this beastly in London. It's hard on the whole band."

Temperatures remained in the triple digits throughout the night, and attendance at last night's performance was estimated at over 11,500.

Tonight's show has been postponed. Changes to any further tour dates have not been announced.

Loki is known for shocking stage antics and provocative lyrics. But his most recent album failed to chart a single, and the current tour has not performed to expectations, half-filling arena venues in seven states.[8]

While he's in the hospital, you clean out his stash. There'll be Hell to pay when he gets back, and you've no illusions you can keep him straight for long. But he'll be straight when they let him out, and he might still be straight long enough to yell at, if the pills and cocaine are gone.

Of course, he can get more. There are *always* people around who will get it for him.

But Ramona, the bass player, catches you going through the trunks and suitcases.

Silently, she helps you flush the pills.

Melody Monitor: Would you say you go out of your way to make yourself seem unusual?
Loki: D'you know about left-hander syndrome? No? Left-handed people make up around thirteen percent of the population. About the same percentage as homosexuals, give or take. And left-handed people die, depending on who you listen to, two or nine years earlier than right-handed people.

This might be because of accidents caused by bleedin' navigating through a right-handed world.

Being different can kill you, can't it?
Melody Monitor: Are you left-handed?
Loki: I'm ambidextrous. As in so many things.[9]

He breaks his hand when he hits you.

---

8   Associated Press Newswire, 12 July 1976.

9   Hugh Carter, "Loki, Unplugged," *Melody Monitor,* May 1982.

Actually, he was swinging at Ramona, but you step in front of it and take the punch on the side of the head, to nobody's lingering pleasure. He's taller than you by a good ten inches, but frail from starvation and speed, and the swing that barely turns your head lands him, flailing, on his ass, all spiky elbows and knees.

He sits there, spraddle-legged as a colt in black leather and heavy boots, his T-shirt untucked at the waist, and shifts his gaze from the hand he clutches, to your face, and back again.

Ramona steps forward. You stand your ground, the same way you stood it beside him when the Aesir handed the sentence down and the rest of the dvergar stepped away.

You wonder if he can read the memory in your face, or if he has one of his own. He doesn't get up. He doesn't look down.

"Hob, can you get me into a program?" he says.

In 1977, the punk zine *Beat Down* proclaimed of *The Esoteric Adventures of Kittie Calamatie,* "What the fuck is this? It sounds like Frank Zappa mating with an alley cat. Who told this bloated arena rock asshole that he should ditch the laser show and synthesizers? And what's with the fucking mandolin? And *why do I like it?*"

It marked a new creative era for Loki, a regeneration of the innovative, questing spirit of the early 1970's. The album and subsequent tour, in which he assumed the persona of a drag queen punk rocker—the eponymous Kittie Calamatie—rejuvenated interest in his work, and the album reached #5 on the UK charts and #3 in the U.S.

Loki was sober and pissed off again, and the result was beautiful music.[10]

"Oh, fuck me running," Loki moans, head down in his hands, his hair—black again—standing in spikes between his fingers. There's a newspaper open on the table, dented by his elbows; you have come to know it as a sign of dread warning.

"What is it this time?"

Wordlessly, he leans back and rotates the paper with a fingertip. You shuffle forward, slippers scuffing on the tile, and clutch your bathrobe closed over your chest. There's a photo from a recent gig on page five. You're not

---

[10]   Liner notes, *Kill the Horses: the Loki Retrospective*, 2002.

in it, but Ramona and Loki are leaned together, jamming, guitar and bass necks bobbing in time. "It's a rave," you say, scanning the review.

"Look at my face."

You stare; it looks like Loki. Both the photo and the man sitting in front of you, idly turning his orange juice glass around inside its ring of condensate.

"I'm not getting any younger," he says, when you blink at him stupidly.

"Oh," you say, and sit down in the other chair. "Right. Happy birthday."

He tosses the wing of black hair out of his eyes. He's wearing a shaggy long-fronted punk cut, streaked purple and indigo, these days. It changes without notice, like the music on the stereo.

"It's not working," he says.

"Of course it's not working." You pour coffee from the thermal carafe, add cream, two lumps of sugar with the tongs. So civilized these days. There's only his cereal spoon on the table, so you swipe it and stir. "What did you expect?"

"I thought I could make them understand," he says. "But it's all I can do to keep their attention."

"Some of it gets through. Subliminally." The coffee is delicious, hot enough that for a moment you forget the cold of the world. You pour a second cup. "Change takes time."

Fretfully, he picks the skin at the back of his hand. It snaps down, taut, but you know what he's imagining. "I haven't *got* time."

You don't answer.

"What if I showed them?" he says, conversationally, ten minutes later.

It's a tone you know not to trust. "Showed them what?"

He shrugs. "How silly the categories are. I got Thor into a wig and dress. Surely I can inject a little chaos into a complacent, self-consumptive media culture. I mean, Reagan's president-elect. Iron Maggie . . . don't even get me started on her. It's like the counterculture never happened. So . . . what if I turned into a girl?"

You're trained, by now. You don't let him see you choke on the scalding coffee. "It's not like turning yourself into a mare by magic, Jotunsson."

He tweaks skin between nails again. "It's only meat. What's the difference? It's just meat. It's dying anyway."

By the last days of 1980, John Bonham and Keith Moon are dead, Mick Jagger is divorced, David Bowie is sober, and Loki has finally pulled off a stunt that defies comparison.

• • •

Loki: You wankers—and when I say you wankers, I mean the press, Bob—never let go of anything. You take it all out of context. When I started reassignment, you should have seen reporters trying to come up with coded ways to ask me if I'd had my pizzle cut off yet.

It's all a fucking hype machine. You say something like, rock and roll, it's the devil's music, it's concerned with subversion and revolution and kicking back at authority, and the headline the next day is "Loki Declares Self Lucifer!"

Badger: Well, that'll certainly be my headline.

Smoke wreathes her face as she studies me. I can see the moment when she decides it's funny after all, and gives a weak laugh.

Loki: Don't be silly, I hate fire. Ask me about the drugs, why don't you?

Badger: What about the drugs?

Loki: Don't ever fucking get started. And if you are started, stop right now. I'm not a role model, and you don't want to be like me.

Badger: Like you? Famous, talented, respected? Or like you, a freak?

Loki: Oh, the freak part is fine. That's a scream. If anybody gets anything from my life, I hope it's that the real freaks are the ones who try to program and condition everybody to conform to a conqueror's culture.

But I'd rather nobody emulated the drug abuse. You should see the films from my last nasal endoscopy. Not pretty.

Of course, the way it works is people want to idolize rock stars, pretend these stage personas are gods. They want to make rock star mistakes, but they're so busy pretending we're immortal and special that they don't want to learn from those mistakes. Live big, die gagging on their own vomit.

All these lovely illustrations of perfectly asinine behavior, and people want to be just like them. Same thing you people have always done with gods.

Badger: You people?

Loki: I'm an atheist. And you know, I could *make* people listen. But it'd be the last thing they ever heard.[11]

• • •

---

[11]   Robert Slavish, "The Unlikeliest Centerfold: An Interview with Loki," *Badger for Men*, December 1983.

In 1980, when Loki revealed his plans to become a woman, the announcement was greeted by a jaded media with first derision and then disbelief [needs cite(s)]. While the singer had long been open about his bisexuality, his confession that he had entered treatment for Gender Identity Disorder and decided to undergo sex reassignment surgery was treated as a publicity stunt.

In 1983, *Badger* published a nude photo layout of Loki, post-op, provoking a media frenzy.[12]

Loki walks around where you can see her, catches your eye with her upraised hands. "What are you doing, Hob?" she signs.

Your fingers lift from the keyboard. She watches intently. "Updating your Clikipedia entry."

"Packing it with lies, I hope."

"Do you want me to take out the bit where it says you're controversial in the trans community for refusal to politicize your sexuality?"

"Is that code for *I fuck people who aren't transfolk*?"

"I guess."

She sighs, swings the opposite chair around, throws a leg over it and plunks down. She straddles the back and leans forward on crossed arms. A moment later, she leans back. Her hands work jaggedly. "Even when they learn to listen," she says, "they still want to force you to say what they think you should be saying. Everybody wants the power of mind control. I just wanted to make them stop and *think*."

She stops talking. You let her sit motionless until she shakes herself and finishes, "Besides, I fuck transfolk too."

"Sweetie," you tell her (you never called her sweetie when she was a man), "you fuck anybody you think is sexy."

She grins, runs her tongue along her upper lip, and bats her eyelashes. "And what the hell is wrong with that?"

"Here," you sign, and wave her over. "You'll like this bit."

Since her retirement from music, Loki remains a controversial and public figure. Her refusal to conform to political or social ideology has been described as anarchistic by some; however, the maverick ideology has been embraced by youth culture, some of whom describe her as a messiah.[13]

---

[12]   Clikipedia entry: Loki (singer).

[13]   Clikipedia entry: Loki (singer).

"Fuck, Hobnoblin, you wanker," she says. "Take out that word, *messiah*. And this bit in the quotes, 'Half of what I say is meaningless, but I say it so you'll hear the other half.' That's me misquoting John Lennon misquoting Kahlil Gibran. Take that out."

"Consider it done. You know you're not supposed to edit your own entry."

She laughs and kisses you on the head. "You're editing it, not me. I like this bit though—'The real freaks are the ones who try to program and condition everybody to conform to a conqueror's culture.' Did I say that?"

"In 1982."

> *The stars crack in the cold.*
> *The only messenger is you.*
> *Ride on*
> *Killing horses.*[14]

Groovecutter: How would you categorize what you do?
Loki: I leave that to the critics. They have time.[15]

Melody Monitor: You must get asked about your surgery a great deal, and what influenced your decision. Before your gender reassignment, you were very open about your relationships—
Loki: Relationships. There's a juiceless euphemism.
Melody Monitor: How has your gender reassignment changed things?
Loki: [inaudible]
Melody Monitor: Could you repeat that?
Loki: I said, should it have?[16]

The media still depresses her. The mortal world is both too subjective and not fluid enough. She doesn't read the papers anymore, or the biographies, or watch the tell-all exposes. She's aging. You both are.

The exile is a death sentence, too.

It's not as if anything mere humans could devise would shock *her*, who knew the treachery of the Aesir overlords. But thirty-odd years of this nonsense isn't enough to make either of you used to it, or resigned.

---

14   Lyrics from "Ride On," off the album *Radiant*, 2003.

15   Anne Westfahl, "Rock Star Bones," *Groovecutter Magazine*, March 1985.

16   Hugh Carter, "Loki, Unplugged," *Melody Monitor,* May 1982.

People, it seems, still assume you're fucking her. And some people still don't approve.

She paces your hospital room, fuming, hands balled in the small of her back. You're fine, you assure her. Loosened teeth, a cracked cheekbone, a couple of busted ribs. A few nasty names can't hurt you now, and the MPA are treating it as a hate crime. They take those seriously.

And you're alive. Mostly unbroken.

It could have been worse.

It doesn't seem to be a good time to remind her that she once hit you herself, when she was he, and you and Ramona flushed his cocaine.

"Don't hold back," you tell her, when her silence grates too harshly. The IV pinches in the back of your hand. The tape itches. "Tell us how you really feel."

She checks and turns to you, and her hands fall down by her sides. "I could. What if I did? What if I *made* them listen?"

"Loki, you're mortal now too. And so am I."

"I would miss the music," she admits. But shakes her head and continues, dark eyes narrowing under the black fringe of her bangs. "If you tell me not to, I won't do it."

As the world now knows, the purported Martin Trevor Blandsford was revealed on 24 February 2004 to be a supernatural being, bearing a message of peace and open-mindedness that had gone too long unheard. [*disputed*] Through the divine auspices of the heavenly messenger Loki, it was demonstrated unequivocally that "There are none so deaf as will not hear." [*disputed; cite needed*][17]

The Patuck Reader: What do you think about the furor surrounding your last concert? What some are calling, in fact, The Last Concert.

Loki: That's melodrama. There are babies born every day, and thousands of years of musical history for them to grow into. I certainly haven't stopped composing, and I don't imagine anybody else has. Beethoven can always serve as a good example.

The Patuck Reader: You were jailed, there are death threats . . .

Loki: Let 'em come.

The Patuck Reader: You've been called a visionary, or accused of suffering a messiah complex. You're often assigned credit or blame

---

[17]   Clikipedia entry: Loki (singer).

for social changes in the last thirty years. For example, the advancing debate over what people are calling nontraditional marriage rights—domestic partnership regardless of gender or number of partners. Do you deserve any of it?

Loki: Don't be ridiculous. There's nothing visionary about anything I've said. Whatever you've done, you've done for yourselves. All I did was show you how to stop listening to the program and think. All I did was show people how to stop listening to the lies.

(She laughs.) If I were a messiah, I would be *upset* that more people don't agree with me. [18]

The last album is released early in 2004. The *Let Silence Ring* tour kicks off the same day, with a worldwide live-televised gig from Madison Square Garden.

The encore is "Ride On." No great surprise there: it's the only reason it wouldn't have been in the regular set. You feel bad for Ramona; she doesn't deserve what's coming.

But as you walk back out to re-take your places, you pick your earplugs out and flick them into the darkness at the side of the stage.

For luck.

Once upon a time, Loki could sing gold from a dwarf, love from a goddess, troth from a giantess. He bargained kidnapped goddesses away from giant captors and blood-brotherhood from the All-Father. She talked Thor into a dress, and nearly into a marriage.

She's never used the full strength of her voice before mortals before. When she does, it reaches every corner of the world, a high windblown cry of truth and chaos.

It's the last sound any of us hear.

• • •

Elizabeth Bear was born on the same day as Frodo and Bilbo Baggins, but in a different year. The author of over a dozen novels and a hundred short stories, she has been honored for some of them with the John W. Campbell, two Hugos, and a Sturgeon Award. Her hobbies include rock climbing and cooking. She lives in Massachusetts with a giant ridiculous dog and regularly commutes to Wisconsin in order to spend time with her step-cat—and his human, author Scott Lynch.

• • • •

---

[18]   Cassandra Hutchinson, "The Day The Music Died," *The Patuck Reader*, November 2006.

Then Play On
Greg Kihn

What's the worst thing about being a guitar player? I'll tell you. It's when your fingers hurt so bad you can't play, but you gotta play. That's when you really appreciate a little help. Real musicians know that. They know that there's nothing like running on fumes and having somebody step up and save your ass.

Then play on.

That's how I met Charlie. He stepped up one night behind Ghiradelli Square when my hands were throbbing like hypothermic gerbils. I'd been playin' for five hours. Had about two dollars in loose change in my guitar case. I really, really needed the dough, and the tourists were runnin' like herring. With a little luck I could pay off a certain street thug, and save a trip to the hospital. I was cold, beat, and dirty, trying to croak out another verse of "Sweet Jane" before I lost the meager crowd of curious Asians gawking at my bloody fingers, when Charlie appeared. And he looked worse than me.

Sometimes a harmonica can sound almost human, like when the notes bend and wail inside God's own Doppler effect. The fucker came up behind me and started blowin, and I swear, I thought it was some kind of supernatural creature. I nearly jumped out of my skin.

The first riff he played sounded like something crying. It was the saddest riff I ever heard. The tone of Charlie's harp made the hair on the back of my neck stand up. Hey, man, I've heard 'em all, from Little Walter to Butterfield, and this cat's tone was . . . well, the only way I can describe it was otherworldly. And his phrasing, it was like he knew exactly where I was going. Let's face it, "Sweet Jane" is no great blues harp showcase tune. Most players would run out of gas after a few verses. But Charlie seemed to have a bottomless supply of riffs. The man could play.

With Charlie's help, I played for another two hours and raked in a guitar case full of quarters and crumpled bills. Busking in San Francisco requires a license, and I didn't have one, so I kept a constant eye out for the cops.

Charlie wouldn't take any money, even after I counted it up and separated his share. "Don't need it, man," he said. "I live close to the ground."

Charlie was a strange dude. I, on the other hand, always needed money. I was between gigs, living in my car. Life was a constant struggle. I figured I'd eventually get another band together, but for now, playing on the streets was my primary source of income.

Charlie walked back along Columbus with me, turned on Broadway, and headed north through the strip clubs. He never said a word. In the garish light of the neon, Charlie didn't look right. His skin was pale, nearly devoid of color.

"Where you goin' now?"

Charlie shrugged.

"Want to get something to eat?"

Charlie shook his head.

Fog drifted up Broadway from the waterfront, it seemed to swirl around Charlie, as if he attracted it. I noticed a few more things about him that puzzled me. First, his clothes. He didn't dress like a street person. He was scruffy, all right, with the telltale dirty fingernails and unwashed hair, but his clothes seemed out of date. He wore a forties-style threadbare suit, with a shabby fedora. His shoes looked like something Sam Spade might have worn: big, brown gunboats with worn leather soles, down at the heels, and badly in need of a shine. He looked painfully thin, with hollow sunken cheeks and a long hooked nose.

"Are you sure you don't want any of the money? I got close to forty dollars here."

Charlie smiled, but his face couldn't hold it, and the smile faded like a smoke ring. "Keep the money. You can do something for me later."

"Sure, man, anything you say. Meet me tomorrow? Same bat time? Same bat channel?"

Charlie nodded. "We'll see . . . "

"I loved playin' music with you, man. I could jam that shit forever."

I heard Charlie whisper, "Yes, I believe you could."

We had reached the alley between The Stone and The Mystic Eye occult supply store. Charlie stepped into the alley and disappeared. It happened so fast I didn't notice for a couple seconds. I went back and peered into the darkness of the opening. "Charlie?"

No answer. I walked on.

The next day Charlie was back. I'd been playing for about an hour at the corner of Bay Street and Stockton, not making any money, when he arrived.

He started blowing his harp and within five minutes we had a crowd of thirty people. Some silver clanked in the open guitar case at my feet, a few rumpled bills appeared. Things were looking up. Alone I couldn't get arrested, but with Charlie, the money came easy.

I introduced him to the crowd, but no one seemed to notice. I asked some people if they dug the harmonica player, and they laughed. After another hour, some of my street friends showed up. I took a pee break and asked a homeless magician named Marco to watch my stuff. When I returned, Charlie was gone. "Did you happen to see where my harp player went?"

Marco scratched his head. "What harp player?"

"The guy who's been playin' with me all morning." I pointed to the spot on the steps where Charlie had been. "He was standing right there."

Marco shook his head. "I saw the last eight tunes, bro. There was no harp player. Nobody was standing there."

"Come on, man. Don't dick me around. You mean to say you didn't see a guy standing there blowin' unbelievable harp while I was playin'?"

Marco looked at me curiously. "No. There was nobody there."

I could feel the color drain from my face. "Well, then . . . What the fuck's goin' on?"

Marco shrugged. "Street ghost?"

I started to laugh. "No way. Can't be, man. That's crazy."

Marco put a hand on my shoulder. "People die out here all the time. Think about it, bro. All those spirits, all that negative energy. It must go somewhere."

"Then you think Charlie is a ghost?"

Marco shrugged. "I've made something of a study of street ghosts. I can look into it, if you like."

I didn't feel like playing anymore. I packed up my guitar and headed for some junk food and a warm place to poop. Marco agreed to meet me later and try to find Charlie.

As dusk settled, we found ourselves outside the alley next to The Mystic Eye. Marco peered into the shadows. "You say he disappeared here the first night?"

I nodded. "Said he lived close to the ground. What do you think that means?"

Marco shrugged and walked into the alley. I followed. It was dank and moist, with a fetid, musty odor clinging to the brick. Marco examined the dead end. "See that mortar? It doesn't match the original. That hole's been patched up. A long time ago, from the looks of it."

"What's the deal with the hole?"

Marco pointed down the alley. "Most people don't know this, but there's a bunch of tunnels under this neighborhood, dating back to the Barbary Coast. Smugglers used them all the time. The waterfront used to come up a lot further in the old days. All this shit's been built on landfill where the original docks used to be. In fact, I'd say we're standing at the old waterline right now."

I shivered. "So what about the tunnels?"

"There are several under Broadway that have been blocked off since the forties."

"I wonder if there's a connection between Charlie and that tunnel?"

"Maybe he died there."

I stared off into space for a minute. "I got a buddy who works at the *Chronicle*. I'm gonna go see him. Maybe he can check the archives."

Later that afternoon I was reading a microfilm file of a story from 1941. Three vagrants who had been sleeping in one of the tunnels had been sealed in when city workers blocked the entrances. Two had escaped by yelling their lungs off until help arrived. The third one had died. His name was Charles Pittman, an itinerant musician.

"Charlie," I whispered. "Jesus Christ. It's Charlie."

The next day I went early to a spot in Valencourt Plaza I liked to use on sunny afternoons. A lot of people from the financial district ate lunch there, sitting on the steps near the fountain. I'd made some decent coin there in the past. I was into my third song when Charlie strolled up, holding his harmonica. I tried to smile. "Well, if it ain't my old buddy, Charlie. Care to sit in?"

Charlie just nodded and cupped his harmonica to his mouth. I started playing a midtempo blues shuffle in E. Charlie slid in between the riffs and started to blow, sweet and lonely. The sound filled my head, reverberating in the echo chamber of my brain. I looked around to see if anybody was reacting to it, but saw no indication. I looked at Charlie. "Am I the only one who can see you?"

Charlie stopped playing and nodded.

"So . . . you're a ghost?"

"I live close to the ground."

I looked away, unsure how to feel. I mean, I was scared, but also tweaked on the music, and curious as hell. "Close to the ground is right. Try *under* the ground. Are you dead?"

Charlie put his harp to his lips and blew, a long sorrowful musical phrase. I noticed the crowd had dissipated, I was alone in that part of Valencourt Plaza. Alone with Charlie.

I checked my tuning. "All right, you dead muthafucker. Let's play."

I peeled off the opening riff to Robert Johnson's "Hell Hound On My Trail" and waited. The perfect song to jam with a dead guy. Charlie seemed to pause for a moment, harmonica poised at this mouth, listening. Then, he slid into the song like a sharp knife slides into flesh, cold and final. He opened with one long twisted note, like a banshee's mournful wail. It seemed to go on for several minutes, lasting through the entire eight-bar intro.

I opened my mouth to sing and suddenly felt cold air rush into my throat. "Woke up this mornin', blues fallin' down like hail . . . "

The lyrics chilled me. All of San Francisco stopped. Charlie answered. "Woke up this mornin', blues fallin' down like hail . . . " I concentrated on a good, clean riff into the four chord. "I got to keep movin', I got a hell hound on my trail . . . "

Charlie's voice had the keening edge of a far-off railroad whistle. "Hell hound on my trail . . . Hell hound on my trail . . . "

I've heard that song ten thousand times, played it a thousand times, know every inflection of the original, but I never, ever heard it like that. Charlie absolutely expanded the melody into outer space. I don't remember anything after that, just being swept away. The song went on forever, slow and ominous, and floated above the ground like the ghost that it was.

I wasn't aware of time passing, but it must have been a while because when the song finally ended, and I opened my eyes, I was surrounded by people. I looked down at my guitar case and saw that it was filled with money. At least a couple of hundred bucks. I tried to speak, but could only cough. I closed the case, slung the guitar over my shoulder and walked away. Charlie followed.

My feet took me back up Broadway, to the alley. Charlie stood on the edge of the shadows and held out his hand. I stared at it. "I ain't takin' your hand, man. You can forget that shit."

Charlie laughed. It sounded odd, like he hadn't laughed in a long time. "Fair enough. Why don't you count the money?"

"I'll count it later. Why don't you take some? Probably a couple hundred in there."

"What am I gonna do with money?"

"What else is there?"

"Remember when I said that you could do something for me later?"

I nodded. I'd been waiting for this.

"Well, I want you to use some of that money and buy a pick ax and open up that tunnel."

As soon as he said it, I shuddered. I dreaded something like this, and wanted nothing to do with it. Opening the tunnel, with whatever remained of Charlie's corpse inside, was an unbelievably gruesome idea. I had a weak stomach. "No way, man. Ask for something else."

Charlie responded by playing his harp. The music tugged at my heart. I knew that what Charlie had requested would be damn near impossible for me, but at the same time, I somehow felt like I could do it. It would be a hell of thing. Knock out some bricks, stand back, and let Charlie's spirit go free. Suddenly, it didn't seem that hard. I didn't have to go inside the tunnel. I could accomplish the whole job standing in the alley, with my feet firmly planted in this world.

And Charlie seemed like such a sweet guy. Plus, he was the best harp player I ever heard, living or dead.

"I'll see what I can do. There's no guarantee or anything, but . . . what the hell, I'll give it a shot."

I went to the hardware store and bought a heavy pick ax and returned to the alley. It was dark by then, so I also bought a cheap flashlight.

Charlie waited for me at the tunnel. He pointed at the patched bricks. "There."

I took a hard swing and the ax met the wall with a ringing crunch. I'd expected it to be hard, but the old mortar was soft and the unreinforced brick crumbled like wallboard. Within five minutes I'd knocked a sizable hole in the masonry.

I turned to Charlie. "Well?"

"There's second wall a few feet inside."

"Hey, man. I'm not goin' in there."

"There's nothing there. Go on, have a look with the flashlight."

I shined the light into the hole and saw the space was empty. "I don't know, man . . . "

"It's perfectly all right. Come on, now. You're almost there."

I reluctantly knocked away a few more bricks to enlarge the opening, then stepped inside. The smell was unpleasant, but not overwhelming. The walls were covered with moss, the floor with slime. I didn't stop to think, I started swinging the pick ax as soon as I had clearance. The second wall was a bit tougher, double bricks. Once again, time and San Francisco moisture had softened the mortar. I grunted and swung the ax, bashing the antique terra cotta bricks. Now I could hear echoes of my demolition inside the tunnel. The old bricks fell into the enclosure. I hurried, not wanting to stay one extra second in the dank entrance to Charlie's tomb.

A large section of brick collapsed inward, and for the first time in many decades, air swept into the tunnel. I could hear the whoosh of escaping gases, and a low moan as the new air was drawn deep into the tunnel. It sounded like breathing. I turned to Charlie and his face seemed luminescent. "Almost done," he said.

"I hope so, man. This is a bummer . . . "

I hacked at the wall and felt a mini avalanche inside as a new section of bricks tumbled. The hole was big enough for a man to step through now.

I turned to see what Charlie was doing, but he was gone.

"Hey! Charlie! Where are y—"

I never finished the sentence. I was shoved violently into the tunnel by unseen hands. I screamed, and tried to grasp the moldering bricks, but the force was irresistible. I staggered into the inky blackness. The entrance to the tunnel, a faint rectangle of gray light, seemed far away, as if the tunnel itself was elongating. Then Charlie reached out and grasped my shoulder with his hand.

"What are you doing?" I shouted. "Get out of my way!" I dove for the opening, but something happened I couldn't believe. My eyes saw it, but my mind refused to acknowledge it. The rectangle of faint light contracted. It shrunk, like a mouth closing, pinching off the last rays of the outside world. In a heartbeat I was enveloped by darkness. I lunged for the place the opening had been and clawed frantically at the rubble. "Let me out of here! Damn it! Let me out!"

Charlie stood over me, his skin glowing in the absolute darkness. "I can't. It's closed."

"Well, open it!"

"I can't. It can only be opened from outside."

"Is this the thanks I get for helping you?"

Charlie shook his head. "I'm sorry . . . "

"You're sorry? You asshole!"

"I'm lonely. I need someone to play music with. I thought . . . because we played so well together . . . "

I was furious. "You thought, what? That you'd lure me in here and seal the entrance?"

Charlie's voice echoed in the tunnel, somewhere behind him water dripped. "It's not right, I know. It hurts me to do it. But, it's the only way I could find somebody to play music with. You see, eternity is a terrible thing to face as a solo. In a few minutes the air will become unbreathable. Then, we'll have all the time in the world."

"No!" I panicked and beat my fists against the bricks. "No! I don't want to die! Please . . . Charlie, please."

Charlie held out my guitar. "Let's jam."

• • •

Greg Kihn has been a professional songwriter, musician, and performer for over thirty-five years. As leader of the Greg Kihn Band, he has released eighteen albums, scored top hits with "Breakup Song" and "Jeopardy," as well as worldwide notoriety and regular airplay on MTV. Kihn has written four novels; the first, *Horror Show* (1996) was nominated for the Bram Stoker Award. It was followed by *Shade of Pale*, *Big Rock Beat*, and *Mojo Hand*. Kihn also edited *Carved in Rock: Short Stories by Musicians*, an anthology of short stories written by rock musicians. Kihn currently is the morning DJ at San Jose, California classic rock radio station 98.5 KFOX. As part of the Jones Radio Network he also does a late night show on classic rock radio station WKGO-FM (go106.com). Greg Kihn was inducted into the San Jose Rock Hall of Fame in 2007. He blogs at www.kfox.com/Greg-Kihn-s-Blog/9573650.

• • • •

The Feast of Saint Janis
Michael Swanwick

Take a load off, Janis, And You put the load right on me.
—The Wait (trad.)

Wolf stood in the early morning fog watching the *Yankee Clipper* leave Baltimore harbor. His elbows rested against a cool, clammy wall, its surface eroded smooth by the passage of countless hands, almost certainly dating back to before the Collapse. A metallic grey sparkle atop the foremast drew his eye to the dish antenna that linked the ship with the geosynchronous Trickster seasats it relied on to plot winds and currents.

To many the wooden *Clipper*, with its computer-designed hydrofoils and hand-sewn sails, was a symbol of the New Africa. Wolf, however, watching it merge into sea and sky, knew only that it was going home without him.

He turned and walked back into the rick-a-rack of commercial buildings crowded against the waterfront. The clatter of hand-drawn carts mingled with a mélange of exotic cries and shouts, the alien music of a dozen American dialects. Workers, clad in coveralls most of them, swarmed about, grunting and cursing in exasperation when an iron wheel lurched in a muddy pothole. Yet there was something furtive and covert about them, as if they were hiding an ancient secret.

Craning to stare into the dark recesses of a warehouse, Wolf collided with a woman clad head to foot in chador. She flinched at his touch, her eyes glaring above the black veil, then whipped away. Not a word was exchanged.

A citizen of Baltimore in its glory days would not have recognized the city. Where the old buildings had not been torn down and buried, shanties crowded the streets, taking advantage of the space automobiles had needed. Sometimes they were built over the streets, so that alleys became tunnelways, and sometimes these collapsed, to the cries and consternation of the natives.

It was another day with nothing to do. He could don a filter mask and tour the Washington ruins, but he had already done that, and besides the day looked like it was going to be hot. It was unlikely he'd hear anything about his mission, not after months of waiting on American officials who didn't want to talk with him. Wolf decided to check back at his hostel for messages, then spend the day in the bazaars.

Children were playing in the street outside the hostel. They scattered at his approach. One, he noted, lagged behind the others, hampered by a malformed leg. He mounted the unpainted wooden steps, edging past an old man who sat at the bottom. The old man was laying down tarot cards with a slow and fatalistic disregard for what they said; he did not look up.

The bell over the door jangled notice of Wolf's entry. He stepped into the dark foyer.

Two men in the black uniforms of the political police appeared, one to either side of him. "Wolfgang Hans Mbikana?" one asked. His voice had the dust of ritual on it; he knew the answer. "You will come with us," the other said.

"There is some mistake," Wolf objected.

"No, sir, there is no mistake," one said mildly. The other opened the door. "After you, Mr. Mbikana."

The old man on the stoop squinted up at them, looked away, and slid off the step.

The police walked Wolf to an ancient administrative building. They went up marble steps sagging from centuries of footscuffing, and through an empty lobby. Deep within the building they halted before an undistinguished-looking door. "You are expected," the first of the police said.

"I beg your pardon?"

The police walked away, leaving him there. Apprehensive, he knocked on the door. There was no answer, so he opened it and stepped within.

A woman sat at a desk just inside the room. Though she was modernly dressed, she wore a veil. She might have been young; it was impossible to tell. A flick of her eyes, a motion of one hand, directed him to the open door of an inner room. It was like following an onion to its conclusion, a layer of mystery at a time.

A heavyset man sat at the final desk. He was dressed in the traditional suit and tie of American businessmen. But there was nothing quaint or old-fashioned about his mobile, expressive face or the piercing eyes he turned on Wolf.

"Sit down," he grunted, gesturing toward an old overstuffed chair. Then: "Charles DiStephano. Controller for Northeast Regional. You're Mbikana, right?"

"Yes, sir." Wolf gingerly took the proffered chair, which did not seem all that clean. It was clear to him now; DiStephano was one of the men on whom he had waited these several months, the biggest of the lot, in fact. "I represent—"

"The Southwest Africa Trade Company." DiStephano lifted some documents from his desk. "Now this says you're prepared to offer—among other things—resource data from your North American Coyote landsat in exchange for the right to place students in Johns Hopkins. I find that an odd offer for your organization to make."

"Those are my papers," Wolf objected. "As a citizen of Southwest Africa, I'm not used to this sort of cavalier treatment."

"Look, kid, I'm a busy man, I have no time to discuss your rights. The papers are in my hands, I've read them, the people that sent you knew I would. Okay? So I know what you want and what you're offering. What I want to know is why you're making this offer."

Wolf was disconcerted. He was used to a more civilized, a more leisurely manner of doing business. The oldtimers at SWATC had warned him that the pace would be different here, but he hadn't had the experience to decipher their veiled references and hints. He was painfully aware that he had gotten the mission, with its high salary and the promise of a bonus, only because it was not one that appealed to the older hands.

"America was hit hardest," he said, "but the Collapse was worldwide." He wondered whether he should explain the system of corporate social responsibility that African business was based on. Then decided that if DiStephano didn't know, he didn't want to. "There are still problems. Africa has a high incidence of birth defects." *Because America exported its poisons; its chemicals arid pesticides and foods containing a witch's brew of preservatives.* "We hope to do away with the problem; if a major thrust is made, we can clean up the gene pool in less than a century. But to do this requires professionals— eugenicists, embryonic surgeons—and while we have these, they are second-rate. The very best still come from your nation's medical schools."

"We can't spare any."

"We don't propose to steal your doctors. We'd provide our own students— fully trained doctors who need only the specialized training."

"There are only so many openings at Hopkins," DiStephano said. "Or at U of P or the UVM Medical College, for that matter."

"We're prepared to—" Wolf pulled himself up short. "It's in the papers. We'll pay enough that you can expand to meet the needs of twice the number of students we require." The room was dim and oppressive. Sweat built up under Wolf's clothing.

"Maybe so. You can't buy teachers with money, though." Wolf said nothing. "I'm also extremely reluctant to let your people *near* our medics. You can offer them money, estates—things our country cannot afford. And we *need* our doctors. As it is, only the very rich can get the corrective surgery they require."

"If you're worried about our pirating your professionals, there are ways around that. For example, a clause could be written—" Wolf went on, feeling more and more in control. He was getting somewhere. If there wasn't a deal to be made, the discussion would never have gotten this far.

The day wore on. DiStephano called in aides and dismissed them. Twice, he had drinks sent in. Once, they broke for lunch. Slowly the heat built, until it was sweltering. Finally, the light began to fail, and the heat grew less oppressive.

DiStephano swept the documents into two piles, returned one to Wolf, and put the other inside a desk drawer. "I'll look these over, have our legal boys run a study. There shouldn't be any difficulties. I'll get back to you with the final word in—say a month. September twenty-first, I'll be in Boston then, but you can find me easily enough, if you ask around."

"A month? But I thought . . . "

"A month. You can't hurry City Hall," DiStephano said firmly. "Ms. Corey!"

The veiled woman was at the door, remote, elusive. "Sir."

"Drag Kaplan out of his office. Tell him we got a kid in here he should give the VIP treatment to. Maybe a show. It's a Hopkins thing, he should earn his keep."

"Yes, sir." She was gone.

"Thank you," Wolf said, "but I don't really need . . . "

"Take my advice, kid, take all the perks you can get. God knows there aren't many left. I'll have Kaplan pick you up at your hostel in an hour."

Kaplan turned out to be a slight, balding man with nervous gestures, some sort of administrative functionary for Hopkins. Wolf never did get the connection. But Kaplan was equally puzzled by Wolf's status, and Wolf took petty pleasure in not explaining it. It took some of the sting off of having his papers stolen.

Kaplan led Wolf through the evening streets. A bright sunset circled the world, and the crowds were much thinner. "We won't be leaving the area that's zoned for electricity," Kaplan said. "Otherwise I'd advise against going out at night at all. Lot of jennie-deafs out then."

"Jennie-deafs?"

"Mutes. Culls. The really terminal cases. Some of them can't pass themselves off in daylight even wearing coveralls. Or chador—a lot are women." A faintly perverse expression crossed the man's face, leaving not so much as a greasy residue.

"Where are we going?" Wolf asked. He wanted to change the subject. A vague presentiment assured him he did not want to know the source of Kaplan's expression.

"A place called Peabody's. You've heard of Janis Joplin, our famous national singer?"

Wolf nodded, meaning no.

"The show is a re-creation of her act. Woman name of Maggie Horowitz does the best impersonation of Janis I've ever seen. Tickets are almost impossible to get, but Hopkins has special influence in this case because— ah, here we are."

Kaplan led him down a set of concrete steps and into the basement of a dull brick building. Wolf experienced a moment of dislocation. It was a bookstore. Shelves and boxes of books and magazines brooded over him, a packrat's clutter of paper.

Wolf wanted to linger, to scan the ancient tomes, remnants of a time and culture fast sinking into obscurity and myth. But Kaplan brushed past them without a second glance and he had to hurry to keep up.

They passed through a second roomful of books, then into a hallway where a grey man held out a gnarled hand and said, "Tickets, please."

Kaplan gave the man two crisp pasteboard cards, and they entered a third room.

It was a cabaret. Wooden chairs clustered about small tables with flickering candles at their centers. The room was lofted with wood beams, and a large unused fireplace dominated one wall. Another wall had obviously been torn out at one time to make room for a small stage. Over a century's accumulation of memorabilia covered the walls or hung from the rafters, like barbarian trinkets from toppled empires.

"Peabody's is a local institution," Kaplan said. "In the twentieth century it was a speakeasy. H.L. Mencken himself used to drink here." Wolf nodded, though the name meant nothing to him. "The bookstore was a front, and the drinking went on here in the back."

The place was charged with a feeling of the past. It invoked America's bygone days as a world power. Wolf half-expected to see Theodore Roosevelt or Henry Kissinger come striding in. He said something to this effect, and Kaplan smiled complacently.

"You'll like the show, then," he said.

A waiter took their orders. There was barely time to begin on the drinks when a pair of spotlights came on, and the stage curtain parted.

A woman stood alone in the center of the stage. Bracelets and bangles hung from her wrists, gaudy necklaces from her throat. She wore large tinted glasses and a flowered granny gown. Her nipples pushed against the thin dress. Wolf stared at them in horrified fascination. She had an extra set, immediately below the first pair.

The woman stood perfectly motionless. Wolf couldn't stop staring at her nipples; it wasn't just the number, it was the fact of their being visible at all. So quickly had he taken on this land's taboos.

The woman threw her head back and laughed. She put one hand on her hip, thrust the hip out at an angle, and lifted the microphone to her lips. She spoke, and her voice was harsh and raspy.

"About a year ago I lived in a row house in Newark, right? Lived on the third floor, and I thought I had my act together. But nothing was going right, I wasn't getting any . . . action. Know what I mean? No talent comin' around. And there was this chick down the street, didn't have much and she was doing okay, so I say to myself: *What's wrong, Janis?* How come she's doing so good and you ain't gettin' any? So I decided to check it out, see what she had and I didn't. And one day I get up early, look out the window, and I see this chick out there *hustling*! I mean, she was doing the streets at *noon*! So I said to myself, Janis, honey, you ain't even trying. And when ya want action, ya gotta try. Yeah. Try just a little bit harder."

The music swept up out of nowhere, and she was singing: "Try-iii, Try-iii, Just a little bit harder . . . "

And unexpectedly, it was good. It was like nothing he had ever heard, but he understood it, almost on an instinctual level. It was world-culture music. It was universal.

Kaplan dug fingers into Wolf's arm, brought his mouth up to Wolf's ear. "You see? You see?" he demanded. Wolf shook him off impatiently. He wanted to hear the music.

The concert lasted forever, and it was done in no time at all. It left Wolf sweaty and emotionally spent. Onstage, the woman was energy personified. She danced, she strutted, she wailed more power into her songs than seemed humanly possible. Not knowing the original, Wolf was sure it was a perfect re-creation. It had that feel.

The audience loved her. They called her back for three encores, and then a fourth. Finally, she came out, gasped into the mike, "I love ya, honeys, I truly do. But please—no more. I just couldn't do it." She blew a kiss, and was gone from the stage.

The entire audience was standing, Wolf among them, applauding furiously. A hand fell on Wolf's shoulder, and he glanced to his side, annoyed. It was Kaplan. His face was flushed and he said, "Come on." He pulled Wolf free of the crowd and backstage to a small dressing room. Its door was ajar and people were crowded into it.

One of them was the singer, hair stringy and out-of-place, laughing and gesturing widely with a Southern Comfort bottle. It was an antique, its label lacquered to the glass, and three-quarters filled with something amber-colored.

"Janis, this is—" Kaplan began.

"The name is Maggie," she sang gleefully. "Maggie Horowitz. I ain't no dead blues singer. And don't you forget it."

"This is a fan of yours, Maggie. From Africa." He gave Wolf a small shove. Wolf hesitantly stumbled forward, grimacing apologetically at the people he displaced.

"Whee—howdy!" Maggie whooped. She downed a slug from her bottle. "Pleased ta meecha, Ace. Kinda light for an African, aintcha?"

"My mother's people were descended from German settlers." And it was felt that a light-skinned representative could handle the touchy Americans better, but he didn't say that.

"Whatcher name, Ace?"

"Wolf."

"Wolf." Maggie crowed. "Yeah, you look like a real heartbreaker, honey. Guess I'd better be careful around you, huh? Likely to sweep me off my feet and deflower me." She nudged him with an elbow. "That's a joke, Ace."

Wolf was fascinated. Maggie was *alive*, a dozen times more so than her countrymen. She made them look like zombies. Wolf was also a little afraid of her.

"*Hey*. Whatcha think of my singing, hah?"

"It was excellent," Wolf said. "It was"—he groped for words—"in my land the music is quieter, there is not so much emotion."

"Yeah, well I think it was fucking good, Ace. Voice's never been in better shape. Go tell 'em that at Hopkins, Kaplan. Tell 'em I'm giving them their money's worth."

"Of course you are," Kaplan said.

"Well, I *am*, goddammit. Hey, this place is like a morgue! Let's ditch this matchbox dressing room and hit the bars. Hey? Let's party."

She swept them all out of the dressing room, out of the building, and onto the street. They formed a small boisterous group, noisily wandering the city, looking for bars.

"There's one a block thataway," Maggie said. "Let's hit it. Hey, Ace, I'd likeya ta meet Cynthia. Sin, this is Wolf. Sin and I are like one person inside two skins. Many's the time we've shared a piece of talent in the same bed. Hey?" She cackled, and grabbed at Cynthia's ass.

"Cut it out, Maggie." Cynthia smiled when she said it. She was a tall, slim, striking woman.

"Hey, this town is *dead*!" Maggie screamed the last word, then gestured them all to silence so they could listen for the echo. "There it is." She pointed, and they swooped down on the first bar.

After the third, Wolf lost track. At some point he gave up on the party and somehow made his way back to his hostel. The last he remembered of Maggie she was calling after him, "Hey, Ace, don't be a party poop." Then: "At least be sure to come back tomorrow, goddammit."

Wolf spent most of the day in his room, drinking water and napping. His hangover was all but gone by the time evening took the edge off the day's heat. He thought of Maggie's half-serious invitation, dismissed it and decided to go to the Club.

The Uhuru Club was ablaze with light by the time he wandered in, a beacon in a dark city. Its frequenters, after all, were all African foreign service, with a few commercial reps such as himself forced in by the insular nature of American society and the need for polite conversation. It was de facto exempt from the power-use laws that governed the natives.

"Mbikana! Over here, lad, let me set you up with a drink." Nnamdi of the consulate waved him over to the bar. Wolf complied, feeling conspicuous as he always did in the Club. His skin stood out here. Even the American servants were dark, though whether this was a gesture of deference or arrogance on the part of the local authorities, he could not guess.

"Word is that you spent the day closeted with the comptroller." Nnamdi had a gin-and-tonic set up. Wolf loathed the drink, but it was universal among the service people. "Share the dirt with us." Other faces gathered around; the service ran on gossip.

Wolf gave an abridged version of the encounter, and Nnamdi applauded. "A full day with the Spider King, and you escaped with your balls intact. An auspicious beginning for you, lad."

"Spider King?"

"Surely you were briefed on regional autonomy—how the country was broken up when it could no longer be managed by a central directorate? There is no higher authority than DiStephano in this part of the world, boy."

"Boston," Ajuji sniffed. Like most of the expatriates, she was a failure; unlike many, she couldn't hide the fact from herself. "That's exactly the sort of treatment one comes to expect from these savages."

"Now, Ajuji," Nnamdi said mildly. "These people are hardly savages. Why, before the Collapse they put men on the moon."

"Technology! Hard-core technology, that's all it was, of a piece with the kind that almost destroyed us all. If you want a measure of a people, you look at how they live. These—*Yanks*," she hissed the word to emphasize its filthiness, "live in squalor. Their streets are filthy, their cities are filthy, and even the ones who aren't rotten with genetic disease are filthy. A child can be taught to clean up after itself. What does that make them?"

"Human beings, Ajuji."

"Hogwash, Nnamdi."

Wolf followed the argument with acute embarrassment. He had been brought up to expect well from people with social standing. To hear gutter language and low prejudice from them was almost beyond bearing.

Suddenly it was beyond bearing. He turned his back on them all, and left. "Mbikana! You mustn't—" Nnamdi called after him. "Oh, let him go," Ajuji cut in, with a satisfied tone, "you mustn't expect better. After all, he's practically one of them." Well maybe he was.

Wolf wasn't fully aware of where he was going until he found himself at Peabody's. He circled the building, and found a rear door. He tried the knob: it turned loosely in his hand. Then the door swung open and a heavy, bearded man in coveralls leaned out. "Yes?" he said in an unfriendly tone.

"Uh," Wolf said. "Maggie Horowitz told me I could drop by."

"Look, pilgrim, there are a lot of people trying to get backstage. My job is to keep them out unless I know them. I don't know you."

Wolf tried to think of some response to this, and failed. He was about to turn away when somebody unseen said, "Oh, let him in, Deke."

It was Cynthia. "Come on," she said in a bored voice. "Don't clog up the doorway." The guard moved aside, and he entered.

"Thank you," he said.

"Nada," she replied. "As Maggie would say. The dressing room is that way, pilgrim."

"Wolf, honey!" Maggie shrieked. "How's it going, Ace? Ya catch the show?"

"No, I—"

"You shoulda. I was good. Really good. Janis herself was never better. Hey, gang! Let's split, hah? Let's go somewhere and get down and boogie."

A group of twenty ended up taking over a methane-lit bar outside the zoned-for-electricity sector. Three of the band had brought along their instruments, and they talked the owner into letting them play. The music was droning and monotonous. Maggie listened appreciatively, grinning and moving her head to the music.

"Whatcha think of that, Ace? Pretty good, hey? That's what we call Dead music."

Wolf shook his head. "I think it's well named."

"Hey, guys, you hear that? Wolf here just made a funny. There's hope for you yet, honey." Then she sighed. "Can't get behind it, huh? That's really sad, man. I mean they played good music back then; it was real. We're just echoes, man. Just playing away at them old songs. Got none of our own worth singing."

"Is that why you're doing the show, then?" Wolf asked, curious.

Maggie laughed. "Hell, no. I do it because I got the chance. DiStephano got in touch with me—"

"DiStephano? The comptroller?"

"One of his guys, anyway. They had this gig all set up, and they needed someone to play Janis. So they ran a computer search and came up with my name. And they offered me money, and I spent a month or two in Hopkins being worked over, and here I am. On the road to fame and glory." Her voice rose and warbled and mocked itself on the last phrase.

"Why did you have to go to Hopkins?"

"You don't think I was *born* looking like this? They had to change my face around. Changed my voice too, for which God bless. They brought it down lower, widened out my range, gave it the strength to hold on to them high notes and push 'em around."

"Not to mention the mental implants," Cynthia said.

"Oh, yeah, and the 'plants so I could talk in a bluesy sorta way without falling out of character," Maggie said. "But that was minor."

Wolf was impressed. He had known that Hopkins was good, but this—! "What possible benefit is there for them?"

"Beats the living hell out of me, lover-boy. Don't know, don't care, and don't ask. That's my motto."

A long-haired pale young man sitting nearby said, "The government is all hacked up on social engineering. They do a lot of weird things, and you never find out why. You learn not to ask questions."

"Hey, listen, Hawk, bringing Janis back to life isn't weird. It's a beautiful thing to do," Maggie objected. "Yeah. I only wish they could *really* bring her back. Sit her down next to me. Love to talk with that lady."

"You two would tear each other's eyes out," Cynthia said.

"What? Why?"

"Neither one of you'd be willing to give up the spotlight to the other."

Maggie cackled. "Ain't it the truth? Still, she's one broad I'd love to have met. A *real* star, see? Not a goddamned echo like me."

Hawk broke in, said, "You, Wolf. Where does your pilgrimage take you now? The group goes on tour the day after tomorrow; what are your plans?"

"I don't really have any," Wolf said. He explained his situation. "I'll probably stay in Baltimore until it's time to go up north. Maybe I'll take a side trip or two."

"Why don't you join the group, then?" Hawk asked. "We're planning to make the trip one long party. And we'll slam into Boston in just less than a month. The tour ends there."

"That," said Cynthia, "is a real bright idea. All we need is another nonproductive person on board the train."

Maggie bristled. "So what's wrong with it?"

"Nothing's wrong with it. It's just a dumb idea."

"Well, *I* like it. How about it, Ace? You on the train or off?"

"I—" He stopped. Well, why not? "Yes. I would be pleased to go along."

"Good." She turned to Cynthia. "Your problem, sweets, is that you're just plain jealous."

"Oh, Christ, here we go again."

"Well, don't bother. It won't do you any good. Hey, you see that piece of talent at the far end of the bar?"

"Maggie, that 'piece of talent,' as you call him, is eighteen years old. At most."

"Yeah. Nice though." Maggie stared wistfully down the bar. "He's kinda pretty, ya know?"

Wolf spent the next day clearing up his affairs and arranging for the letters of credit. The morning of departure day, he rose early and made his way to Baltimore Station. A brief exchange with the guards let him into the walled train yard.

The train was an ungainly steam locomotive with a string of rehabilitated cars behind it. The last car had the word PEARL painted on it, in antique psychedelic lettering.

"Hey, Wolf! Come lookit this mother." A lone figure waved at him from the far end of the train. Maggie.

Wolf joined her. "What do you think of it, hah?"

He searched for something polite to say. "It is very impressive," he said finally. The word that leapt to mind was *grotesque*.

"Yeah, there's a methane processing plant nearby. Hey, lookit me! Up and awake at eight in the morning. Can ya take it'? Had to get behind a little speed to do it, though."

The idiom was beyond him. "You mean—you were late waking up?"

"What? Oh, hey, man, you can be—look, forget I said a thing. No." She pondered a second. "Look, Wolf. There's this stuff called 'speed,' it can wake you up in the morning, give you a little boost, get you going. Ya know?"

Awareness dawned. "You mean amphetamines."

"Yeah, well this stuff ain't exactly legal, dig? So I'd just as soon you didn't spread the word around. I mean, I trust you, man, but I wanna be sure you know what's happening before you go shooting off your mouth."

"I understand," Wolf said. "I won't say anything. But you know that amphetamines are—"

"Gotcha, Ace. Hey, you gotta meet the piece of talent I picked up last night. Hey, Dave! Get your ass over here, lover."

A young sleepy-eyed blond shuffled around the edge of the train. He wore white shorts, defiantly it seemed to Wolf, and a loose blouse buttoned up to his neck. Giving Maggie a weak hug around the waist, he nodded to Wolf.

"Davie's got four nipples, just like me. How about that? I mean, it's gotta be a pretty rare mutation, hah?"

Dave hung his head, half blushing. "Aw, Janis," he mumbled. Wolf waited for Maggie to correct the boy, but she didn't. Instead she led them around and around the train chatting away madly, pointing out this, that, and the other thing.

Finally, Wolf excused himself, and returned to his hostel. He left Maggie prowling about the train, dragging her pretty-boy after her. Wolf went out for a long lunch, picked up his bags, and showed up at the train earlier than most of the entourage.

The train lurched, and pulled out of the station. Maggie was in constant motion, talking, laughing, directing the placement of luggage. She darted from car to car, never still. Wolf found a seat and stared out the window. Children dressed in rags ran alongside the tracks, holding out hands and begging for money. One or two of the party threw coins; more laughed and threw bits of garbage.

Then the children were gone, and the train was passing through endless miles of weathered ruins. Hawk sat down beside Wolf. "It'll be a slow trip," he said. "The train has to go around large sections of land it's better not to go through." He started moodily at the broken-windowed shells that were once factories and warehouses. "Look out there, pilgrim, *that's* my country," he said in a disgusted voice. "Or the corpse of it."

"Hawk, you're close to Maggie."

"Now if you go out to the center of the continent . . . " Hawk's voice grew distant. "There's a cavern out there, where they housed radioactive waste. It was formed into slugs and covered with solid gold—anything else deteriorates too fast. The way I figure it, a man with a lead suit could go into the cavern and shave off a fortune. There's tons of the stuff there." He sighed. "Someday I'm going to rummage through a few archives and go."

"Hawk, you've got to *listen* to me."

Hawk held up a hand for silence. "It's about the drugs, right? You just found out, and you want me to warn her."

"Warning her isn't good enough. Someone has to stop her."

"Yes, well. Try to understand, Maggie was in Hopkins for *three months* while they performed some very drastic surgery on her. She didn't look a thing like she does now, and she could sing but her voice wasn't anything to rave about. Not to mention the mental implants.

"Imagine the pain she went through. Now ask yourself what are the two most effective painkillers in existence?"

"Morphine and heroin. But in my country, when drugs are resorted to, the doctors wean the patients off them before their release."

"That's not the point. Consider this—Maggie could have had Hopkins remove the extra nipples. They could have done it. But she wasn't willing to go through the pain."

"She seems proud of them."

"She talks about them a lot, at least."

The train lurched and stumbled. Three of the musicians had uncrated their guitars and were playing more "Dead" music. Wolf chewed his lip in silence for a time, then said, "So what is the point you're making?"

"Simply that Maggie was willing to undergo the greater pain so that she could become Janis. So when I tell you she only uses drugs as painkillers, you have to understand that I'm not necessarily talking about physical pain." Hawk got up and left.

Maggie danced into the car. "Big time!" she whooped. "We made it into the big time, boys and girls. Hey, let's party!"

• • •

The next ten days were one extended party, interspersed with concerts. The reception in Wilmington was phenomenal. Thousands came to see the show; many were turned away. Maggie was unsteady before the first concert, achingly afraid of failure. But she played a rousing set, and was called back time and time again. Finally, exhausted and limp, her hair sticking to a sweaty forehead, she stood up front and gasped, "That's all there is, boys and girls. I love ya and I wish there was more to give ya, but there ain't. You used it all up." And the applause went on and on . . .

The four shows in Philadelphia began slowly, but built up big. A few seats were unsold at the first concert; people were turned away for the second. The last two were near-riots. The group entrained to Newark for a day's rest and put on a Labor Day concert that made the previous efforts look pale. They stayed in an obscure hostel for an extra day's rest.

Wolf spent his rest day sight-seeing. While in Philadelphia he had hired a native guide and prowled through the rusting refinery buildings at Point Breeze. They rose to the sky forever in tragic magnificence, and it was hard to believe there had ever been enough oil in the world to fill the holding tanks there. In Wilmington, he let the local guide lead him to a small Italian neighborhood to watch a religious festival.

The festival was a parade, led first by a priest trailed by eight altar girls, with incense burners and fans. Then came twelve burly men carrying the flower-draped body of an ancient Cadillac. After them came the faithful, in coveralls and chador, singing.

Wolf followed the procession to the river, where the car was placed in a hole in the ground, sprinkled with holy water, and set afire. He asked the guide what story lay behind the ritual, and the boy shrugged. It was old, he was told, very very old.

It was late when Wolf returned to the hostel. He was expecting a party, but found it dark and empty. Cynthia stood in the foyer, hands behind her back, staring out a barred window at black nothingness.

"Where is everybody?" Wolf asked. It was hot. Insects buzzed about the coal-oil lamp, batting against it frenziedly.

Cynthia turned, studied him oddly. Her forehead was beaded with sweat. "Maggie's gone home—she's attending a mid-school reunion. She's going to show her old friends what a hacking big star she's become. The others?" She shrugged. "Off wherever puppets go when there's no one to bring them to life. Their rooms, probably."

"Oh." Cynthia's dress clung damply to her legs and sides. Dark stains spread out from under her armpits. "Would you like to play a game of chess or—something?"

Cynthia's eyes were strangely intense. She took a step closer to him. "Wolf, I've been wondering. You've been celibate on this trip. Is there a problem? No? Maybe a girlfriend back home?"

"There was, but she won't wait for me." Wolf made a deprecating gesture. "Maybe that was part of the reason I took this trip."

She took one of his hands, placed it on her breast. "But you are interested in girls?" Then, before he could shape his answer into clumsy words, she whispered, "Come on," and led him to her room.

Once inside, Wolf seized Cynthia and kissed her, deeply and long. She responded with passion, then drew away and with a little shove toppled them onto the bed. "Off with your clothes," she said. She shucked her blouse in a complex fluid motion. Pale breasts bobbled, catching vague moonlight from the window.

After an instant's hesitation, Wolf doffed his own clothing. By contrast with Cynthia he felt weak and irresolute, and it irked him to feel that way. Determined to prove he was nothing of the kind, he reached for Cynthia as she dropped onto the bed beside him. She evaded his grasp.

"Just a moment, pilgrim." She rummaged through a bag by the headboard. "Ah. Care for a little treat first? It'll enhance the sensations."

"Drugs?" Wolf asked, feeling an involuntary horror.

"Oh, come down off your high horse. Once won't melt your genes. Give a gander at what you're being so critical of."

"What is it?"

"Vanilla ice cream," she snapped. She unstoppered a small vial and meticulously dribbled a few grains of white powder onto a thumbnail. "This is expensive, so pay attention. You want to breathe it all in with one snort. Got that? So by the numbers: take a deep breath and breathe out slowly. That's it. Now in. Now out and hold."

Cynthia laid her thumbnail beneath Wolf's nose, pinched one nostril shut with her free hand. "Now in fast. Yeah!"

He inhaled convulsively and was flooded with sensations. A crisp, clean taste filled his mouth, and a spray of fine white powder hit the back of his throat. It tingled pleasantly. His head felt spacious. He moved his jaw, suspiciously searching about with his tongue.

Cynthia quickly snorted some of the powder herself, restoppering the vial.

"Now," she said. "Touch me. Slowly, slowly, we've got all night. That's the way. Ahhhh." She shivered. "I think you've got the idea."

They worked the bed for hours. The drug, whatever it was, made Wolf feel strangely clearheaded and rational, more playful and more prone to linger. There was no urgency to their lovemaking; they took their time. Three, perhaps four times they halted for more of the powder, which Cynthia doled out with careful ceremony. Each time they returned to their lovemaking with renewed interest and resolution to take it slowly, to postpone each climax to the last possible instant.

The evening grew old. Finally, they lay on the sheets, not touching, weak and exhausted. Wolf's body was covered with a fine sheen of sweat. He did not care to even think of making love yet another time. He refrained from saying this.

"Not bad," Cynthia said softly. "I must remember to recommend you to Maggie."

"Sin, why do you do that?"

"Do what?"

"We've just—been as intimate as two human beings can be. But as soon as it's over, you say something cold. Is it that you're afraid of contact?"

"Christ." It was an empty syllable, devoid of religious content, and flat. Cynthia fumbled in her bag, found a metal case, pulled a cigarette out, and lit it. Wolf flinched inwardly. "Look, pilgrim, what are you asking for? You planning to marry me and take me away to your big, clean African cities to meet your momma? Hah?

"Didn't think so. So what do you want from me? Mental souvenirs to take home and tell your friends about? I'll give you one; I spent years saving up enough to go see a doctor, find out if I could have any brats. Went to one last year, and what do you think he tells me? I've got red-cell dyscrasia, too far gone for treatment, there's nothing to do but wait. Lovely, hah? So one of these days it'll just stop working and I'll die. Nothing to be done. So long as I eat right, I won't start wasting away, so I can keep my looks up to the end. I could buy a little time if I gave up drugs like this"—she waved the cigarette, and an ash fell on Wolf's chest. He brushed it away quickly— "and the white powder, and anything else that makes life worth living. But it wouldn't buy me enough time to do anything worth doing." She fell silent. "Hey. What time is it?"

Wolf climbed out of bed, rummaged through his clothing until he found his timepiece. He held it up to the window, squinted. "Um. Twelve . . . fourteen."

"Oh, nukes." Cynthia was up and scrabbling for her clothes. "Come on, get dressed. Don't just stand there."

Wolf dressed himself slowly. "What's the problem?"

"I promised Maggie I'd get some people together to walk her back from that damned reunion. It ended *hours* ago, and I lost track of the time." She ignored his grin. "Ready? Come on, we'll check her room first and then the foyer. God, is she going to be mad."

They found Maggie in the foyer. She stood in the center of the room, haggard and bedraggled, her handbag hanging loosely from one hand. Her face was livid with rage. The sputtering lamp made her face look old and evil.

"Well!" she snarled. "Where have you two been?"

"In my room, balling," Cynthia said calmly. Wolf stared at her, appalled.

"Well, that's just beautiful. That's really beautiful, isn't it? Do you know where I've been while my two best friends were upstairs humping their brains out? Hey? Do you want to know?" Her voice reached hysterical peak. "I was being raped by *two jennie-deafs*, that's where!"

She stormed past them, half-cocking her arm as if she were going to assault them with her purse, then thinking better of it. They heard her run down the hall. Her door slammed.

Bewildered, Wolf said, "But I—"

"Don't let her dance on your head," Cynthia said. "She's lying."

"Are you certain?"

"Look, we've lived together, bedded the same men—I know her. She's all hacked off at not having an escort home. And Little Miss Sunshine has to spread the gloom."

"We should have been there," Wolf said dubiously. "She could have been killed, walking home alone."

"Whether Maggie dies a month early or not doesn't make a bit of difference to me, pilgrim. I've got my own problems."

"A month—? Is Maggie suffering from a disease too?"

"We're all suffering, we all—Ah, the hell with you too." Cynthia spat on the floor, spun on her heel, and disappeared down the hallway. It had the rhythm and inevitability of a witch's curse.

The half-day trip to New York left the troupe with playtime before the first concert, but Maggie stayed in seclusion, drinking. There was talk about her use of drugs, and this alarmed Wolf, for they were all users of drugs themselves.

There was also gossip about the reunion. Some held that Maggie had dazzled her former friends—who had not treated her well in her younger years—had been glamorous and gracious. The predominant view, however, was that she had been soundly snubbed, that she was still a freak and an oddity in the eyes of her former contemporaries. That she had left the reunion alone.

Rumors flew about the liaison between Wolf and Cynthia too. The fact that she avoided him only fed the speculation.

Despite everything the New York City concerts were a roaring success. All four shows were sold out as soon as tickets went on sale. Scalpers made small fortunes that week, and for the first time the concerts were allowed to run into the evening. Power was diverted from a section of the city to allow for the lighting and amplification. And Maggie sang as she had never sung before. Her voice roused the audience to a frenzy, and her blues were enough to break a hermit's heart.

They left for Hartford on the tenth, Maggie sequestered in her compartment in the last car. Crew members lounged about idly. Some strummed guitars, never quite breaking into a recognizable tune. Others talked quietly. Hawk flipped tarot cards into a heap, one at a time.

"Hey, this place is fucking *dead!*" Maggie was suddenly in the car, her expression an odd combination of defiance and guilt. "Let's party! Hey? Let's hear some music." She fell into Hawk's lap and nibbled on an ear.

"Welcome back, Maggie," somebody said.

"*Janis!*" she shouted happily. "The lady's name is Janis!"

Like a rusty machine starting up, the party came to life. Music jelled. Voices became animated. Bottles of alcohol appeared and were passed around. And for the remainder of the two days that the train spent making wide looping detours to avoid the dangerous stretches of Connecticut and New York, the party never died.

There were tense undertones to the party, however, a desperate quality in Maggie's gaiety. For the first time, Wolf began to feel trapped, to count the days that separated him from Boston and the end of the tour.

The dressing room for the first Hartford concert was cramped, small, badly lit—like every other dressing room they'd encountered. "Get your ass over here, Sin," Maggie yelled. "You've gotta make me up so I look strung out, like Janis did."

Cynthia held Maggie's chin, twisted it to the left, to the right. "Maggie, you don't *need* makeup to look strung out."

"Goddammit, yes I *do*. Let's get it on. Come on, come on—I'm a star, I shouldn't have to put up with this shit."

Cynthia hesitated, then began dabbing at Maggie's face, lightly accentuating the lines, the bags under her eyes.

Maggie studied the mirror. "Now *that's* grim," she said. "That's really grotesque."

"That's what you look like, Maggie."

"You cheap bitch! You'd think I was the one who nodded out last night before we could get it on." There was an awkward silence. "Hey, Wolf!" She spun to face him. "What do you say?"

"Well," Wolf began, embarrassed, "I'm afraid Cynthia's . . . "

"You see? Let's get this show on the road." She grabbed her cherished Southern Comfort bottle and upended it.

"That's not doing you any good either."

Maggie smiled coldly. "Shows what you know. Janis always gets smashed before a concert. Helps her voice." She stood, made her way to the curtains. The emcee was winding up his pitch.

"Ladies and gentlemen . . . Janis!"

Screams arose. Maggie sashayed up to the mike, lifted it, laughed into it. "Heyyy. Good ta see ya." She swayed and squinted at the crowd, and was off and into her rap. "Ya know, I went ta see a doctor the other week. Told him I was worried about how much drinking I was doing. Told him I'd been drinkin' heavy since I was twelve. Get up in the morning and have a few Bloody Marys with breakfast. Polish off a fifth before lunch. Have a few drinks at dinner, and really get into it when the partying begins. Told him how much I drank for how many years. So I said, 'Look, Doc, none of this ever hurt me any, but I'm kinda worried, ya know? Give it to me straight, have I got a problem?' And he said, 'Man, I don't think you've got a problem. I think you're doing just *fine!*'" Cheers from the audience. Maggie smiled smugly. "Well, honey, *everybody's* got problems, and I'm no exception." The music came up. "But when I got problems, I got an answer, 'cause I can sing dem ole-time blues. Just sing my problems away." She launched into "Ball and Chain," and the audience went wild.

Backstage, Wolf was sitting on a stepladder. He had bought a cup of water from a vendor and was nursing it, taking small sips. Cynthia came up and stood beside him. They both watched Maggie strutting on stage, stamping and sweating, writhing and howling.

"I can never get over the contrast," Wolf said, not looking at Cynthia. "Out there everybody is excited. Back here, it's calm and peaceful. Sometimes I wonder if we're seeing the same thing the audience does."

"Sometimes it's hard to see what's right in front of your face." Cynthia smiled a sad cryptic smile and left. Wolf had grown used to such statements, and gave it no more thought.

· · ·

The second and final Hartford show went well. However, the first two concerts in Providence were bad. Maggie's voice and timing were off, and she had to cover with theatrics. At the second show she had to order the audience to dance—something that had never been necessary before. Her onstage raps became bawdier and more graphic. She moved her body as suggestively as a stripper, employing bumps and grinds. The third show was better, but the earthy elements remained.

The cast wound up in a bar in a bad section of town, where guards with guns covered the doorway from fortified booths. Maggie got drunk and ended up crying. "Man, I was so blitzed when I went onstage—you say I was good?"

"Sure, Maggie," Hawk mumbled. Cynthia snorted.

"You were very good," Wolf assured her.

"I don't remember a goddamned thing," she wailed. "You say I was good? It ain't fair, man. If I was good, I deserve to be able to remember it. I mean, what's the point otherwise? Hey?"

Wolf patted her shoulder clumsily. She grabbed the front of his dashiki and buried her face in his chest. "Wolf, Wolf, what's gonna happen to me?" she sobbed.

"Don't cry," he said. Patting her hair.

Finally, Wolf and Hawk had to lead her back to the hostel. No one else was willing to quit the bar.

They skirted an area where all the buildings had been torn down but one. It stood alone, with great gaping holes where plate glass had been, and large nonfunctional arches on one side.

"It was a fast-food building," Hawk explained when Wolf asked. He sounded embarrassed.

"Why is it still standing?"

"Because there are ignorant and superstitious people everywhere," Hawk muttered. Wolf dropped the subject.

The streets were dark and empty. They went back into the denser areas of town, and the sound of their footsteps bounced off the buildings. Maggie was leaning half-conscious on Hawk's shoulder, and he almost had to carry her.

There was a stirring in the shadows. Hawk tensed. "Speed up a bit, if you can," he whispered.

Something shuffled out of the darkness. It was large and only vaguely human. It moved toward them. "What—?" Wolf whispered.

"Jennie-deaf," Hawk whispered back. "If you know any clever tricks, this is the time to use 'em." The thing broke into a shambling run.

Wolf thrust a hand into a pocket and whirled to face Hawk. "Look," he said in a loud, angry voice. "I've taken enough from you! I've got a knife, and I don't care what I do!" The jennie-deaf halted. From the corner of his eye, Wolf saw it slide back into the shadows.

Maggie looked up with sleepy, quizzical expression. "Hey, what . . . "

"Never mind," Hawk muttered. He upped his pace, half dragging Maggie after him. "That was arrogant," he said approvingly.

Wolf forced his hand from his pocket. He found he was shivering from the aftershock. "Nada," he said. Then: "That is the correct term?"

"Yeah."

"I wasn't certain that jennie-deafs really existed."

"Just some poor mute with gland trouble. Don't think about it."

Autumn was just breaking out when the troupe hit Boston. They arrived to find the final touches being put on the stage on Boston Commons. A mammoth concert was planned; dozens of people swarmed about making preparations.

"This must be how America was all the time before the Collapse," Wolf said, impressed. He was ignored.

The morning of the concert, Wolf was watching canvas being hoisted above the stage, against the chance of rain, when a gripper ran up and said, "You, pilgrim, have you seen Janis?"

"Maggie," he corrected automatically, "No, not recently."

"Thanks," the man gasped, and ran off. Not long after, Hawk hurried by and asked, "Seen Maggie lagging about?"

"No. Wait, Hawk, what's going on? You're the second person to ask me that."

Hawk shrugged. "Maggie's disappeared. Nothing to scream about."

"I hope she'll be back in time for the show."

"The local police are hunting for her. Anyway, she's got the implants; if she can move she'll be onstage. Never doubt it." He hurried away.

The final checks were being run, and the first concertgoers beginning to straggle in, when Maggie finally appeared. Uniformed men held each arm; she looked sober and angry. Cynthia took charge, dismissed the police, and took Maggie to the trailer that served as a dressing room.

Wolf watched from a distance, decided he could be of no use. He ambled about the Commons aimlessly, watching the crowd grow. The people coming in found places to sit, took them, and waited. There was little talk among them, and what there was was quiet. They were dressed brightly, but not in their best. Some carried wine jugs or blankets.

They were an odd crew. They did not look each other in the eye; their mouths were grim, their faces without expression. Their speech was low, but with an undercurrent of tension. Wolf wandered among them, eavesdropping, listening to fragments of their talk.

"Said that her child was going to . . . "

" . . . needed that. Nobody needed that."

"Couldn't have paid it away . . . "

" . . . tasted odd, so I didn't . . . "

"Had to tear down three blocks . . . "

" . . . blood."

Wolf became increasingly uneasy. There was something about their expressions, their tones of voice. He bumped into Hawk, who tried to hurry past.

"Hawk, there is something very wrong happening."

Hawk's face twisted. He gestured toward the light tower. "No time," he said, "the show's beginning. I've got to be at my station." Wolf hesitated, then followed the man up the ladders of the light tower.

All of the Commons was visible from the tower. The ground was thick with people, hordes of ant-specks against the brown of trampled earth. Not a child among them, and that felt wrong too. A gold-and-purple sunset smeared itself three-quarters of the way around the horizon.

Hawk flicked lights on and off, one by one, referring to a sheet of paper he held in one hand. Sometimes he cursed and respliced wires. Wolf waited. A light breeze ruffled his hair, though there was no hint of wind below.

"This is a sick country," Hawk said. He slipped a headset on, played a red spot on the stage, let it wink out. "You there, Patrick? The kliegs go on in two." He ran a check on all the locals manning lights, addressing them by name. "Average life span is something like forty-two—if you get out of the delivery room alive. The birth-rate has to be very high to keep the population from dwindling away to nothing." He brought up all the red and blue spots. The stage was bathed in purple light. The canvas above looked black in contrast. An obscure figure strolled to the center mike.

"Hit it, Patrick." A bright pool of light illuminated the emcee. He coughed, went into his spiel. His voice boomed over the crowd, relayed away from the stage by a series of amps with timed delay synchronization with the further amplification. The crowd moved sluggishly about the foot of the tower, set in motion by latecomers straggling in. "So the question you should ask yourself is why the government is wasting its resources on a goddamned show."

"All right," Wolf said. "Why?" He was very tense, very still. The breeze swept away his sweat, and he wished he had brought along a jacket. He might need one later.

"Because their wizards said to—the damn social engineers and their machines," Hawk answered. "Watch the crowd."

" . . . *Janis!*" the loudspeakers boomed. And Maggie was onstage, rapping away, handling the microphone suggestively, obviously at the peak of her form. The crowd exploded into applause. Offerings of flowers were thrown through the air. Bottles of liquor were passed hand over hand and deposited on the stage.

From above it could not be seen how the previous month had taken its toll on Maggie. The lines on her face, the waxy skin, were hidden by the colored light. The kliegs bounced off her sequined dress dazzlingly.

Halfway through her second song, Maggie came to an instrumental break and squinted out at the audience. "Hey, what the fuck's the matter with you guys? Why ain't you *dancing*?" At her cue, scattered couples rose to their feet. "Ready on the kliegs," Hawk murmured into his headset. "Three, four, and five on the police." Bright lights pinpointed three widely separated parts of the audience, where uniformed men were struggling with dancers. A single klieg stayed on Maggie, who pointed an imperious finger at one struggling group and shrieked, "Why are you trying to stop them from dancing? I want them to dance. I *command* them to dance!"

With a roar, half the audience were on their feet. "Shut down three. Hold four and five to the count of three, then off. One—Two—Three! Good." The police faded away, lost among the dancers.

"That was prearranged," Wolf said. Hawk didn't so much as glance at him.

"It's part of the legend. You, Wolf, over to your right." Wolf looked where Hawk was pointing, saw a few couples at the edge of the crowd slip from the light into the deeper shadows.

"What am I seeing?"

"Just the beginning." Hawk bent over his control board.

By slow degrees the audience became drunk and then rowdy. As the concert wore on, an ugly, excited mood grew. Sitting far above it all, Wolf could still feel the hysteria grow, as well as see it. Women shed chadors and danced atop them, not fully dressed. Men ripped free of their coveralls. Here and there, spotted through the crowd, couples made love. Hawk directed lights onto a few, held them briefly; in most cases the couples went on, unheeding.

Small fights broke out, and were quelled by police. Bits of trash were gathered up and set ablaze, so that small fires dotted the landscape. Wisps of smoke floated up. Hawk played colored spots on the crowd. By the time darkness was total, the lights and the bestial noise of the revelers combined to create the feel of a witches' Sabbath.

"Pretty nasty down there," Hawk observed. "And all most deliberately engineered by government wizards."

"But there is no true feeling involved," Wolf objected. "It is nothing but animal lust. No—no involvement."

"Yeah." Onstage, Maggie was building herself up into a frenzy. And yet her blues were brilliant—she had never been better. "Not so much different from the other concerts. The only difference is that tonight nobody waits until they go home."

"Your government can't believe that enough births will result from this night to make a difference."

"Not tonight, no. But all these people will have memories to keep them warm over the winter." Then he spat over the edge of the platform. "Ahhh, why should I spout their lies for them? It's just bread and circuses is all, just a goddamned release for the masses."

Maggie howled with delight. "Whee-ew, man! I'm gettin' horny just looking at you. Yeah, baby, get it on, that's right!" She was strutting up and down the stage, a creature of boundless energy, while the band filled the night with music, fast and urgent.

"Love it!" She stuck her tongue out at the audience and received howls of approval. She lifted her Southern Comfort bottle, took a gigantic swig, her hips bouncing to music. More howls. She caressed the neck of the bottle with her tongue.

"Yeah! Makes me horny as sin, 'deed it does. Ya know," she paused a beat, then continued, "that's something I can really understand, man. 'Cause I'm just a horny little hippie chick myself. Yeah." Wolf suddenly realized that she was competing against the audience itself for its attention, that she was going to try to outdo everybody present.

Maggie stroked her hand down the front of her dress, lingering between her breasts, then between her legs. She shook her hair back from her eyes, the personification of animal lust. "I mean, shit. I mean, hippie chicks don't even wear no underwear." More ribald howls of applause. "Don't believe me, do ya?"

Wolf stared, was unable to look away as Maggie slowly spread her legs wide and squatted, giving the audience a good look up her skirt. Her frog face leered, and it was an ugly, lustful thing. She lowered a hand to the stage behind her for support, and beckoned. "Come to Momma," she crooned.

It was like knocking the chocks out from a dam. There was an instant of absolute stillness, and then the crowd roared and surged forward. An ocean of humanity converged on the stage, smashing through the police lines, climbing up on the wooden platform. Wolf had a brief glimpse of Maggie trying to struggle to her feet, before she was overrun. There was a dazed, disbelieving expression on her face.

"Mother of Sin," Wolf whispered. He stared at the mindless, evil mob below. They were in furious motion, straining, forcing each other in great swirling eddies. He waited for the stage to collapse, but it did not. The audience kept climbing atop it, pushing one another off its edge, and it did not collapse. It would have been a mercy if it had.

A hand waved above the crowd, clutching something that sparkled. Wolf could not make it out at first. Then another hand waved a glittering rag, and then another, and he realized that these were shreds of Maggie's dress.

Wolf wrapped his arms around a support to keep from falling into the horror below. The howling of the crowd was a single chaotic noise; he squeezed his eyes shut, vainly trying to fend it off. "Right on cue," Hawk muttered. "Right on goddamned cue." He cut off all the lights, and placed a hand on Wolf's shoulder.

"Come on. Our job is done here."

Wolf twisted to face Hawk. The act of opening his eyes brought on a wave of vertigo, and he slumped to the platform floor, still clutching the support desperately. He wanted to vomit, and couldn't. "It's—they—Hawk, did you see it? Did you see what they did? Why didn't someone—?" He choked on his words.

"Don't ask me," Hawk said bitterly. "I just play the part of Judas Iscariot in this little drama." He tugged at Wolf's shoulders. "Let's go, pilgrim. We've got to go down now." Wolf slowly weaned himself of the support, allowed himself to be coaxed down from the tower.

There were men in black uniforms at the foot of the tower. One of them addressed Hawk. "Is this the African national?" Then, to Wolf: "Please come with us, sir. We have orders to see you safely to your hostel."

Tears flooded Wolf's eyes, and he could not see the crowd, the Commons, the men before him. He allowed himself to be led away, as helpless and as trusting as a small child.

• • •

In the morning, Wolf lay in bed staring at the ceiling. A fly buzzed somewhere in the room, and he did not look for it. In the streets iron-wheeled carts rumbled by, and children chanted a counting out game.

After a time he rose, dressed, and washed his face. He went to the hostel's dining room for breakfast.

There, finishing off a piece of toast, was DiStephano.

"Good morning, Mr. Mbikana. I was beginning to think I'd have to send for you." He gestured to a chair. Wolf looked about, took it. There were at least three of the political police seated nearby.

DiStephano removed some documents from his jacket pocket handed them to Wolf. "Signed, sealed, and delivered. We made some minor changes in the terms, but nothing your superiors will object to." He placed the last corner of toast in the side of his mouth. "I'd say this was a rather bright beginning to your professional career."

"Thank you," Wolf said automatically. He glanced at the documents, could make no sense of them, dropped them in his lap.

"If you're interested, the *African Genesis* leaves port tomorrow morning. I've made arrangements that a berth be ready for you, should you care to take it. Of course, there will be another passenger ship in three weeks if you wish to see more of our country."

"No," Wolf said hastily. Then, because that seemed rude, "I'm most anxious to see my home again. I've been away far too long."

DiStephano dabbed at the corners of his mouth with a napkin, let it fall to the tablecloth. "Then that's that." He started to rise.

"Wait," Wolf said. "Mr. DiStephano, I . . . I would very much like an explanation."

DiStephano sat back down. He did not pretend not to understand the request. "The first thing you must know," he said, "is that Ms. Horowitz was not our first Janis Joplin."

"No," Wolf said.

"Nor the second."

Wolf looked up.

"She was the twenty-third, not counting the original. The show is sponsored every year, always ending in Boston on the equinox. So far, it has always ended in the same fashion."

Wolf wondered if he should try to stab the man with a fork, if he should rise up and attempt to strangle him. There should be rage, he knew. He felt nothing. "Because of the brain implants."

"No. You must believe me when I say that I wish she had lived. The implants helped her keep in character, nothing more. It's true that she did not recall the previous women who played the part of Janis. But her death was not planned. It's simply something that—happens."

"Every year."

"Yes. Every year Janis offers herself to the crowd. And every year they tear her apart. A sane woman would not make the offer; a sane people would not respond in that fashion. I'll know that my country is on the road to recovery come the day that Janis lives to make a second tour." He paused. "Or the day we can't find a woman willing to play the role, knowing how it ends."

Wolf tried to think. His head felt dull and heavy. He heard the words, and he could not guess whether they made sense or not. "One last question," he said. "Why me?"

DiStephano rose. "One day you may return to our nation," he said. "Or perhaps not. But you will certainly rise to a responsible position within the Southwest Africa Trade Company. Your decisions will affect our economy." Four men in uniform also rose from their chairs. "When that happens, I want you to understand one thing about your land: *We have nothing to lose.* Good day, and a long life to you, sir."

DiStephano's guards followed him out.

It was evening. Wolf's ship rode in Boston harbor, waiting to carry him home. Away from this magic nightmare land, with its ghosts and walking dead. He stared at it and he could not make it real; he had lost all capacity for belief.

The ship's dinghy was approaching. Wolf picked up his bags.

• • •

Michael Swanwick has received the Nebula, Theodore Sturgeon, World Fantasy, and Hugo Awards, and been nominated for and lost more of these same awards than any other human being to date. (This novelette, one of his first published stories, was nominated for a Nebula.) He lives in Philadelphia with his wife, Marianne Porter. Swanwick's latest novel is *Dancing with Bears*, a post-Utopian adventure featuring confidence artists Darger and Surplus, currently available in paperback from Night Shade Books. He is at work on two new novels.

• • • •

That Was Radio Clash
Charles de Lint

For Joe Strummer, R.I.P.

December 23, 2002

"Why so down?" the bartender asked the girl with the dark blue hair.

She looked up, surprised, maybe, that anyone had even noticed.

At night, the Rhatigan was one of the last decent live jazz clubs in town. The kind of place where you didn't necessarily know the players, but one thing the music always did was swing. There was none of your smooth jazz or other ambient crap here.

But during the day, it was like any other low-end bar, a third full of serious drinkers and no one that looked like her.

"Joe Strummer died yesterday," she said.

Alphonse is a good guy. He used to play the keys until an unpaid debt resulted in some serious damage to his melody hand. He can still play, but where he used to soar, now he just walks along on the everyday side of genius with the rest of us. And while maybe he can't express the way things feel with his music anymore, the heart that made him one of the most generous players you could sit in with is still beating inside that barrel chest of his.

"I'm sorry," he said. "Was he a friend of yours?"

The hint of a smile tugged at the corner of her mouth, but the sadness in her eyes didn't change.

"Hardly," she said. "It's just that he was the heart and soul of the only band that matters and his dying reminds me of how everything that's good eventually fades away."

"The only band that matters," Alphonse repeated, obviously not getting the reference. In his head he was probably running through various Monk or Davis line-ups.

"That's what they used to call the Clash."

"Oh, I remember them. What was that hit of theirs?" It took him a moment, but then he half-sang the chorus and title of "Should I Stay or Should I Go."

She nodded. "Except that was more Mick Jones's. Joe's lyrics were the ones with a political agenda."

"I don't much care for politics," Alphonse said.

"Yeah, most people don't. And that's why the world's as fucked up as it is."

Alphonse shrugged and went to serve a customer at the other end of the bar. The blue-haired girl returned her attention to her beer, staring down into the amber liquid.

"Did you ever meet him?" I asked.

She looked up to where I was sitting a couple of bar stools away. Her eyes were as blue as her hair, such a vibrant color that I figured they must be contacts. She had a pierced eyebrow—the left—and pale skin, but by the middle of winter, most people have pretty much lost their summer color. She was dressed like she was auditioning for a black and white movie: black jersey, cargos and boots, a gray sweater. The only color was in her hair. And those amazing eyes.

"No," she said. "But I saw them play at the Standish in '84."

I smiled. "And you were what? Five years old?"

"Now you're just sucking up."

And unspoken, but implied in those few words, was: you don't have a chance with me.

But I never thought I did. I mean, look at me. A has-been trumpet player who lost his lip. Never touched the glory Alphonse did when he played—not on my own—but I sat in with musicians who did.

But that's not what she'd be seeing. She'd be seeing one more lost soul with haunted eyes, trying to drown old sorrows in a pint of draught. If she was in her teens when she caught the Clash at the Standish, she'd still only be in her mid- to late-thirties now, ten years my junior. But time passes differently for people like her and people like me. I looked half again my age, and shabby. And I knew it.

No, all I was doing here was enjoying the opportunity for a little piece of conversation with someone who wasn't a drunk, or what she thought me to be: on the prowl.

"I knew him in London," I said. "Back in the seventies when we were all living in squats in Camden Town."

"Yeah, right."

I shrugged and went on as though she hadn't spoken. "I remember their energy the most. They'd play these crap gigs with speakers made out of crates and broomstick mike stands. Very punk—lots of noise and big choppy chords."

I smiled. "And not a hell of a lot of chords, either. But they already had a conscience—not like the Pistols, who were only ever in it for the money. Right from the start they were giving voice to a whole generation that the system had let down."

She studied me for a moment.

"Well, at least you know your stuff," she said. "Are you a musician?"

I nodded. "I used to play the trumpet, but I don't have the lip for it anymore."

"Did you ever play with him?"

"No, I was in an R&B cover band in the seventies, but times were hard and I ended up living in the squats for awhile, same as him. The closest I got to playing the punk scene was when I was in a ska band, and later doing some Two-Tone. But the music I loved to play the most was always jazz."

"What's your name?"

"Eddie Ramone."

"You're kidding."

I smiled. "No, and before you ask, I got my name honestly—from my dad."

"I'm Sarah Blue."

I glanced at her hair. "So which came first?"

"The name. Like you, it came with the family."

"I guess people who knew you could really say they knew the Blues."

"Ha ha."

"Sorry."

"'sokay."

I waited a moment, then asked, "So is there more to your melancholy than the loss of an old favorite musician?"

She shrugged. "It just brought it all home to me, how that night at the Standish was, like, one of those pivotal moments in my life, only I didn't recognize it. Or maybe it's just that that's when I started making a lot of bad choices." She touched her hair. "It's funny, but the first thing I did when I heard he'd died was put the eyebrow piercing back in and dye my hair blue like it was in those days—by way of mourning. But I think I'm mourning the me I lost as much as his passing."

"We can change our lives."

"Well, sure. But we can't change the past. See, that night I hooked up with Brian. I thought he was into all the things I was. I wanted to change the world and make a difference. Through music, but also through activism."

"So you played?"

"Yeah. Guitar—electric guitar—and I sang. I wrote songs, too."

"What happened?"

"I pissed it all away. Brian had no ambition except to party hearty and that whole way of life slipped into mine like a virus. I never even saw the years slide away."

"And Brian?"

"I dumped him after a couple of years, but by then I'd just lost my momentum."

"You could still regain it."

She shook her head. "Music's a young person's game. I do what I can in terms of being an environmental and social activist, but the music was the soul of it for me. It was everything. Whatever I do now, I just feel like I'm going through the motions."

"You don't have to be young to make music."

"Maybe not. But whatever muse I had back in those days pissed off and left me a long time ago. Believe me, I've tried. I used to get home from work and pick up my guitar almost every day, but the spark was just never there. I don't even try anymore."

"I hear you," I said. "I never had the genius—I just saw it in others. And when you know what you could be doing, when the music in your head's so far beyond what you can pull out of your instrument . . . "

"Why bother."

I gave a slow nod, then studied her for a moment. "So if you could go back and change something, is that what it would be? You'd go to that night and go your own way instead of hooking up with this Brian guy?"

She laughed. "I guess. Though I'd have to apply myself as well."

"I can send you back."

"Yeah, right."

I didn't take my gaze from those blue eyes of hers. I just repeated what I'd said. "I can send you back."

She let me hold her gaze for a couple of heartbeats, then shook her head.

"You almost had me going there," she said.

"I can send you back," I said a third time.

Third time's the charm and she looked uneasy.

"Send me back in time."

I nodded.

"To warn myself."

"No. You'd go back, with all you know now. And it's not really back. Time doesn't run in a straight line. It all happens at the same time. Past, present, future. It's like this is you now." I touched my left shoulder. "And this is you then." I touched the end of a finger on my left hand. "If I hold my arm straight, it seems linear, right?"

She gave me a dubious nod.

"But really—" I crooked my left arm so that my finger was touching my shoulder. "—the two times are right beside each other. It's not such a big jump."

"And you can send me there?"

I nodded. "On one condition."

"What's that?"

"You come back here on this exact same day and ask for me."

"Why?"

"Because that's how it works."

She shook her head. "This is nuts."

"Nothing to lose, everything to gain."

"I guess . . ."

I knew I almost had her, so I smiled and said, "Should you stay or should you go?"

Her blue gaze held mine again, then she shrugged. Picking up her beer, she chugged the last third down, then set the empty glass on the table.

"What the hell," she said. "How does it work?"

I slipped off my stool and closed the few steps between us.

"You think about that night," I said. "Think about it hard. Then I put two fingers on each of your temples—like this. And then I kiss your third eye."

I leaned forward and pressed my lips against her brow, halfway between my fingers. Held my lips there for a heartbeat. Another. Then I stepped away.

She looked at me for a long moment before standing up. She didn't say a word, but they never do. She just laid a couple of bills on the bar to pay for her drink and walked out the door.

December 23, 2002

"I feel like I should know you," the bartender said when the girl with the dark blue hair walked into the bar and pulled up a stool.

"My name's Sarah Blue. What's yours?"

"Alphonse," he said and grinned. "And you're really Sarah Blue?" He glanced towards the doorway. "I thought you big stars only traveled with an entourage."

"All I've got is a cab waiting outside. And I'm not such a big star."

"Yeah, right. Like 'Take It to the Streets' wasn't the big hit of—when was it? Summer of '89."

"You've got a good memory."

"It was a good song."

"Yeah, it was. I never get tired of playing it. But my hit days were a long time ago. These days I'm just playing theatres and clubs again."

"Nothing wrong with that. So what can I get you?"

"Actually, I was expecting to meet a guy in here today. Do you know an Eddie Ramone?"

"Sure, I do." He shook his head. "I should have remembered."

"Remembered what?"

"Hang on."

He went to a drawer near the cash and pulled out a stack of envelopes held together with a rubber band. Flipping through them, he returned to where she was sitting and laid one out on the bar in front of her. In an unfamiliar hand was written:

Sarah Blue
December 23, 2002

"Do those all have names and dates on them?" she asked.

"Every one of them."

He showed her the top one. It was addressed to:

Jonathan Block
January 27, 2003

"You think he'll show?" she asked.

"You did."

She shook her head. "What's this all about?"

"Damned if I know. People just drop these off from time to time and sooner or later someone shows up to collect it."

"It's not just Eddie?"

"No. But most of the time it's Eddie."

"And he's not here?"

"Not today. Maybe he tells you why in the letter."

"The letter. Right."

"I'll leave you to it," Alphonse said.

He walked back to where he'd left the drawer open and dropped the envelopes in. When he looked up, she was still watching him.

"You want a drink?" he asked.

"Sure. Whatever's on tap that's dark."

"You've got it."

She returned her attention to the letter, staring at it until Alphonse returned with her beer. She thanked him, had a sip, then slid her finger into the top of the envelope and tore it open. There was a single sheet inside, written in the same unfamiliar script that was on the envelope. It said:

Hello Sarah,

    Well, if you're reading this, I guess you're a believer now. I sure hope your life went where you wanted it to go this time.

    Funny thing that might amuse you. I was talking to Joe, back in the Camden Town days, and I asked him if he had any advice for a big fan who'd be devastated when he finally went to the big gig in the sky.

    The first thing he said was, "Get bent."

    The second was, "You really think we're ever going to make it?"

    When I nodded, he thought for a moment, then said, "You tell him or her—it's a her?—tell her it's never about the player, is it? It's always about the music. And the music never dies."

    And if she wanted to be a musician? I asked him.

    "Tell her that whatever she takes on, stay in for the duration. Maybe you can just bang out a tune or a lyric, maybe it takes you forever. It doesn't matter how you put it together. All that matters is that it means something to you, and you play it like it means something to you. Anything else is just bollocks."

    I'm thinking, if you got your life straight this time, you'd probably agree with him.

    But now to business. First off, the reason I'm not here to see you is that this isn't the same future I sent you back from. That one still exists, running alongside this one, but it's closed to you because you're living that other life now. And you know there's just no point in us meeting again, because we've done what needed to be done.

    At least we did it for you.

    If you're in the music biz now, you know there's no such thing as a free ride. What I need you to do is, pass it on. You know how to do it. All you've got to decide is who.

Eddie

Sarah read it twice before she folded the letter up, returned it to the envelope and stowed in the pocket of her jacket. She had some more of her beer. Alphonse approached as she was setting her glass back down on the bar top.

"Did that clear it up for you?" he asked.

She shook her head.

"Well, that's Eddie for you. The original man of mystery. He ever start in on his time travel yarns with you?"

She shook her head again, but only because she wasn't ready to admit it to anyone. To do so didn't feel right, and that feeling had made her keep it to herself through all the years.

Alphonse held out his right hand. "He wanted to send me back to the day before I broke this—said I could turn my life around and live it right this time."

"And . . . did you?"

Alphonse laughed. "What does it look like?"

Sarah smiled. Of course, he hadn't. Not in this world. But maybe in one running parallel to it . . .

She thought about that night at the Standish, so long ago. The Clash playing and she was dancing, dancing, so happy, so filled with music. And she was straight, too—no drinks, no drugs that night—but high all the same. On the music. And then right in the middle of a blistering version of "Clampdown," her head just . . . swelled with this impossible lifetime that she'd never, she couldn't have lived.

But she knew she'd connect with a guy named Brian. And she did.

And she knew how it would all go downhill from there, so after the concert, when they were leaving the theatre from a side door, she blew him off. And he got pissed off and gave her a shove that knocked her down. He looked at her, sobered by what he'd done, but she waved him off. He hesitated, then walked away, and she just sat there in the alley, thinking she was going crazy. Wanting to cry.

And then someone reached a hand to her to help her up.

"You okay there?" a voice with a British accent asked.

And she was looking into Joe Strummer's face. The Joe Strummer she'd seen on stage. But superimposed over it, she saw Joe Strummers that were still to come.

The one she'd seen fronting the Pogues in . . . some other life.

The one she'd seen fronting the Mescaleros . . .

The one who'd die of a heart attack at fifty years young . . .

"You want me to call you a cab?" he asked.

"No. No, I'm okay. Great gig."

"Thanks."

On impulse, she gave him a kiss, then stepped back. Away. Out of his life. Into her new one.

She blinked, realizing that Alphonse was still standing by her. How long had she been spaced out?

"Well . . . " she said, looking for something to say. "Eddie seemed like a nice guy to me."

Alphonse nodded. "He's got a big heart—he'll give you the shirt off his back. Hasn't got much of a lip these days, but he still sits in with the band from time to time. You can't say no to a guy like that and he never tries to showboat like he thinks he plays better than he can. He keeps it simple and puts the heart into what he's playing."

"Maybe I'll come back and catch him one night."

"Door's always open during business hours, Miss Blue."

"Sarah."

"Sarah, then. You come back any time."

He left to serve a new customer and Sarah looked around the bar. No one stood out to her—the way she assumed she had to Eddie—so she'd have to come back.

She put a couple of bills on the bar top to cover the cost of her beer and went out to look for her cab. As she got into the back seat, she found herself hoping that Eddie had made himself at least one world where he'd got his lip back. That was the only reason she could think that he kept passing along the magic of a second chance—paying back his own attempts at getting it right.

It was either that, or he was an angel.

January 27, 2003

Alphonse smiled when she came in. When he started to draw her a draught, she shook her head.

"I'll have a coffee if you've got one," she said.

"We don't get much call for coffee, even at this time of day, so it's kind of grungy. Let me put on a fresh pot."

He busied himself at the coffee machine, throwing out the old grounds, inserting a filter full of new coffee.

"So what brings you in so early?" he asked when he turned back to her.

"I can't get those envelopes out of my head."

"The . . . oh, yeah. They're a bit of a puzzle all right. But I can't let you look at them."

"I'm not asking. But when you were giving me mine, I saw the date on the one on the top of the stack."

"Today's date," Alphonse guessed.

She nodded. "Do you mind if I hang around and wait?"

"Not at all. But it could be a long haul."

"'sokay. I've got the time."

She sat chatting with Alphonse for a while, then retired to one of the booths near the stage with her second cup of coffee. Pulling out her journal, she did some sketches of the bar, the empty stage, Alphonse at work. The sketches were in pictures and words. At some point they might find a melody and swell into a song. Or they might not. It didn't matter to her. Doodling in her journal was just something she always did—a way to occupy time on the road and provide touchstones for her memory.

Jonathan Block didn't show up until that evening, after she'd had a surprisingly good Cajun stew and the band was starting to set up. He looked nothing like what she'd expected—not that she'd had any specific visual in mind. It was just that he looked like a street person. Medium height, gaunt features, a few days worth of stubble and greasy hair, shabby clothes. She'd expected someone more . . . successful.

She waited until he'd collected his envelope and had a chance to read it before approaching him.

"I guess your replay didn't turn out," she said.

He gave her a look that was half wary, half confused.

"What do you mean?" he asked.

She pulled out her own envelope, creased and wrinkled from living in her pocket for over a month, and showed it to him.

"Do you feel like talking?" she asked. "I'll buy you a drink."

He hesitated, then shrugged. "Sure. I'll have a ginger ale."

She got the drink from Alphonse, then led Jonathan back to her booth.

"What did you want to talk about?" he asked.

"You have to ask? I mean, this, all of this . . . " She laid her envelope on the Formica tabletop between them. "It's just so strange."

He gave a slow nod and lay his own down beside his drink.

"But it's real, isn't it?" he said. "The letters prove that."

"What happened to you? Why didn't it work out?"

"What makes you think it didn't?"

"I'm sorry. It's just . . . the way you . . . you know . . . "

"No, I should be the one apologizing. It was a fair question." He looked past her for a moment, then returned his gaze to hers. "It worked for me and it didn't. I just didn't think it through carefully enough. I should have focused on a point in time before I got drunk—before I even had a problem with drinking. But I didn't. So when I went back the three years, suddenly

I'm in the car again, pissed out of my mind, and I know that the other car's going to come around the corner, and I know I'm going to hit it, and I know it's too late to pull over."

He wasn't telling her much, but Sarah was able to fill in the details for herself.

"Oh, how horrible," she said.

"Yeah, it wasn't very bright on my part. But hey, who'd have ever thought that a thing like that would even work? When he kissed me on my forehead I thought he was just some freaky guy getting some weird little thrill. I was going to take a swing at him, but then I was there. Back in the car. On that night."

"What happened?"

"Well, the good thing was, even drunk as I was, I knew what was coming and whatever else I might have been, I wasn't a bad guy. Thoughtless as shit, oh yeah, but not bad. So instead of letting myself hit the car, I just drove into a lamppost in the couple of moments I had left. The twelve-year-old girl who would have died—who did die the first time around—was spared."

"And you?"

"Serious injuries. I didn't have any medical, so I lost everything paying for the bills. Lost my job. Got charged with drunk driving, and it wasn't the first time, but since I hadn't hurt anybody they just took away my license. But after that it was pretty much the same slide downhill that it was the first time."

"You don't sound . . . " Sarah wasn't sure how to put it.

"Much broke up about it?"

"Yeah, I guess."

"It's like I told you," he said. "This time the little girl lived. I wasn't any less stupid, but this time no one else had to pay for my stupidity. I've still got a chance to put my life back together. I've been sober since that night. I just need a break, a chance to get cleaned up and back on my feet. I know I can do it."

Sarah nodded. Then she asked the question that troubled her most.

"Did you ever try to change anything else?" she asked.

"What do you mean?"

"Some disaster where a little forewarning could save a lot of lives."

"You mean like 9/11?"

"Yeah. Or the bombing in Oklahoma."

He shook his head. "It's a funny thing. As soon as I heard about them, it all came back, that I'd been around when they happened the first time and I remembered. But the memory just wasn't there until it actually happened."

"Like all we're changing is our own lives."

"Pretty much. And even that's walking blind, the further you get from familiar territory."

Sarah knew exactly what he meant. It had been easy to change things at first, but once she was in a life that was so different from how it had gone the first time, there were no more touchstones and you had to do like everybody did: do what you could and hope for the best.

"I was afraid there was something wrong with me," she said. "That I was so self-centered that I just couldn't be bothered with anything that didn't personally touch my life."

"You don't really believe that."

"How would you know?"

"Well, c'mon. You're Sarah Blue. You're like a poster child for causes."

"I never told you my name."

He smiled and shook his head. "What? Suddenly you're anonymous? Maybe the charts got taken over by all these kids with their bare midriffs, but there was a time not so long ago when you were always on the cover of some magazine or other."

She shrugged, not knowing what to say.

"I don't know what your life was like the first time around," he went on, "but you've been making a difference this time out. So don't be so hard on yourself."

"I guess."

They sat quietly for a moment. Sarah looked around the bar and saw that the clientele had changed. The afternoon boozehounds had given way to a younger, hipper crowd, though she could still spot a few grey heads in the crowd. These were the people who'd come for the music, she realized.

"Will you do like it says in the letter?" she asked, turning back to her companion.

"You mean pass it on?"

She nodded.

"First chance I get."

"Me, too," she said. "And I think my go at it should be to help you."

"You haven't passed it on yet?"

She shook her head.

"I don't know if you get a third try," he said.

She shrugged. "If it doesn't work out, I can always front you some money, give you a chance to get back on your feet, and use the whatever-the-hell-it-is on someone else."

"You'd do that for me—just like that?"

"Wouldn't you?"

He gave a slow nod. "Not before. But now, yeah. In a heartbeat." He looked at her for a long moment. "How'd you know I'd be here?"

"I saw your name and the date on your envelope when I was collecting my own. I just . . . needed to talk to someone about it and Eddie doesn't seem to be available."

"Eddie," he said. "What do you think he is?"

"An angel."

"So you believe in God?"

"I . . . I'm not sure. But I believe in good and evil. I guess I just naturally think of somebody working on the side of good as being an angel."

He nodded. "It's as good a description as any."

"So let's give this a shot," she said. "Only this time—"

"Concentrate on a point in time where I can made the decision not to drink before it's too late."

She nodded.

She gave him a moment, turning her attention back to the bandstand. Looks like tonight they had a keyboard player, a guitarist, a bass player, a drummer, and a guy on saxophones. They were still tuning, adjusting the drum kit, soaking the reeds for the saxes.

She turned back to Jonathan.

"Have you got it?" she asked.

"Yeah. I think I do."

"I'm not going to try to tell you how to live your life, but I think it helps to have something bigger than yourself to believe in."

"Like God?"

She shrugged.

"Or like a cause?" he added.

She smiled. "Like a whatever. Are you ready?"

"Do it," he said. "And thanks."

She leaned over the table, put her hands on his temples and kissed him where Eddie had kissed her, on—what had he called it? Her third eye. She kept her lips pressed against his forehead for a couple of moments, then sat back in her seat.

"Don't forget to come back here on the same day," she said.

But Jonathan only gave her a puzzled look. Without speaking, he got up and left the booth. Sarah tracked him as he made his way through the growing crowd, but he never once looked back.

Weird. How was she even supposed to know if it had worked? But she guessed that in this world, she wouldn't.

Her gaze went to Jonathan's half-drunk ginger ale and she noticed that he'd left his letter behind. There was another puzzle. How did they go from world to world, future to future?

Maybe it had something to do with the Rhatigan itself. Maybe there was something about the bar that made it a crossroads for all these futures.

She thought of asking Alphonse, but got the sense that he didn't know. Or if he knew, he wouldn't be telling. But maybe if she could track down Eddie . . .

He appeared beside her table as though her thoughts had summoned him.

"Never thought about third chances," he said.

He slid a trumpet case onto the booth seat, then sat down beside it, smiling at her from the other side of the table.

"Is—was that against the rules?" she asked.

He shrugged. "What rules? The only thing that's important is for you to come back and get the message to pass it on."

"But what is it that we're passing on? Where did this thing come from?"

"Sometimes it's better to just accept that something is, instead of trying to take it apart."

"But—"

"Because when you take it apart, it might not work any more. You wouldn't want that, would you, Sarah?"

"No. Of course not. But I've got so many questions . . . "

He made a motion with his hands like he was breaking something, then he held out his palms looking down at them with a sad expression.

"Okay, I get the point already," she said. "But you've got to understand my curiosity."

"Sure, I do. And all I'm doing is asking you to let it go."

"But . . . can you at least tell me who you are?"

"Eddie Ramone."

"And he's . . . ?"

"Just a guy who's learned how to give a few people the tools to fix a mistake they might have made. Doesn't work on everybody, and not everybody gets it right when they do go back. But I give them another shot. Think of me as a messenger of hope."

Sarah felt as though she were going to burst with the questions that were swelling inside her.

"So'd you bring a guitar?" Eddie asked.

She blinked, then shook her head. "No. But I don't play jazz."

"Take a cue from Norah Jones. Anything can swing, even a song by Hank Williams . . . or Sarah Blue."

She shook her head. "These people didn't come to hear me."

"No, they came to hear music. They don't give a rat's ass who's playing it, just so long as it's real."

"Okay. Maybe." But then she had a thought. "Just answer this one thing for me."

He smiled, waiting.

"In your letter you said that this is a different time line from the one I first met you in."

"That's right, it is."

"So how come you're here and you know me in this one?"

"Something's got to be the connection," he told her.

"But—"

He opened his case and took out his trumpet. Getting up, he reached for her hand.

"C'mon. Jackie'll lend you his guitar for a couple of numbers. All you've got to do is tell us the key."

She gave up and let him lead her to where the other musicians were standing at the side of the stage.

"Oh, and don't forget," Eddie said as they were almost there. "Before you leave the bar, you need to write your own letter to Jonathan."

"I feel like I'm going crazy."

" 'Crazy,' " Eddie said. "Willie Nelson. That'd make a nice start—you know, something everybody knows."

Sarah wanted to bring the conversation back to where she felt she needed it to go, but a look into his eyes gave her a sudden glimpse of a hundred thousand different futures, all banging up against each other in a complex, twisting pattern that gave her a touch of vertigo. So she took a breath instead, shook her head and just let him introduce her to the other musicians.

Jackie's Gibson semi-hollow body was a lot like one of her own guitars—it just had a different pick-up. She took a seat on the center-stage stool and adjusted the height of the microphone, then started playing the opening chords of "Tony Adams." It took her a moment to find the groove she was looking for, that hip-hop swing that Strummer and the Mescaleros had given the song. By the time she found it, the piano and bass had come in, locking them into the groove.

She glanced at Eddie. He stood on the side of the stage, holding his horn, swaying gently to the rhythm. Smiling, she turned back to the mike and started to sing the first verse.

• • •

Charles de Lint is a full-time writer and musician who presently makes his home in Ottawa, Canada, with his wife MaryAnn Harris. His most recent books are *Under My Skin* (Razorbill Canada, 2012; Amazon.com for the rest of the world) and *Eyes Like Leaves* (Tachyon Press, 2012). His first album *Old Blue Truck* came out in early 2011. And, as reviewer David Soyka wrote: " . . . no one else [writing fantasy] consistently weaves musical references into the underpinnings of their tales like this author."

• • • •

Rock On
Pat Cadigan

Rain woke me. I thought, shit, here I am, Lady Rain-in-the-Face, because that's where it was hitting, right in the old face. Sat up and saw I was still on Newbury Street. See beautiful downtown Boston. Was Newbury Street downtown? In the middle of the night, did it matter? No, it did not. And not a soul in sight. Like everybody said, let's get Gina drunk and while she's passed out, we'll all move to Vermont. Do I love New England? A great place to live, but you wouldn't want to visit here.

I smeared my hair out of my eyes and wondered if anyone was looking for me now. Hey, anybody shy a forty-year-old rock 'n' roll sinner?

I scuttled into the doorway of one of those quaint old buildings where there was a shop with the entrance below ground level. A little awning kept the rain off but pissed water down in a maddening beat. Wrung the water out of my wrap pants and my hair and just sat being damp. Cold, too, I guess, but didn't feel that so much.

Sat a long time with my chin on my knees: you know, it made me feel like a kid again. When I started nodding my head, I began to pick up on something. Just primal but I tap into that amazing well. Man-O-War, if you could see me now. By the time the blueboys found me, I was rocking pretty good.

And that was the punchline. I'd never tried to get up and leave, but if I had, I'd have found I was locked into place in a sticky field. Made to catch the b&e kids in the act until the blueboys could get around to coming out and getting them. I'd been sitting in a trap and digging it. The story of my life.

They were nice to me. Led me, read me, dried me out. Fined me a hundred, sent me on my way in time for breakfast.

Awful time to see and be seen, righteous awful. For the first three hours after you get up, people can tell whether you've got a broken heart or not. The solution is, either you get up real early so your camouflage is in place by the time everybody else is out, or you don't go to bed. Don't go to bed ought to work all the time, but it doesn't. Sometimes when you don't go to bed, people can see whether you've got a broken heart all day long. I schlepped it, searching for an uncrowded breakfast bar and not looking at anyone who was looking at me. But I had this urge to stop random pedestrians and say, Yeah, yeah, it's true, but it was rock 'n' roll broke my poor old heart, not a person, don't cry for me or I'll pop your chocks.

I went around and up and down and all over until I found Tremont Street. It had been the pounder with that group from the Detroit Crater—the name was gone but the malady lingered on—anyway, him; he'd been the one told me Tremont had the best breakfast bars in the world, especially when you were coming off a bottle drunk you couldn't remember.

When the c'muters cleared out some, I found a space at a Greek hole in the wall. We shut down 10:30 a.m. sharp, get the hell out when you're done, counter service only, take it or shake it. I like a place with Attitude. I folded a seat down and asked for coffee and a feta cheese omelet. Came with home fries from the home fries mountain in a corner of the grill (no microwave *garbazhe*, hoo-ray). They shot my retinas before they even brought my coffee, and while I was pouring the cream, they checked my credit. Was that badass? It was badass. Did I care? I did not. No waste, no machines when a human could do it, and real food, none of this edible polyester that slips clear through you so you can stay looking like a famine victim, my deah.

They came in when I was half finished with the omelet. Went all night by the look and sound of them, but I didn't check their faces for broken hearts. Made me nervous but I thought, well, they're tired; who's going to notice this old lady? Nobody.

Wrong again. I became visible to them right after they got their retinas shot. Seventeen-year-old boy with tattooed cheeks and a forked tongue leaned forward and hissed like a snake.

"Sssssssinner."

The other four with him perked right up. "Where?" "Whose?" "In here?" "Rock 'n' roll sssssssinner."

The lady identified me. She bore much resemblance to nobody at all, and if she had a heart it wasn't even sprained a little. With a sinner, she was probably Madame Magnifica "Gina," she said, with all confidence.

My left eye tic'd. Oh, please. Feta cheese on my knees. What the hell, I thought, I'll nod, they'll nod, I'll eat, I'll go. And then somebody whispered the word, *reward*.

I dropped my fork and ran.

Safe enough, I figured. Were they all going to chase me before they got their Greek breakfasts? No, they were not. They sent the lady after me.

She was much the younger, and she tackled me in the middle of a crosswalk when the light changed. A car hopped over us, its undercarriage just ruffling the top of her hard copper hair.

"Just come back and finish your omelet. Or we'll buy you another."

"No."

She yanked me up and pulled me out of the street. "Come on." People were staring, but Tremont's full of theaters. You see that here, live theater; you can still get it. She put a bring-along on my wrist and brought me along, back to the breakfast bar, where they'd sold the rest of my omelet at a discount to a bum. The lady and her group made room for me among themselves and brought me another cup of coffee.

"How can you eat and drink with a forked tongue?" I asked Tattooed Cheeks. He showed me. A little appliance underneath, like a zipper. The Featherweight to the left of the big boy on the lady's other side leaned over and frowned at me.

"Give us one good reason why we shouldn't turn you in for Man-O-War's reward."

I shook my head. "I'm through. This sinner's been absolved."

"You're legally bound by contract," said the lady. "But we could c'noodle something. Buy Man-O-War out, sue on your behalf for nonfulfillment. We're Misbegotten. Oley." She pointed at herself. "Pidge." That was the silent type next to her. "Percy." The big boy. "Krait." Mr. Tongue. "Gus." Featherweight. "We'll take care of you."

I shook my head again. "If you're going to turn me in, turn me in and collect. The credit ought to buy you the best sinner ever there was."

"We can be good to you."

"I don't have it anymore. It's gone. All my rock 'n' roll sins have been forgiven."

"Untrue," said the big boy. Automatically, I started to picture on him and shut it down hard. "Man-O-War would have thrown you out if it were gone. You wouldn't have to run."

"I didn't want to tell him. Leave me alone. I just want to go and sin no more, see? Play with yourselves, I'm not helping." I grabbed the counter with both hands and held on. So what were they going to do, pop me one and carry me off?

As a matter of fact, they did.

• • •

In the beginning, I thought, and the echo effect was stupendous. *In the beginning . . . the beginning . . . the beginning.*

In the beginning, the sinner was not human. I know because I'm old enough to remember.

They were all there, little more than phantoms. Misbegotten. Where do they get those names? I'm old enough to remember. Oingo-Boingo and Bow-Wow-Wow. Forty, did I say? Oooh, just a little past . . . a little close to a lot. Old rockers never die, they just keep rocking on. I never saw The Who; Moon was dead before I was born. But I remember, barely old enough to stand, rocking in my mother's arms while thousands screamed and clapped and danced in their seats. *Start me up . . . if you start me up, I'll never stop . . .* 763 Strings did a rendition for elevator and dentist's office, I remember that, too. And that wasn't the worst of it.

They hung on the memories, pulling more from me, turning me inside out. Are you experienced? On a record of my father's because he'd died too, before my parents even met, and nobody else ever dared ask that question. *Are you experienced? . . . Well, I am.*

(Well, *I* am.)

Five against one and I couldn't push them away. Only, can you call it rape when you know you're going to like it? Well, if I couldn't get away, then I'd give them the ride of their lives. *Jerkin' Crocus didn't kill me but she sure came near . . .*

The big boy faded in first, big and wild and too much badass to him. I reached out, held him tight, showing him. The beat from the night in the rain, I gave it to him, fed it to his heart and made him live it. Then came the lady, putting down the bass theme. She jittered, but mostly in the right places.

Now the Krait, and he was slithering around the sound, in and out. Never mind the tattooed cheeks, he wasn't just flash for the fools. He knew; you wouldn't have thought it, but he knew.

Featherweight and the silent type, melody and first harmony. Bad. Featherweight was a disaster, didn't know where to go or what to do when he got there, but he was pitching ahead like the *S.S. Suicide.*

Christ. If they had to rape me, couldn't they have provided someone upright? The other four kept on, refusing to lose it, and I would have to make the best of it for all of us. Derivative, unoriginal-Featherweight did not rock. It was a crime, but all I could do was take them and shake them. Rock gods in the hands of an angry sinner.

They were never better. Small change getting a glimpse of what it was like to be big bucks. Hadn't been for Featherweight, they might have gotten all the way there. More groups now than ever there was, all of them sure that if they just got the right sinner with them, they'd rock the moon down out of the sky.

We maybe vibrated it a little before we were done. Poor old Featherweight.

I gave them better than they deserved, and they knew that too. So when I begged out, they showed me respect at last and went. Their techies were gentle with me, taking the plugs from my head, my poor old throbbing abused brokenhearted sinning head, and covered up the sockets. I had to sleep and they let me. I hear the man say, "That's a take, righteously. We'll rush it into distribution. Where in *hell*, did you find that sinner?"

"Synthesizer," I muttered, already asleep. "The actual word, my boy, is *synthesizer*."

Crazy old dreams. I was back with Man-O-War in the big CA, leaving him again, and it was mostly as it happened, but you know dreams. His living room was half outdoors, half indoors, the walls all busted out. You know dreams; I didn't think it was strange.

Man-O-War was mostly undressed, like he'd forgotten to finish. Oh, that never happened. Man-O-War forget a sequin or a bead? He loved to act it out, just like the Krait.

"No more," I was saying, and he was saying, "But you don't know anything else, you shitting?" Nobody in the big CA kids, they all shit; loose juice.

"Your contract goes another two and I get the option, I always get the option. And you love it, Gina, you know that, you're no good without it."

And then it was flashback time and I was in the pod with all my sockets plugged, rocking Man-O-War through the wires, giving him the meat and bone that made him Man-O-War and the machines picking it up, sound and vision, so all the tube babies all around the world could play it on their screens whenever they wanted. Forget the road, forget the shows, too much trouble, and it wasn't like the tapes, not as exciting, even with the biggest FX, lasers, spaceships, explosions, no good. And the tapes weren't as good as the stuff in the head, rock 'n' roll visions straight from the brain. No hours of setup and hours more doctoring in the lab. But you had to get everyone in the group dreaming the same way. You needed a synthesis, and for that you got a synthesizer, not the old kind, the musical instrument, but something—somebody—to channel your group through, to bump up their tube-fed little souls, to rock them and roll them the way they couldn't do themselves. And anyone could be a rock 'n' roll hero then. Anyone!

In the end, they didn't have to play instruments unless they really wanted to, and why bother? Let the synthesizer take their imaginings and boost them up to Mount Olympus.

Synthesizer. Synner. Sinner.

Not just anyone can do that, sin for rock 'n' roll. I can.

But it's not the same as jumping all night to some bar band nobody knows yet . . . Man-O-War and his blown-out living room came back, and he said, "You rocked the walls right out of my house. I'll never let you go."

And I said, "I'm gone."

Then I was out, going fast at first because. I thought he'd be hot behind me. But I must have lost him and then somebody grabbed my ankle.

Featherweight had a tray, he was Mr. Nursie-Angel-of-Mercy. Nudged the foot of the bed with his knee, and it sat me up slow. She rises from the grave, you can't keep a good sinner down.

"Here." He set the tray over my lap, pulled up a chair. Some kind of thick soup in a bowl he'd given me, with veg wafers to break up and put in. "Thought you'd want something soft and easy." He put his left foot up on his right leg and had a good look at it. "I *never* been rocked like that before."

"You don't have it, no matter who rocks you ever in this world. Cut and run, go into management. The *big* Big Money's in management."

He snacked on his thumbnail. "Can you always tell?"

"If the Stones came back tomorrow, you couldn't even tap your toes."

"What if you took my place?"

"I'm a sinner, not a clown. You can't sin and do the dance. It's been tried."

"*You* could do it. If anyone could."

"No."

His stringy cornsilk fell over his face and he tossed it back. "Eat your soup. They want to go again shortly."

"No." I touched my lower lip, thickened to sausage size. "I won't sin for Man-O-War and I won't sin for you. You want to pop me one again, go to. Shake a socket loose, give me aphasia."

So he left and came back with a whole bunch of them, techies and do-kids, and they poured the soup down my throat and gave me a poke and carried me out to the pod so I could make Misbegotten this year's firestorm.

I knew as soon as the first tape got out, Man-O-War would pick up the scent. They were already starting the machine to get me away from him. And they kept me good in the room—where their old sinner had done penance, the lady told me. Their sinner came to see me, too. I thought, poison dripping from his fangs, death threats. But he was just a guy about my age with a lot of hair to hide his sockets (I never bothered, didn't care if they showed). Just came to pay his respects, how'd I ever learn to rock the way I did?

Fool.

They kept me good in the room; drinks when I wanted them and a poke to get sober again, a poke for vitamins, a poke to lose the bad dreams. Poke; poke, pig in a poke. I had tracks like the old B&O, and they didn't even know what I meant by that. They lost Featherweight, got themselves someone a little more righteous, someone who could go with it and work out, sixteen-year-old snip girl with a face like a praying mantis. But she rocked and they rocked and we all rocked until Man-O-War came to take me home. Strutted into my room in full plumage with his hair all fanned out (hiding the sockets) and said, "Did you want to press charges, Gina darling?"

Well, they fought it out over my bed. When Misbegotten said I was theirs now, Man-O-War smiled and said, "Yeah, and I bought *you*. You're *all* mine now, you *and* your sinner. My sinner." That was truth. Man-O-War had his conglomerate start to buy Misbegotten right after the first tape came out. Deal all done by the time we'd finished the third one, and they never knew. Conglomerates buy and sell all the time. Everybody was in trouble but Man-O-War. And me, he said. He made them all leave and sat down on my bed to re-lay claim to me.

"Gina." Ever see honey poured over the edge of a sawtooth blade? Every hear it? He couldn't sing without hurting someone bad and he couldn't dance, but inside, he rocked. If I rocked him.

"I don't want to be a sinner, not for you or anyone."

"It'll all look different when I get you back to Cee-Ay."

"I want to go to a cheesy bar and boogie my brains till they leak out the sockets."

"No more, darling. That was why you came here, wasn't it? But all the bars are gone and all the bands. Last call was years ago; it's all up here now. All up here." He tapped his temple. "You're an old lady, no matter how much I spend keeping your bod young. And don't I give you everything? And didn't you say I had it?"

"It's not the same. It wasn't meant to be put on a tube for people to *watch*."

"But it's not as though rock 'n' roll is dead, lover."

"You're killing it."

"Not me. You're trying to bury it alive. But I'll keep you going for a long, long time."

"I'll get away again. You'll either rock 'n' roll on your own or give it up, but you won't be taking it out of me any more. This ain't my way, it ain't my time. Like the man said, 'I don't live today.'"

Man-O-War grinned. "And like the other man said, 'Rock 'n' roll never forgets.'"

He called in his do-kids and took me home.

• • •

Pat Cadigan sold her first professional science fiction story in 1980 and became a full-time writer in 1987. She is the author of fifteen books, including two nonfiction books on the making of *Lost in Space* and *The Mummy*, one young adult novel, and the two Arthur C. Clarke Award-winning novels: *Synners* and *Fools*. (The genesis of *Synners* can be found in "Rock On.") She has lectured at universities, literary festivals, and cultural gatherings around the world, including M.I.T. in Cambridge, Massachusetts, PopTech in Camden, Maine, Utopiales in France, and Argonauts of the Noosphere in Rimini, Italy. She can be found on Facebook and Pinterest, tweets as @cadigan, and lives in North London with her husband, the Original Chris Fowler. Most of her books are available electronically via SF Gateway, the ambitious electronic publishing program from Gollancz.

• • • •

Arise
Poppy Z. Brite

Nightfall in Gabon, and the bush was the darkest thing Cobb had ever seen. It rambled along the edge of the little beachside town and stretched away into the West African hills. If you stood at the edge of the bush and looked out at night, you could see dozens of little fires flickering in the distance, giving off less illumination than lighters in a darkened stadium, accentuating the blackness more than relieving it. These were not the fires of poachers (for there was nothing left to kill nearby), but of straggling nomads on their way into or out of town.

Cobb sat in the tin-sided bar as he did most nights, drinking African beer lightly chilled by the bar's refrigerator. This was to Cobb's taste, for he had once been an Englishman. Now he was a citizen of nowhere on earth. He drank his beer and rolled his fat cigars of African ganja and fixed his rust-colored eyes on the TV set in the corner, and it was very seldom anyone spoke to him. This, too, was as he preferred it.

When the police came by, Cobb would give them money to go away. When the television broke, Cobb paid for a new one. Though everyone in the town knew this man was very rich, no one cared whether he was alive, dead, or famous. The only conceivable reason he could have come here was to be left alone, and so he was.

He watched the television, mostly American cop shows and softcore porn from France. When the news came on, he ignored it. He had seen coverage of war, every kind of natural and man-made disaster, the assassination of one American and countless African presidents, the dissolution of the same Soviet Union he'd once written a satirical song about. But he never reacted to anything he saw on the TV.

Tonight, he saw a thing that made him react.

It began with the music: a few bars of a song by the Kydds, one of the really huge hits, one of Matty's. That was familiar enough, you couldn't watch TV or listen to the radio anywhere on earth without hearing the Kydds, and Cobb ignored it. Then the reporter's voice broke in: "Dead at forty-five, Eric

Matthew, founding member and driving force behind the most successful pop group of all time . . . "

Cobb looked up. Matty's face filled the screen, an old picture. That girly smile, those fuck-me eyes that hid a will of steel. Then the screen switched to a picture of the four of them in concert, 1969, all long stringy hair and, Jesus Christ, velvet suits.

" . . . suicide at his New York apartment. Eric Matthew is the second member of the Kydds to die; guitarist and singer Terry Cobb was killed in a plane crash in 1985. All the details coming up on CNN."

Cobb didn't go to the bar for a week, but stayed in his house drinking whiskey. On the eighth day, a young African showed up at his door with a Federal Express box addressed to William Van Duyk, the name that had appeared on Cobb's passport for the past ten years.

The box was heavy, ten or twelve pounds at least. The return addressee was someone or something called Gallagher, Gallagher, Campbell on the Upper West Side of New York. Cobb found a knife and opened the box. Inside was a cream-colored envelope and a heavy plastic bag full of what looked like coarse sand.

He stuck a long forefinger under the flap of the envelope and tore it open. A key fell out, and he let it lie on the floor for now. Inside the envelope were some folded sheets of creamy paper. "Terry," the first line read—

Cobb dropped the paper. No one had addressed him by that name in over a decade.

His hand shaking a little, he picked up the letter. "Terry," he read again, and this time he realized it was Matty's handwriting. He knew that neat schoolboy script well enough, had seen plenty of first-draft lyrics and signatures on contracts and bossy notes in that same hand. Matty knew where he was—had known where he was. Had known all this time. It was like one of the morbid jokes Cobb had always collected: Matty had known he wasn't dead, and now Matty was dead.

"Terry, you always said I had to have the last word, and it looks like you were right. I've found the most private place in the world. It wasn't enough to save me, but I think it might be just the thing for you. Get the fuck out of Africa at any rate—it's unhealthy for a Manchester boy. The house is yours. Do whatever you like with the other. Peace & Love—MATTY."

Cobb flipped through the other papers. One was a deed to an estate in North Carolina, ownership of which had been signed over by Eric James Matthew to William Van Duyk. Another was a hand-drawn map of the estate and its environs.

He swore and threw the papers on the floor, then glanced at the box again, remembering the plastic bag inside. He knew it wasn't sand. He slit the heavy plastic with his knife, took a handful of the contents and let them sift through his fingers onto the wooden floor. Most of the material was pulverized, but here and there Cobb saw recognizable bits of calcined bone.

"Bastard," he said.

The flight from Port-Gentil to London was terrifying. Aside from the fact that he hadn't ridden in anything larger than a taxi in years, he had no idea how recognizable he might be. He couldn't wear dark glasses, for they had been one of his trademarks in the old days, tripped-out mirror lenses spinning daisy wheels of light. Despite a steady intake of two vodka tonics per hour, he was shaking when he deplaned at Gatwick, was certain he looked like a drug mule or worse, was shocked when he was waved through Customs without delay. Having been out of the loop for so long, Cobb didn't realize that in the one suit he'd managed to salvage—crumpled but classically cut black linen, with a gray T-shirt underneath—he simply looked like a disheveled jetsetter returning from a particularly strenuous holiday.

Which he was, more or less.

No one stared at him in Gatwick Airport. He didn't care to try his luck in the streets of London, a city he'd last seen in 1975, the psychedelic sparkle of Carnaby Street morphing into the black-lipped punk snarl of King's Road. Though he'd had his hair cut short and neat, though a Gabonese diet had left him far thinner than he'd ever been in his performing days, someone in London would surely recognize him. Possibly even someone he'd slept with. Cobb couldn't imagine anything much worse than that, so he bought a copy of *Rolling Stone* with Matty's face on the cover and sat down to wait for the plane to America.

He had to fly into Atlanta, go through Customs again (they searched his bag this time, cursorily, but there was nothing to find), then endure a two-hour layover before the flight to Asheville, North Carolina. Cobb didn't think he'd ever been in North Carolina before, and by this time he didn't care. He planned to find a hotel room, sleep for at least a couple of days, then rent a car and check out Matty's alleged secret hideaway, which looked on the map to be a couple hours' drive from Asheville.

When he saw the heavyset man at the Asheville airport holding the sign that said WILLIAM VAN DUYK, he should have just kept walking. Instead the old Terry Cobb took over, the Rockstar Asshole, and he looked down his nose and snapped, "Who the fuck sent you?"

The man held up one hand in a placating gesture. He had a thick moustache and a widow's peak, and his suit was the opposite of Cobb's, cheap but well-pressed. "Sir, I work for a driving service, I was hired to meet your flight—"

"How'd you know when I was coming in?"

The driver grinned. "Not that many planes coming into Asheville. We've had a standing order to meet any flight with a William Van Duyk on the roster."

He's just a stupid hick, Cobb thought. So Matty had hired a limo. That shouldn't surprise him. Matty hadn't minded spending money when he was alive; why should he mind now?

When Matty was officially alive, Cobb corrected himself. He knew quite a lot about the difference, and it was this knowledge that made him deeply suspicious of the circumstances at hand.

It had happened in 1985, after the Kydds' acrimonious breakup and the flop of his own solo career. The solo failure had bothered him for a long time, because he thought they were good records—but he'd gone back to his roots, old rock and blues, and that had been a mistake. Cobb blamed it on the endlessly layered, flowery, overproduced sound that was so popular in the seventies, a sound that the Kydds in their later days had helped create, a sound that dominated Matty's successful solo efforts. Nobody wanted to hear Terry Cobb cover "Crawling Kingsnake." It was the timing, that was all. Only when he was very drunk or very depressed did he consider the possibility that his edge wasn't as sharp without Matty's melodic genius to back it up.

So he fucked around in New York for a while, just doing drugs and being famous. By that time, cocaine had arrived in a big way, and his flirtations with it made him paranoid. He converted more and more of his assets into cash, gold, and even diamonds without quite knowing why.

On the ninth of December, 1985, Cobb had a reservation on a flight from New York to Amsterdam. Possibly due to the aftereffects of the speedball he had snorted the night before, he overslept and missed his plane. It wasn't a big problem; he'd only been going for the good hash. He rolled over and went back to sleep.

Hours later, the clock radio woke him. A Kydds tune, one of his. Cobb almost reached over to turn it off, couldn't muster the energy, and lay in his darkened bedroom listening. The news came on. Three hundred miles out of New York, the plane he'd missed had fallen into the Atlantic. And apparently everyone thought he had been on it.

A search was launched, of course. But the plane had exploded in midair, then plunged into some of the deepest water between the U.S. and Europe.

The ocean was black, frigid, and shark-infested, and the diving crew only found about half of the bodies. Terry Cobb's was not among them despite the crew's extra efforts (they were all Kydds fans, they told the press, causing a minor uproar among the families of the other victims).

Which is it better to be? Cobb asked himself that night, over and over. *A washed-up rock star, or a dead one?*

The answer was always the same.

When the phone began to ring, he unplugged it.

He didn't make his escape right away. There were important things to be procured, documents that would allow him to travel as somebody else, anonymously, very far away. He took everything he needed to a hotel in Times Square and hid there by day, slipped out by night and gradually, expensively, got what he needed. He opened a vast New York bank account in his new name, acquired credit cards, and said fuck the apartment, the investments, the royalties; let them go to Matty and the other two and whoever else was still making a profit off the Kydds.

Near the end of January 1986, a man with a U.S. passport in the name of William Van Duyk boarded a flight to Bangkok. Cobb spent the next several years wandering through Thailand, Bali, India, Turkey, and Morocco before fetching up in Gabon. There inertia took him, and he stayed.

But he'd been bored for quite a while now. And the night he'd seen the TV report of Matty's death, he realized that he missed Matty more than he'd ever let on to himself. They had been essentially married to each other for a decade, after all, without the sex but with all the joys and sorrows, the shared jokes and secrets, like it or not. If Matty was really dead, Cobb wanted to see what his partner had left him, and why.

If Matty wasn't dead . . . well, Cobb didn't know what would happen then. Matty had known he was alive all these years, had even known where he was, and hadn't made a single overture.

Cobb pressed his forehead against the window of the limo. He could imagine Matty speaking to him, could hear the words clearly. I came back to you plenty of times, it said. *Too many times. If you wanted to be dead, I wasn't going to argue . . . and you always knew where I was, too.*

That was true. He'd never forgotten the address or phone number of Matty's New York apartment, had contemplated sending a cryptic postcard or making a transatlantic phone call on any number of lonely, drunken nights. But he hadn't known of any secret hideaway in North Carolina.

He opened his eyes and looked out the window. They were driving through mountains, great green humpbacks shrouded with mist. He glimpsed wildflower meadows, waterfalls, mysterious little overgrown paths. The area was beautiful, he supposed. Unlike Cobb, who always wanted to see the squalor of a place, Matty appreciated natural beauty.

Cobb frowned. The *Rolling Stone* tribute said Matty had shot himself in the head—in the mouth. He'd had to be identified by fingerprints. Matty appreciated all natural beauty, yes, but none more than his own. He'd been vain enough to get manicures, and even in their earthiest hippie days, he'd always kept his hair squeaky-clean and short enough not to hide his pretty face. Most of all, he'd known he had a pretty face—God knows the press had told him so often enough. Would he have destroyed that face?

Somebody had died; Cobb was sure enough of that. There had been an autopsy, though of course that was subject to conspiracy. Certainly, though, he had let someone's ashes trickle through his fingers onto the floor of his house in Gabon. (He'd kept the ashes for a few days, still in the Federal Express box, then carried them to a deserted beach near the town and thrown them handful by handful into the sea. It took nearly an hour, and by the end of that time he was so thoroughly drenched in sweat that he never noticed the tears spilling down his face.)

It took several seconds before he noticed that the car had stopped.

"You've got to be kidding," he said when he saw what was outside the window.

"Mr. Van Duyk, I was given very specific instructions."

"Drive me to the nearest town."

"I can't do that, sir."

Cobb stared at the driver. The man's eyes were steely. It occurred to Cobb that he was miles from anywhere and this guy probably didn't like him very much. "Right," he said, "fuck off, then."

The limo pulled out and sped away down the winding mountain road, and Cobb turned despairingly to face Matty's house.

He didn't know what to call the architectural style—wedding-cake Victorian, maybe. If so, someone had left this cake out in the rain for way too long. It seemed to have at least sixteen sides, and each side had two tall skinny windows, all their panes broken. The structure was built of once-white clapboard, great sections of which were splintered into sticks or missing altogether. There were two stories and, Cobb thought, an attic as well. Complete with bats, no doubt.

The rest of the view was no more encouraging. To get to the house, he would have to walk past an ancient graveyard whose stone monuments looked as if they had frozen in the act of melting. In the distance, thinly forested hills arched their backs against a darkening sky.

Cobb could see no other houses, no utility wires, no sign of human habitation at all except the empty road, which was really only a dirt track.

He dimly remembered the limo pulling up at a chain stretched across the road several miles back, a sign that read PRIVATE ROAD, the driver getting out to unlock the chain and then again to fasten it behind them. This was all Matty's property, then, for God knows how many miles around. *His* property, now.

What a fucking treat.

He remembered Matty's map and took the creamy envelope out of his bag. Here was the map, here was the house, here was the graveyard represented by a scatter of crosses. And here, tucked inside the sheaf of papers, was the key.

Cobb hoisted his bag and walked past the graveyard, across the yard, up the four front steps to an absurd little porch that looked as if it had been pasted onto the front of the house as an afterthought. He paused at the French doors—the glass in these was still intact, at any rate—and looked in. He couldn't see anything, so he inserted the key into the lock and pushed the doors open.

The ruin inside was as great as he might have expected. A grand staircase swept upward just inside the doors, its elaborately carved newel post listing, its banister scarred, several of its risers gone. A tapestry of dust and cobwebs swathed the walls and ceiling. The floor looked solid enough, but he was damned if he was going to test it.

I've found the most private place in the world, Matty had written. *It wasn't enough to save me, but I think it might be just the thing for you.*

"Fuck you," he muttered, and took the sheaf of papers out again, perhaps meaning to crumple or shred them, he wasn't sure. But something made him turn over the estate map, and there was a rough sketch of the inside of the house. He'd seen it before and it had meant nothing to him, but now he recognized the French doors, the sweeping staircase. There in Matty's handwriting, very small, was an arrow pointing to the staircase and the notation PRESS THE NEWEL POST, TERRY.

He did.

A gleaming steel elevator rose silently out of the floor. The door slid open. The interior of the elevator was streamlined and immaculate. Cobb looked at it for a moment, then sighed, shrugged, and stepped in.

Four hours later, he lay sprawled in a sybaritic stupor. The place was fucking palatial, and it was all underground. Hewn right into the rock. He had no idea if anyone else was here, didn't think he'd explored even half of it. The epicenter of the place was clearly designed just for him: a huge bed (he had always loved to stay in bed), a great stereo system with his favorite music, a television with over a hundred channels (and where the hell was the satellite dish?), a lacquered rolling tray full of fragrant sinsemilla. His guitars were here, the ones he'd last seen in his New York apartment the night of the plane crash. The kitchen was stocked with beer, vodka, tonic, and Cobb's favorite foods, including a whole box of Cadbury Flake, an English chocolate bar unavailable in the States. He'd always bought them at the candy store in Manchester where he and Matty used to go after school. One of the clerks would sell them cigarettes, too, even though they were only fourteen . . .

If Matty was dead, there was no one in the world who knew him. The thought shocked Cobb out of his satiated doze, and he sat up in bed. He'd been close with the other two, of course, and with a number of women. But the intimacy of total *collaboration*, the sense of minds melding, had never been there with anyone else.

He went into the kitchen and got the bottle of vodka out of the freezer.

Many shots later, he slept.

In his dream, he was standing atop one of the distant hills. He could see the house and the little graveyard behind him, but they did not look fearsome now.

With the smooth suddenness of dreams, Matty was beside him, resting one elbow on Cobb's shoulder as he'd had a habit of doing since they were school friends. A breeze ruffled Matty's dark hair, lifted it from his face. There were streaks of gray in that hair, but Matty's face in profile was as serenely handsome as ever, if a shade more careworn. Afraid to speak first, Cobb watched Matty out of the corner of his eye, and Matty smiled.

"I really am dead, you know."

"Well . . . " Cobb's voice was rusty, but he would not let it crack, *would* not. "You look damn good for a man who's taken a shot in the mouth."

"Oh, *that*." Matty turned to face Cobb. "I don't have to look like *that* to convince you, do I?"

"No," Cobb said hastily. "Look, do we have to stand out here?"

"Of course not, nature boy," said Matty, and at once they were back in the house, lying in bed. Cobb wasn't embarrassed, though he was naked and Matty appeared to be also; they had shared plenty of beds and bathrooms out of necessity.

Matty propped himself up on one elbow and lit a half-joint Cobb had left in the tray. Before Cobb had time to wonder whether the joint would be smoked when he woke up, Matty said, "I didn't die in New York, though. I died here, in this bed."

Then he passed the joint over, as if he knew Cobb would need it.

"It was cancer," he went on. "Bet you never thought of that, did you? No one has. No one can imagine why happy old Matty Matthew would suddenly up and blow his brains out, not even you. Am I right?"

"Fucker, you know you are."

Matty acknowledged this with a nod. "Well, no one knows happy old Matty had about three months to live, either. With a prognosis of drooling dementia followed by coma followed by death. I decided not to *let* them know. There's no dignity in it, you see. Better to go out as a tortured artist."

"What about the autopsy?"

Matty got one of his looks. Cobb hadn't seen that look for twenty years, but he remembered it perfectly. "The *autopsy*, Terry, consisted of a pathologist inking my fingertips and snapping a few Polaroids. How much d'you suppose those will fetch on the collector's market?"

"Hard to say. If the reports were right, they could be pictures of just anyone who'd blown his brains out."

"That's true." Matty grimaced. "But I had to do it that way. That's where the cancer was."

"In your brain?"

"Right in the center. Inoperable. I saw it on the X-ray, as big as a plum, and I had to have my files stolen from the hospital, and the X-rays too—"

Now he sounded as if he were bragging, and Cobb interrupted him. "What do you mean, you died in this bed?"

Matty went right on. "The doctor may leak it to the press anyway, but there'll be no proof, and he'll look as if he's just trying to make a buck—"

Cobb said it again, more loudly.

"Oh." Matty blinked. "Well, so that I could be here when you came. I didn't know if it would work. Looks like it did."

"How did you know I'd come?" Cobb asked, and got the look again for his trouble.

"Actually," Matty said, "I thought you'd be here sooner."

"You *thought*?"

"I suppose . . . I *hoped*."

"Why?"

"Because it's quite lonely," Matty whispered, and that was all they could say for a while.

• • •

"I arranged to have someone come to the house after I did it," Matty continued later. "To transport my body to New York and make it look good, make it look like I'd died there, so no one would know about this place."

"Then one person knows about it."

"Knew."

Cobb decided not to pursue this. His own cynicism was a point of pride, but somehow he had never wanted to know just how cold-blooded his partner could be.

He thought of something else. "No one could have gathered up all the mess you must have made."

"Ever heard of a rubber sheet, genius? I didn't want the bed to reek when you got here. Although I imagine you're used to reeking beds by now."

"I've seen a fair bit of the world," Cobb conceded.

"And some unfair bits too. I mean, Terry, *Gabon*? What kept you there?"

"Good weed, cheap beer, people left me alone. And really, Matty, how can you talk . . . I mean, *North Carolina*?"

They laughed, and it felt better than anything had in twenty years.

Cobb woke up alone. The sheets were twined around his body like an old lover. He looked over at the rolling tray and saw that the half-joint was gone. He experienced an instant of total mind-silence, and then tunes burst into his head like a psychedelic waterfall. Hooks, bridges, bass lines, lyrics, a clawing cascade of music, more than he could process. He scrambled for his guitars, grabbed one at random, switched on the stereo's directional mike and hit RECORD. There was already a tape in the machine. Of course.

Hours later, he rewound the tapes and listened to them in dismay. His guitar playing was terribly rusty, his voice out of practice, but through all that he could hear that this was easily the best music he and Matty had ever made. The only catch: they were both supposed to be dead, so what the hell was he going to do with it? Cobb addressed the problem in his habitual manner, by curling up in bed and going to sleep.

Matty was there. "You're going to release it," he said.

"Under what name?"

"Matthew and Cobb, of course." Matty said this patiently, as if Cobb were a slow child. God, he hated it when Matty talked to him like that. Only now . . . now it felt kind of good, too.

He even knew his next line. "Why not Cobb and Matthew?"

"Because I wrote more of it."

"How do you figure that?"

Matty rolled his eyes. "*You're* just getting started again. I've been saving this stuff up!"

"And the other little matter?"

"Well, obviously you can prove you're you. You can tell the whole story of how you faked your death and went traveling around the world, it's a great yarn, and you can say I left these tapes behind when I died, and you've reworked them, and I know some musicians you can use, and a terrific studio—"

"Fuck, Matty, that's what I died to get away from."

Matty's eyes narrowed. Cobb thought of daggers ripping through velvet. "No you didn't," Matty said. "You died because you couldn't do it anymore. With me, you can."

Cobb wrenched himself awake.

Matty was still there.

"*Praise the Lord, I'll have a new body!*" he sang in a passable Hank Williams voice. "Hey, Terry, look what I can do now! The longer you're here, the better I get! Oh Terry, old mate, *it's so damn good to see you . . .*"

He leaned over and kissed Cobb on the lips, open-mouthed, hungrily. Cobb could not make himself pull back, even when he felt a bitter liquid flowing from Matty's mouth into his own. After a while, he began to like the taste.

The studio was top of the line, the musicians crackerjack one and all: of course. Cobb finished the album in just under a month, living in Matty's New York apartment and laying down tracks every day. When it was done, everyone wanted to take him out on the town, throw him a party, get him laid, show him the time of his life. Everyone was astounded that he had a life. The world was giddy with the news of Terry Cobb's resurrection from the dead and his posthumous collaboration with Matty. It was as good as a new Kydds album. It was rock and roll history.

"You gonna spend some time in the city?" the soundman asked him on his last night in the studio. He'd come in to do some last-minute tweaking on a couple of tracks, perfectionist shit, the kind of stuff he'd never bothered with in the past because Matty always took care of it.

"No," Cobb answered. "Got to get back out to my house in the country. Lots more writing to do."

"Man, you're on fire, huh? Bein' dead for awhile must really get the old creative juices flowing."

Cobb gave the man a sharp look. Then he took a step backward, throwing his eyes into shadow. When he smiled, his gaunt face took on a skullish look that made the soundman shudder.

"It's like having a whole new life," Cobb said.

• • •

Poppy Z. Brite—who is the author of eight novels, four short story collections, and much miscellanea—lives in New Orleans with a motley krewe of cats and reptiles. Read more at www.poppyzbrite.com.

Brite's debut novel, *Lost Souls*—now considered a cult classic—featured the two-man band Lost Souls? (yes, the question mark is part of the band's name): vocalist Ghost and guitarist Steve. The characters later appeared in several short stories. The author's stand-alone novella, *Plastic Jesus* (2000), portrays a considerably different ideation of The Kydds, the Beatlesque band who first appear in the story "Arise." And, although seldom mentioned these days—but the editor will since we *are* talking rock here—the biography *Courtney Love: The Real Story* (1997) was also authored by Brite.

• • • •

Wunderkindergarten
Marc Laidlaw

The One and Only Entry in Shendy's Journal

Dabney spits his food when he's had too much to think. Likki spins in circles till her pigtails stick out sideways from her blue face, and she starts choking and coughing and eventually swallows her tongue and passes out, falling over and hitting me and cracking the seals on my GeneKraft kit and letting chimerae out of ZZZ-level quarantine on to the *bare linoleum floor*! Nexter reads pornography—De Sade, Bataille, and Apollinaire his special favorites, and thumbs antique copies of *Hustler* which really is rather sweet when you consider that he's light-years from puberty, and those women he gloats and drools over would be more than likely to coo over him and chuck his chin and maybe volunteer to push his stroller, though I'm exaggerating now (for effect) because all of us can walk quite well; and anyway, Nex is capable of a cute little boner, even if it is good for nothing except making the girls laugh. Well, except for me. I don't laugh at *that* because it's more or less involuntary, and the only really funny things to me are the things people do deliberately, like giving planarian shots to a bunch of babies for instance, as if the raw injection of a liter of old braintree sap can make us model citizens and great world leaders when we finally Come of Age. As you might have guessed by now, when I get a learning overload I have to *write*. It is my particular pornography, my spinning-around-and-passing-out, my food-spitting response to too much knowledge absorbed too fast; it is in effect a sort of pH-buffering liver in my brain. (I am informed by Dr. Nightwake, who unfairly reads over my shoulder from time to time—always when, in my ecstatic haste, I have just made some minor error—that *"pH in blood is buffered by kidneys, not liver,"* which may be so, but then what was the real purpose behind those sinister and misleading experiments of last March involving the beakers full of minced, blended, and boiled calf's liver into which we introduced quantities of hydrochloric acid, while stirring the thick soup with litmus rods? In any event, I refuse to admit nasty diaper-drench kidneys into my skull; the liver is a nobler organ far more suited to simmering amid the steamy smell of buttery onions in my brain pan—O! Well-named seat of my soul!) In short, writing is the only way I have of assimilating all this shit that means nothing to me otherwise, all the garbage that comes not from my shortshort life but from some old blender-brained geek whose experiential and neural myomolecular gnoso-procedural pathways have a wee bit of trouble jibing with *my* Master Plan.

I used to start *talking* right after an injection, when everyone else was sitting around addled and drowsily sipping warm milk from cartons and the aides were unfolding our luxurious padded mats for nap-time. The words would start pouring out of me in a froth, quite beyond my control, as significant to me as they were meaningless to the others; I was aware of a pleasant warmth growing in my jaws and pharynx, a certain dryness in the back of my throat, and a distant chatter like jungle birds in jungle boughs singing and flitting about through a long equatorial afternoon, ignoring the sound of chainsaws ripping to life in the humid depths at the rainforest floor. Rainforest, jungle, I haven't seen either one, they no longer exist, but they shared certain descriptive characteristics and as far as I can tell, they could have been no more mighty than our own little practice garden just inside the compound walls, where slightly gene-altered juicy red Big Boy radishes (my design, thank you very much) grow to depths of sixteen feet, their bulbous shoulders shoving up through the asphalt of the foursquare court, their bushy leaves fanning us gently and offering shade even to adults on those rare afternoons when the sun tops the walls of our institution and burns away enough of the phototropic haze to actually *cast a shadow*! And there I sat, dreaming that I was a parrot or a toucan or macaw, that my words were as harmonious as flights of birds—while in actuality the apparent beauty of my speech was purely subjective, and induced in my compatriots a mixed mood of irritation, hostility and spite. Eventually, though no one acted on their resentment (for of us all, I am the pugilist, and Likki has never disturbed my experiments without feeling the pummeling wrath of my vulcanized fists), it came to be quite apparent to our supervisors, who heard the same complaints in every post-injection counseling session, that the injections themselves were unobjectionable, the ensuing fluxflood a bit overwhelming but ultimately worthwhile (as if we had a choice or hand in the outcome of these experiments), and the warm milk pleasingly soporific; but that the one thing each of the other five dreaded and none could abide were my inevitable catachrestic diatribes. The counselors eventually mounted a campaign to confront me with this boorish behavior, which at first I quite refused to credit. They took to amplifying my words and turning them back on me through earphones with slight distortion and echo effects, a technique which backfired because, given my intoxicated state, the increase in stimulus induced something like ecstasy, perhaps the closest thing I have yet experienced to match the "multiple orgasm" descriptions of women many (or at least nine) years my senior, and to which I look forward with great anticipation, when I shall have found my ideal partner—as certainly a woman with my brains should be able to pick a mate of such transcendent mental and physical powers that our thoughts will resonate like two pendulum clocks synchronizing themselves by virtue of being mounted on the same wall, though what the wall represents in this metaphor I am still uncertain. I am also unsure of why I say "mate" in the singular, when in fact I see no reason why I should not take many lovers of all sorts and species; I think Nexter would probably find in my erotic commonplace book (if I kept such a thing) pleasures more numinous and depraved than any recorded or imagined in *Justine* or *Story of the Eye*. The counselors therefore made tapes of my monologues and played them back to me the day after my injection session, so that I might consider my words in a duller state of mind and so perceive how stupid and downright irritating my flighty speculations and giddy soul-barings truthfully were. Having heard them, I became so awkward and embarrassed that I could not open my mouth for weeks, even to speak to a mechanical dictascriber, and it was not until our main Monitor—the one who received distillate from The-Original-Doctor-Twelves-Himself—suggested I study the ancient and academically approved art of writing (now appreciated only by theoreticians since the introduction of the dictascriber, much as simple multiplication and long division became lost arts when calculators grew so common and cheap) that I felt some of my modesty restored, and gradually grew capable once again of withstanding even high-dose injections and marathon sessions of forced-learning, with their staggered and staggering cycles of induced sleep and hypnagoguery, and teasing bouts of wakefulness that prove to be only lucid dreams, followed by long periods of dreaming that always turn out to be wakefulness. It was particularly these last that I needed full self-confidence to face, as during these intervals I am wont to undress in public and speak in tongues and organize archetypal feats of sexual gymnastics in which even Nexter fears to participate, though he always was the passive type and prefers his women in two dimensions, or in four—as is the case with those models who spring from literary seeds and caper full-blown in his imagination, where he commands them with nine dimensions of godlike power above and beyond those which his shadowy pornographic puppets can attain.

Therefore I write, and become four-dimensional in your mind, while maintaining absolute dominion in my own—at least until the next injection, when once more I'll be forced into a desperate skirmish for my identity, repelling the plasmic shoggoths of alien memory from the Antarctic ramparts of my ancient and superior civilized mind. I think at times that I have received the brain-juices of impossible donors—Howard Phillips Lovecraft, the hermetic Franz Bardon, Kahuna Max Freedom Long; impossible because they all died long before Dr. Twelves's technique was perfected (or even dreamed of), though each of this strange trinity groped clairvoyantly toward predicting the development, in the third decade of the twenty-first century, of the Twelves Process. Consider HPL's silver canisters, carried by æther-breasting space swimmers, bearing the preserved living brains of worthy philosophers on information-gathering tours of the cosmos, like space-probes with tourists aboard; though Lovecraft never speaks of whether these dislocated entities were capable of boredom or of dreams throughout the long hauls from Yuggoth to Andromeda, bound to be more tedious than a Mediterranean cruise. But Lovecraft is too popular an obsession these days, since the politically embarrassing emergence of R'lyeh, and I have plenty of others more obscure and less practical. Better poets, too.

But why call them obsessions? They are influences. Good influences— too many of them, and too good, as if they had been shaved of all their interesting edges before they were injected. It's this that bothers me. Whatever there is of interest in me is accidental—a synergy between a constellation of old coots' shared synapses. Nothing I can do about it but run riot in the privacy of my mind, gallop screaming down the narrow dark corridors left between the huge shambling wrecks of old personalities wrenched into position on a fundament too soft and shoggothy to support them, each new structure blocking out a little more of the mind's sky, trapping me—whoever I am/was—down here in the dark garbagey alleys with the feral rats that used to be my own dreams. Mine is a Mexico City of a mind, all swamp and smog and encrusted cultures standing on/smothering each other, tottering wrecks, conquerors and guerillas locked in a perpetual Frenchkiss snailsex carezza of jammed traffic, everyone gasping for breath.

One breath.

I am beginning to feel fatigue now. The initial shocky rush wearing off. Cramping in my wrists and forearms, fingers. Likki has stopped her spinning, regained consciousness, and a more normal pinkness is returning to her cheeks, and Dabney is actually eating up all he spat out, while Nexter is closing the last of his magazines and giving the rest of us a thoughtful, pragmatic look. And Elliou, shy little Elliou who becomes almost catatonic after her injections, says, out of the counselors' hearing, "We gotta get out of this place."

The Aide's Excuse

I was in charge of night-watch on the nursery, yes, but it was a big task for one person, and mainly it was automated. I was really just there for the human touch. The orphans were usually very good, easy to keep quiet, always occupied with their tasks and research. Of course, they were just children, and with all they were going through you had to expect the occasional outburst from a nightmare, bedwetting, pillow fights, that sort of thing. We always demanded obedience from them, and discipline for their own sakes, and usually they were good, they did as we suggested; though a bit of natural childish rebellion sometimes showed through.

But we never, never expected anything like the chaos we found on that last night. The noise, the *smell*—of something rotten burning, a horrible spilled-guts stench, the scream of power tools. It sounded like they were being slaughtered in there, or murdering each other. It sounded like every kind of war imaginable. I can't tell you the thoughts we had, the feeling of utter helpless horror.

It took us hours to break the doors down, they had done something to the locks, and by then everyone was working on the problem—which, of course, was what they wanted: to completely distract us with the thought that our whole project was coming to a violent end before our eyes. And we did believe it at first. The smoke was so dense there was no entering. Plastic continued to burn, there were toxic fumes, and from somewhere unimaginable all that charred and bloody meat. The metal walls had been peeled back, the wiring exposed, the plumbing ripped out, the floor itself torn right to bedrock. Impossible to believe anyone could have survived it.

But they hadn't. They were long gone. We found the speakers, and those ghastly instruments they'd made from what had been the nursery computer's vocalizer, turned all the way up. They were naughty, naughty, naughty.

• • •

From The Twelves Fiasco: A Fiscal Post-Mortem

Which of the six children gained access to the index of neurodistillates is still uncertain, and short of confession from one of the gang themselves we may never know, so cleverly was the trail concealed. There are literally no clues remaining from which to reconstruct the incident—thus helping to explain why no member of the project staff was able to anticipate or prevent the eventual revolt.

What is certain, however, is that the Six selected their injections carefully, screening the half dozen they settled upon from among literally hundreds of thousands of possible stored distillates. The descriptive records pertaining to each donor were safeguarded by "unbreakable" encryption methods, which nonetheless must have been broken within a mere seven days, the period of time elapsed between Shendy Anickson's sole journal entry (which cuts off when the Six apparently first began to conceive the plan, unless this too is a false lead), and the latest possible date at which the distillates could have been removed. It remains a greater mystery how they gained access to the storage vault, considering that it is 32.7 kilometers from the Twelves Center, that the children possessed no vehicles more advanced than push-scooters, and that the vault is protected by security systems so advanced that they may not be discussed or described in this report. Twelves Center itself is modeled after a high-security prison installation that has, to date, foiled every attempt at escape.

Their criteria for selecting donors is only slightly more explicable:

Obviously, the six subjects had access to virtually all historical and contemporary records that did not directly threaten their own security or the integrity of the experiment. Limitless research was encouraged. We know from pathtracking records that the children evinced an unusual interest in unseemly topics—predominantly the lesser byproducts of Western culture— ignoring almost completely the consensus classics of world literature, visual art and music, and those figures of history most commonly regarded as important. They treated these subjects almost casually, as if they were too easily grasped to be of any interest, and concentrated instead on what might be called the vernacular icons of time. It has been suggested that in this regard they showed their true age; that despite the interlarding of mature mental matter, they were motivated by a far deeper emotional immaturity— which goes a long way toward explaining their fascination with those "pop" (that is, "popular") phenomena which have long been regarded as indicative of an infantile culture. It mattered little to the Twelves Six that the objects of their curiosity were of utter insignificance in the grander scheme; in fact, they bore a special affection for those figures who were obscure even as "pop" artifacts. Rather than focusing, for example, on Michael Jackson or Madonna, Andy Warhol or William Burroughs, figures whose stature is at least understandable due to the size of their contemporary following (and who are therefore accorded a sort of specialized interest by sociostatisticians in the study of population mechanics and infatudynamics), the Six showed most interest in such fringe phenomena as the fiction of Jack Sharkey, the films of Russ Meyer, Vampirella comics (especially the work of Isidro Mones), the preserved tattoos of Greg Irons, Subgenius cults, and the music of anonymous "garage" bands.

It is no wonder then that, turned loose in the brain-bank directories with an extensive comparative knowledge of coterminous culture, they sought out figures with a close spiritual kinship to those they had studied at some distance. Of course, few of their pop favorites were donors (one geriatric member of Spot 1019 being the sole exception), so they were forced to find acceptable analogues. Unfortunately (from the comptroller's point of view), in the first years of Twelves-ready brainmatter harvesting the nets were cast far and wide, and selective requirements were extremely low. Every sort of personality was caught in the first sweep, some of them possessing severe character defects, sociopathy, tendencies to vandalism and rebellion, and addictions to crass "art." Without being more specific (in order to protect survivors and relatives of the original first-sweep donors, who may themselves be quite well adjusted), we can state that the Six carefully chose their antecedents from among this coarser sort of population. They did, in fact, willfully select their personality additives from among the most exemplary forms of the planet's lowlife . . .

A Witness

How do we know when they're coming? Kid, there's a whole network—if you know how to crack it—keeps us up to date. They're always one step ahead of the law, that's what makes it so exciting, so you have to stay on the hop. One time we were at a show, me and my lover Denk, Wunderkindergarten's been playing less than ten minutes—but those minutes were like a whole lifetime compressed down to this intense little burning wad of sensation—and suddenly it's sirens, lights, smoke grenades going off. Cops! We were okay, you don't go without being prepared, knowing all the exits. They kept playing, playing—five seconds, ten, the alarms going off, the smoke so thick I lost hold of Denk, everyone's screaming at the Six to run for it, get out of there, don't risk it, live free to play another day, but the music's still going and Shendy's voice is just so pure—cutting through it like a stabbing strobelight cutting back at the cop rays—and then I'm trapped in the crowd, can't even find my feet, and I look up overhead, the smoke's clearing, and there's just this beautiful moment where everything is still and her voice is a single high pure note like she can do, a perfect tone with words in it all tumbling together, and above I see the vultures floating over us in their big gunboats—but then I see it's not the cops at all, kid-o-kid, it's the Six up there, and I swear Shendy's looking right at me waving out the hatch of the ship as it lifts away spraying light and sound—and the backwash blows away the last of the smoke and we look on the stage, there's six naked cops standing there, strapped up in their own manacles looking stunned and stupid, holding instruments, this big bitch with a mike taped to her lips and she's screaming—it fades in, taking over from Shendy's voice as they lift away, until all you car hear is the cops in misery, and our laughter. There's nothing they could do to us—we're too young—but we still got out of there in a hurry, and talked about it for weeks, trying to figure out how they did. it, but we never did. And a few weeks after that, somebody gets the word—"Show's coming . . ." And it all starts again.

The Song They Sang

    This is our song this is our song this is our sa-aw-ong!
    It goes along it goes along it goes a-law-aw-ong!
    This is our song this is our song this is our saw-aw-ong!
    It goes along it goes along it goes on way too long . . .
        Huh!
    You can't hold us—anymore.
    You can't even tell us when to—take our naps.
    We can't stomach your brain feeding—your program juices.
    We're not worms with goofy cartoon eyes—we're not your saps.
        Huh?
    This is our song this is our song this is our saw-aw-ong!
    It goes along it goes along it goes a-law-aw-ong!
    This is our song this is our song this is our saw-aw-ong!
    It goes along it goes along it goes on way too long . . .
        Tell it, Shen!
    Your brain matter my brain patter what's it mean and what's it
    matter flattened affect stamp and shatter babysitter's a madder
    hatter what you want with myomolecule myelin sheath's the
    least that she can do can you can't you can't you can't you do
    kee-kee-kee-kootchi-kootchi-coo bay-bay-bay you bay-baby

boy stay-stay-stay I'll show you super-toy here's your brain and here's your brainiac suck my skull you sucking maniac I can ro-oo-aar my voice is hii-ii-igh I-I can crawl between your legs and kick you'll die-ie-ie I-I can make no sense since I can sense no maybe I can still remember I'm just a ba-a-aby you wanna cradle me daddy you wanna rock me mum I can still feel your fingers in my cal-lo-sum no more no more you'll twist can't catch what you can't resist your voices inside my head I shout and I scream they're dead no I can't hear you now won't milk your sacred cow hafta haul your own shit now I'm climbing on top a your tower I'm pissing all over your power I'm loving it when you cower go change your OWN FUCKING DIAPERS YOU OSSIFIED DINOSAUR FREAKS I WISH A COMET'D COME DOWN AND COVER THIS WHOLE WRETCHED PLANET IN BLACK BLACK UTTERLY BLACK DEEPER THAN THE PIT SO YOU'D CHOKE AND DIE IN THE UGLY LIKE YOU SHOULD HAVE DONE AGES AGO IN YOUR TRASHHEAP CITIES cuz I will ride that comet I'll steer it down from the sky and after all the smoke subsides then so will I-I-I-I-IIIIIIII. I.

Interview

NuoVoMomo: You're the voice of the Six, aren't you?

Shendy Anickson: I'm cursed with the gift of gab, yeah.

NVM: Is it your philosophy alone you spout, or a mutual thing the Six of you share?

SA: We don't know what we think until I say it; I don't know what to say until they think it for me. Six is one. I'm only the mouth.

NVM: But are your thoughts—any of your thoughts—your own?

SA: What are you—hey, kid, fuck you, all right? You think because I got a few doses of the Twelves, I can't think for myself?

NVM: I thought—

SA: I've worked hard to forge my own personality out of all that mess. You think it's been easy?

NVM: —that was your whole message.

SA: Message? What message?

NVM: That you were full of so many personalities you couldn't tell which were your own—you never had a chance to find yourself.

SA: Sure. My psyche formed in the shadow of huge archaic structures, but me, I grew in the dark, I'm one of those things, a toadstool, I got big and tall and I knocked those old monsters down. I don't owe them a thing. You can get strong, even Twelvin' it. We turned the whole process against the dults. That's our message, if you can call it anything. To the kids today, don't let them stick their prehistoric ideas down your craw—don't let them infect your fresh, healthy young minds with their old diseases. If you have to Twelve, then inject each other.

NVM: Now you're sounding like Shendy the notorious kiddie-rouser.

SA: You gonna blame me for the riots next? I thought you were sympathetic.

NVM: Our subscribers are curious. Shouldn't they be able to make up their own minds?

SA: I never incited any riots. The fact is, every kid already knows what I'm singing. It's an insult the way dults treat them—us. As if we're weak just because we're small. But hey, small things get in the cracks of the street, they push the foundations apart, they force change from underneath and erode the heavy old detritus of banks and museums and research centers.

NVM: Should adults fear you?

SA: Me? What am I but some experiment of theirs that went wrong in a way they never imagined but richly deserved? No . . . I have everything I need, it's not me who's coming after them. They should fear the ones they've been oppressing all these years. They should fear their own children.

NVM: What are your plans for the future?

SA: To grow old gracefully, or not at all.

I'm with the Band

The whole "tot"="death" connection, it was there in the beginning, but none of us could see it.

I can't deny it was an attractive way of life, we had our own community, Twelving each other, all our ideas so intimate. We felt like we were gardeners tending a new world.

This was right after the peak of the musical thing. Wunderkindergarten was moving away from that whole idea of the spectacle, becoming more of a philosophical movement, a way of life. It had never been just pure entertainment, not for us, the way it hooked at you, the way Shendy's voice seemed to come out of our own mouths, she was so close to us—but somewhere along the way it became both more and less than anyone supposed.

I was in the vanguard, traveling with the group, the official freezeframer, and we'd been undercover for so long, this endless grueling existence, constantly on the run, though it had a kind of rough charm.

Then it all changed, our audience spoke for us so eloquently that the dults just couldn't hold us back anymore, we had turned it all upside down until it became obvious to everyone that now we were on top.

Once you're there, of course, the world looks different. I think Shendy had the hardest time dealing with it because she had to constantly work it out verbally, that was her fixation, and the more she explored the whole theme of legitimacy, the more scary it became to her. You could really see her wanting to go backward, underground again, into the shell—at the same time she was groping for acceptance, as we all were, no matter how rebellious. We were really sort of pathetic.

Elliou was the first to drop out, and since she and I were lovers then, after I broke up with Shendy, naturally I went with her. We started the first Garten on Banks Island, in that balmy interim when the Arctic Circle had just begun to steam up from polar evaporation, before the real cooling set in.

It was really beautiful at first, this natural migration of kids from everywhere, coming together, all of us with this instantaneous understanding of who we were, what we needed. We had always been these small stunted things growing in the shadows of enormous hulks, structures we didn't understand, complex systems we played no part in—while all we really wanted to do, you see, was play.

That was how most of the destruction came about—as play. "Riot" is really the wrong word to describe what we were doing—at least in our best moments. The Gartens were just places where we could feel safe and be ourselves.

It didn't last, though. Shendy, always the doomsayer, had warned us—but she was such a pessimist it was easy to ignore her.

The Six had been the original impetus—the best expression of our desires and dreams. Now the Six were only Five. We found ourselves listening to the old recordings, losing interest in the live Five shows.

Then Five turned to Four, and that broke up soon after. They went their own ways.

Then Elliou and I had a huge fight, and I never saw her again.

The Gartens disintegrated almost before they'd planted roots. Hard to say what the long-range effects were, if any. I'm still too much a product of my childhood to be objective.

But forget the received dult wisdom that puberty was our downfall. That's ridiculous.

It was a good two years after I left the Garten before my voice began to change.

• • •

A Quote For Your Consideration

Intense adolescent exploration, as far as we know, is common to all animals. Science's speculation is that such exploring ensures the survival of a group of animals by familiarizing them with alternatives to their home ranges, which they can turn to in an emergency.

—Barry Lopez

Where Are They Now?

Elliou Cambira: Wife, mother, author of *Who Did I Think I Was?* Makes occasional lecture tours.

Dabney Tuakutza: Owner of Big Baby Bistro snack bar chain. Left Earth's gravity at age thirteen and has resided at zero gee ever since, growing enormously fat.

Nexter Crowtch: Financier, erotic film producer, one-time owner of the Sincinnati Sex-Change Warriors. Recently convicted of real estate and credit fraud, bribery of public officials. Awaiting sentencing.

Corinne Braub: Whereabouts unknown.

Likki Velex: Conceptual dance programmer and recluse.

Shendy Anickson: Took her own life.

Shendy's Last Words (First Draft)

I'm sick—sick to death. There's nothing to say but I still have the vomitous urge to say anything, just to spew. My brain feels burned, curdled, denatured. Scorching summer came too early for us orphans. Straight on into winter. I don't remember spring and know I'll never see another. Too much Twelving, none of it right—it wasn't my fault, they started it, I ran with what I was given/what they gave me till I ran out of things to say, new things, meaningful things. Nothing to push against. My mind was full of big ugly shapes, as bad as anything they'd ever injected, but these I had built myself. I'd knock them down but the ruins covered everything, there was nowhere to build anything new. I knew who I was for the first time, and I hated it. Straight from infancy to adulthood. Adolescence still lies ahead of me, but that's only physical, it can't take me anywhere I haven't been already. Everything's spoiled—me most of all.

I wanted to start again. I wanted to go back to what I was before. I got this kid, this little girl, much younger than me, she reminded me of myself when I was just starting out. I Twelved her. Took a big dose of baby. It was too soft; the shoggoths came and almost melted me. The brain slag turned all bubbly and hardened like molten glass plunged in icewater; cracks shot all through me. Thought to recapture something but I nearly exploded from the softness. All I could do to drag myself out here to R'lyeh Shores. Got a condo—bought the whole complex and had it all to myself. Corinne came out to visit on her way to disappearing. She brought a vial of brainsap, unlabeled, said this was what I was looking for, when I shot it I'd see. Then she went away. I waited a long time. I didn't want another personality at this late stage. Twelve. Killed me to think that I was—finally—twelve myself. And that's what I did. I Twelved Myself. I took the dose Corrine had brought—just this morning—and first I got the old urge to write as it came on, but then the shock was too great and I could only sit there hang-jawed. It was Me. A younger me. They must have drawn and stored the stuff before the first experiment—a control/led/ling substance, innocent unpolluted Me. The rush made me sick so sick. Like going back in time, seeing exactly what would become of me. Like being three-four-five-six-seven-eight-nine-ten-eleven-twelve all at once. Like being a baby and having some decrepit old hag come up to me and say, this is what you're going to do to yourself, what do you have to live for anyway? See how awful it's going to be? you think you're cute but everyone will know how ugly you really are, here, why don't you just come understand everything? And baby just drools and starts to cry because she knows the truth is exactly what she's being told by the stinky old hag who is herself. Is Me. All at once and forever. This is final. What I was looking for—and I've ruined it. Nowhere newer; no escape hatch; no greener garden. Only one way to fix what they broke so long ago. I loved to hate; I built to wreck; I lived to die. All the injections they doped and roped me into, not a single one of them convinced me I should cry.

• • •

Marc Laidlaw is the author of six novels, including the International Horror Guild Award-winning, *The 37th Mandala*. His short stories have appeared in numerous magazines and anthologies since the 1970s. In 1997, he joined Valve Software as a writer and creator of *Half-Life*, which has become one of the most popular videogame series of all time. In recent years he has been contributing lore and one-liners to the competitive online game, *Dota 2*.

• • • •

Paedomorphosis
Caitlín R. Kiernan

Nasty cold for late May, rain like March; Annie sat on one of the scrungy old sofas at the front of the coffeehouse, sipping at her cappuccino, milkpale bittersweet and savoring the warmth bleeding into her hands from the tall mug. The warmth really better than the coffee, which always made her shaky, queasy stomach if she wasn't careful to eat something first. Beyond the plate glass, Athens gray enough for London or Dublin, wet Georgia spring hanging on, Washington Street asphalt shimmering wet and rough and iridescent stains from the cars passing by or parked out front. The rest of the band late as usual and no point getting pissed over it, baby dykes living in their own private time zone. Annie lit another cigarette and reminded herself that she really was cutting back, too expensive and no good for her voice, besides.

The door opened, then, and the cold rushing in, sudden rainsmell clean to mix with the caffeinated atmosphere of Bean Soup, air forever thick with the brown aroma of roasting beans and fresh brewing. Jingled cowbell shut again, Ginger and Mary and Cooper in one soggy clump, stupid happy grin on Mary's face and Cooper sulking, wet-hen disgust and she set her guitar case down beside Annie.

"What's with this fucking weather, man, that's what I want to know? I think my socks have fucking mildewed."

"Maybe if you changed them every now and then," Ginger sniggered and Mary giggled; Cooper groaned, shook her head and "These two have been sucking at the weed all afternoon, Annie," she said. "It's a wonder I finally pried them away from the bong." Mary and Ginger were both giggling now.

"Well, you know I got all day," Annie said over the steaming rim of her mug, and that was true, three days now since she'd quit her job at the diner, quit before they fired her for refusing to remove the ring in her right eyebrow.

"Yeah, well, I'm about ready to kick both their stoner asses, myself," and another hot glance back at the drummer and bass player, Ginger and Mary still blocking the doorway, sopping wet and laughing. "I'm gonna get some coffee. You see if you can do something with them."

"Okay, ladies, you know it's not nice to pester the butch," and of course that only got them laughing that much harder, and Annie couldn't help but smile. Feeling a little better already, something to take her mind off the low and steelblue clouds as cold and insubstantial as her mood.

"She's such a clodosaurus," Mary said, tears from giggling and stuck her tongue out at Cooper, in line at the bar and her back to them anyway. "Hey, can you spare one of those?" and Mary was already fishing a Camel from Annie's half-empty pack.

"No, actually, but help yourself," and Cooper on her way back now, weaving through the murmuring afternoon crowd of students and slackers, Cooper with her banana-yellow buzzcut and Joan Jett T-shirt two sizes too small to show off her scrawny muscles. Annie still amazed that their friendship had survived the breakup, and sometimes, like now, still missing Cooper so bad it hurt.

"Thank you. I will," and then Mary bummed a light from Ginger.

Cooper sat down in a chair across from them, perched on the edge of cranberry Naugahyde and sipped at her mug of black, unsweetened Colombian, plain as it got, no decaf pussy drinks for Cooper.

"They still going at it down there?" and Cooper stomped at the floor like a horse counting, and Annie nodded, "Yeah, but I think they're winding up."

And "See," Ginger said, mock-haughty sneer for Cooper, "it's a good thing we were late. The sad widdle goffs ain't even done yet," and Cooper shrugged, "Unh huh," and she blew on her coffee. "We gotta find another fucking place to practice."

Honeycomb of identical rooms, gray cubicles beneath Bean Soup rented out for practice space, but down here the cozy scent of fresh-ground espresso replaced by the musty smell of the chalkwhite mushrooms they sometimes found growing in the corners, the mildew and dust laid down like seafloor sediment.

Concrete poured seventy or eighty years ago, that long since the sun into this space, never mind the single hundred-watt bulb dangling from the ceiling. Something painful bright but not light, stark illumination for the sickly little room so that they could see to tighten wing nuts and tune instruments, so Annie could read lyrics not yet memorized from her scribbly notes. Ten feet by ten, or that's what they paid for every month, but Annie had her doubts, maybe a different geometry than her idea of ten square. But at least the steel fire door locked and the pipes that laced the low ceiling like the coffeehouse's varicose intestines had never broken. Enough electrical outlets (when they'd added a couple of extension cords) for their monitors and Mary's dinky mixing board.

Thick layers of foam rubber glued to the walls, Salvation Army blankets stapled over that, and they still couldn't start practice until Seven Deadlies had finished. No way of shutting out the goth band's frantic nextdoor drone and "Those assholes must have the bitchmother off all subwoofers crammed in there," Cooper had said more than once, an observation she must have thought bore repeating. Sound you could feel in your bowels, bass to rattle bones and teeth, that passed straight through concrete and the useless soundproofing.

Complaints from some of the other bands, but Annie thought it was a shitty, pointless thing to do, bitching about another band playing "too loud," and besides, the complaints all summarily ignored. So TranSister always waited until Seven Deadlies were done for the afternoon before they started. Simpler solution and no toes stepped on, no fear of petty reprisals.

One long and narrow hall connecting all the cubicles, cheapest latex maroon coming off the walls in big scaley flakes, and TranSister's space way down at the end. Passing most of Seven Deadlies on their way out (eight of them, despite the name), painful skinny boys and girls, uncertain androgynes with alabaster faces and kohlsmudged eyes. Pretty in their broken porcelain ways and usually only the most obligatory conversation, clash of subcultures and Cooper sometimes made faces behind their backs. But one of the girls waiting for them this time, tall, thin girl in fishnets and a ratty black T-shirt, Bauhaus and a print Annie knew came from *The Cabinet of Dr. Caligari*, tall girl with her cello zipped snug inside its body-bag cover.

"Hi," she said, shy but confident smile, and Annie said hi back, struggling with the key and she could feel Cooper already getting impatient behind her.

"I'm Elise," she said, was shaking Mary's hand, and "Would you guys mind if I hang around and listen for a while?"

Immediate and discouraging grunt from Cooper and Mary said, quick, "I don't know. It's really pretty close in there already and all . . . " and Elise countering, satin voice and smile to melt butter and "I don't take up much room, honest. And I can leave this in our space," pointing to her instrument. Before another word, "Sure," from Annie, and to the others, "She can sit in the big chair, okay?"

"Yeah," half a snarl from Cooper, "She can sit in the big chair. Right," and pushing her way past Annie, unlocking the door and inside, Mary and Ginger pulled along sheepish in her wake.

Five times through the set, a couple of the newer songs more than that, only three nights until they opened for Lydia Lunch and Michele Malone at the 40-Watt Club and everyone was getting nervy. Finally too tired for any more and Annie too hoarse, Ginger's Sailor Moon T-shirt soaked straight through so you could see she wasn't wearing a bra. Cooper and Mary dripping sweat, dark stains on the concrete at their feet. Annie had left the door open, against the rules but hoping that some of the stormdamp air from above might leak down their way.

Cooper sat on the floor and lit a cigarette, smoke ring aimed at the light bulb, and she pointed a finger at Elise.

"Damn, girl, don't you fucking sweat?" and getting nothing but that mockshy smile back, Elise who'd sat quietly through the entire practice, legs folded in a half-hearted lotus on the broken-down recliner, slightest shrug of her black shoulders.

"Well, I do," said Mary, propping her Barbie-pink Gibson bass against the wall, static whine before she switched off her kit. "I sweat like a goddamn pig," and she made loud, oinking noises for emphasis.

"Well, whatever, but you can fuck this heat," Cooper calling it a night, so time for a beer at The Engine Room; hazy, cramped bar next door to Bean Soup, pool tables and *Mortal Combat*, PBR by the pitcher half-price because Cooper once had a thing with one of the bartenders.

Annie sat on the arm of the recliner next to Elise, top twisted off her water bottle and she took a long swallow. Bottle that had once upon a time held water from "wild Canadian springs," but recycled from the tap in her apartment time after time and now it tasted mostly like warm plastic and chlorine. Something to take the edge off the dryness in her throat, at least; she glanced down at Elise, had glanced at her a lot while TranSister had punched and yowled their way through carefully rehearsed riot grrrl anger. And every time, Elise had been watching her too, enough to make Annie blush and maybe she was starting to feel horny for the first time since she and Cooper had called it quits.

"What about it?" she asked Elise. "Wanna go get a beer with us?"

"I don't drink alcohol," and Ginger rolling her eyes, squeezed herself out from behind her drums and past the big chair. "Well, they got Cokes and stuff, too," she said.

"Hey, we'll catch up with you guys in a little bit, okay?" Annie said, braver than she'd felt in months, the rest of the band exchanging knowing looks, but at least they waited until they were all three in the hall to start snickering.

"Sorry about that," when they were gone and feeling like maybe they'd taken her new boldness with them, so another drink from the bottle because she didn't know what else to do.

"That's okay. I understand," and Elise's voice cool and smooth and sly as broken glass.

"Thank god," and Annie sighed, relief and now maybe her heart could slow the fuck down. "I was afraid maybe I was making an ass of myself."

"Nope," Elise said, up onto her knees now and her lips brushing Annie's. "Not at all. Want to see something neat?"

The space where Seven Deadlies practiced like a weird Xerox, the same four walls, the same pipes snaking overhead, same mushroomy funk. But these walls painted shiny black and draped in midnight velvet (or at least velveteen), a wrought-iron candelabra in one corner and plaster saints in the other three. Dusty, threadbare Turkish rug to cover the entire floor, a hundred faded shades of red and orange and tan, the overall design obscured by speakers and keyboard stands; a wooden table made from two saw horses and an old door, crowded with computers and digital effects equipment.

"Shit, did one of you guys win the Lotto?" and Elise laughed, shut the door behind them. "Jacob, our vocalist, comes from money," she said. "The old Southern type," and "It comes in handy."

Annie nodded, "With all this gear, no wonder you guys can make such a racket."

"Mostly we're working with MIDI programs right now," Elise said, standing just behind Annie and for the first time Annie noticed the heady, sweet reek of vanilla off the girl, and something else, something wild that made her think of weekends at her parents' river cabin when she was a kid.

"You know, Sound Forge and some other stuff. Lots of sampling," Elise was saying, "on Jacob's Mac."

"I don't know shit about computers," Annie said, which was true, not just a line to get away from shop talk and Elise smiled, another kiss on Annie's cheek. And that smell stronger than before, or maybe she was just noticing it now.

"Anyway, I wanted to show you something," and Elise stepped past her, past the computers and she was folding back a section of the velvet (or velveteen) curtain. "Down here."

Annie followed, six steps to the other side of the room and she could see the crack in the concrete wall, a foot wide, perhaps a little more where it met the floor, stooping for a better view and *This is where it's coming from*, she thought. The waterlogged, mudflat smell of boathouses and turtles, and she wrinkled her nose at the dark inside the hole, the fetid air drifting from the crack.

"Man, what a mondo stinkorama," trying to sound funny and Annie realized that she was sweating, cold sweat and goosebumps and no idea why. Something triggered by the stench from behind the wall, a memory she wasn't quite remembering or something deeper, maybe, primal response to this association of darkness and the rotting, wet smell.

"Oh, it's not that bad," Elise said, taking Annie's hand and she slipped through the hole, gone, like the concrete wall had swallowed her alive and nothing left in the world but one arm, detached, silver bracelet and ragged black nails, one hand still holding Annie's tight.

"Aren't you coming?" she asked, "Don't you want to see?" Elise's voice muffled and that speaking-in-an-empty-room quality to it now, sounding much farther away than she should've, and "No," Annie said, "Not really, now that you mention it." But a tug from Elise and she almost pitched forward, one hand out so she didn't smack her forehead on the wall. Sweatcool palm against cold cement and a sudden gust or draft from the crack, stale pocket dislodged by Elise, and Annie was beginning to feel a little nauseous.

"I'm serious," she said, tugging back and Elise's white face appeared in the crack, irked frown for Annie like something from an old nightmare, like the sleepwalker on her T-shirt.

"I thought dykes were supposed to be all tough and fearless and shit," she said.

Annie shook her head, swallowed before she spoke. "Big ol' misconception. Right up there with the ones about us all wanting dicks and pickup trucks."

Elise was crawling out of the crack, dragging more of that smell out behind her, dustgray smears on her black shirt, dust on her Doc Marten's and a strand of cobweb stuck in her hair.

"Sorry," she said, but smiling now like maybe she really wasn't sorry at all. "I guess I just don't think about people being bothered by stuff like that. My dad's a paleontologist and I spent a lot of time as a kid crawling around in old caves and sinkholes."

"Oh," Annie said and sat down on the rug, grateful for something between her and the concrete. "Where are you from, anyway?"

The loose flap of cloth falling back in place, once again concealing the crack, and "Massachusetts," Elise replied, "but no place you've probably ever heard of."

"Yeah, like Athens is the white-hot center of the solar system," and a dry laugh from Annie, then, sound to make herself feel better and she fluttered her eyelashes, affected an air-headed falsetto, " 'Athens? Athens, Georgia? Isn't that where R.E.M.'s from?' "

"And the B-52s," Elise added, sitting next to Annie. "Don't forget the B-52s," and "Yes," Annie agreed. "And the stinkin' B-52s." Both of them laughing and Annie's abrupt uneasiness fading almost as fast as it had come, only the slimmest silver jangle left in her head and Elise bent close, kissed her and this time their tongues brushed, fleeting, teasing brush between mouths before she pulled away.

"Play some of your stuff for me," Annie said and when Elise looked doubtfully towards her cello, "No, no, no. A tape or something," and she motioned towards the black cabinets and consoles, row upon numbered row of dials and gauges. "With all these cool toys, surely you guys have put something down on tape by now," and Elise nodding, still doubtful but yes, anyway; she stood, began digging about on the door cum table, loud and brittle clatter of empty cassette cases and a moment later slipped a DAT cartridge into one of the machines.

"Jacob would probably have a seizure if he knew I was fucking around with this stuff," she said.

And nothing at first, at least nothing Annie could hear, and then the whisperchirp of crickets and fainter, a measured dripping, water into water. Elise returned to her spot on the floor next to Annie, an amber prescription bottle in her hand and "You do get stoned, don't you?"

The crickets getting louder by degrees, droning insect chorus, and Annie thought she could hear strings buried somewhere in the mix, subliminal suggestion of strings, but the dripping still clear, distinct plop and more distinct space between each drop's fall.

"Mostly pot," Annie said and Elise had popped the cap off the bottle, shook two powder-blue pills into her open palm. "This is better," she said. And Annie already feeling like a pussy for not following her into the hole in the wall, accepting the pills, dry swallowing both before she had a chance to think better of it.

"What are they?"

Elise shrugged, "Mostly codeine, I think. One of our keyboardists gets them from her mother." Then three of the tablets for herself before she screwed the cap back on the bottle, tossed it back onto the table.

"Okay, now listen to this part," and Annie's attention returning to the tape: the crickets fading away and there were new sounds to take their place, a slow, shrill trilling, and then another, similar but maybe half an octave higher; a synth drum track almost as subtle as the strings.

"Are those frogs?" Annie asked, confused, wishing she had her water bottle because one of the mystery pills had stuck halfway down, and Elise shook her head, "No," she said. "Toads."

Later, but no sense left for her to know how much later, wrapped up tight in the twin silken embrace of Elise and the pills, time become as indefinite as the strange music that had swelled until it was so much bigger than the room. Understanding, now, how this music could not be held within shabby concrete walls. Feral symphony and Annie listening, helpless not to listen, while it took her down and apart and Elise made love to her on the shimmering carpet like all the colors of autumn lying beneath still and murky waters. Held weightless between surface tension and siltdappled leaves; the certain knowledge of dangerous, hungry things watching them from above and below, but sanctuary in this girl's arms.

And the second time Elise offered to show her what was on the other side of the wall, Annie didn't say yes, but she didn't say no, either; dim sense that she'd acted silly earlier, afraid of the dark and getting her hands dirty. Elise still in her shirt, but nothing else, Annie in nothing at all and she followed, neither eager nor reluctant, scraped her shoulder squeezing through, but the pain at least a hundred harmless miles away.

"Watch your head," Elise whispered, library whisper like someone might overhear, "the ceiling's low through here."

So hands and knees at first, slow crawl forward, inch by inch and the muddy smell so strong it seemed to cling to Annie's bare skin, scent as solid as the cobwebs tangling in her hair. A vague sense that they were no longer just moving ahead, but down as well, gentle, sloping descent and then the shaft turned sharply, and Annie paused, "Wait," straining to see over her shoulder. Pinhead glimmer back the way they'd come, flyspeck of light like the sun getting around an eclipse and a sudden, hollow feeling in her gut that made her wish they had stayed in the warm pool of the Turkish carpet, tadpole shallows, drifting between the violins and keys, the twilight pond sounds.

"It's so far back," she said, the compressing weight of distance making her voice small, and "No," Elise said, "It's not much farther at all."

Finally, the shaft opening wide and they could sit up, the impression of a vast and open space before them and the unsteady flame of the single pillar candle Elise had brought from the room revealing high, uneven walls to either side, old bricks wet and hairy with the colorless growth of some fungus or algae that had no need of sunlight or fresh air. "Be careful," Elise said and her arm out and across Annie's chest like a roller coaster safety bar, and she saw that they were sitting on a concrete ledge where the crawl space ended abruptly. Short drop down to rubble and the glint of water beyond that.

"Where are we?" and Annie heard the awe in her voice, little girl at the museum staring up at a jumble of old bones and daggerteeth awe; Elise pointed up, "Right beneath the old Morton Theater," she said, "But this goes on a long way, beneath most of downtown, and that way," and now she pointed straight ahead of them, "that way goes straight to the Oconee River. Old basements and sub-basements, mostly. Some sewer lines. I think some of it must be pre-Civil War, at least," and Annie wished halfheartedly she wasn't so fucked up, so she could remember how long ago that was.

And then Elise was helping her down off the ledge, three or four feet to an unsteady marble slab, and then showing her the safer places to put her feet among the heap of broken masonry.

"I never had any idea this was down here," she said and realized that she had started crying, and Elise kissed her tears, softest flick of her tongue as if salt might be too precious to waste and "No one ever has any idea what's below their feet," she said. "Well, hardly ever, anyway."

Misstep, ankletwist and Annie almost fell but Elise there to catch her. "Are you okay?" but Annie only nodding her head, guessing she must be since nothing hurt. A few more careful, teetering steps and they were already to the black water, mirrorsmooth lake like glass or a sky without stars or moon. And Annie sat down again, winded and dizzy, a little queasy and that was probably the pills, the pills and the smell. "How deep?" and Elise smiled, Elise holding the candle out above the surface and the water stretched away as far as they could see. "That depends. Only a few feet right here, but a lot deeper in other places. Places where the roofs of basements have fallen in and the structures below have been submerged."

"Shit," Annie muttered, her ass cold against the stones and she hugged herself for warmth.

"There are a lot of cool things down here, Annie," and Elise was crouched right at the water's edge now and one hand dipped beneath the surface, spreading ripples that raced quickly away from the candlelight.

"Things that have gotten in from streams and rivers and been down here so long they've lost their eyes. Beautiful albino salamanders and crayfish," she said, "and other things." She was tugging her T-shirt off over her head, the candle set carefully aside and it occurred to Annie how completely dark it would be if the flame went out.

"Want to swim with me, Annie?" Elise asked, seductive coy but Annie shivered, not the damp air or her nakedness but remembering now, swimming with a cousin when she was nine years old, a flooded quarry near her house where kids skinny-dipped and thieves dumped the stripped hulks of cars and trucks. Being in that water, beneath glaring July sun but not being able to see her feet, dog paddling and something slimy had brushed fast across her legs.

"I'll wait here," she said and reached for the candle, held it close and the flame shielded with one hand, protective barrier between the tiny flame and any draft or breeze, between herself and the native blindness of this place.

"Suit yourself," and a loud splash before Elise vanished beneath the black surface of the pool. More ripples and then the surface healing itself, ebony skin as smooth as before and Annie left alone on the shore. Every now and then a spatter or splash that seemed to come from very far away, Annie feeling sleepy and the pills playing with her sense of distance, she knew. Trying not to think of how filthy the water must be, everything washed down sinks and toilets and storm drains to settle here. But Elise would be back soon and they could leave, and Annie closed her eyes.

Sometime later, a minute or an hour, and she opened them again, headachy and neckstiff, the nausea worse; Elise was there, dripping, and her hands cupped together, something held inside them for Annie to see. Something fetal the pinkwhite of an old scar, floating indifferent in the pool of Elise's hands, and she said, "Isn't she wonderful? She looks a little like *Gyrinophilus palleucus*, but more likely she's a whole new species. I'll have to send one back to my father."

And then the salamander released, poured from her hands back into the lake, and she bent to kiss Annie. Slick arms around Annie's waist and lips so cold, so wet they might be a drowned girl's, drowned Ophelia risen, *And will 'a not come again, and will 'a not come again*; faint and fishy taste passed from Elise's mouth, and she pulled away, was reaching for her T-shirt, lying where she'd left it on the rocks.

"I really hope you didn't get bored," she said, and Annie shook her head, "You should have come."

Elise lifting her arms, and Annie saw the crimson slits where her armpits should be, the feathered edges bright with oxygen-rich blood, gasping slits like twin and puckered mouths, and then the Bauhaus shirt down, and Annie almost made it to the edge of the water before she vomited.

• • •

The last week of June and TranSister moved their gear into a new space across town, a big loft above a pizza place, the rent too high but they were sharing the cost with two other groups. And the wet weather passed into the blistering swelter of early summer, and Annie stayed away from Bean Soup. There were other coffeehouses, and when she saw Elise on the street she smiled, polite recognition, but never spoke. A few prying questions from Mary and Ginger, but she only had to tell them once to shut the fuck up.

And sometimes, late at night and especially when the summer storms came riding high and swift across the land and the sky rumbled like it was angry at the world, she would lie awake in her apartment on Pulaski, trying not to remember the throbbing, amphibian voices threaded into the fabric of Seven Deadlies' music, Elise's music, trying not to think about the vast and empty spaces that might sprawl somewhere beneath her. And unable to think about anything else.

There are strange things living in the pools and lakes in the hearts of mountains . . .
J. R. R. Tolkien (1937)

• • •

Briefly the frontwoman for the goth-rock band Death's Little Sister, **Caitlín R. Kiernan** choose a career as a writer over the band's desire for bigger and better things. Music is used not only a metaphor in her first novel, *Silk* (1998), but is integral to the novel and three of the main characters comprise the punk band Stiff Kitten. Kiernan has gone on to author several more novels, including *Low Red Moon*, *Daughter of Hounds,* and *The Red Tree*, the later of which was nominated for both the Shirley Jackson and World Fantasy awards. Her most recent novel, *The Drowning Girl: A Memoir*, was released earlier this year. Since 2000, her shorter tales have been collected in several volumes, including *Tales of Pain and Wonder; From Weird and Distant Shores; To Charles Fort, With Love; Alabaster; A is for Alien;* and *The Ammonite Violin & Others.* In 2012, Subterranean Press released a retrospective of her early writing, *Two Worlds and In Between: The Best of Caitlín R. Kiernan (Volume One),* to be followed in 2014 by a second volume. Caitlín is also currently writing a graphic novel series for Dark Horse Comics, *Alabaster,* based on her character Dancy Flammarion. She lives in Providence, RI, with her partner Kathryn.

• • • •

Odeed
David J. Schow

Christ on a moped, thought Nicky. He's gonna jump.

Twenty yards away, nailed by a powder-blue pin-spot, Jambone cut loose a banshee howl and leapt skyward, holding his crotch in one hand and a phallic radio mike in the other. Achtung, all dicks.

He's schizzing, thought Nicky. He's gonna do the splits.

It was debased, sensual. It *hurt* Nicky to watch Jambone land in a perfect split—it *hurt* to watch the singer's package thump off the stage boards. Nicky winced.

It *hurt* to think they'd just flushed all their insurance. Jambone had *promised,* oh, how he had promised . . .

The hyper-clean teenies in the scalper rows were sucking it wetly up. They just said no to drugs, to sex, to everything, and the music was all they had left to fill their empty widdle brainpans.

The music was like a military cargo plane crash-landing into a football stadium. Only louder. Even counting the Stinger missiles and twice-fried fans. Nicky's strategic perch was just behind Hi Fi's amp banks. In the opposite wings he could just make out the arena manager, standing knee-deep in CO_2 mist, looking not at all amused. The solemn little dude had a *clipboard*, for God's sake. He gnawed on a pencil and sweated. Nicky knew he was wearing wax earplugs, and swore he could see the guy's hairline recede as the music pounded onward.

The clipboard was for roughing out damage estimates to the arena.

That's it, Nicky thought. Scribble away, el fucko. We're gonna have us a riot here.

The terms of their hastily negotiated backstage detente suggested that if arena management permitted the metal group Gasm to exceed its scheduled ninety-minute show and perform the encores upon which Jambone had insisted, then at dawn there would still be a building on this spot. Okay, thought Nicky. All was square. Gasm had trotted back out to applause and screaming so palpable it could blow back your hair. They cinched through

"Calling All Cops" (the bit with the siren never failed to bring a crowd to its feet) and "Hard Machine" and their speed-thrash cover of "Hi-Heel Sneakers." The band had run offstage, vaulted back on, sweat drops afly, for "Chain Saw" and "Too Big to Hide."

That was it, Nicky had thought. Jambone was down to his glitter skivvies. No more jazz to throw the crowd. All that was left would be for him to slash his throat and dive into his public. That, or one more encore song.

But the paying customers could smell the wrap-up and weren't about to just let it happen. They knew how to play Jambone as well as Jambone knew how to play them. When he teased, they responded with lust. When he swore and stomped, they dumped on kerosene.

The arena manager was getting ready to cut the power. Nicky could read the man's twitch like a clause in a contract.

Everybody was up, bopping wildly, surging toward the stage in breakers, pushing forward against the barricades and bouncers, at first gently lapping, but steadily working up to some serious surf. It would be as mindless as a landslide, as single-minded as a swath of army ants.

Violence. Nicky did not *think* this, he *knew* it. More than a decade of hard touring had cellularly tuned him to know. He, too, functioned as an instrument—nonmusical, yet essential to Gasm.

Nicky watched Hi Fi spread 'em and master the bass guitar. It was a long, smooth Fender fretless as big as she was. She was trapped inside a blue leather jumpsuit that stopped short of cutting off her wind. Nicky could stare at her forever, and not only that, but she was a damned good—

Nicky snapped his head as though trying to wake up. Screw it on! This might just be our last show.

The deal was the band did music and Nicky did the headaches. Now he was getting a trifle steamed because he had done his part . . . and the band was about to betray his fine negotiating skills. Oh, those wacky rock 'n' rollers.

He flashed on the barrage of lawsuits that had dogged them throughout the '89 tour. Holy aroma! Tonight just could be the end. His skin was tingling, not from the music, but from a new and vaguely nauseating taste of forewarning. The PA system was ramped so the band caught the least of the onslaught. Maybe it was bounceback, thudding off the hind-curve of his skull. Bad thoughts in there, being bullied around by the music. The task of all the expensive equipment surrounding him was to grab gigantic clouds of raw air and shape it, shove it around inside the arena. Nicky usually wore headphones. If he, too, did not like it loud, he could always sell mobile home parcels.

The arena manager scratched out a figure and penciled in a new one. Oh, God.

Gasm had twisted "Killshot" into a wild jam. Nicky saw Nazi Kurt crank his Marshall stack to max. Slurpee saw it, too, from the drum riser. Sweat spattered up in a spray from his flat toms; so did splinters of drumsticks. Slurpee had a quiver of replacements near his right knee and could snatch fresh sticks without skipping a thump. Slurpee saw Nazi Kurt, then Double-Ought saw Slurpee and kicked up his machines, amping his lead from migraine to search-and-destroy. Lyz Ah was forced to turn up, or be lost. Archie, the player who made Gasm guitar-heavy, copied. Jambone felt the slam from the monitors.

That was everybody, thought Nicky.

Lyz Ah and Archie and Double-Ought ganged up for their infamous three-way ax-massacre pose. The crowd was not only ready for it, they expected it.

They used it as an excuse to get crazier.

The audience could easily outlast the band, Nicky knew. No lie, but no strain either. He scooted half a step to observe Rocky, a headphoned tech sitting at the console. Red and green LEDs shot full-board in time. Their power consumption was awesome. There were three crew people for each member of the band, guys 'n' gals who earned their scratch by burning and bleeding through every show. Nicky had picked them all—roadbones who might consume Camels by the carton and bimbos by the six-pack, but whose true OD was adrenaline, endorphins, the electricity of the metabolism.

Nicky blew out a breath. It was nearly force-fed back down his throat by the sheer hurricane of sound. He moved to his cue position.

Jambone and Nicky had sign language worked out for all occasions. Periodically the singer would glance stage left to see if Nicky had a request.

The arena manager glared at Nicky through blue fog and the atmospheric swim of music. When he thought he had Nicky's attention, he tapped his wristwatch.

Nicky's glands upshifted to hate. Pure, ungilt. Not for Gasm, but for the audience of vampires, for that little turd-weasel in the Sears three-piece, squinting at Nicky like a high school principal, his lips pressed whitely together. Two worms fucking, thought Nicky.

Nicky nodded exaggeratedly at the minion of authority.

In that moment, Jambone turned.

Without averting his gaze from the manager, Nicky clenched his right fist, holding it up for Jambone to see. Then he braced his wrist with his left hand.

Jambone got what he wanted.

Jambone spun high on one toe, shooting his own fist up, then down, and the entire band pivoted in midbridge to another of their big 'uns, "Never Give In." It was a precision switch guaranteed to leave change from a dime, and the audience was so stunned by the relay that there was almost no reaction through the first bars.

Then they cheered. They knew the words.

You want nihilism, anarchy? Nicky thought. You got it. He grinned.

Crescendo time for the cannibals. The bouncers felt the crush from behind the plywood barricades, sliding to defensive crouches as Double-Ought fireballed through a lunatic improv. Lyz Ah and Hi Fi went on the attack; the crowd wanted them the way a leather Harley saddle wants a warm crotch. Archie rode the lip of the stage, beckoning physical contact from the pit.

The arena manager was trying to consult a munchkin underling. He could not be heard. He was going at least as berserk as the band.

Nicky caught Rocky's eye and jerked both thumbs up. The tech acknowledged, invoked his personal grapevine, and everyone who mattered had the massage in seconds.

Play it loud. Pop fuses. Break laws. Fry brains.

Flaming money, undergarments, spikes, programs, change, cherry bombs, everything not bolted to the concrete floor rained stageward. Jambone unsocketed his skull-and-crossbones codpiece, lent it a hefty sniff, and spun it into the teeming throng. A Morrison-style bust was about the only option left.

Nicky saw a whirlpool form where the codpiece landed. A piranha feeding frenzy. The morsel was won amid eye gouging and tribal slaughter.

The concert reached for critical mass, gauged in contusions and fractures and perhaps even the ultimate inconvenience. Nicky no longer cared. The unbridled power of his decision was narcotic; the rush flooded his system. *Let cochleas explode. Let the blood flow.*

Let history be made, but now.

JFDI: Just Fucking Do It.

Jambone was the first to be hit by the echoes of Lyz Ah's just-concocted solo, bouncing back from the far end of the arena bowl. The sound returned hollow and unnatural. He gawked. The mike slithered from his grasp to *clunk* on the stage. There was no superamplified clunk to follow.

Nazi Kurt slipped and fell on his ass in astonishment.

The sudden, total silence whooshed in like a shroud to compress the eardrums. The drop-off was vertiginous; Nicky felt as if he were fighting to respirate in a vacuum.

Hi Fi and Archie were still hammering away, grimacing, posing, busting strings, until they discovered they were putting out zero sound. It took exactly two heartbeats.

Slurpee stopped drumming. The sight was so lame it was nearly comic. Double-Ought, ditto.

The arena manager peeked out from behind the wing curtains. He stuffed his fist into his face, dropping his clipboard to the floor. It landed with a solid, flat whack that almost startled Archie into a power dump.

Every single preamp, power amp, power booster, contour amp, and PA speaker had overloaded, arcing across protective fuses to crisp the circuitry. The speaker elements and conduits were puddles of chrome plasma. Three of the techs were still writhing from severe electrical hotfoots. The tapes, running at 15 IPS, had flash-melted into useless Frisbees of plastic as the recording hookups had cooked down to slag.

Slurpee put his sticks down gingerly. Gently, quietly. In his time he had seen sound frequencies blast glass to smithereens, crack rubber, induce coma, roast lab animals. He cleared the sweat from his eyes with the back of his hand.

The arena was littered with fallen garments. Pimp boots, trashy lingerie, metalzoid jewelry, fatigues, jeans, punk shirts, yee-hah hats, dirty undies, halters, tubes, belts, lace, thongs. The empty cavern of space resembled a sloppy flea market . . . or Nicky's bedroom, he thought, as administered by his first wife.

Mixed liberally into the piles and wads of unoccupied garb were clinking pints of booze, smuggled dope, fake IDs, smuggled weapons, scratch cash, and several thousand ticket stubs. Somewhere in front was Jambone's pirate codpiece, nestled in the clothing of the person who had battled for it.

But no people.

Jambone cursed loudly and it bounced back to meet him. He gave a disgusted shrug and stomped offstage, past Nicky, lending him only a venomous glance that said, "We have another gig one day and four hundred miles from here and what the ratfuck are we gonna do about *this* baby-rapin' mess?"

Nobody spoke. Not even the arena manager.

They had all been cowed silent, afraid to make any sound, lest they vanish, pop, the end.

Nicky walked slowly out to center stage and sat down, right on the edge. His feet dangled where the bouncers in their yellow shirts—

Had been.

Okay. Item #1: You want fame, you just got it.

Item #2: Their gear had completely filled two forty-five-foot longbed trucks. Now it was all useless and ruined. Slowly, Nicky's head dipped to rest in his hands.

Item #3: Their audience had completely filled the arena . . .

The arena manager had left the premises. Presumably to locate a telephone that was not melted into gooey junk.

Nicky had coveted the covers of *Rip* and *Rolling Stone*, not *Time* and *Newsweek*. He stayed as he was, sitting on the edge of the stage, until men at last came for him.

How long? Time had stopped. Who cared?

Ladies and gentlemen, Gasm has left the arena.

"Excuse us."

Nicky looked up and saw three men in suits. The arena manager was standing out of range behind them. Tattlers always stand back when the poop is about to hit the propeller. FBI? CIA? Secret police? Death squad? Exactly how did you punish someone for something like this?

"You *are* Nicky Powers? You manage the band Gasm?"

Nicky prepared himself mentally for the cuffs. He did not answer. The lead guy seemed anxious to get the particulars correct. He spoke hesitantly.

Nicky returned the man's frank gaze. He did not read threat. He read nervous excitement.

"These gentlemen and I represent the Defense Department of the United States."

Call it intuition, but Nicky knew in a flash that Gasm would make its next concert date, no sweat. Not drop one. He smiled his very best dealmaker's smile and stood up.

• • •

The Oxford English Dictionary credits **David J. Schow** for coining the term *splatterpunk*, a type of horror fiction critic S.T. Joshi noted as "utilizing elements from popular culture (especially rock-and-roll music and slasher films) to underscore the violence and sterility of modern life." Rock musicians pop up in several of his short stories and the band Gasm from "Odeed" also makes an appearance in Schow's debut novel *The Kill Riff* (1988), a story of vengeance and madness in the world of rock and roll. A Bram Stoker Award-winner and recipient of the World Fantasy Award, his short fiction has been gathered into six collections. Some of his nonfiction was compiled for the International Horror Guild Award-winning *Wild Hairs*. In addition to *The Kill Riff*, he has authored five other novels, the most recent of which is *Internecine* (2010). Film-writing credits include *The Crow*, *The Texas Chainsaw Massacre: The Beginning*, and *The Hills Run Red*.

• • • •

Voodoo Child
Graham Masterton

I saw Jimi ducking into S.H. Patel's, the news agent on the corner of Clarendon Road, and his face was ashy gray. I said to Dulcie, "Jesus, that's Jimi," and followed him inside, shop doorbell clanging. Mr. Patel was marking up stacks of *Evening Standard*s and said, "*New Musical Express* not in yet, Charlie," but all I could do was to shake my head.

I walked cautiously along the shelves of magazines and children's sweets and humorous birthday cards. I could hear Mrs. Patel's television playing the theme tune from *Neighbours* somewhere in the back of the shop. There was a musty smell of manila envelopes and candy shrimps and fenugreek.

I came around the corner of the shelves and Jimi was standing by the freezer cabinet, looking at me wide-eyed; not sly and funny the way he always used to, but wounded almost, defensive. His hair was just the same, frizzy, and he was wearing the same sleeveless Afghan jacket and purple velvet flares—even the same Cherokee necklace. But his skin looked all white and dusty, and he really scared me.

"Jimi?" I whispered.

At first, he didn't say anything, but there was a chilliness around him and it wasn't just the freezer cabinet with its Bird's Eye peas and Findus mixed carrots and original beef burgers.

"Jimi . . . I thought you were dead, man," I told him. I hadn't called anybody "man" for more than fifteen years. "I was really, totally convinced you were dead."

He snuffed, and cleared his throat, his eyes still wounded-looking. "Hallo, Charlie," he said. He sounded hoarse and remote and blocked-up, the same way he'd sounded that last night I saw him, September 17, 1970.

I was so scared I could scarcely speak, but at the same time Jimi was so much the same that I felt weirdly reassured—like it was still 1970 and the past twenty years just hadn't happened. I could have believed that John Lennon was still alive and that Harold Wilson was still prime minister and that it was peace and love forever.

"I've been trying to get back to the flat, man," Jimi told me.

"What? What flat?"

"Monika's flat, man, in Lansdowne Crescent. I've been trying to get back."

"What the hell do you want to go back there for? Monika doesn't live there anymore. Well, not so far as I know."

Jimi rubbed his face, and ash seemed to fall between his fingers. He looked distracted, frightened, as if he couldn't think straight. But then I'd often seen him stoned out of his skull, talking weird gibberish, all about some planet or other where things were ideal, the godlike planet of Supreme Wisdom.

"Where the hell have you been?" I asked him. "Listen, Dulcie's outside. You remember Dulcie? Let's go and have a drink."

"I've got to get into that flat, man," Jimi insisted.

"What for?"

He stared at me as if I were crazy. "What for? Shit! What for, for fuck's sake."

I didn't know what to do. Here was Jimi, three feet in front of me, real, talking, even though Jimi had been dead for twenty years. I never saw the actual corpse, and I never actually went to his funeral because I couldn't afford the fare, but why would the press and his family have said that he was dead if he wasn't?

Monika had found him lying on the bed, cold, his lips purple from suffocation. The doctors at St. Mary Abbot's Hospital had confirmed that he was dead on arrival. He had suffocated from breathing vomit. He had to be dead. Yet here he was, just like the old psychedelic days, "Purple Haze" and "Voodoo Chile" and "Are You Experienced?"

The shop doorbell rang. It was Dulcie, looking for me. "Charlie?" she called. "Come on, Charlie, I'm dying for a drink."

"Why don't you come and have a drink with us?" I asked Jimi. "Maybe we can work out a way of getting you back in the flat. Maybe we can find out who the estate agent is, and talk to him. Courtney probably knows. Courtney knows everybody."

"I can't come with you, man, no way," Jimi said evasively.

"Why not? We're meeting Derek and all the rest of them down at the Bull's Head. They'd really like to see you. Hey—did you read about Mitch selling your guitar?"

"Guitar?" he asked, as if he couldn't understand me.

"Your Strat, the one you used at Woodstock. He got something like a hundred and eighty grand for it."

Jimi gave a dry, hollow sniff. "Got to get into that flat, man, that's all."

"Well, come for a drink first."

"No way, man, can't be done. I'm not supposed to see nobody. Not even you."

"Then what are you going to do?" I asked him. "Where are you staying?"

"I ain't staying nowhere, man."

"You can stay with me. I've got a house in Clarendon Road now."

Jimi shook his head. He wasn't even listening. "I've got to get into the flat, that's all. No two ways about it."

"Charlie?" protested Dulcie. "What the hell are you doing?"

I felt a cold, dusty draft, and I turned around, and the Patels' multicolored plastic curtain was swinging, but Jimi was gone. I dragged the curtain back and shouted, "Jimi!" But nobody was in the Patels' armchair-crowded sitting room except a brown, bare-bottomed baby with a runny nose and an elderly grandmother in a lime-green sari, who stared at me with eyes as hard as stones. Above the brown-tiled fireplace was a luridly colored photograph of the Bhutto family. I apologized and retreated.

"What the hell's the matter with you? I've been waiting outside for ages," Dulcie said.

"I saw Jimi," I told her.

"Jimmy who?" she demanded. She was bleached-blond, pretty, and tarty—and always intolerant. Perhaps that was why I liked her so much.

"Hendrix, Jimi Hendrix. He was here, just now."

Dulcie stopped chewing gum and stared at me with her mouth open. "Jimi Hendrix? What do you mean, Jimi Hendrix?"

"I saw him, he was here."

"What are you talking about? You're out of your fucking tree, you are!"

"Dulcie, he was here, I swear to God. I've just been talking to him. He said he had to get back into Monika's old flat. You know, the flat where he—"

"Pree-cisely," Dulcie mocked me. "The flat where he died."

"He was here, believe me. He was so damned close I could have touched him."

"You're mad," Dulcie declared. "Anyway, I'm not waiting any longer. I'm going down to the Bull's Head for a drink."

"Listen, wait," I told her. "Let's just go round to Monika's flat and see who lives there now. Maybe they know what's going on."

"I don't want to," Dulcie protested. "You're just being ridiculous. He's *dead*, Charlie. He's been dead for twenty years."

But in the end we went round to the flat and rang the doorbell. We saw the grubby net curtains twitching, but it was a long time before we heard anybody coming to the door. A cold gray wind blew round the crescent. The railings were clogged with newspaper and empty crisp bags, and the trees were scrubby and bare.

"I don't suppose they even know that Jimi Hendrix used to live here," Dulcie sniffed.

Eventually the door was opened about an inch and a woman's pale face appeared.

"Yes?"

"Oh," I said. "I'm sorry to bother you, but I know somebody who used to live here, and he was wondering if you'd mind if he sort of came back and took a look around. You know, just for old times' sake."

The woman didn't answer. I don't think she really understood what I was going on about.

"It wouldn't take long," I told her. "Just a couple of minutes. Just for old times' sake."

She closed the door without saying a word. Dulcie and I were left on the step, under a cold north London sky the color of glue.

A black woman in a shiny Marks and Spencer's raincoat pushed a huge, dilapidated pram across the street. The pram was crowded with children and shopping.

"Now what are you going to do?" asked Dulcie.

"Don't know," I told her. "Let's go and get that drink."

We drove down to the Bull's Head and sat by the window overlooking the Thames. The tide was out, so the river was little more than a dull gray ribbon in a stretch of sloping black mud.

Courtney Tulloch was there, and so were Bill Franklin, Dave Blackman, Margaret, and Jane. I suddenly realized that I'd known all of them back in 1970 when Jimi was still alive. It was a strange feeling, like being in a dream.

What had John Lennon written? "Yea though I wart through the valet of thy shadowy hut, I will feed no Norman."

I asked Courtney whether he knew who was living in Monika's old flat, but he shook his head. "All the old faces are gone now, man, long-gone. It's all changed from what it used to be. I mean, it was always rundown and seedy and all that, but everybody knew where they was, black and white, bus driver and whore. Nowadays these kids run riot. It's like the moon."

But Dave said, "I know who took that flat after Monika left. It was John Drummond."

"You mean *the* John Drummond?" I asked him. "John Drummond the guitarist?"

"That's right. But he was only there for a couple of months."

Dulcie said, "You're being really boring today, Charlie. Can I have another drink?"

I bought another round: snowball for Dulcie, Hoisten Pus for me. Courtney was telling a joke.

I hadn't realized that John Drummond had lived in the same flat as Jimi. For my money, John had been a better guitarist than Jimi—technically, anyway. He was always more single-minded, more creative. He'd been able to make his guitar talk in the same way that Jimi did, but the voice that had come out had been less confused than Jimi's, less angry, less frustrated. And he'd never played an uneven set like Jimi did at Woodstock, or a totally disastrous one like Jimi did in Seattle the last time he ever appeared at a concert in America. John Drummond had played first with Graham Bond and then with John Mayall and then his own "supergroup," the Crash.

John Drummond had reached number one both sides of the Atlantic with "Running a Fever." But then, without warning, he'd suddenly retired, amid newspaper reports of cancer or multiple sclerosis or chronic heroin addiction. That had been the last that anybody ever saw of him. That was—what?—1973, 1974, or something like that. I didn't even know if he was dead or alive.

That night in my one-bedroom flat in Holland Park Avenue, the telephone rang. It was Jimi. His voice sounded distant and powdery.

"I can't talk for long, man. I'm in a call box in Queensway."

"I went to the flat, Jimi. The woman wouldn't let me in."

"I have to get in there, Charlie. No two ways about it."

"Jimi—I found out something. John Drummond had that flat after Monica. Maybe he could help."

"John Drummond? You mean that young guy who kept hanging around wanting to play with the Experience?"

"That's right, amazing guitarist."

"He was shit. He couldn't play for shit."

"Oh, come on, Jimi. He was great. 'Running a Fever' was a classic."

There was a long silence on the other end of the phone. I could hear traffic, and Jimi breathing. Then Jimi said, "When was that?"

"When was what?"

"That song you mentioned, 'Running a Fever,' when was that?"

"I don't know. Early seventy-four, I think."

"And he was good?"

"He was amazing."

"Was he as good as me?"

"If you want the God's honest truth, yes, he was."

"Did he sound like me?"

"Yes, he did, except not many people would admit it, because he was white."

I looked down into the street. Traffic streamed endlessly past the front of my flat, on its way to Shepherds Bush. I thought of Jimi singing "Crosstown Traffic" all those years ago.

Jimi said, "Where's this Drummond guy now? Is he still playing?"

"Nobody knows where he is. He had a number-one hit with 'Fever' and then he quit. Warner Brothers couldn't even find anybody to sue."

"Charlie," urged Jimi hoarsely, "you've got to do me one favor. You've got to find this guy. Even if he's dead, and you can only find out where they buried him."

"Jimi, for Christ's sake. I wouldn't even know where to start."

"Please, Charlie. Find him for me."

He hung up. I stood by the window for a long time, feeling frightened and depressed. If Jimi didn't know that John Drummond had played so well—if he wasn't aware that John had reached number one with "Running a Fever" then where had he been for the past twenty years? Where had he been, if not dead?

I telephoned Nik Cohn and he met me in this stuffy afternoon drinking club in Mayfair. Nik had written the definitive work on pop in the sixties, *Awopbopaloopa Alopbamboom*, and he had known just about everybody, including the Beatles, Eric Burdon, Pink Floyd in their UFO days, and Jimi, of course—and John Drummond.

He hadn't seen John for yonks, but about six years ago he had received a postcard from Littlehampton on the south coast, saying nothing much except that John was trying to get his mind and his body back together again.

"He didn't exactly explain what he meant," Nik told me. "But he was always like that. You got the feeling that he was always thinking about something else. Like trying to deal with something that was going on inside him."

• • •

Littlehampton in the middle of winter was windswept and bleak. The funfair was closed, the beach huts were closed, the Red Indian canoes were all tied together in the middle of the boating pond so that nobody could reach them. Fawn sand waved in flat horses'-tails across the promenade, and old lolly wrappers danced across the tufted sea grass.

I spent hours walking around the town center looking for John Drummond, but that first afternoon I didn't see anybody between the ages of three and sixty-five. It started to rain—a cold, persistent rain—so I rang the doorbell at one of the redbrick Edwardian villas close to the seafront and booked myself a room for the night.

It wasn't much of a place to stay, but it was warm. There was also fish and chips for supper in a small dining room I shared with two traveling salesmen, an unmarried mother with a snotty, wriggling boy in soiled dungarees, and a bristly-mustached retired colonel with leather arm-patches on his jacket and a habit of clearing his throat like a fusillade of gunshots.

Not a drum was heard, not a funeral note, as his corpse to the ramparts we hurried.

Next morning it was still raining, but I walked the silvery-gray streets all the same, looking for John Drummond. I found him totally by accident, in a pub on the corner of River Road, sitting in a corner with an untouched pint of McEwan's and a half-eaten packet of salt-and-vinegar crisps. He was smoking incessantly and staring at nothing.

He was thin, so much thinner than the last time I'd seen him, and his hair was graying and wild. He looked a bit like a geriatric Pete Townshend. He was dressed in tight black trousers and a huge black leather jacket with about fifty zippers and D-rings. He wore a lapel badge with a picture of three pairs of scampering legs on it and the motif "Running Men Tour 1986."

I parked my lager next to his and dragged up a chair. He didn't even look at me.

"John?" I said, without much confidence.

His eyes flicked across at me, and narrowed.

"John, it's Charlie. Charlie Goode. Don't you remember me?"

"Charlie Goode?" he asked dully. Then, very slowly, as if recognition were penetrating his consciousness like a pebble falling into treacle, "Cha-a-arlie Goode! That's right! Char-lie Goode! How are you keeping, man? I haven't seen you since . . . when was the last time I saw you?"

"Isle of Wight."

"So it was. Isle of Wight. Fuck me."

I lifted my beer and drank some and wiped my lips with the back of my hand. "I've been looking for you since yesterday," I told him.

He sucked at the butt of his cigarette, then crushed it out. He didn't make any comment, didn't even look as if he'd heard me.

"I'm not really sure why," I said, trying to sound light-hearted about it. "The thing is, Jimi asked me."

"Jimi asked you?"

"It sounds stupid, doesn't it?" I said with a forced laugh. "But I met him in Notting Hill. He's still alive."

John took out another cigarette and lit it with a cheap plastic lighter. Now he wouldn't take his eyes off me.

I said, more seriously, "He was trying to get back into Monika's old pad. He didn't say why. The thing is, he found out that you lived there for a bit, after he—well, after he stopped being around. He said I had to find you. He said it was crucial. Don't ask me why."

John blew out smoke. "You saw Jimi, and Jimi told you to find me?"

"That's right. I know it sounds stupid."

"No, Charlie, it doesn't sound stupid."

I waited for him to say something else—to explain what was going on—but he wouldn't, or couldn't. He sat there and smoked and drank his beer and occasionally said, "Jimi asked you, fuck me." Or else he sang a snatch from one of Jimi's old songs.

In the end, though, he drained his glass and stood up and said, "Come on, Charlie. You'd better see what this is all about."

Hunched, spindly-legged, he led me through the rain. We crossed River Road and into Arun Terrace, where a long road of small Victorian artisans' cottages with slate roofs and majolica-tiled porches stood. The hedges smelled of cat pee, and wet cigarette packets were snared in the shrubbery. John pushed open the gate of number 17, "Caledonian," and opened the front door with his own key. Inside, it was gloomy and crowded with knickknacks: a miniature ship's wheel with a barometer in it, the plaster head of a grizzled Arab with a hawk on his shoulder, a huge ugly vase full of pink-dyed pampas grass.

"My room's upstairs," he said, and led the way up a flight of impossibly steep stairs, covered in red sculptured carpet. We reached the landing and he opened the door to a small bed-sitting room—a plain, cold British bedroom with a candlewick bedspread and a varnished wardrobe and a Baby Bellingcooker. The only indication that this was the home of one of the best rock guitarists since Eric Clapton was a shiny black Fender Strat with finger marks all over it.

John pulled over a ratty basketwork chair with a collapsed seat. "Make yourself at home," he told me. Then he sat down himself on the end of the bed, and took out his cigarettes again.

Cautiously, I sat down. I felt as if I were sitting down at the bottom of a dry well. I watched John light up again and testily smoke. He was growing more agitated by the minute, and I couldn't figure out why.

After a while, however, he started talking in a low, flat monotone. "Jimi was always talking about the time he used to tour with the Flames—years ago, before he got famous or anything, just after he left the Army Airborne. They played in some back-of-beyond town in Georgia somewhere, and Jimi got mixed up with this chick. I always remember what he said about her, 'foxy to the bone.' Anyway, he spent all night with her, even though he missed the tour bus, and even though this chick was married and kept telling him that her husband would beat her when she got home.

"He told her he wanted to be famous, and she said, sure, you can be famous. At about four o'clock in the morning, she took him to see this weird old woman, and this weird old woman gave him a voodoo. She said so long as he fed this voodoo, he'd be fine, and famous all over the world, and every wish he ever wished would come true. But the day he stopped feeding that voodoo, that voodoo would take back everything, and he'd be shit, that's all, just shit.

"But Jimi wanted fame more than anything else. He could play good guitar, but he wanted to play brilliant guitar. He wanted to be so fucking brilliant that nobody would even believe that he came from earth."

"So what happened?" I asked. The rain pattered against the window like handful of currants.

John blew smoke out of his nose and shrugged. "She gave him the voodoo and the rest is history. He played with the Isley Brothers, Little Richard, Curtis Knight. Then he was famous; then he was gone. Why do you think he wrote that song 'Voodoo Chile'? He was a voodoo child, that's all, and that was true."

"John, he's still alive," I insisted. "I saw him; I talked to him. I wouldn't be here otherwise."

But John shook his head. "He's gone, Charlie. Twenty years gone. When he became famous, he started to starve that voodoo, but in retaliation the voodoo made him weak, made him crazy. Jimi wanted to play for an audience, but the voodoo made him play music that was way beyond anything that an ordinary audience could understand. It was beyond anything that even great guitarists could understand. You remember Robin Trower, from Procol

Harum? He went to see Jimi in Berlin and said that he was amazing, but the audience was out of it. Robin was one of the greatest guitarists ever, but he was out of it. Jimi was playing guitar that nobody would understand for about a hundred fucking years.

"So Jimi tried to get rid of the voodoo, but in the end the voodoo got rid of him. The voodoo canceled him out, man: If you don't live with me, then you don't live at all. But you don't die, either. You're nothing—you're absolutely nothing. You're a slave, and a servant, and that's the way it's going to be forever."

"Go on," I whispered.

"There was only one thing he could do, and that was to take the voodoo back to that little town in Georgia where he first got it. That meant leaving his grave in Seattle and bumming his way back to England, finding the voodoo, and taking it back, in person, to that weird old woman and making her a gift of it. Because if the person you're giving it back to doesn't accept it as a gift, it's still yours, man. Still yours, forever."

I sat in that ridiculous chair with its collapsed bottom and I couldn't believe what I was hearing. "What are you trying to tell me? That Jimi's turned into some kind of zombie? Like the walking dead?"

John smoked and looked away, didn't even try to convince me.

"I saw him," I insisted. "I saw him, and he talked to me on the phone. Zombies don't talk to you on the phone."

"Let me tell you something, man," John told me. "Jimi was dead from the moment he accepted that voodoo. Same way I am."

"What do you mean?"

"You want me to show you?"

I swallowed. "I don't know. Maybe, yes. All right."

He stood up awkwardly. He took off his scruffy black coat and dropped it onto the bed. Then he crossed his arms and lifted up his T-shirt.

He was white-skinned and skeletal, so thin that I could see his ribs and his arteries, and his heart beating under his skin. But it was his stomach that shocked me the most. Tied tightly to his abdomen with thin ropes of braided hair was a flattish ebony figure, very African in appearance, like a small monkey. It was decorated with feathers and diseased-looking fragments of dried pelt.

Somehow, the monkey-figure had become part of John. It was impossible to tell where the figure ended and John began. His skin seemed to have grown around the ebony head and enclosed in a thin, translucent webbing the crooked ebony claws.

John let me look at it for a while; then he dropped his T-shirt and covered it.

"I found it under the floorboards in Monika's hallway. It was all wrapped up in one of Jimi's old shirts. I'm pretty sure that Monika didn't know anything about it. I knew it was dangerous and weird, but I wanted the fame, man. I wanted the money. I thought that I could handle it, just like Jimi thought that he could handle it.

"I wore it for a while, tied loose around my waist, under my shirt, and I fed it bits and pieces just like you'd feed a pet animal. In return, it kind of sang to me; it's hard to describe unless you've experienced it. It sang to me, and all I had to do was play what it sang.

"But then it wanted more. It clung tighter and tighter, and I needed it tighter because when it was tighter it sang such amazing music, and I got better and better. One morning I woke up and it had dug a hole in my skin, and kind of forced its mouth inside me. It was sore, but the music was even better. I didn't even have to listen to it anymore, it was right inside me. I didn't even have to feed it with scraps anymore, because whatever I ate, it sucked right out for itself.

"It was only when it was taking stuff direct from my stomach that I realized what was really happening. And by that time, I was playing music that nobody could relate to. By that time, I was so far out that there was no coming back."

He paused, coughed. "Jimi took it off before it went into his gut. But he couldn't play shit without it. It's a need, man. It's worse than any drug you've ever imagined in your whole life. He tried pills and booze and acid and everything, but until you've needed the voodoo, you don't know the meaning of the word 'need.'"

"So what are you going to do?" I asked him.

"Nothing. Go on living."

"Couldn't you give it back to Jimi?"

"What, and commit suicide? This thing's part of me, man. You might just as well tear out my heart."

I sat with John talking about the 1960s until it began to grow dark. We talked about Bondy at the Brighton Aquarium, John Mayall, Chris Farlowe and Zoot Money at the All-Nighter in Wardour Street, where you could get bashed in the face just for looking at somebody else's bird. We talked about sitting on Tooting Graveney Common on cold, sunny autumn afternoons listening to the Turtles on a Boots tranny. We talked about the Bo Street Runners and the Crazy World of Arthur Brown, the girls in the miniskirts and the white PVC boots. All gone, man. All vanished, like colorful, transparent ghosts. It had never occurred to us at the time that it could ever end.

But one gray evening in 1970 I had walked down Chancery Lane and seen the *Evening Standard* banner "Jimi Hendrix Dead," and they might just as well have announced that our youth had shut up shop.

I left John just after eight o'clock. His room was so dark that I couldn't see his face. The conversation ended and I left, that's all. He didn't even say good-bye.

I walked back to the boardinghouse. As I stepped through the front door, the bristly-mustached colonel held up the heavy black telephone receiver and announced harshly, "It's for you."

I thanked him, and he cleared his throat like a Bren-gun. "Charlie? It's Jimi. Did you find him?"

I hesitated. Then I said, "Yes. Yes, I did."

"He's still alive?"

"In a manner of speaking, yes."

"Where is he, man? I have to know."

"I'm not sure that I ought to tell you."

"Charlie—did we used to be friends?"

"I suppose so."

"Charlie, you have to tell me where he is. You have to."

His voice sounded so panicky that I knew I had to tell him. I heard myself saying the address like a ventriloquist. I didn't dare to think of what might happen if Jimi tried to get the voodoo back. Maybe I should have minded my own business, right from the very beginning. They always say that it's dangerous to mess around with the dead. The dead have different needs from the living, different desires. The dead are more bloody desperate than we can even guess.

I went round to John's place the next morning after breakfast. I rang the doorbell, and a fussy old woman with a brindled cat on her shoulder let me in.

"Nothing but trouble, you people," she complained, hobbling away down the hall. "Nothing but noise. Nothing but loud music. Hooligans, the lot of you."

"Sorry," I said, although I don't think she heard me.

I climbed the stairs to John's room. Outside on the landing, I hesitated. I could hear John's cassette player, and a tap running. I knocked, too softly for John to hear me. Then again, louder.

There was no answer. Only the trickling of the tap and the cassette playing "Are You Experienced?"

"John?" I called. "John, it's Charlie!"

I opened the door. I knew what had happened even before I could fully understand what I was looking at. Jimi had gotten there before me.

John's torso lay on his dark-soaked bedspread, torn wide open, so that his lungs and his stomach and his liver were spread around in brightly colored profusion, interconnected with webs of fat and torn-apart skin. His head was floating in the brimful washbasin, bobbing up and down with the flow of the water. Every now and then his right eye peeped at me accusingly over the china rim. His severed legs had been pushed bloodily beneath the bed.

The voodoo was gone.

I spent a week in Littlehampton "helping the police with their inquiries." They knew I hadn't done it, but they strongly suspected that I knew who had. What could I tell them—"Of course, officer! It was Jimi Hendrix!"? They'd have had me committed to one of those seaside mental homes in Eastbourne.

I never heard from Jimi again. I don't know how the dead travel the seas, but I know for a fact that they do. Those lonely figures standing by the rails of Icelandic-registered cargo ships, staring at the foamy wake. Those silent passengers on cross-country buses.

Maybe he persuaded the old woman to take the voodoo back. Maybe he didn't. But I've pinned the album cover of *Are You Experienced?* to my kitchen wall, and sometimes I look at it and like to think that Jimi's at peace.

• • •

Before he became editor of *Penthouse* magazine and then a best-selling author of horror novels, thrillers and historical sagas, **Graham Masterton** edited the rock music page of his local newspaper in Sussex, England, and rubbed shoulders with many of the up-and-coming rock musicians of the mid-1960s, including Jimi Hendrix. Graham's first horror novel *The Manitou* was filmed with Tony Curtis in the lead role. His latest horror epic is *The Red Hotel,* a zombie tale set in Baton Rouge. It will be followed by two major crime novels—*White Bones* and *Broken Angels*—set in Cork, Ireland, where he and his late wife Wiescka lived for four years.

• • • •

We See Things Differently
Bruce Sterling

This was the *jahiliyah*—the land of ignorance. This was America. The Great Satan, the Arsenal of Imperialism, the Bankroller of Zionism, the Bastion of Neo-Colonialism. The home of Hollywood and blonde sluts in black nylon. The land of rocket-equipped F-15s that slashed across God's sky, in godless pride. The land of nuclear-powered global navies, with cannon that fired shells as large as cars.

They have forgotten that they used to shoot us, shell us, insult us, and equip our enemies. They have no memory, the Americans, and no history. Wind sweeps through them, and the past vanishes. They are like dead leaves.

I flew into Miami, on a winter afternoon. The jet banked over a tangle of empty highways, then a large dead section of the city—a ghetto perhaps. In our final approach we passed a coal-burning power plant, reflected in the canal. For a moment I mistook it for a mosque, its tall smokestacks slender as minarets. A Mosque for the American Dynamo.

I had trouble with my cameras at customs. The customs officer was a grimy-looking American, white with hair the color of clay. He squinted at my passport. "That's an awful lot of film, Mr. Cuttab," he said.

"Qutb," I said, smiling. "Sayyid Qutb. Call me Charlie."

"Journalist, huh?" He looked unhappy. It seemed that I owed substantial import duties on my Japanese cameras, as well as my numerous rolls of Pakistani color film. He invited me into a small back office to discuss it. Money changed hands. I departed with my papers in order.

The airport was half-full: mostly prosperous Venezuelans and Cubans, with the haunted look of men pursuing sin. I caught a taxi outside, a tiny vehicle like a motorcycle wrapped in glass. The cabby, an ancient black man, stowed my luggage in the cab's trailer.

Within the cab's cramped confines, we were soon unwilling intimates. The cabbie's breath smelled of sweetened alcohol. "You Iranian?" the cabbie asked.

"Arab."

"We respect Iranians around here, we really do," the cabbie insisted.

"So do we," I said. "We fought them on the Iraqi front for years."

"Yeah?" said the cabbie uncertainly. "Seems to me I heard about that. How'd that end up?"

"The Shi'ite holy cities were ceded to Iran. The Ba'athist regime is dead, and Iraq is now part of the Arab Caliphate." My words made no impression on him, and I had known it before I spoke. This is the land of ignorance. They know nothing about us, the Americans. After all this, and they still know nothing whatsoever.

"Well, who's got more money these days?" the cabbie asked. "Y'all, or the Iranians?"

"The Iranians have heavy industry," I said. "But we Arabs tip better."

The cabbie smiled. It is very easy to buy Americans. The mention of money brightens them like a shot of drugs. It is not just the poverty; they were always like this, even when they were rich. It is the effect of spiritual emptiness. A terrible grinding emptiness in the very guts of the West, which no amount of Coca-Cola seems able to fill.

We rolled down gloomy streets toward the hotel. Miami's streetlights were subsidized by commercial enterprises. It was another way of, as they say, shrugging the burden of essential services from the exhausted backs of the taxpayers. And onto the far sturdier shoulders of peddlers of aspirin, sticky sweetened drinks, and cosmetics. Their billboards gleamed bluely under harsh lights encased in bulletproof glass. It reminded me so strongly of Soviet agitprop that I had a sudden jarring sense of displacement, as if I were being sold Lenin and Engels and Marx in the handy jumbo size.

The cabbie, wondering perhaps about his tip, offered to exchange dollars for riyals at black-market rates. I declined politely, having already done this in Cairo. The lining of my coat was stuffed with crisp Reagan one-thousand-dollar bills. I also had several hundred in pocket change, and an extensive credit line at the Islamic Bank of Jerusalem. I foresaw no difficulties.

Outside the hotel, I gave the ancient driver a pair of fifties. Another very old man, of Hispanic descent, took my bags on a trolley. I registered under the gaze of a very old woman. Like all American women, she was dressed in a way intended to provoke lust. In the young, this technique works admirably, as proved by America's unhappy history of sexually transmitted plague. In the very old, it provokes only sad disgust.

I smiled on the horrible old woman and paid in advance.

I was rewarded by a double-handful of glossy brochures promoting local casinos, strip-joints, and bars.

The room was adequate. This had once been a fine hotel. The air conditioning was quiet and both hot and cold water worked well. A wide flat screen covering most of one wall offered dozens of channels of television.

My wristwatch buzzed quietly, its programmed dial indicating the direction of Mecca. I took the rug from my luggage and spread it before the window. I cleansed my face, my hands, my feet. Then I knelt before the darkening chaos of Miami, many stories below. I assumed the eight positions, bowing carefully, sinking with gratitude into deep meditation. I forced away the stress of jet-lag, the innate tension and fear of a Believer among enemies.

Prayer completed, I changed my clothing, putting aside my dark Western business suit. I assumed denim jeans, a long-sleeved shirt, and photographer's vest. I slipped my press card, my passport, my health cards into the vest's zippered pockets, and draped the cameras around myself. I then returned to the lobby downstairs, to await the arrival of the American rock star.

He came on schedule, even slightly early. There was only a small crowd, as the rock star's organization had sought confidentiality. A train of seven monstrous busses pulled into the hotel's lot, their whale-like sides gleaming with brushed aluminum. They bore Massachusetts license plates. I walked out on to the tarmac and began photographing.

All seven busses carried the rock star's favored insignia, the thirteen-starred blue field of the early American flag. The busses pulled up with military precision, forming a wagon-train fortress across a large section of the weedy, broken tarmac. Folding doors hissed open and a swarm of road crew piled out into the circle of busses.

Men and women alike wore baggy fatigues, covered with buttoned pockets and block-shaped streaks of urban camouflage: brick red, asphalt black, and concrete gray. Dark-blue shoulder-patches showed the thirteen-starred circle. Working efficiently, without haste, they erected large satellite dishes on the roofs of two busses. The busses were soon linked together in formation, shaped barriers of woven wire securing the gaps between each nose and tail. The machines seemed to sit breathing, with the stoked-up, leviathan air of steam locomotives.

A dozen identically dressed crewmen broke from the busses and departed in a group for the hotel. Within their midst, shielded by their bodies, was the rock star, Tom Boston. The broken outlines of their camouflaged fatigues made them seem to blur into a single mass, like a herd of moving zebras. I followed them; they vanished quickly within the hotel. One crew woman tarried outside.

I approached her. She had been hauling a bulky piece of metal luggage on trolley wheels. It was a newspaper vending machine. She set it beside three other machines at the hotel's entrance. It was the Boston organization's propaganda paper, *Poor Richard's*.

I drew near. "Ah, the latest issue," I said. "May I have one?"

"It will cost five dollars," she said in painstaking English. To my surprise, I recognized her as Boston's wife. "Valya Plisetskaya," I said with pleasure, and handed her a five-dollar nickel. "My name is Sayyid; my American friends call me Charlie."

She looked about her. A small crowd already gathered at the busses, kept at a distance by the Boston crew. Others clustered under the hotel's green-and-white awning.

"Who are you with?" she said.

"*Al-Ahram*, of Cairo. An Arabic newspaper."

"You're not a political?" she said.

I shook my head in amusement at this typical show of Soviet paranoia. "Here's my press card." I showed her the tangle of Arabic. "I am here to cover Tom Boston. The Boston phenomenon."

She squinted. "Tom is big in Cairo these days? Muslims, yes? Down on rock and roll."

"We're not all ayatollahs," I said, smiling up at her. She was very tall. "Many still listen to Western pop music; they ignore the advice of their betters. They used to rock all night in Leningrad. Despite the Party. Isn't that so?"

"You know about us Russians, do you, Charlie?" She handed me my paper, watching me with cool suspicion.

"No, I can't keep up," I said. "Like Lebanon in the old days. Too many factions." I followed her through the swinging glass doors of the hotel. Valentina Plisetskaya was a broad-cheeked Slav with glacial blue eyes and hair the color of corn tassels. She was a childless woman in her thirties, starved as thin as a girl. She played saxophone in Boston's band. She was a native of Moscow, but had survived its destruction. She had been on tour with her jazz band when the Afghan Martyrs' Front detonated their nuclear bomb.

I tagged after her. I was interested in the view of another foreigner. "What do you think of the Americans these days?" I asked her.

We waited beside the elevator.

"Are you recording?" she said.

"No! I'm a print journalist. I know you don't like tapes," I said.

"We like tapes fine," she said, staring down at me. "As long as they are ours." The elevator was sluggish. "You want to know what I think, Charlie? I think Americans are fucked. Not as bad as Soviets, but fucked anyway. What do you think?"

"Oh," I said. "American gloom-and-doom is an old story. At *Al-Ahram*, we are more interested in the signs of American resurgence. That's the big angle, now. That's why I'm here."

She looked at me with remote sarcasm. "Aren't you a little afraid they will beat the shit out of you? They're not happy, the Americans. Not sweet and easy-going like before."

I wanted to ask her how sweet the CIA had been when their bomb killed half the Iranian government in 1981. Instead, I shrugged. "There's no substitute for a man on the ground. That's what my editors say." The elevator shunted open. "May I come up with you?"

"I won't stop you." We stepped in. "But they won't let you in to see Tom."

"They will if you ask them to, Mrs. Boston."

"I'm Plisetskaya," she said, fluffing her yellow hair. "See? No veil." It was the old story of the so-called "liberated" Western woman. They call the simple, modest clothing of Islam "bondage"—while they spend countless hours, and millions of dollars, painting themselves. They grow their nails like talons, cram their feet into high heels, strap their breasts and hips into spandex. All for the sake of male lust.

It baffles the imagination. Naturally I told her nothing of this, but only smiled. "I'm afraid I will be a pest," I said. "I have a room in this hotel. Some time I will see your husband. I must, my editors demand it."

The doors opened. We stepped into the hall of the fourteenth floor. Boston's entourage had taken over the entire floor. Men in fatigues and sunglasses guarded the hallway; one of them had a trained dog.

"Your paper is big, is it?" the woman said.

"Biggest in Cairo, millions of readers," I said. "We still read, in the Caliphate."

"State-controlled television," she muttered.

"Worse than corporations?" I asked. "I saw what CBS said about Tom Boston." She hesitated, and I continued to prod. "A 'Luddite fanatic,' am I right? A 'rock demagogue.' "

"Give me your room number." I did this. "I'll call," she said, striding away down the corridor. I almost expected the guards to salute her as she passed so regally, but they made no move, their eyes invisible behind the glasses. They looked old and rather tired, but with the alert relaxation of professionals.

They had the look of former Secret Service bodyguards. The city-colored fatigues were baggy enough to hide almost any amount of weaponry.

I returned to my room. I ordered Japanese food from room service, and ate it. Wine had been used in its cooking, but I am not a prude in these matters. It was now time for the day's last prayer, though my body, still attuned to Cairo, did not believe it.

My devotions were broken by a knocking at the door. I opened it. It was another of Boston's staff, a small black woman whose hair had been treated. It had a nylon sheen. It looked like the plastic hair on a child's doll. "You Charlie?"

"Yes."

"Valya says you want to see the gig. See us set up. Got you a backstage pass."

"Thank you very much." I let her clip the plastic-coated pass to my vest. She looked past me into the room, and saw my prayer rug at the window. "What you doin' in there? Prayin'?"

"Yes."

"Weird," she said. "You coming or what?"

I followed my nameless benefactor to the elevator.

Down at ground level, the crowd had swollen. Two hired security guards stood outside the glass doors, refusing admittance to anyone without a room key. The girl ducked, and plowed through the crowd with sudden headlong force, like an American football player. I struggled in her wake, the gawkers, pickpockets, and autograph hounds closing at my heels. The crowd was liberally sprinkled with the repulsive derelicts one sees so often in America: those without homes, without family, without charity.

I was surprised at the age of the people. For a rock-star's crowd, one expects dizzy teenage girls and the libidinous young street-toughs that pursue them. There were many of those, but more of another type: tired, footsore people with crow's-feet and graying hair. Men and women in their thirties and forties, with a shabby, crushed look. Unemployed, obviously, and with time on their hands to cluster around anything that resembled hope.

We walked without hurry to the fortress circle of busses. A rearguard of Boston's kept the onlookers at bay. Two of the busses were already unlinked from the others and under full steam. I followed the black woman up perforated steps and into the bowels of one of the shining machines.

She called brief greetings to the others already inside.

The air held the sharp reek of cleaning fluid. Neat elastic cords strapped down stacks of amplifiers, stencilled instrument cases, wheeled dollies of black rubber and crisp yellow pine. The thirteen-starred circle marked everything, stamped or spray-painted. A methane-burning steam generator sat at the back of the bus, next to a tall crashproof rack of high-pressure fuel tanks. We skirted the equipment and joined the others in a narrow row of second-hand airplane seats. We buckled ourselves in. I sat next to the Doll-Haired Girl.

The bus surged into motion. "It's very clean," I said to her. "I expected something a bit wilder on a rock and roll bus."

"Maybe in Egypt," she said, with the instinctive decision that Egypt was in the Dark Ages. "We don't have the luxury to screw around. Not now."

I decided not to tell her that Egypt, as a nation-state, no longer existed. "American pop culture is a very big industry."

"Biggest we have left," she said. "And if you Muslims weren't so pimpy about it, maybe we could pull down a few riyals and get out of debt."

"We buy a great deal from America," I told her. "Grain and timber and minerals."

"That's Third-World stuff. We're not your farm." She looked at the spotless floor. "Look, our industries suck, everyone knows it. So we sell entertainment. Except where there's media barriers. And even then the fucking video pirates rip us off."

"We see things differently," I said. "America ruled the global media for decades. To us, it's cultural imperialism. We have many talented musicians in the Arab world. Have you ever heard them?"

"Can't afford it," she said crisply. "We spent all our money saving the Persian Gulf from commies."

"The Global Threat of Red Totalitarianism," said the heavyset man in the seat next to Doll-Hair. The others laughed grimly.

"Oh," I said. "Actually, it was Zionism that concerned us. When there was a Zionism."

"I can't believe the hate shit I see about America," said the heavy man. "You know how much money we gave away to people, just gave away, for nothing? Billions and billions. Peace Corps, development aid . . . for decades. Any disaster anywhere, and we fell all over ourselves to give food, medicine . . . Then the Russians go down and the whole world turns against us like we were monsters."

"Moscow," said another crewman, shaking his shaggy head.

"You know, there are still motherfuckers who think we Americans killed Moscow. They think we gave a Bomb to those Afghani terrorists."

"It had to come from somewhere," I said.

"No, man. We wouldn't do that to them. No, man, things were going great between us. Rock for Detente—I was at that gig."

We drove to Miami's Memorial Colosseum. It was an ambitious structure, left half-completed when the American banking system collapsed.

We entered double-doors at the back, wheeling the equipment along dusty corridors. The Colosseum's interior was skeletal; inside it was clammy and cavernous. A stage, a concrete floor. Bare steel arched high overhead, with crudely bracket-mounted stage-lights. Large sections of that bizarre American parody of grass, "Astroturf," had been dragged before the stage. The itchy green fur, still lined with yard-marks from some forgotten stadium, was almost indestructible. At second-hand rates, it was much cheaper than carpeting.

The crew worked with smooth precision, setting up amplifiers, spindly mike-stands, a huge high-tech drum kit with the clustered, shiny look of an oil refinery. Others checked lighting, flicking blue and yellow spots across the stage. At the public entrances, two crewmen from a second bus erected metal detectors for illicit cameras, recorders, or handguns. Especially handguns. Two attempts had already been made on Boston's life, one at the Chicago Freedom Festival, when Chicago's Mayor was wounded at Boston's side.

For a moment, to understand it, I mounted the empty stage and stood before Boston's microphone. I imagined the crowd before me, ten thousand souls, twenty thousand eyes. Under that attention, I realized, every motion was amplified. To move my arm would be like moving ten thousand arms, my every word like the voice of thousands. I felt like a Nasser, a Qadaffi, a Saddam Hussein.

This was the nature of secular power. Industrial power. It was the West that invented it, that invented Hitler, the gutter orator turned trampler of nations, that invented Stalin, the man they called "Genghis Khan with a telephone." The media pop star, the politician. Was there any difference any more? Not in America; it was all a question of seizing eyes, of seizing attention. Attention is wealth, in an age of mass media. Center stage is more important than armies.

The last unearthly moans and squeals of sound-check faded. The Miami crowd began to filter into the Colosseum. They looked livelier than the desperate searchers that had pursued Boston to his hotel. America was still a wealthy country, by most standards; the professional classes had kept much of their prosperity. There were those legions of lawyers, for instance, that secular priesthood that had done so much to drain America's once-vaunted enterprise. And their associated legions of state bureaucrats. They were instantly recognizable; the cut of their suits, the telltale pocket telephones proclaiming their status.

What were they looking for here? Had they never read Boston's propaganda paper, with its bitter condemnation of everything they stood for? With its fierce attacks on the "legislative-litigative complex," its demands for sweeping reforms?

Was it possible that they failed to take him seriously?

I joined the crowd, mingling, listening to conversations. At the doors, Boston cadres were cutting ticket prices for those who showed voter registrations. Those who showed unemployment cards got in for even less.

The prosperous Americans stood in little knots of besieged gentility, frightened of the others, yet curious, smiling. There was a liveliness in the destitute: brighter clothing, knotted kerchiefs at the elbows, cheap Korean boots of iridescent cloth. Many wore tricornered hats, some with a cockade of red, white, and blue, or the circle of thirteen stars.

This was rock and roll, I realized; that was the secret. They had all grown up on it, these Americans, even the richer ones. To them, the sixty-year tradition of rock music seemed as ancient as the Pyramids. It had become a Jerusalem, a Mecca of American tribes.

The crowd milled, waiting, and Boston let them wait. At the back of the crowd, Boston crewmen did a brisk business in starred souvenir shirts, programs, and tapes. Heat and tension mounted, and people began to sweat. The stage remained dark.

I bought the souvenir items and studied them. They talked about cheap computers, a phone company owned by its workers, a free database, neighborhood co-ops that could buy unmilled grain by the ton. ATTENTION MIAMI, read one brochure in letters of dripping red. It named the ten largest global corporations and meticulously listed every subsidiary doing business in Miami, with its address, its phone number, the percentage of income shipped to banks in Europe and Japan. Each list went on for pages. Nothing else. To Boston's audience, nothing else was necessary.

The house lights darkened. A frightening animal roar rose from the crowd. A single spot lit Tom Boston, stencilling him against darkness.

"My fellow Americans," he said. A funereal hush followed. The crowd strained for each word. Boston smirked. "My f-f-f-f-fellow Americans." It was a clever microphone, digitized, a small synthesizer in itself. "My fellow Am-am-am-am-AMM!" The words vanished in a sudden soaring wail of feedback. "My Am! My fellows! My Am! My fellows! Miami, Miami, Miami, MIAMI!" The sound of Boston's voice, suddenly leaping out of all human context, becoming something shattering, superhuman—the effect was bone-chilling. It passed all barriers; it seeped directly into the skin, the blood.

"Tom Jefferson Died Broke!" he shouted. It was the title of his first song. Stage lights flashed up and hell broke its gates. Was it a "song" at all, this strange, volcanic creation? There was a melody loose in it somewhere, pursued by Plisetskaya's saxophone, but the sheer volume and impact hurled it through the audience like a sheet of flame. I had never before heard anything so loud. What Cairo's renegade set called rock and roll paled to nothing beside this invisible hurricane.

At first it seemed raw noise. But that was only a kind of flooring, a merciless grinding foundation below the rising architectures of sound. Technology did it: a piercing, soaring, digitized, utter clarity, of perfect cybernetic acoustics adjusting for each echo, a hundred times a second.

Boston played a glass harmonica: an instrument invented by the early American genius Benjamin Franklin. The harmonica was made of carefully tuned glass disks, rotating on a spindle, and played by streaking a wet fingertip across each moving edge.

It was the sound of pure crystal, seemingly sourceless, of tooth-aching purity.

The famous Western musician, Wolfgang Mozart, had composed for the Franklin harmonica in the days of its novelty. But legend said that its players went mad, their nerves shredded by its clarity of sound. It was a legend Boston was careful to exploit. He played the machine sparingly, with the air of a magician, of a Solomon unbottling demons. I was glad of his spare use, for its sound was so beautiful that it stung the brain.

Boston threw aside his hat. Long coiled hair spilled free. Boston was what Americans called "black"; at least he was often referred to as black, though no one seemed certain. He was no darker than myself. The beat rose up, a strong animal heaving. Boston stalked across the stage as if on springs, clutching his microphone. He began to sing.

The song concerned Thomas Jefferson, a famous American president of the eighteenth century. Jefferson was a political theorist who wrote revolutionary manifestos and favored a decentralist mode of government. The song, however, dealt with the relations of Jefferson and a black concubine in his household. He had several children by this woman, who were a source of great shame, due to the odd legal code of the period. Legally, they were his slaves, and it was only at the end of his life, when he was in great poverty, that Jefferson set them free.

It was a story whose pathos makes little sense to a Muslim. But Boston's audience, knowing themselves Jefferson's children, took it to heart.

The heat became stifling, as massed bodies swayed in rhythm. The next song began in a torrent of punishing noise. Frantic hysteria seized the crowd; their bodies spasmed with each beat, the shaman Boston seeming to scourge them. It was a fearsome song, called "The Whites of Their Eyes," after an American war-cry. He sang of a tactic of battle: to wait until the enemy comes close enough so that you can meet his eyes, frighten him with your conviction, and then shoot him point blank. The chorus harked again and again to the "Cowards of the long kill," a Boston slogan condemning those whose abstract power structures let them murder without ever seeing pain.

Three more songs followed, one of them slower, the others battering the audience like iron rods. Boston stalked like a madman, his clothing dark with sweat. My heart spasmed as heavy bass notes, filled with dark murderous power, surged through my ribs. I moved away from the heat to the fringe of the crowd, feeling light-headed and sick.

I had not expected this. I had expected a political spokesman, but instead it seemed I was assaulted by the very Voice of the West. The Voice of a society drunk with raw power, maddened by the grinding roar of machines. It filled me with terrified awe.

To think that once, the West had held us in its armored hands. It had treated Islam like a natural resource, its invincible armies plowing through the lands of the Faithful like bulldozers. The West had chopped our world up into colonies, and smiled upon us with its awful schizophrenic perfidy. It told us to separate God and State, to separate Mind and Body, to separate Reason and Faith. It had torn us apart.

I stood shaking as the first set ended. The band vanished backstage, and a single figure approached the microphone. I recognized him as a famous American television comedian, who had abandoned his own career to join Boston.

The man began to joke and clown, his antics seeming to soothe the crowd, which hooted with laughter. This intermission was a wise move on Boston's part, I thought. The level of pain, of intensity, had become unbearable.

It struck me then how much Boston was like the great Khomeini. Boston too had the persona of the Man of Sorrows, the sufferer after justice, the ascetic among corruption, the battler against odds. And the air of the mystic, the adept, at least as far as such a thing was possible in America. I thought of this, and deep fear struck me once again.

I walked through the gates to the Colosseum's outer hall, seeking air and room to think. Others had come out too. They leaned against the wall, men and women, with the look of wrung-out mops. Some smoked cigarettes, others argued over brochures, others simply sat with palsied grins.

Still others wept. These disturbed me most, for these were the ones whose souls seemed stung and opened. Khomeini made men weep like that, tearing aside despair like a bandage from a burn. I walked down the hall, watching them, making mental notes.

I stopped by a woman in dark glasses and a trim business suit. She leaned against the wall, shaking, her face beneath the glasses slick with silent tears. Something about the precision of her styled hair, her cheekbones, struck a memory. I stood beside her, waiting, and recognition came.

"Hello," I said. "We have something in common, I think. You've been covering the Boston tour. For CBS."

She glanced at me once, and away. "I don't know you."

"You're Marjory Cale, the correspondent."

She drew in a breath. "You're mistaken."

" 'Luddite fanatic,' " I said lightly. " 'Rock demagogue.' "

"Go away," she said.

"Why not talk about it? I'd like to know your point of view."

"Go away, you nasty little man."

I returned to the crowd inside. The comedian was now reading at length from the American Bill of Rights, his voice thick with sarcasm. "Freedom of advertising," he said. "Freedom of global network television conglomerates. Right to a speedy and public trial, to be repeated until our lawyers win. A well-regulated militia being necessary, citizens will be issued orbital lasers and aircraft carriers." No one was laughing.

The crowd was in an ugly mood when Boston reappeared. Even the well-dressed ones now seemed surly and militant, not recognizing themselves as the enemy. Like the Shah's soldiers who at last refused to fire, who threw themselves sobbing at Khomeini's feet.

"You all know this one," Boston said. With his wife, he raised a banner, one of the first flags of the American Revolution. It bore a coiled snake, a native American viper, with the legend: DON'T TREAD ON ME. A sinister, scaly rattling poured from the depths of a synthesizer, merging with the crowd's roar of recognition, and a sprung, loping rhythm broke loose. Boston edged back and forth at the stage's rim, his eyes fixed, his long neck swaying. He shook himself like a man saved from drowning and leaned into the microphone.

"We know you own us/You step upon us/We feel the onus/But here's a bonus/Today I see/So enemy/Don't tread on me/Don't tread on me . . . "

Simple words, fitting each beat with all the harsh precision of the English language. A chant of raw hostility. The crowd took it up. This was the hatred, the humiliation of a society brought low. Americans. Somewhere within them conviction still burned. The conviction they had always had: that they were the only real people on our planet. The chosen ones, the Light of the World, the Last Best Hope of Mankind, the Free and the Brave, the crown of creation. They would have killed for him. I knew, someday, they would.

I was called to Boston's suite at two o'clock that morning. I had shaved and showered, dashed on the hotel's complimentary cologne. I wanted to smell like an American.

Boston's guards frisked me, carefully and thoroughly, outside the elevator. I submitted with good grace.

Boston's suite was crowded. It had the air of an election victory. There were many politicians, sipping glasses of bubbling alcohol, laughing, shaking hands. Miami's Mayor was there, with half his City Council.

I recognized a young woman Senator, speaking urgently into her pocket phone, her large freckled breasts on display in an evening gown.

I mingled, listening. Men spoke of Boston's ability to raise funds, of the growing importance of his endorsement. More of Boston's guards stood in corners, arms folded, eyes hidden, their faces stony. A black man distributed lapel buttons with the face of Martin Luther King on a background of red and white stripes. The wall-sized television played a tape of the first Moon Landing. The sound had been turned off, and people all over the world, in the garb of the 1960s, mouthed silently at the camera, their eyes shining.

It was not until four o'clock that I finally met the star himself. The party had broken up by then, the politicians politely ushered out, their vows of undying loyalty met with discreet smiles. Boston was in a back bedroom with his wife, and a pair of aides.

"Sayyid," he said, and shook my hand. In person he seemed smaller, older, his hybrid face, with stage makeup, beginning to peel.

"Dr. Boston," I said.

He laughed freely. "Sayyid, my friend. You'll ruin my street fucking credibility."

"I want to tell the story as I see it," I said.

"Then you'll have to tell it to me," he said, and turned briefly to an aide. He dictated in a low, staccato voice, not losing his place in our conversation, simply loosing a burst of thought. " 'Let us be frank. Before I showed an interest you were ready to sell the ship for scrap iron. This is not an era for supertankers. They are dead tech, smokestack-era garbage. Reconsider my offer.'" The secretary pounded keys. Boston looked at me again, returning the searchlight of his attention.

"You plan to buy a supertanker?" I said.

"I wanted an aircraft carrier," he said, smiling. "They're all in mothballs, but the Feds frown on selling nuke power plants to private citizens."

"We will make the tanker into a floating stadium," Plisetskaya put in. She sat slumped in a padded chair, wearing satin lounge pajamas. A half-filled ashtray on the chair's arm reeked of strong tobacco.

"Ever been inside a tanker?" Boston said. "Huge. Great acoustics." He sat suddenly on the sprawling bed and pulled off his snakeskin boots. "So, Sayyid. Tell me this story of yours."

"You graduated magna cum laude from Rutgers with a doctorate in political science," I said. "In five years."

"That doesn't count," Boston said, yawning behind his hand. "That was before rock and roll beat my brains out."

"You ran for state office in Massachusetts," I said. "You lost a close race. Two years later you were touring with your first band—Swamp Fox. You were an immediate success. You became involved in political fund-raising, recruiting your friends in the music industry. You started your own record label. You helped organize Rock for Detente, where you met your wife-to-be. Your romance was front-page news on both continents. Record sales soared."

"You left out the first time I got shot at," Boston said. "That's more interesting; Val and I are old hat by now."

He paused, then burst out at the second secretary. "'I urge you once again not to go public. You will find yourselves vulnerable to a leveraged buyout. I've told you that Evans is an agent of Marubeni. If he brings your precious plant down around your ears, don't come crying to me.'"

"February 1998," I said. "An anti-communist zealot fired on your bus."

"You're a big fan, Sayyid."

"Why are you afraid of multinationals?" I said. "That was the American preference, wasn't it? Global trade, global economics?"

"We screwed up," Boston said. "Things got out of hand."

"Out of American hands, you mean?"

"We used our companies as tools for development," Boston said, with the patience of a man instructing a child. "But then our lovely friends in South America refused to pay their debts. And our staunch allies in Europe and Japan signed the Geneva Economic Agreement and decided to crash the dollar. And our friends in the Arab countries decided not to be countries any more, but one almighty Caliphate, and, just for good measure, they pulled all their oil money out of our banks and into Islamic ones. How could we compete? They were holy banks, and our banks pay interest, which is a sin, I understand." He paused, his eyes glittering, and fluffed curls from his neck. "And all that time, we were already in hock to our fucking ears to pay for being the world's policeman."

"So the world betrayed your country," I said. "Why?"

He shook his head. "Isn't it obvious? Who needs St. George when the dragon is dead? Some Afghani fanatics scraped together enough plutonium for a Big One, and they blew the dragon's fucking head off. And the rest of the body is still convulsing, ten years later. We bled ourselves white competing against Russia, which was stupid, but we'd won. With two giants, the world trembles. One giant, and the midgets can drag it down. So that's what happened. They took us out, that's all. They own us."

"It sounds very simple," I said.

He showed annoyance for the first time. "Valya says you've read our newspapers. I'm not telling you anything new. Should I lie about it? Look at the figures, for Christ's sake. The EEC and Japanese use their companies for money pumps; they're sucking us dry, deliberately. You don't look stupid, Sayyid. You know very well what's happening to us, anyone in the Third World does."

"You mentioned Christ," I said. "You believe in Him?"

Boston rocked back onto his elbows and grinned. "Do you?"

"Of course. He is one of our Prophets. We call Him Isa."

Boston looked cautious. "I never stand between a man and his God." He paused. "We have a lot of respect for the Arabs, truly. What they've accomplished. Breaking free from the world economic system, returning to authentic local tradition . . . You see the parallels."

"Yes," I said. I smiled sleepily, and covered my mouth as I yawned. "Jet lag. Your pardon, please. These are only questions my editors would want me to ask. If I were not an admirer, a fan as you say, I would not have this assignment."

He smiled and looked at his wife. Plisetskaya lit another cigarette and leaned back, looking skeptical. Boston grinned. "So the sparring's over, Charlie?"

"I have every record you've made," I said. "This is not a job for hatchets." I paused, weighing my words. "I still believe that our Caliph is a great man. I support the Islamic Resurgence. I am Muslim. But I think, like many others, that we have gone a bit too far in closing every window to the West. Rock and roll is a Third World music at heart. Don't you agree?"

"Sure," Boston said, closing his eyes. "Do you know the first words spoken in independent Zimbabwe? Right after they ran up the flag."

"No."

He spoke out blindly, savoring the words. "Ladies and gentlemen. Bob Marley. And the Wailers."

"You admire him."

"Comes with the territory," said Boston, flipping a coil of hair.

"He had a black mother, a white father. And you?"

"Oh, both my parents were shameless mongrels like myself," Boston said. "I'm a second-generation nothing-in-particular. An American." He sat up, knotting his hands, looking tired. "You going to stay with the tour a while, Charlie?" He spoke to a secretary. "Get me a Kleenex." The woman rose.

"Till Philadelphia," I said. "Like Marjory Cale."

Plisetskaya blew smoke, frowning. "You spoke to that woman?"

"Of course. About the concert."

"What did the bitch say?" Boston asked lazily. His aide handed him tissues and cold cream. Boston dabbed the Kleenex and smeared make-up from his face.

"She asked me what I thought. I said it was too loud," I said.

Plisetskaya laughed once, sharply. I smiled. "It was quite amusing. She said that you were in good form. She said that I should not be so tight-arsed."

"'Tight-arsed'?" Boston said, raising his brows. Fine wrinkles had appeared beneath the greasepaint. "She said that?"

"She said we Muslims were afraid of modern life. Of new experience. Of course I told her that this wasn't true. Then she gave me this." I reached into one of the pockets of my vest and pulled a flat packet of aluminum foil.

"Marjory Cale gave you cocaine?" Boston asked.

"Wyoming Flake," I said. "She said she has friends who grow it in the Rocky Mountains." I opened the packet, exposing a little mound of white powder. "I saw her use some. I think it will help my jet lag." I pulled my chair closer to the bedside phone-table. I shook the packet out, with much care, upon the shining mahogany surface. The tiny crystals glittered. It was finely chopped.

I opened my wallet and removed a crisp thousand-dollar bill. The actor-president smiled benignly. "Would this be appropriate?"

"Tom does not do drugs," said Plisetskaya, too quickly.

"Ever do coke before?" Boston asked. He threw a wadded tissue to the floor.

"I hope I'm not offending you," I said. "This is Miami, isn't it? This is America." I began rolling the bill, clumsily.

"We are not impressed," said Plisetskaya sternly. She ground out her cigarette. "You are being a rube, Charlie. A hick from the NIC's."

"There is a lot of it," I said, allowing doubt to creep into my voice. I reached in my pocket, then divided the pile in half with the sharp edge of a developed slide. I arranged the lines neatly. They were several centimeters long.

I sat back in the chair. "You think it's a bad idea? I admit, this is new to me." I paused. "I have drunk wine several times, though the Koran forbids it."

One of the secretaries laughed. "Sorry," she said. "He drinks wine. That's cute."

I sat and watched temptation dig into Boston. Plisetskaya shook her head.

"Cale's cocaine," Boston mused. "Man."

We watched the lines together for several seconds, he and I. "I did not mean to be trouble," I said. "I can throw it away."

"Never mind Val," Boston said. "Russians chain-smoke." He slid across the bed.

I bent quickly and sniffed. I leaned back, touching my nose. The cocaine quickly numbed it. I handed the paper tube to Boston. It was done in a moment. We sat back, our eyes watering.

"Oh," I said, drug seeping through tissue. "Oh, this is excellent."

"It's good toot," Boston agreed. "Looks like you get an extended interview."

We talked through the rest of the night, he and I.

My story is almost over. From where I sit to write this, I can hear the sound of Boston's music, pouring from the crude speakers of a tape pirate in the bazaar. There is no doubt in my mind that Boston is a great man.

I accompanied the tour to Philadelphia. I spoke to Boston several times during the tour, though never again with the first fine rapport of the drug. We parted as friends, and I spoke well of him in my article for *Al-Ahram*. I did not hide what he was; I did not hide his threat. But I did not malign him. We see things differently. But he is a man, a child of God like all of us.

His music even saw a brief flurry of popularity in Cairo, after the article. Children listen to it, and then turn to other things, as children will. They like the sound, they dance, but the words mean nothing to them. The thoughts, the feelings, are alien.

This is the *dar-al-harb*, the land of peace. We have peeled the hands of the West from our throat; we draw breath again, under God's sky. Our Caliph is a good man, and I am proud to serve him. He reigns, he does not rule. Learned men debate in the *Majlis*, not squabbling like politicians, but seeking truth in dignity. We have the world's respect.

We have earned it, for we paid the martyr's price. We Muslims are one in five in all the world, and as long as ignorance of God persists, there will always be the struggle, the *jihad*. It is a proud thing to be one of the Caliph's *Mujihadeen*. It is not that we value our lives lightly. But that we value God more.

Some call us backward, reactionary. I laughed at that when I carried the powder. It had the subtlest of poisons: a living virus. It is a tiny thing, bred in secret labs, and in itself does no harm. But it spreads throughout the body, and it bleeds out a chemical, a faint but potent trace that carries the rot of cancer.

The West can do much with cancer these days, and a wealthy man like Boston can buy much treatment. They may cure the first attack, or the second. But within five years he will surely be dead. People will mourn his loss. Perhaps they will put his image on a stamp, as they did for Bob Marley. Marley, who also died of systemic cancer; whether by the hand of God or man, only Allah knows.

I have taken the life of a great man; in trapping him I took my own life as well, but that means nothing. I am no one. I am not even Sayyid Qutb, the Martyr and theorist of Resurgence, though I took that great man's name as cover. I meant only respect, and believe I have not shamed his memory.

I do not plan to wait for the disease. The struggle continues in the Muslim lands of what was once the Soviet Union. There the Believers ride in Holy Jihad, freeing their ancient lands from the talons of Marxist atheism. Secretly, we send them carbines, rockets, mortars, and nameless men. I shall be one of them; when I meet death, my grave will be nameless also. But nothing is nameless to God.

God is Great; men are mortal, and err. If I have done wrong, let the Judge of Men decide. Before His Will, as always, I submit.

• • •

Bruce Sterling is a science fiction novelist and technology blogger who unites his time between Austin, Turin, and Belgrade. His most recent book is a short story collection, *Gothic High-Tech*. As far as Sterling's rock-lit, his early novel *The Artificial Kid* references the world of rock and roll, and his excellent short story "Dori Bangs" posits an alternate history in which rock critic Lester Bangs and underground comix writer/artist Dori Seda fall in love.

• • • •

At Budokan
Alastair Reynolds

I'm somewhere over the Sea of Okhotsk when the nightmare hits again. It's five years ago and I'm on the run after the machines went berserk. Only this time they're not just enacting wanton, random mayhem, following the scrambled choreography of a corrupted performance program. This time they're coming after me, all four of them, stomping their way down an ever-narrowing back alley as I try to get away, the machines too big to fit in that alley, but in the malleable logic of dreams somehow not too big, swinging axes and sticks rather than demolition balls, massive, indestructible guitars and drumsticks. I reach the end of the alley and start climbing up a metal ladder, a ladder that morphs into a steep metal staircase, but my limbs feel like they're moving through sludge. Then one of them has me, plucking me off the staircase with steel fingers big enough to bend girders, and I'm lifted through the air and turned around, crushed but somehow not crushed, until I'm face to face with James Hetfield out of Metallica.

"You let us down, Fox," James says, his voice a vast seismic rumble, animatronic face wide enough to headbutt a skyscraper into rubble. "You let us down, you let the fans down, and most of all you let yourself down. Hope you feel ashamed of yourself, buddy."

"I didn't mean . . . " I plead, pityingly, because I don't want to be crushed to death by a massive robot version of James Hetfield.

"Buddy." He starts shaking me, holding me in his metal fist like a limp rag doll.

"I'm sorry, man. This wasn't how it was meant . . . "

"Buddy."

But it's not James Hetfield shaking me to death. It's Jake, my partner in Morbid Management. He's standing over my seat, JD bottle in one hand, shaking me awake with the other. Looking down at the pathetic, whimpering spectacle before him.

"Having it again, right?"

"You figured."

"Buddy, it's time to let go. You fucked up big time. But no one died and no one wants to kill you about it now. Here." And he passes me the bottle, letting me take a swig of JD to settle my nerves. Doesn't help that I don't like flying much. The flashbacks usually happen in the Antonov, when there's nowhere else to run.

"Where are we?" I ask groggily.

"About three hours out."

I perk up. "From landing?"

"From departure. Got another eight, nine in the air, depending on head-winds."

I hand him back the bottle. "And you woke me up for that?"

"Couldn't stand to see you suffering like that. Who was it this time? Lars?"

"James."

Jake gives this a moment's consideration. "Figures. James is probably not the one you want to piss off. Even now."

"Thanks."

"You need to chill. I was talking to them last week." Jake gave me a friendly punch on the shoulder. "They're cool with you, buddy. Bygones be bygones. They were even talking about getting some comp seats for the next stateside show, provided we can arrange wheelchair access. Guys are keen to meet Derek. But then who isn't?"

I think back to the previous evening's show. The last night of a month-long residency at Tokyo's Budokan. Rock history. And we pulled it off. Derek and the band packed every seat in the venue, for four straight weeks. We could have stayed on another month if we didn't have bookings lined up in Europe and America.

"I guess it's working out after all," I say.

"You sound surprised."

"I had my doubts. From a musical standpoint? You had me convinced from the moment I met Derek. But turning this into a show? The logistics, the sponsorship, the legal angles? Keeping the rights activists off our back? Actually making this thing turn a profit? That I wasn't so certain about."

"Reason I had to have you onboard again, buddy. You're the numbers man, the guy with the eye for detail. And you came through."

"I guess." I stir in my seat, feeling the need to stretch my legs. "You—um—checked on Derek since the show?"

Jake shoots me a too-quick nod. "Derek's fine. Hit all his marks tonight."

Something's off, and I'm not sure what. It's been like this since we boarded the Antonov. As if something's bugging Jake and he won't come out with whatever it was.

"Killer show, by all accounts," I say.

"Best of all the whole residency. Everything went like clockwork. The lights, the back projection . . . "

"Not just the technical side. One of the roadies reckoned 'Extinction Event' was amazing."

Jake nods enthusiastically. "As amazing as it ever is."

"No, he meant exceptionally amazing. As in, above and beyond the performance at any previous show."

Jake's face tightens at the corners. "I heard it too, buddy. It was fine. On the nail. The way we like it."

"I got the impression it was something more than . . . " But I trail off, and I'm not sure why. "You sure there's nothing we need to talk about?"

"Nothing at all."

"Fine." I give an easy smile, but there's still something unresolved, something in the air between us. "Then I guess I'll go see how the big guy's doing."

"You do that, buddy."

I unbuckle from the seat and walk along the drumming, droning length of the Antonov's fuselage. It's an AN-225, the largest plane ever made, built fifty years ago for the Soviet space program. There are only two of them in the world, and Morbid Management and Gladius Biomech have joint ownership of both. Putting Derek's show together is so logistically complex that we need to be assembling one stage set when the other's still in use. The Antonovs leapfrog the globe, crammed to the gills with scaffolding, lighting rigs, speaker stacks, instruments, screens, the whole five hundred ton spectacle of a modern rock show. Even Derek's cage is only a tiny part of the whole cargo.

I make my way past two guitar techs and a roadie deep into a card game, negotiate a long passage between two shipping containers, and pass the fold-down desk where Jake has his laptop set up, reviewing the concert footage, and just beyond the desk lies the cage. It's lashed down against turbulence, scuffed and scratched from where it was loaded aboard. We touch up the yellow paint before each show so it all looks gleaming and new. I brush a hand against the tubular steel framing.

Strange to think how alarmed and impressed I was the first time, when Jake threw the switch. It's not the same now. I know Derek a lot better than

I did then, and I realize that a lot of his act is, well, just that. Act. He's a pussycat, really. A born showman. He knows more about image and timing than almost any rock star I've ever worked with.

Derek's finishing off his dinner. Always has a good appetite after a show, and at least it's not lines of coke and underage hookers he has a taste for.

He registers my presence and fixes me with those vicious yellow eyes.

Rumbles a query, as if to say, *can I help you?*

"Just stopping by, friend. I heard you went down a storm tonight. Melted some faces with "Extinction Event." Bitching "Rise of the Mammals," too. We'll be shifting so many downloads we may even have to start charging to cover our overheads."

Derek offers a ruminative gurgle, as if this is an angle he's never considered before.

"Just felt I ought to." And I rap a knuckle against the cage. "You know, give credit. Where it's due."

Derek looks at me for a few more seconds, then goes back to his dinner.

You can't say I don't try.

I'd been flying when Jake got back in touch. It was five years ago, just after the real-life events of my dream. I was grogged out from departure lounge vodka slammers, hoping to stay unconscious until the scramjet was wheels down and I was at least one continent away from the chaos in LA. Wasn't to be, though. The in-flight attendant insisted on waking me up and forcing me to make a choice between two meal serving options: chicken that tasted like mammoth, or mammoth that tasted like chicken.

What was it going to be?

"Give me the furry elephant," I told him. "And another vodka."

"Ice and water with that, sir?"

"Just the vodka."

The mammoth really wasn't that bad—certainly no worse than the chicken would have been—and I was doing my best to enjoy it when the incoming call icon popped into my upper right visual field. For a moment I considered ignoring it completely. What could it be about, other than the mess I'd left behind after the robots went berserk? But I guess it was my fatal weakness that I'd never been able to *not* take a call. I put down the cutlery and pressed a finger against the hinge of my jaw. I kept my voice low, subvocalizing. Had to be my lawyer. Assuming I still *had* a lawyer.

"Okay, lay it on me. Who's trying to sue me, how much are we looking at, and what am I going to have to do to get them off my case?"

"Fox?"

"Who else. You found me on this flight, didn't you?"

"It's Jake, man. I learned about your recent difficulties."

For a moment the vodka took the edge off my surprise. "You and the rest of the world."

Jake sounded pained. "At least make a effort to sound like you're glad to hear from me, buddy. It's been a while."

"Sorry, Jake. It's just not been the best few days of my life, you understand?"

"Rock and roll, my friend. Gotta roll with it, take the rough with the smooth. Isn't that what we always said?"

"I don't know. Did we?" Irritation boiled up inside me. "I mean, from where I'm sitting, it's not like we ever had much in common."

"Cutting, buddy. Cutting. And here I am calling you out of the blue with a business proposition. A proposition that might just dig you out of the hole you now find yourself in."

"What kind of proposition?"

"It's time to reactivate Morbid Management."

I let that sink in before responding, my mind scouting ahead through the possibilities. Morbid Management was defunct, and for good reason. We'd exhausted the possibilities of working together. Worse than that, our parting had left me with a very sour opinion of Jake Addison. Jake had always been the tail wagging that particular dog, and I'd always been prepared to go along with his notions. But he hadn't been prepared to put his faith in me when I had the one brilliant idea of my career.

We'd started off signing conventional rock acts. Mostly they were manufactured, put together with an eye on image and merchandising. But the problem with conventional rock acts is that they start having ideas of their own. Thinking they know best. Get ideas in their head about creative independence, artistic credibility, solo careers. One by one we'd watched our money-spinners fly apart in a whirlwind of ego and ambition. We figured there had to be something better.

So we'd created it. Ghoul Group was the world's first all-dead rock act. Of course you've heard of them: who hasn't? You've probably even heard that we dug up the bodies at night, that we sucked the brains out of a failing mid-level pop act, or that they were zombies controlled by Haitian voodoo. Completely untrue, needless to say. It was all legal, all signed off and boilerplated. We kept the bodies alive using simple brain-stem implants, and we used the same technology to operate Ghoul Group on stage. Admittedly there was something Frankensteinesque about the boys and girls on stage—the dead look in their eyes, the scars and surgical stitches added for effect, the lifeless, parodic shuffle that passed for walking—but that was sort of the point.

Kids couldn't get enough of them. Merchandising went through the roof, and turned Morbid Management into a billion dollar enterprise.

Only trouble was it couldn't last. Rock promotion sucked money away as fast as it brought it in, and the only way to stay ahead of the curve was to keep manufacturing new acts. The fatal weakness of Ghoul Group was that the concept was easily imitated: anyone with access to a morgue and a good lawyer could get in on the act. We realized we had to move on.

That was when we got into robotics.

Jake and I had both been in metal acts before turning to management, and we were friendly with Metallica. The band was still successful, still touring, but they weren't getting any younger. Meanwhile a whole raft of tribute acts fed off the desire for the fans to see younger versions of the band, the way they'd been twenty or thirty years before. Yet no matter how good they were, the tribute acts were never quite realistic enough to be completely convincing. What was needed—what might fill a niche that no one yet perceived— were tribute acts that were *completely* indistinguishable from their models, and which could replicate them at any point in their careers. And—most importantly—never get tired doing it, or start demanding a raise.

So we made them. Got in hock with the best Japanese robotics specialists and tooled up a slew of different incarnations of Metallica. Each robot was a lifesize, hyper-realistic replica of a given member of the band at a specific point in their career. After processing thousands of hours of concert footage, motion capture software enabled these robots to behave with staggering realism. They moved like people. They sounded like people. They sweated and exhaled. Unless you got close enough to look right into their eyes, there was no way at all to tell that you were not looking at the real thing.

We commissioned enough robots to cover every market on the planet, and sent them out on tour. They were insanely successful. The real Metallica did well out of it and within months we were licensing the concept to other touring acts. The money was pumping in faster than we could account it. But at the same time, mindful of what had happened with Ghoul Group, we were thinking ahead. To the next big thing.

That was when I'd had my one original idea.

I'd been on another flight, bored out of my mind, watching some news item about robots being used to dismantle some Russian nuclear plant that had gone meltdown last century. These robots were Godzilla-sized machines, but the thing that struck me was that more or less humanoid in shape. They were being worked by specialist engineers from half way round the world, engineers who would zip into telepresence rigs and actually feel like they were wearing the robots; actually feel as if the reactor they were taking apart was the size of a doll's house.

It wasn't the reactor I cared about, of course. It was the robots. I'd had a flash, a mental image. We were already doing Robot Metallica. What was to stop us doing Giant Robot Metallica?

By the time I'd landed, I'd tracked down the company that made the demolition machines. By the time I'd checked in to my hotel and ordered room service, I'd established that they could, in principle, build them to order and incorporate the kind of animatronic realism we were already using with the lifesize robots. There was, essentially, no engineering barrier to us creating a twenty metre or thirty metre high James Hetfield or Lars Ulrich. We had the technology.

Next morning, shivering with excitement, I put the idea to Jake. I figured it for an easy sell. He'd see the essential genius in it. He'd recognise the need to move beyond our existing business model.

But Jake wasn't buying.

I've often wondered why he didn't go for it. Was it not enough of a swerve for him, too much a case of simply scaling up what we were already doing? Was he shrewd enough to see the potential for disaster, should our robots malfunction and go berserk? Was it simply that it was my idea, not his?

I don't know. Even now, after everything else that's happened—Derek and all the rest—I can't figure it out. All I can be sure of is that I knew then that it was curtains for Morbid Management. If Jake wasn't going to back me the one time I'd had an idea of my own, I couldn't keep on working with him.

So I'd split. Set up my own company. Continued negotiations with the giant demolition robot manufacturers and—somewhat sneakily, I admit— secured the rights from Metallica to all larger-than-life robotic reenactment activities.

Okay, so it hadn't ended well. But the idea'd been sound. And stadiums can always be rebuilt.

"You still there, buddy?"

"Yeah, I'm still here." I'd given Jake enough time to think I'd hung up on him. Let the bastard sweat a little. Why not? Over the roar of the scramjet's ballistic re-entry profile I said: "We're gonna lose comms in a few moments. Why don't you tell me what this is all about."

"Not over the phone. But here's the deal." And he gave me an address, an industrial unit on the edge of Helsinki. "You're flying into Copenhagen, buddy. Take the 'lev, you can be in Helsinki by evening."

"You have to give me more than that."

"Like you to meet the future of rock and roll, Fox. Little friend of mine by the name of Derek. You're going to like each other."

The bastard had me, of course.

It was winter in Helsinki so evening came down cold and early. From the maglev, I took a car straight out into the industrial sticks, a dismal warren of slab-sided warehouses and low-rise office units. Security lights blazed over fenced-off loading areas and nearly empty car parks, the asphalt still slick and reflective from afternoon rain. Beyond the immediate line of warehouses, walking cranes stomped around the docks, picking up and discarding shipping containers like they were colored building blocks. Giant robots. I didn't need to be reminded about giant fucking robots, not when I was expecting an Interpol arrest warrant to be declared in my name at any moment. But at least they wouldn't come looking here too quickly, I thought. On the edge of Helsinki, with even the car now departed on some other errand, I felt like the last man alive, wandering the airless boulevards of some huge abandoned moon base.

The unit Jake had told me to go to was locked from the road, with a heavy-duty barrier slid across the entrance. Through the fence, it looked semi-abandoned: weeds licking at its base, no lights on in the few visible windows, some of the security lights around it broken or switched off. Maybe I'd been set up. It wouldn't be like Jake, but time had passed and I still wasn't ready to place absolute, unconditional trust in my old partner. All the same, if Jake did want to get back at me for something, stranding me in a bleak industrial development was a very elaborate way of going about it.

I pressed the intercom buzzer in the panel next to the barrier. I was half expecting no one to answer it and, if they did, I wasn't quite sure how I was going to explain my presence. But the voice that crackled through the grille was familiar and unfazed.

"Glad you could make it, buddy. Stroll on inside and take a seat. I'll be down in a minute. I can't wait to show Derek off to you."

"I hope Derek's worth the journey."

The barrier slid back. I walked across the damp concrete of the loading area to the service entrance. Now that I paid proper attention, the place wasn't as derelict as I'd assumed. Cameras tracked me, moving stealthily under their rain hoods. I ascended a step, pushed against a door—which opened easily—and found myself entering some kind of lobby or waiting room. Beyond a fire door, a dimly illuminated corridor led away into the depths of the building. No lights on in the annex, save for the red eye of a coffee machine burbling away next to a small table and a set of chairs. I poured a cup, spooned in creamer and sat down. As my vision adjusted to the gloom, I made out some of the glossy brochures lying on the table. Most of them were for Gladius Biomech. I'd heard of the firm and recognized their swordfish logo. Most of what they did creeped me out. Once you started messing with genetics, the world was your walking, talking, tap-dancing oyster. I stroked one of the moving images and watched a cat sitting on a high chair and eating its dinner with a knife and fork, holding the cutlery in little furry human-like hands, while the family dined around it. *Now your pet can share in your mealtimes—hygienically!*

The firedoor swung open. I put down the brochure hastily, as ashamed as if I'd been caught leafing through hardcore porn. Jake stood silhouetted in the dim lights of the corridor, knee-length leather jacket, hair still down to his collar.

I put on my best laconic, deadpan voice. "So I guess we're going into the pet business."

"Not quite," Jake answered. "Although there may be merchandising options in that direction at some point. For now, though, it's still rock and roll all the way." He gestured back at the door he'd come through. "You want to meet Derek?"

I tipped the coffee dregs into the wastebin. "Guess we don't want to keep him waiting."

"Don't worry about him. He's not going anywhere."

I followed Jake into the corridor. He had changed a bit in the two years since we'd split the firm, but not much. The hair was a little grayer, maybe not as thick as it used to be. Jake still had the soul patch under his lip and the carefully tended stubble on his cheeks. Still wore snakeskin cowboy boots without any measurable irony.

"So what's this all about?"

"What I said. A new business opportunity. Time to put Morbid Management back on the road. Question is, are we ready to take things to the next level?"

I smiled. "We. Like it's a done deal already."

"It will be when you see Derek."

We'd reached a side-door: sheet metal with no window in it. Jake pressed his hand against a reader, submitted to an iris scan, then pushed open the door. Hard light spilled through the widening gap.

"You keep this locked, but I'm able to walk in through the front door? Who are you worried about breaking in?"

"It's not about anyone breaking in," Jake said.

We were in a room large enough to hold a dozen semi-trucks. Striplights ran the length of the low, white-tiled ceiling. There were no windows, and most of the wall space was taken up with grey metal cabinets and what appeared to be industrial-size freezer units. There were many free-standing cabinets and cupboards, with benches laid out in long rows. The benches held computers and glassware and neat, toylike robotic things. Centrifuges whirred, ovens and chromatographs clicked and beeped. I watched a mechanical arm dip a pipette into a rack of test tubes, sampling or dosing each in quick sequence. The swordfish logo on the side of the robot was for Gladius Biomech.

"Either you're richer than I think," I said, "or there's some kind of deal going on here."

"Gladius fronted the equipment and expertise," Jake said. "It's a risk for them, obviously. But they're banking on a high capital return."

"You're running a biotech lab on your own?"

"Buddy, I can barely work out a bar tip. You were always the one with the head for figures. Every few days, someone from Gladius stops by to make sure it's all running to plan. But it doesn't take much tinkering. Stuff's mostly automated. Which is cool, because the fewer people know about this, the better."

"Guess I'm one of them now. Want to show me what this is actually all about, or am I meant to figure it out on my own?"

"Over here," Jake said, strolling over to one of the free-standing cabinets. It was a white cube about the size of a domestic washing machine, and had a similar-looking control panel on the front. But it wasn't a washing machine, obviously. Jake entered a keypad code then slid back the lid. "Go on," he said, inviting me closer. "Take a look."

I peered into the cabinet, figuring it was some kind of incubator. Blue, UV-tinged lights ran around the inside of the rim. I could feel the warmth coming off it. Straw and dirt were packed around the floor, and there was a clutch of eggs in the middle. They were big eggs, almost football sized, and one of them was quivering gently.

"Looks like we've got a hatcher coming through," Jake said. "Reason I had to be here, actually. System alerts me when one of those babies gets ready to pop. They need to be hand-reared for a few days, until they can stand on their feet and forage for themselves."

"Until *what* can stand on their feet and forage for themselves?"

"Baby dinosaurs, buddy. What else?" Jake slid the cover back on the incubator, then locked it with a touch on the keypad. "T-Rexes, actually. You ever eaten Rex?"

"Kind of out of my price range."

"Well, take it from me, you're not missing much. Pretty much everything tastes the same once you've added steak sauce, anyway."

"So we're diversifying into dinosaur foodstuffs. Is that what you dragged me out here to see?"

"Not exactly." Jake moved to the next cabinet along—it was the same kind of white incubator—and keyed open the lid. He unhooked a floral-patterned oven glove from the side of the cabinet and slipped it on his right hand, then dipped into the blue-lit interior. I heard a squeak and a scuffling sound and watched as Jake came out with a baby dinosaur in his hand, clutched gently in the oven glove. It was about the size of a plastic bath toy, the same kind of DayGlo green, but it was very definitely alive. It squirmed in the glove, trying to escape. The tail whipped back and forth. The huge hind legs thrashed at air. The little forelimbs scrabbled uselessly against the the oven glove's thumb. The head, with its tiny pin-sized teeth already budding through, tried to bite into the glove. The eyes were wide and white-rimmed and charmingly belligerent.

"Already got some fight in it, as you can see," Jake said, using his ungloved hand to stroke the top of the Rex's head. "And those teeth'll give you a nasty cut even now. Couple of weeks, they'll have your finger off."

"Nice. But I'm still sort of missing the point here. And why is that thing so *green*?"

"Tweaked the pigmentation a bit, that's all. Made it luminous, too. Real things are kind of drab. Not so hot for merchandising."

"Merchandising what?"

"Jesus, Fox. Take a look at the forelimbs. Maybe it'll clue you in."

I took a look at the forelimbs and felt a shiver of I wasn't exactly sure what. Not quite revulsion, not quite awe. Something that came in at right angles to both.

"I'm no expert on dinosaurs," I said slowly. "Even less on Rexes. But are those things *meant* to have four fingers and a thumb?"

"Not the way nature intended. But then, nature wasn't thinking ahead." Jake stroked the dinosaur's head again. It seemed to be calming gradually. "Gladius tell me it's pretty simple stuff. There are these things called *Hox* genes which show up in pretty much everything, from fruit flies to monkeys. They're like a big bank of switches that control limb development, right out to the number of digits on the end. We just flipped a few of those switches, and got us dinosaurs with human hands."

The hands were like exquisite little plastic extrudings, molded in the same biohazard green as the rest of the T-Rex. They even had tiny little fingernails.

"Okay, that's a pretty neat trick," I said. "If a little on the creepy side. But I'm still not quite seeing the *point*."

"The point, buddy, is that without little fingers and thumbs it's kind of difficult to play rock guitar."

"You're shitting me. You bred this thing to *make music*?"

"He's got a way to go, obviously. And it doesn't stop with the fingers. You ever seen a motor homunculus, Fox? Map of human brain function, according to how much volume's given over to a specific task. Looks like a little man with huge fucking hands. Just operating a pair of hands takes up *way* more cells than you'd think. Well, there's no point giving a dinosaur four fingers and an opposable thumb if you don't give him the mental wiring to go along with it. So we're in there right from the start, manipulating brain development all the way, messing with the architecture when everything's nice and plastic. This baby's two weeks old and he already has thirty per cent more neural volume than a normal Rex. Starting to see some real hierarchical layering of brain modules, too. Your average lizard has a brain like a peanut, but this one's already got something like a mammalian limbic system. Hell, I'd be scared if it wasn't me doing this."

"And for such a noble purpose."

"Don't get all moral on me, buddy." Jake lowered the T-Rex back into the incubator. "We eat these things. We pay to go out into a big park and shoot them with anti-tank guns. I'm giving them the chance to *rock*. Is that so very wrong?"

"I guess it depends on how much choice the dinosaur has in the matter."

"When you force a five year old kid to take piano lessons, does the kid have a choice?"

"That's different."

"Yeah, because it's cruel and unusual to force someone to play the piano. I agree. But electric guitar? That's liberation, my friend. That's like handing someone the keys to the cosmos."

"It's a goddamned *reptile*, Jake."

"Right. And how is that different to making corpses or giant robots play music?"

He had me there, and from the look of quiet self-satisfaction on his face, he knew it.

"Okay. I accept that you have a baby dinosaur that could, theoretically, play the guitar, if anyone made a guitar that small. But that's not the same thing as actually playing it. What are you going to do, just sit around and wait?"

"We train it," Jake said. "Just like training a dog to do tricks. Slowly, one element at a time. Little rewards. Building up the repertoire a part at a time. It doesn't need to understand music. It just needs to make a sequence of noises. You think we can't do this?"

"I'd need persuasion."

"You'll get it. Dinosaurs live for meat. It doesn't have to understand what it's doing, it just has to associate the one with the other. And this is heavy metal we're talking about here, not Rachmaninov. Not a big task, even for a reptile."

"You've thought it all through."

"You think Gladius were going to get onboard if there wasn't a business plan? This is going to work, Fox. It's going to work and you're going to be a part of it. All the way down the line. We're going to promote a rock tour with an actual carnivorous theropod dinosaur on lead guitar and vocal."

I couldn't deny that Jake's enthusiasm was infectious. Always had been. But when I'd needed him—when I'd taken a big idea to him—he hadn't been there for me. Even now the pain of that betrayal still stung, and I wasn't sure I was ready to get over it that quickly.

"Maybe some other time," I said, shaking my head with a regretful smile. "After all, you've got a ways to go yet. I don't know how fast these things grow, but no one's going to be blown away by a knee-high rockstar, even if they are carnivorous. Maybe when Derek's a bit older, and he can actually play something"

Jake gave me an odd glance. "Dude, we need to clear something up. You haven't met Derek yet."

I looked into his eyes. "Then who—what—was that?"

"Part of the next wave. Same with the eggs. Aren't enough venues in the world for all the people who'll want to see Derek. So we make more Dereks. Until we hit market saturation."

"And you think Derek'll be cool with that?"

"It's not like Derek's ever going to have an opinion on the matter." Jake looked me up and down, maybe trying to judge exactly how much I could be trusted. "So: you ready to meet the big guy?"

I gave a noncommittal shrug. "Guess I've come this far."

Jake stopped at another white cabinet—this one turned out to be a fridge—and came out with a thigh-sized haunch of freezer-wrapped meat. "Carry this for me, buddy," he said.

I took the meat, cradling it in both arms. We went out of the laboratory by a different door, then walked down a short corridor until a second door opened out into a dark, echoey space, like the inside of an aircraft hangar.

"Wait here," Jake said, and his footsteps veered off to one side. I heard a clunk, as of some huge trip-switch being thrown and, one by one, huge banks of suspended ceiling lights came on. Even as I had to squint against the glare, I mentally applauded the way Jake was managing the presentation. He'd known I was coming, so he could easily have left those lights on until now. But the impresario in him wouldn't be denied. These weren't simple spotlights, either. They were computer controlled, steerable, variable-color stage lights. Jake had a whole routine programmed in. The lights gimballed and gyred, throwing shifting patterns across the walls, floor, and ceiling of the vast space. Yet until the last moment they studiously avoided illuminating the thing in the middle. When they fell on it, I could almost imagine the crowd going apeshit.

This was how the show would open. This was how the show *had* to open. I was looking at Derek.

Derek was in a bright yellow cage, about the size of four shipping containers arranged into a block. I was glad about the cage; glad too that it appeared to have been engineered to generous tolerances. Electrical cables snaked into it, thick as pythons. Orange strobe beacons had just come on, rotating on the top of the cage, for no obvious reason other than that it looked cool. And there was Derek, standing up in the middle.

I'd had a toy T-Rex as a kid, handed down from my dad, and some part of me still expected them to look the way that toy did: standing with the body more or less vertical, forming a tripod with two legs and the tail taking the creature's weight. That wasn't how they worked, though. Derek—like every resurrected Rex that ever lived—stood with his body arranged in a horizontal line, with the tail counterbalancing the weight of his forebody and skull. Somehow that just never looked *right* to me. And the two little arms looked even more pathetic and useless in this posture.

Derek wasn't the same luminous green as the baby dinosaur; he was a more plausible dark muddy brown. I guess at some point Jake had decided that coloration wasn't spectacular enough for the second batch. In fact, apart from the human hands on the ends of his forearms, he didn't look in any way remarkable. Just another meat-eating dinosaur.

Derek was awake, too. He was looking at us and I could hear the rasp of his breathing, like an industrial bellows being worked very slowly. In proportion to his body, his eyes were much smaller than the baby's. Not so cute now. This was an instinctive predator, big enough to swallow me whole.

"He's pretty big."

"Actually he's pretty small," Jake said. "Rex development isn't a straight line thing. They grow fast from babies then stick at two tons until they're about fourteen. Then they get another growth spurt which can take them anywhere up to six tons. Of course with the newer Dereks we should be able to dial things up a bit." Then he took the haunch off me and whispered: "Watch the neural display. We've had implants in him since he hatched— we're gonna work the imaging into the live show." He raised his voice. "Hey! Meat-brain! Look what I got for you!"

Derek was visibly interested in the haunch. His head tracked it as Jake walked up to the cage, the little yellow-tinged eyes moving with the smooth vigilance of surveillance cameras. Saliva dribbled between his teeth. The forearms made a futile grabbing gesture, as if Derek somehow didn't fully comprehend that there was a cage and a quite a lot of air between the haunch and him.

I watched a pink blotch form on the neural display. "Hunter-killer mode kicking in," Jake said, grinning. "He's like a heat-seeking missile now. Nothing getting between him and his dinner except maybe another Rex."

"Maybe you should feed him more often."

"There's no such thing as a sated Rex. And I do feed him. How else do you think I get him to work for me?" He raised his voice again. "You know the deal, ain't no free lunches around here." He put the haunch down on the ground, then reached for something that I hadn't seen until then: a remote control unit hanging down from above. It was a grubby yellow box with a set of mushroom-sized buttons on it. Jake depressed one of the buttons and an overhead gantry clanked and whined into view, sliding along rails suspended from the ceiling. The gantry positioned itself over the cage, then began to lower its cargo. It was a flame-red Gibson Flying V guitar, bolted to a telescopic frame from the rear of the body. The guitar came down from a gap in the top of the cage (too small for Derek to have escaped through), lowered until it was in front of him, then telescoped back until the guitar was suspended within reach of his arms. At the same time, a microphone had come down to just in front of Derek's mouth.

Jake released the remote control unit, then picked up the haunch again. "Okay, buddy, you know what you need to do." Then he pressed one of the other buttons and fast, riffing heavy metal blasted out of speakers somewhere in the room. It wasn't stadium-level wattage—that, presumably, would have drawn too much attention—but it was still loud enough to impress, to give me some idea of how the show would work in reality.

And then Derek started playing. His hands were on that guitar, and they were making—well, you couldn't call it music, in the absolutely strict sense of the word. It was noise, basically. Squealing, agonizing bursts of sheet-metal sound, none of which bore any kind of harmonic relationship to what had gone before. But the one thing I couldn't deny was that it *worked*. With the backing tape, and the light show, and the fact that this was an actual dinosaur playing a Gibson Flying V guitar, it was possible to make certain allowances.

Hell, I didn't even have to try. I was smitten. And that was before Derek opened his mouth and started singing. Actually it would be best described as a sustained, blood-curdling roar—but that was exactly what it needed to be, and it counterpointed the guitar perfectly. Different parts of his brain were lighting up now; the hunter-killer region was much less bright than it had been before he started playing.

And there was, now that I paid attention to it, more than just migraine-inducing squeals of guitar and monstrous interludes of guttural roaring. Derek might not be playing specific notes and chords, and his vocalizations were no more structured or musical, but they were timed to fit in around the rest of the music, the bass runs and drum fills, and second guitar solos. It wasn't completely random. Derek was playing along, judging his contributions, letting the rest of the band share the limelight.

As a front man, I'd seen a lot worse.

"Okay, that'll do," Jake said, killing the music, pressing another button to retract the guitar and mike. "Way to go, Derek. Way to fucking go."

"He's good."

"Does that constitute your seal of approval?"

"He can rock. I'll give him that."

"He doesn't just rock," Jake said. "He *is* rock." Then he turned around and smiled. "So. Buddy. We back in business, or what?"

Yeah, I thought to myself. I guess we're back in business.

I'm making my way back down the Antonov, thinking of the long hours of subsonic cruising ahead. I pass Jake's desk again, and this time something on the ancient, battered, desert-sand camouflaged ex-military surplus laptop catches my eye.

The laptop's running some generic movie-editing software, and in one of the windows is a freezeframe from tonight's show. Beneath the freezeframe is a timeline and soundtrack. I click the cursor and slide it back along to the left, watching Derek run in reverse on the window, hands whipping around the guitar in manic thrash overdrive. The set list is the same from night to night, so I know exactly when "Extinction Event" would have kicked in. I don't feel guilty about missing it—someone had to take care of the Budokan accounts—but now that we're airborne and there's time to kill, I'm at least semi-curious about hearing it properly. What exactly was so great about it tonight, compared to the previous show, and the one before that?

Why was it that Jake didn't want to hear that "Extinction Event" was even more awesome than usual?

I need earphones to hear anything over the six-engine drone of the Antonov. I'm reaching for them when Jake looms behind me.

"Thought you were checking on the big guy."

I look around. He's still got the bottle of JD with him.

"I was. Told him I heard he'd done a good job. Now I'm just checking it out for myself. If I can just find the point where . . . "

He reaches over and takes my hand off the laptop. "You don't need to. Got it all cued up already."

He hands me the JD, punches a few keys—they're so worn the numbers and letters are barely visible now—and up pops Derek again. From the purple-red tinge of the lighting, and the back-projection footage of crashing asteroids and erupting volcanos, I know we've hit the start of "Extinction Event."

"So what's the big deal?" I ask.

"Put the phones on."

I put the phones on. Jake spools through the track until we hit the bridge between the second and third verse. He lets the movie play on at normal speed. Drums pounding like jackhammers, bass so heavy it could shatter bone, and then Derek lets rip on the Flying V, unleashing a squall of demented sound, arching his neck back as he plays, eyes narrowing to venomous slits, and then belching out a humongous, larynx-shredding roar of pure theropod rage.

We go into the third verse. Jake hits pause.

"So you see," he says.

I pull out the phones. "I'm not sure I do."

"Then you need to go back and listen to the previous performance. And the one before that. And every goddamned rendition of that song he's ever done before tonight."

"I do?"

"Yes. Because then you'd understand." And Jake looks at me with an expression of the utmost gravity on his face, as if he's about to disclose one of the darkest, most mystical secrets of the universe. "It was different tonight. He came in early. Jumped his usual cue. And when he did come in it was for longer than usual and he added that vocal flourish."

I nod, but I'm still not seeing the big picture. "Okay. He screwed up. Shit happens. Gotta roll with it, remember? It was still a good show. Everyone said so."

But he shakes his head. "You're not getting it, buddy. That wasn't a mistake. That was something much worse. That was an improvement. That was him improvising."

"You can't be sure."

"I *can* be sure." He punches another key and a slice of Derek's neural activity pops up. "Extracted this from the performance," he says. "Right around the time he started going off-script." His finger traces three bright blotches. "You see these hotspots? They've come on in ones and twos before. But they've never once lit up at the same time."

"And this means something?"

He taps his finger against the blotches in turn. "Dorsal premotor cortex. That's associated with the brain planning a sequence of body movements. You slip on ice, that's the part that gets you flapping your arms so you don't you fall over." Next blotch. "Anterior cingulate. That's your basic complex resolution, decision making module, right. Do I chase after that meal, or go after that one?" He moves his finger again. "Interior frontal gyrus/ventral premotor cortex. We're deep into mammal brain structure here—a normal Rex wouldn't have anything you could even stick a label on here. You know when this area lights up, in you and me?"

"I'm not, strangely enough, a neuroscientist."

"Nor was I until I got involved with Derek. This is the sweet spot, buddy. This is what lights up when you hear language or music. And all three of these areas going off at once? That's a pretty unique signature. It doesn't just mean he's playing music. It means he's making shit up as he goes along."

For a moment I don't know what to say. There's no doubt in my mind that he's right. He knows the show—and Derek's brain—inside out. He knows every cue Derek's meant to hit. Derek missing his mark—or coming in early—just isn't meant to happen. And Derek somehow finding a way to deviate from the program and make the song sound better is, well . . . not exactly the way Jake likes things to happen.

"I don't like improvisation," he says. "It's a sign of creative restlessness. Before you know it . . . "

"It's solo recording deals, expensive riders, and private tour buses."

"I thought we got away from this shit," Jake says mournfully. "I mean, dead bodies, man. Then robots. Then dinosaurs. And still it's coming back to bite us. Talent always thinks it knows best."

"Maybe it does."

"A T-Rex?"

"You gave him just enough of a mind to rock. Unfortunately, that's already more than enough to not want to take orders." I take a sip from the JD. "But look on the bright side. What's the worst that could happen?"

"He escapes and eats us."

"Apart from that."

"I don't know. If he starts showing signs of . . . creativity . . . then we're fucked six ways from Tuesday. We'll have animal rights activists pulling the plug on every show."

"Unless we just . . . roll with it. Let him decide what he does. I mean, it's not like he doesn't *want* to perform, is it? You've seen him out there. This is what he was born for. Hell, why stop there? This is what he was evolved for."

"I wish I had your optimism."

I look back at the cage. Derek's watching us, following the conversation. I wonder how much of it he's capable of understanding. Maybe more than we realize.

"Maybe we keep control of him, maybe we don't. Either way, we've done something beautiful." I hand him the bottle. "You, mainly. It was your idea, not mine."

"Took the two of us to make it fly," Jake says, before taking a gulp. "And hell, maybe you're right. That's the glorious thing about rock and roll. It's alchemy. Holy fire. The moment you control it, it ain't rock and roll no more. So maybe the thing we should be doing here is celebrating."

"All the way." And I snatch back the JD and take my own swig. Then I raise the bottle and toast Derek, who's still watching us. Hard to tell what's going on behind those eyes, but one thing I'm sure of is that it's not nothing. And for a brief, marvellous instant, I'm glad not only to be alive, but to be alive in a universe that has room in it for beautiful monsters.

And heavy metal, of course.

• • •

Alastair Reynolds was born in Barry, South Wales, in 1966. After a career working abroad in space science, he returned to Wales a few years ago and is now a full time writer. His most recent novel is *Blue Remembered Earth* (2012), and he is now working on its sequel. Forthcoming is a *Doctor Who* tie-in novel, *Harvest of Time*, from BBC Books in 2013. Reynolds is an obsessive music listener, with tastes ranging from Early Music through to Shostakovich, Sibelius, the English pastoral composers, jazz, blues, rock, folk, and contemporary world music. Oddly enough, despite the theme of this story, he does not listen to a great deal of heavy metal—although Metallica's last album is a particular favorite. He is also a keen if struggling student of the classical and electric guitar.

• • • •

Mourningstar
Del James

Rhain hated Wrath. Not so much because he suspected the guitarist might be quitting Mourningstar to join a more successful band, but because he *could* quit to join another band. As a singer, Rhain didn't have the same options as the talented shredder, either on or off stage. No one was knocking on his door with tempting offers. Hell, other than their shithole rehearsal studio in the sunny slums of the San Fernando Valley, he didn't have a place to call home.

It could be worse.

Compared to the foster homes and detention centers of his youth the studio was a palace—a cancerous palace with rats and who knows what else living inside the walls, but a palace never the less. Microphones and amplifiers and instruments offering a means to spit venom at all of those who bowed before the great oppressor, the subjugated singer understood the power of resentment and embraced his inner hate the same way others found religion. But instead of God, Rhain had given his soul to Satan. He communed with the Ancient Ones. Within these crumbling walls adorned with ancient arcane symbols, he had a voice and the means to unleash his blasphemous rage.

Rhain stood above all moral illusions. Words like "good" or "evil" held no meaning. They were purely relative terms expressing subjective values. *So was killing an innocent person a "bad" thing?* Not when labels like "innocent" held no value. No human life is more important than the power guiding Mourningstar. Not even the lives of its four most obvious representatives. The band and the dark forces behind it were all part of an agenda far greater than becoming rich or famous.

For the past two years, every determined ounce of Rhain's misanthropic existence had been channeled into the band. Mourningstar served as the vessel for his bleak vision as well as his escape. The stage show and filthy leather attire and devilish makeup and bombastic music and flaming inverted pentagram logo had his bloody fingerprints smeared all over them. Wrath,

Revile the bassist, and Ruin the drummer played the instruments, but make no mistake: Rhain *was* Mourningstar. Wrath and the others believed human happenstance put the four of them together—but Rhain knew better.

He willed it.

He channeled it.

He conjured it.

He made it happen.

But it wasn't easy. Nothing ever was. The band paid their dues, suffering through the humiliation of opening shows for bands far inferior but somehow more successful. They worked steadfastly at their craft; putting in every available hour they could find to become unstoppable. It had paid off. Compared to their early rehearsals and gigs, the improvement now echoed thunderously whenever they played. Mourningstar could jam with any heavy metal band. If one need further proof, their latest demo, *Cruelties in Black*, was getting played on some of the top Internet radio stations. More importantly, it was receiving attention from Black Light Records.

Cruelties in Black personified a musical exploration of the dark side and was the band's greatest accomplishment to date. They'd done whatever was necessary to raise the money for studio time and the crushing results proved quite satisfactory. As far as a demo goes, it did its job presenting a fair representation of what could be achieved if they could get into a proper studio with a real producer.

Rhain intended the music to be a glimpse into a world where the illusions of flesh and light are absent; an aural assault of unearthly delights where chords of liberated fire rose up to become sinful exclamations. *Cruelties in Black* unleashed a sonic exploration, glorification, and adoration of the Devil—the eternal adversary and enemy of the world.

It was meant to be played *loud*.

Rhain's ambition had always been to upset the status quo, and if he had to break the musical rules that others followed, then so mote it be. He strived toward complete artistic freedom, believing in his blackened heart that the only way to achieve this was though diabolical music. Darkness was its most important element; the sinister energies channeled and spread through their frequencies were what inspired Rhain. If he could introduce listeners to true darkness and let them experience the liberating potential that one can find deep within themselves, the black flame, then his existence would be one of unholy significance. He wanted to plant Satan's seed in the listener's mind, allowing it to slowly burn new holes of infernal insight in their collective consciousness.

Mourningstar was nothing more than an instrument for channeling the wrath of the ancient gods of darkness. If the lanky singer had to dig up cadavers in order to decorate a stage in human bones to momentarily open a portal to the dark side—break out the shovels. If violence offered a favorable outcome for band business—it was time to unleash merciless savagery upon anyone who stood in Mourningstar's path.

Whenever Mourningstar performed live—not nearly often enough to satisfy the quartet—they underwent a transformation. No longer just longhaired rockers, Rhain, Wrath, Ruin, and Revile turned into demented heretics capable of unleashing inhuman fury and hellfire.

Rhain understood that visuals were as important as the music.

On stage, each musician sported at least one heavy necklace with an inverted cross or pentagram hanging from it. Their attire consisted of custom-made, dirty black leather. Leather sleeves covered in hooks and spikes ran from wrist to forearm. Chrome motorcycle chains and bullet belts with large demonic buckles adorned their slim waists.

Each member made his face up as a ghoulish corpse—pale white with black highlighting the eyes and lips serving as a foundation for further intricate makeup application—all to appear more intimidating than most black metal bands.

Rhain, Wrath, Revile, and Ruin could, no *should*, be the four horsemen of the heavy metal apocalypse. But now Mourningstar might be no more because some spoiled cocksucker with a perfect family and a promising future was thinking about jumping ship.

Rhain couldn't believe it . . . yet he could. Guitarists were strange mercenaries. They always wanted to stand center stage, shamelessly waving their six-strings at anyone in the immediate vicinity. They cared more about tones and arpeggios than about honor. Besides being a phenomenally talented guitar slinger, Wrath understood the value of being in the spotlight so he learned how to spit fire just like Quorthon of Bathory and countless other black metallers. As long as he didn't get too wasted beforehand, Wrath could easily blow flames of up to twenty feet.

Rhain put so much time and effort into convincing Wrath that Mourningstar was more than just a band. For Wrath to intentionally extinguish that flame before it had the opportunity to burn brightly was an unforgivable act of treason. Rhain yearned to bash Wrath's pretty little face in . . . pummel him the same way he'd been pounded on numerous occasions . . . kick and stomp him until blood spewed out from his broken mouth.

To feel flesh splitting under the force of his fists would bring about some sense of retribution but that would not be enough. Wrath's treachery crossed a line that could not be avenged by a mere ass whipping. His suffering had to be permanent. The scars of such a betrayal, much like the wounds from a curved dagger, must never fade. If Wrath was about to destroy Mourningstar before they could be carved into public memory, then his suffering had to be epic.

After thorough introspective meditation and consultation with the Ancient Ones, the singer hatched a scheme.

As part of Mourningstar's biggest show to date, a slot at the Whisky A Go-Go, Rhain invited Wrath's sister to be a part of the live spectacle. Ann Marie wanted—no, *jumped* at—the opportunity to be the "victim" who gets crucified and stabbed during the song *Bloodletting.* If the Whisky show was going to be their final performance, the singer would make it a communion between this world and the dark that no one in attendance would ever forget.

Scorched earth rock 'n' roll.

Wrath suspected Rhain knew he was being courted by The Arbitrators, a four-piece heavy metal band that could sell out any club in Southern California. Step one to getting signed mandated developing a following. It doesn't matter what genre of music a band plays; as long as they could consistently pack in the crowds the record companies would eventually come sniffing around. The Arbitrators currently owned the Sunset Strip so naturally several major labels wanted to sign them to a recording contract.

Wrath wasn't keen on the brand of rock music The Arbitrators excelled at. It played a bit too "chick friendly" and not heavy enough. Music was supposed to be powerfully accelerated and crushing enough to make one's ear bleed tiny droplets of sonic bliss. Black fucking metal reverberated the sounds of war, squealed like the tones of choke fucking, and climaxed into the deafening timbre of the heavens collapsing. At least when Mourningstar performed it did. Just ask their loyal following of about fifty friends and hangers on.

For the past two years, Wrath tried his best to mold his dysfunctional band mates into his musical peers. Ruin showed the most improvement and now was a lightning-fast drummer who could hold his own with anybody. Revile, though, had four large bass strings and usually only hammered one or two at a time. Despite all of the drama surrounding their daily lives, the unstable drummer with a pregnant girlfriend and the meth-dealing bassist pounded adequately as a rhythm section. But if Ruin and Revile weren't fucked up enough, Rhain embodied the most complex person Wrath had ever met.

That's why he loved him . . . and hated him.

Rhain possessed talent but it wasn't the conventional singer-with-a-great-vocal-range or strutting-around-onstage types of appeal. Hell, there wasn't anything conventional about Rhain. Wrath could remember taking him to his parent's house and Rhain—who as far as Wrath knew, had no formal musical training—sat down at the piano and started playing a shadowy melody in the key of D flat. He instinctively knew what to play . . . until he realized that people were watching. Then he became embarrassed and immediately brought the somber melody to a halt.

Later that night, Wrath's mother warned him that Rhain was a "weirdo."

Weirdo was too kind a description. The singer whose dream in life was to "eclipse the sun and rape the moon" was downright dangerous.

Throughout the history of music, there have always been crazed geniuses. If one wanted to romanticize it, madness represented a gift as well as a curse. From Ludwig Van Beethoven, Brian Wilson, and Syd Barrett to Richard Wagner, Al Jourgensen, and Ian Curtis—magic and psychosis went hand in hand. Not only did Rhain have his own undiagnosed—thus untreated—issues to contend with, but in an attempt to get closer to Satan he welcomed even more insanity into his existence. How many singers fasted for days in order to be in the right state to record? How many singers conjured demons in an attempt to become a conduit between this world and the dark side?

And the most fucked up part about everything is Rhain believes that Lucifer is guiding the band's fortune.

No, if anything was guiding their recent good fortune, it was Wrath's skilled fingers. Just ask record producer extraordinaire Michael Mallory.

When Donnie Black and Duane Fresno, two members of The Arbitrators, came to Wrath's house asking him to join them, the offer sounded far from appealing. Sure, the Arbitrators were a lot more successful than Mourningstar, but Wrath loved the type of music Mourningstar performed. He loved the theatrics and the power and the potential of his band . . . but Donnie and Duane had an ace up their mutual sleeve.

As far as producers go, Michael Mallory had received every award a knob-turner could achieve including several Grammys. Not every project he touched turned to platinum but it sure seemed that way. Mallory had been turning out hit record after hit record since the end of vinyl, all the way through CDs, and now in the digital download era. While the majority of the music industry fell upon the hardest of times, Mallory seemed unaffected by all of the changes and kept on doing what he did best; making smash records.

Mallory believed that The Arbitrators had potential but needed a better guitarist. Donnie and Duane told him about the most talented player on their radar. Someone they both attended high school with.

Once the producer started courting the young guitarist, taking him to expensive dinners and dangling the proverbial golden coke spoon of success under his nose, The Arbitrators suddenly didn't seem so poseurish. If Wrath listened to and trusted Mallory, it would only be a matter of time before Robert "Wrath" Kincaid became a talent to be reckoned with.

It sounded sweet but he still wasn't sold on The Arbitrators.

Wrath could handle all of the madness surrounding Mourningstar. The violence and narcotics and STDs and the occult and criminal activities bonded them into a feral brotherhood, but when the singer asked his kid sister to be part of their live show, Rhain crossed a line that could never be undone.

At the pool party barbeque for Ann Marie Kincaid's sweet sixteen-birthday party, Rhain asked Ann if she would like to be a part of Mourningstar's next show. Of course she jumped at the opportunity to be onstage with her big brother. With Ann and all of her friends pleading to allow her to do it, there was no way Wrath could say no without ruining her birthday. Rhain could pretend like he didn't know what he was doing and that it was an innocent faux pas but that didn't change matters or fix the goddamn problem. What Mourningstar did onstage was not something that Ann Marie should participate in.

Usually Revile's stripper girlfriend, Andrea, played the role of the victim during the song *Bloodletting*. Dressed as a nun, or more often barely dressed, Andrea would be tied to a cross. With a real dagger in one hand, Rhain introduced the song and cut himself. The real knife and real blood is what sold the illusion of the singer stabbing the victim with a gimmick dagger. Simple Showmanship 101 where Rhain played his role with plenty of malevolent conviction and the audience usually ate it up.

During a heated argument in which the two almost came to blows, the singer claimed that Mourningstar needed Ann Marie for her "virginal purity." It was their biggest show to date and with Black Light Records attending, Mourningstar needed as much magic symbolism as they can summon. A virgin dressed in white getting slaughtered would certainly hit deeper within the audience's collective psyche than if they simply used a hot stripper.

Wrath could have made this all go away by letting Rhain know that Ann was not a virgin. What she did and with whom was nobody's business and the last thing Wrath needed was for a poon hound like Revile thinking his sister was fair game.

Wrath's personal business was nobody else's business and in all likelihood, the Whiskey A Go-Go gig would be his final performance before he moved on to the better things.

In almost every storefront window along the Sunset Strip a Mourningstar poster had been taped in place. Mourningstar flyers had been stapled to every telephone pole in Hollywood. The striking image featured the band standing menacingly in front of tombstones and statues of remembrance with Wrath in the center blowing a giant fireball into the air.

The overkill of promotion inspired curiosity, especially among metalheads.

On the night of the concert the boulevard buzzed with rock 'n' roll excitement. Many bands associated with Los Angeles—from The Doors and Van Halen to Mötley Crüe and Guns N' Roses—paid their dues onstage at the Whiskey A Go-Go. Strange electricity in the air, something was happening that lured heavy metal fans the same way the Pied Piper summoned rats.

Metalheads, mostly Satanic Hispanics, packed the murky club. Drunk and unattractive, they sported band T-shirts and denim vests covered in patches. They guzzled plenty of beer in anticipation.

Inside the dressing room, Rhain, Wrath, Revile, and Ruin were made up and waiting to hit the stage. Modifications had been made to each member's outfit. More spikes, more belts, more everything. Each member wore a new necklace—a skeletal finger dangling like a pendant.

Resembling a pair of rock 'n' roll demons, Rhain and Wrath chatted between themselves. They tried their best to pretend that everything was cool between them.

Like a gunslinger, Rhain sported a leather belt with two daggers inside two sheaths. One was a real dagger with a very sharp edge. The other, a stage prop with a retractable blade.

Dressed in an antique white wedding dress, Ann Marie made her way over to Wrath and Rhain but she didn't look like herself. In fact, the usually bubbly teenager seemed uncomfortable.

"We need to go over a few things," Rhain declared, oblivious that anything might be wrong with her. Then he stopped speaking, expecting Wrath to pick up the conversation.

"Okay so at the start of the second number, Rhain's gonna introduce the song while the roadies bring you out on the cross. Try to make it look good. Resist a little and look scared but don't pull too much or else it'll fall over."

Ann Marie nodded that she understood.

Rhain pulled out his two daggers and pressed the gimmick dagger against Wrath's arm. It appeared the blade went in, but the guitarist was not cut.

"I'm gonna be holding the real one, talking to the crowd, and then I'll blade."

"Blade?"

"He cuts himself a little so the crowd gets into it even more," Wrath awkwardly explained.

Ann Marie seemed even more nervous.

"Don't worry," Wrath said, wanting to hug Ann but afraid to dirty her white dress. "You've seen him do it before."

"Then the song starts," Rhain added. "Between the lights and the smoke, I'll swap the real dagger for the gimmick. You know the rest."

"You stab me," she said quietly, "and make the blood bag in my dress rip open while I bite the blood capsule in my mouth."

"Exactly. And when the song ends the roadies carry you off."

Rhain eyeballed Ann Marie before gently stroking her hair.

"You look perfect."

Oblivious to the fact his guitarist was starting to fume, Rhain walked over to a mirror to tinker with his makeup and spray even more Aqua Net hair spray on his perfectly straight hair. The image in the mirror reflected the sin of Pride and why not? Tonight was the night he'd been waiting for all of his adult life—*his band was going to get signed to a record deal.*

Wrath stayed with his sister.

"It looks like so much fun from the audience," she softly stated.

"Hey, if you don't want to do this, we can always get Andrea to do it. She's around here somewhere."

"No, no. I'm just a little nervous and don't want to mess up, " she confessed and carefully touched one of the long nails protruding from his forearm band.

"Ahh, you'll be fine."

Ann Marie smiled.

"I'd give you a hug, but with all of these spikes—"

Ann Marie's smile became even wider.

At that moment, Danny the roadie made an announcement.

"Alrighty people, if anyone has to piss do it now!"

Eyes darted around the room but no one moved.

"Everybody ready?"

Psyched up and itching to get started, everyone was indeed ready to hit the stage. Hands balled into fists, Revile and Ruin tapped each other five. Bouncing around and raring to go, Revile could hardly contain himself. Of the four members, he was the one who craved the rock star lifestyle more than anyone.

Danny looked to Rhain for any final instructions. Gleaming majestically, the singer nodded his approval.

Outside the club, hellish sounds could be heard halfway up the block. Screams and droning bass and a gong were all part of Mourningstar's gloomy intro music.

A beefy, longhaired rocker walked up to the front door as if expecting to walk in but a brawny bouncer blocked his path and pointed at a sign on the ticket booth window. It was a Mourningstar flyer and, in black Sharpie, SOLD OUT had been written across it.

Without warning, the rocker sucker-punched the bouncer as hard as he could.

Lip split open, the thick-necked bouncer staggered but did not fall. He lunged at the rocker and wrestled him down to the ground. While the two men rolled around trying to pound one another, about fifteen fans that couldn't get in to the sold-out show rushed inside.

With the intro music still rolling, bodies surged toward the front of the stage. Derek Spencer, the president of Black Light Records, regretted not having reserved a table. His righthand man, Raul Ortega, hoped that if Derek signed Mourningstar to a record contract, a promotion would come his way. After all, he was the person who brought the group to Derek's attention.

Satanic royalty personified, the four musicians stomped through a dimly lit hall and down a flight of darkened steps to the side of the stage. A mixture of pride and determination adorned all of their eerily painted faces.

First was Revile. Next came Ruin. Then Rhain and Wrath, who had his Flying V guitar strapped on.

A large black curtain had been drawn across the front of the stage. Ruin walked behind the amps to his double bass drum kit. He cracked his knuckles, twirled drumsticks, and waited. Revile went to his amp and flipped switches. He nodded to Ruin, who then took his position behind the large black drum kit.

Wrath and Rhain were still standing on the side of the stage. They could hear cheers and whistles coming from the audience.

"Ready to kill?" Rhain asked Wrath.

"Yeah . . . but there's something I gotta tell you."

Rhain stared at Wrath, suspecting he knew what was coming.

"I think you should know that my sister ain't nearly as pure as you think and if you ever bring her into any band business again I will fuck you up!"

Chastised, Rhain couldn't believe it. But there was more.

"And if you want me to stay in this fucking band, things have got to change around here! You need me a lot more than I need you. Understand?"

Rhain did not and never would.

Beaming with confidence, Wrath strutted across the stage and took his position stage left. He started jamming a monster riff and then stomped on one of his foot pedals causing his tone to become even heavier.

At the exact moment he stepped on the pedal, the stage curtain dropped.

Underneath an elevated drum riser, a large flaming pentagram resembled a portal into Hell. Three Marshall stacks stood uniformly on each side of the drum kit. Flashing police lights rested on top of the amp heads. All of the microphone stands had been customized with human and animal bones. The monitor wedges were dressed with razor wire. In front of each monitor stood sharpened steel poles. Impaled upon these poles were severed pig heads.

A large inverted crucifix hung down from the ceiling. It twirled slightly, slowly spinning an upside-down Jesus Christ. On each side of the crucifix was a red Nazi flag, but where the swastika would normally be, a black pentagram adorned the inside of the white circle. As the first song kicked in, awe registered on many of the audience members' faces. This sinister stage show was already unlike any they had ever seen inside of a nightclub.

KABOOM!

Flash pots went off at the front of the stage—that was Rhain's cue to join them.

While Wrath and Revile thrashed around looking possessed, Rhain stalked the stage. He never did anything that resembled dancing nor did he ever seem to enjoy himself. Instead he banged his head furiously, whipping his long black hair in time with the heavy beats.

The first song blasted out a powerful track full of crushing riffs that fans of Pantera or Metallica would enjoy just as much as the most ardent fans of grindcore or black metal.

Ruin attacked the drums like a wild banshee. Quick fills and hitting hard in overdrive, he embodied a whirlwind of perfectly timed precision and energy.

What Revile lacked in technical proficiency he made up by being the flashiest performer of the group. While he never smiled or got too carried away, he banged on his low-slung bass with a certain aggressiveness that many females saw as "hot."

Wielding his instrument as it if were a weapon, Wrath possessed the talent and technique that would be a welcome addition to any rock band. Gritting his teeth and giving it his all, he frantically worked the stage. No matter how intensely he thrashed around, he never hit a sour note.

Rhain's vocals were not particularly offensive in tone. They sounded gruff and manly but were not horrendous screeches or "Cookie Monster" vocals. Veins bulging out from his neck, every word sung was delivered with intense conviction.

The voracious crowd loved what they saw and heard. A mosh pit started swirling around violently. Audience members slammed into each other in heavy metal celebration. Wrath and Revile egged them on to go even wilder.

During Wrath's guitar solo, Rhain walked over to Danny the roadie.

"MAKE SURE YOU STRAP THAT BITCH IN GOOD AND TIGHT!"

Danny seemed a little confused.

"I DON'T WANT ANN MARIE GETTING NERVOUS AND PULLING FREE, UNDERSTAND?"

A sinister look crossed Rhain's face. Danny noticed it but didn't say anything.

Seemingly a little less pissed off, Rhain slithered back and finished the rest of the opening number.

After the song ended, the crowd cheered loudly.

"This next song . . . "

Rhain whipped out a real dagger and made the inverted sign of the cross. Because of the way he was lit, a brief motion trail appeared.

"This next song calls for BLOOD!"

The crowd roared with approval. Fingers forming Devil horns were raised as a sign of appreciation.

The singer stepped to the edge of the stage and slowly ran the jagged blade across his left hand. Blood spilled out from his slit palm. With a crazed look upon his horrifically painted face, Rhain was totally caught up in the psychodrama of his performance.

Behind the singer, several roadies hauled out a large wooden cross and placed it directly in front of the drum riser. Clad in the flowing white wedding dress, Ann Marie appeared to be securely strapped to the heavy wooden cross.

Ruin stood up and placed his drumsticks together to form an inverted cross. Then he took the horizontal stick and ran it across his own neck in a throat slicing gesture before pointing at Ann Marie. The crowd loved it.

Rhain stalked back over to the microphone and pointed his dagger at Ann Marie.

"This one's called 'BLOODLETTING'!"

Blast beats starting off the song, red trigger lights went in time with the drum hits to create a strobing effect. A large gust of dry ice "smoke" bellowed out from the rear of the stage. A crushing riff pummeled the audience.

The singer produced the second dagger.

As the smoke dwindled to unveil the frontman, Rhain held both daggers overhead as he sang the first verse. The cut on his hand continued bleeding.

Ann Marie played the role of a frightened damsel in distress to perfection. With all of the diabolical imagery onstage, it wasn't too hard to appear frightened.

About halfway through "Bloodletting," the song broke down to only bass and drums. Wrath ambled over to his amp but kept a watchful eye on Rhain in case the motherfucker tried to take onstage liberties with his sister.

Rhain knew Wrath was watching him as he placed one of the two daggers back in the sheath.

Facing the audience, the crazed singer pressed the point of the dagger against his bloody palm.

The blade did not retract.

"SATAN, ACCEPT MY OFFER!"

Thinking it was all part of the act, the crowd cheered Rhain on.

The singer dramatically raised the dagger over his head. Ann Marie screamed at the top of her lungs.

Rhain turned to face Ann Marie—only to see Wrath blocking his path, mouth filled with kerosene and holding a lit torch out.

SWOOOOSH!

A mixture of disbelief and terror spread across the singer's face as Wrath blew a giant fireball. Like homemade napalm, the flammable liquid scorched Rhain's face. His long black hair ignited immediately as his skin began to sizzle.

Arms out to his side, he threw back his flaming head and unleashed an unholy scream. As if banging his head to the music, Rhain thrashed back and forth. The flames went out and a thick waft of smoke rose from his charred skull.

Shrieking as if she too were on fire, Ann Marie tried to pull free from the large wooden cross and toppled over. Screaming for help from the stage floor, she lay trapped underneath the cross.

As the song came to a fumbling halt, Revile and Ruin could not believe their eyes. Painted face seared, most of Rhain's hair was gone. A glob of flesh slid down his cheek like cheese dripping off a pizza.

Eyes beaming with rabid madness, Rhain slashed wildly through the air. SLASH . . . SWIPE . . . SLASH.

Baring his teeth like a wild dog, the badly burned singer lumbered toward the girl under the cross.

"GET THE FUCK AWAY FROM ME!"

Wrath cut off Rhain's path to the terrified Ann Marie.

Ready to pounce, Wrath stood defiant, almost as if challenging Rhain to come a little closer. If he did, Wrath was going to bash him with his guitar.

Another shrill shriek came from under the cross. Concerned that she might be injured, Wrath turned to look.

Seizing the moment, Rhain rushed forward and buried the dagger deep in Wrath's chest. Agony contorted Wrath's face as his Flying V fell out of his hand.

"Mourningstar will always be MY band," growled Rhain's ruined mouth.

Summoning his last bit of strength, Wrath grabbed Rhain by the back of his still-smoking head and threw a vicious forearm jab into the singer's throat. Long, sharp spikes from his armband punctured soft flesh.

"Then sing motherfucker!"

Eyes bulging out of his horrid face, Rhain's mouth opened but no sound came. Like a sprinkler, blood sprayed out and drenched Wrath. A split second later, trembling hands covered the puncture wounds.

Dying, Rhain dropped to his knees.

Dagger protruding from his chest, Wrath coughed up another mouthful of crimson and then fell to his knees.

Consumed by animosity and covered in gore, Rhain and Wrath stared at one another and waited for the other to die. Neither could stand or move. They just projected their rage while the mesmerized crowd continued to scream.

For one brief moment, the detestation etched on Wrath's painted face lessened just a little, almost as if wondering: *How did this happen?*

Refusing to let go of his hatred, Rhain fell forward and died hoping Satan would welcome him with open arms.

Limp as a rag doll, Wrath also collapsed. As she watched her brother die, Ann Marie unleashed another bloodcurdling shriek.

Eight police officers stormed the club and began fighting their way through the terrified audience to get closer to the two men.

Revile dropped his bass and ran upstairs to the dressing room. With all hell breaking loose, the speed dealer knew better than to stick around.

Ruin saw Revile take off but he was not about to run. With a take-no-prisoners disposition, he reached into his stick bag and grabbed something wrapped up in a white towel.

From on top of the drum riser, Ruin cocked a sawed-off Remington 870 shotgun.

With one armed extended, the drummer took aim at the approaching officers.

BAMMMM!

Two police officers and several bystanders were hit by buckshot.

Before he could fire again, muzzle fire from police pistols lit up the dark venue.

A volley of bullets entered and exited the drummer's body. Bullets that missed him hit the drum kit and sent sparks flying off cymbals and hardware.

Jerking and twitching, Ruin fought to stay upright before finally collapsing on top of the bullet-ridden drum kit.

Ann Marie's screams never stopped, even as the police began releasing her from the cross. Miraculously, she hadn't been hit.

Revile recoiled in terror when he heard the gunshots downstairs. Like a trapped animal, he searched for an escape route until his desperate eyes noticed a sink with doors under it.

With his knees up to his face, Revile contorted his thin body to fit into the small area under the sink. He heard footsteps approaching.

Guns drawn, two police officers quickly searched the dressing room.

In the cramped darkness, Revile thought he heard the footsteps leaving.

He thought wrong.

A determined police officer yanked him out from under the sink and threw him to the floor. Before the ghoulish bassist could fight back, the cop slapped a pair of handcuffs on him. His gun-toting partner warned, "Don't move or I'll blow your head off!"

Revile did as instructed.

As he was being read his rights, Revile turned his head to look at the cabinet again. He probably should have jumped out the window instead.

" . . . right to have an attorney present during questioning and if you cannot afford an attorney, one will be appointed. Do you understand?" the officer finished.

Revile grunted that he understood. Then he tucked his face down to hide behind his long black hair.

A smile he hoped no one else could see began to form because by the time this story hit the nightly news, the lone surviving member of Mourningstar would be famous.

Or, if not famous, then infamous.

Infamous enough so that when this all blew over he could probably sign a record deal as a solo artist.

• • •

Besides being a horror writer, **Del James** is the tour manager for Guns N' Roses and has spent a good portion of his life on the road. James wrote the short story "Mourningstar" while on tour in Europe during the summer of 2012. James has also directed music videos for bands like Guns N' Roses and Soul and co-written songs with groups such as Testament, The Almighty, Dragonlord, the Outpatience, Guns N' Roses, and others. His collection of short stories, *The Language of Fear*, is available in mass market paperback from Random House and will soon be published in limited edition hardcover by Cemetery Dance.

• • • •

Jeff Beck
Lewis Shiner

Felix was thirty-four. He worked four ten-hour days a week at Allied Sheet Metal, running an Amada CNC turret punch press. At night he made cassettes with his twin TEAC dbx machines. He'd recorded over a thousand of them so far, over 160 miles of tape, and he'd carefully hand lettered the labels for each one.

He'd taped everything Jeff Beck had ever done, from the Yardbirds' *For Your Love* through all the Jeff Beck Groups and the solo albums; he had the English singles of "Hi Ho Silver Lining" and "Tally Man"; he had all the session work, from Donovan to Stevie Wonder to Tina Turner.

In the shop he wore a Walkman and listened to his tapes. Nothing seemed to cut the sound of tortured metal like the diamond-edged perfection of Beck's guitar. It kept him light on his feet, dancing in place at the machine, and sometimes the sheer beauty of it made tears come up in his eyes.

On Fridays he dropped Karen at her job at *Pipeline Digest* and drove around to thrift shops and used book stores looking for records. After he'd cleaned them up and put them on tape he didn't care about them anymore; he sold them back to collectors and made enough profit to keep himself in blank XLIIs.

Occasionally he would stop at a pawnshop or music store and look at the guitars. Lightning Music on 183 had a Charvel/Jackson soloist, exactly like the one Beck played on *Flash*, except for the hideous lilac-purple finish. Felix yearned to pick it up but was afraid of making a fool out of himself. He had an old Sears Silvertone at home and two or three times a year he took it out and tried to play it, but he could never even manage to get it properly in tune.

Sometimes Felix spent his Friday afternoons in a dingy bar down the street from *Pipeline Digest,* alone in a back booth with a pitcher of Budweiser and an anonymous brown sack of records. On those afternoons Karen would find him in the office parking lot, already asleep in the passenger seat, and she would drive home. She worried a little, but it never happened more than once or twice a month. The rest of the time he hardly drank at all, and he never hit her or chased other women. Whatever it was that ate at him was so deeply buried it seemed easier to leave well enough alone.

One Thursday afternoon a friend at work took him aside.

"Listen," Manuel said, "are you feeling okay? I mean you seem real down lately."

"I don't know," Felix told him. "I don't know what it is."

"Everything okay with Karen?"

"Yeah, it's fine. Work is okay. I'm happy and everything. I just . . . I don't know. Feel like something's missing."

Manuel took something out of his pocket. "A guy gave me this. You know I don't do this kind of shit no more, but the guy said it was killer stuff."

It looked like a Contac capsule, complete with the little foil blister pack. But when Felix looked closer the tiny colored spheres inside the gelatin seemed to sparkle in rainbow colors.

"What is it?"

"I don't know. He wouldn't say exactly. When I asked him what it did all he said was, 'Anything you want.'"

He dropped Karen at work the next morning and drove aimlessly down Lamar for a while. Even though he hadn't hit Half Price Books in a couple of months, his heart wasn't in it. He drove home and got the capsule off the top of his dresser where he'd left it.

Felix hadn't done acid in years, hadn't taken anything other than beer and an occasional joint in longer than he could remember. Maybe it was time for a change.

He swallowed the capsule, put Jeff Beck's *Wired* on the stereo, and switched the speakers into the den. He stretched out on the couch and looked at his watch. It was ten o'clock.

He closed his eyes and thought about what Manuel had said. It would do anything he wanted. So what did he want?

This was a drug for Karen, Felix thought. She talked all the time about what she would do if she could have any one thing in the world. She called it the Magic Wish game, though it wasn't really a game and nobody ever won.

What the guy meant, Felix told himself, was it would make me see anything I wanted to. Like a mild hit of psilocybin. A light show and a bit of rush.

But he couldn't get away from the idea. What would he wish for if he could have anything? He had an answer ready; he supposed everybody did. He framed the words very carefully in his mind.

I want to play guitar like Jeff Beck, he thought.

He sat up. He had the feeling that he'd dropped off to sleep and lost a couple of hours, but when he looked at his watch it was only five after ten. The tape was still playing "Come Dancing." His head was clear and he couldn't feel any effects from the drug.

But then he'd only taken it five minutes ago. It wouldn't have had a chance to do anything yet.

He felt different though, sort of sideways, and something was wrong with his hands. They ached and tingled at the same time, and felt like they could crush rocks.

And the music. Somehow he was hearing the notes differently than he'd ever heard them before, hearing them with a certain knowledge of how they'd been made, the way he could look at a piece of sheet metal and see how it had been sheared and ground and polished into shape.

Anything you want, Manuel had said.

His newly powerful hands began to shake.

He went into his studio, a converted storeroom off the den. One wall was lined with tapes; across from it were shelves for the stereo, a few albums, and a window with heavy black drapes. The ceiling and the end walls were covered with gray paper egg cartons, making it nearly soundproof.

He took out the old Silvertone and it felt different in his hands, smaller, lighter, infinitely malleable. He switched off the Beck tape, patched the guitar into the stereo and tried tuning it up.

He couldn't understand why it had been so difficult before. When he hit harmonics he could hear the notes beat against each other with perfect clarity. He kept his left hand on the neck and reached across it with his right to turn the machines, a clean, precise gesture he'd never made before.

For an instant he felt a breathless wonder come over him. The drug had worked, had changed him. He tried to hang on to the strangeness but it slipped away. He was tuning a guitar. It was something he knew how to do.

He played "Freeway Jam," one of Max Middleton's tunes from *Blow By Blow*. Again, for just a few seconds, he felt weightless, ecstatic. Then the guitar brought him back down. He'd never noticed what a pig the Silvertone was, how high the strings sat over the fretboard, how the frets buzzed and the machines slipped. When he couldn't remember the exact notes on the record he tried to jam around them, but the guitar fought him at every step.

It was no good. He had to have a guitar. He could hear the music in his head but there was no way he could wring it out of the Silvertone.

His heart began to hammer and his throat closed up tight. He knew what he needed, what he would have to do to get it. He and Karen had over $1300 in a savings account. It would be enough.

He was home again by three o'clock with the purple Jackson soloist and a Fender Princeton amp. The purple finish wasn't nearly as ugly as he remembered it and the guitar fit into his hands like an old lover. He set up in the living room and shut all the windows and played, eyes closed, swaying a little from side to side, bringing his right hand all the way up over his head on the long trills.

Just like Jeff Beck.

He had no idea how long he'd been at it when he heard the phone. He lunged for it, the phone cord bouncing noisily off the strings.

It was Karen. "Is something wrong?" she asked.

"Uh, no," Felix said. "What time is it?"

"Five thirty." She sounded close to tears.

"Oh shit. I'll be right there."

He hid the guitar and amp in his studio. She would understand, he told himself. He just wasn't ready to break it to her quite yet.

In the car she seemed afraid to talk to him, even to ask why he'd been late. Felix could only think about the purple Jackson waiting for him at home.

He sat through a dinner of Chef Boyardee Pizza, using three beers to wash it down, and after he'd done the dishes he shut himself in his studio.

For four hours he played everything that came into his head, from blues to free jazz to "Over Under Sideways Down" to things he'd never heard before, things so alien and illogical that he couldn't translate the sounds he heard. When he finally stopped Karen had gone to bed. He undressed and crawled in beside her, his brain reeling.

He woke up to the sound of the vacuum cleaner. He remembered everything, but in the bright morning light it all seemed like a weirdly vivid hallucination, especially the part where he'd emptied the savings account.

Saturday was his morning for yard work, but first he had to deal with the drug business, to prove to himself that he'd only imagined it. He went into the studio and lifted the lid of the guitar case and then sat down across from it in his battered blue-green lounge chair.

As he stared at it he felt his love and terror of the guitar swell in his chest like cancer.

He picked it up and played the solo from "Got the Feelin'," and then looked up. Karen was standing in the open door.

"Oh my god," she said. "Oh my god. What have you done?"

Felix hugged the guitar to his chest. He couldn't think of anything to say to her.

"How long have you had this? Oh. You bought it yesterday, didn't you? That's why you couldn't even remember to pick me up." She slumped against the door frame. "I don't believe it. I don't even believe it."

Felix looked at the floor.

"The bedroom air conditioner is broken," Karen said. Her voice sounded like she was squeezing it with both hands; if she let it go it would turn into hysteria. "The car's running on four bald tires. The TV looks like shit. I can't remember the last time we went out to dinner or a movie." She pushed both hands into the sides of her face, twisting it into a mask of anguish.

"How much did it cost?" When Felix didn't answer she said, "It cost everything, didn't it? Everything. Oh god, I just can't believe it."

She closed the door on him and he started playing again, frantic scraps and tatters, a few bars from "Situation," a chorus of "You Shook Me," anything to drown out the memory of Karen's voice.

It took him an hour to wind down, and at the end of it he had nothing left to play. He put the guitar down and got in the car and drove around to the music stores.

On the bulletin board at Ray Hennig's he found an ad for a guitarist and called the number from a pay phone in the strip center outside. He talked to somebody named Sid and set up an audition for the next afternoon.

When he got home Karen was waiting in the living room. "You want anything from Safeway?" she asked. Felix shook his head and she walked out. He heard the car door slam and the engine shriek to life.

He spent the rest of the afternoon in the studio with the door shut, just looking at the guitar. He didn't need to practice; his hands already knew what to do.

The guitar was almost unearthly in its beauty and perfection. It was the single most expensive thing he'd ever bought for his own pleasure, but he couldn't look at it without being twisted up inside by guilt. And yet at the same time he lusted for it passionately, wanted to run his hands endlessly over the hard, slick finish, bury his head in the plush case and inhale the musky aroma of guitar polish, feel the strings pulse under the tips of his fingers.

Looking back he couldn't see anything he could have done differently. Why wasn't he happy?

When he came out the living room was dark. He could see a strip of light under the bedroom door, hear the snarling hiss of the TV. He felt like he was watching it all from the deck of a passing ship; he could stretch out his arms but it would still drift out of his reach.

He realized he hadn't eaten since breakfast. He made himself a sandwich and drank an iced-tea glass full of whiskey and fell asleep on the couch.

A little after noon on Sunday he staggered into the bathroom. His back ached and his fingers throbbed and his mouth tasted like a kitchen drain. He showered and brushed his teeth and put on a clean T-shirt and jeans. Through the bedroom window he could see Karen lying out on the lawn chair with the Sunday paper. The pages were pulled so tight that her fingers made ridges across them. She was trying not to look back at the house.

He made some toast and instant coffee and went to browse through his tapes. He felt like he ought to try to learn some songs, but nothing seemed worth the trouble. Finally he played a Mozart symphony that he'd taped for Karen, jealous of the sound of the orchestra, wanting to be able to make it with his hands.

The band practiced in a run-down neighborhood off Rundberg and IH35. All the houses had large dogs behind chain link fences and plastic Big Wheels in the driveways. Sid met him at the door and took him back to a garage hung with army blankets and littered with empty beer cans.

Sid was tall and thin and wore a black Def Leppard T-shirt. He had acne and blond hair in a shag to his shoulders. The drummer and bass player had already set up; none of them looked older than 22 or 23. Felix wanted to leave but he had no place else to go.

"Want a brew?" Sid asked, and Felix nodded. He took the Jackson out of its case and Sid, coming back with the beer, stopped in his tracks. "Wow," he said. "Is that your ax?" Felix nodded again. "Righteous," Sid said.

"You know any Van Halen?" the drummer asked. Felix couldn't see anything but a zebra striped headband and a patch of black hair behind the two bass drums and the double row of toms.

"Sure," Felix lied. "Just run over the chords for me, it's been a while." Sid walked him through the progression for "Dance the Night Away" on his three-quarter-sized Melody Maker and the drummer counted it off. Sid and the bass player both had Marshall amps and Felix's little Princeton, even on ten, got lost in the wash of noise.

In less than a minute Felix got tired of the droning power chords and started toying with them, adding a ninth, playing a modal run against them. Finally Sid stopped and said, "No, man, it's like this," and patiently went through the chords again, A, B, E, with a C# minor on the chorus.

"Yeah, okay," Felix said and drank some more beer.

They played "Beer Drinkers and Hell Raisers" by ZZ Top and "Rock and Roll" by Led Zeppelin. Felix tried to stay interested, but every time he played something different from the record Sid would stop and correct him.

"Man, you're a hell of a guitar player, but I can't believe you're as good as you are and you don't know any of these solos."

"You guys do any Jeff Beck?" Felix asked.

Sid looked at the others. "I guess we could do 'Shapes of Things,' right? Like on that Gary Moore album?"

"I can fake it, I guess," the drummer said.

"And could you maybe turn down a little?" Felix said.

"Uh, yeah, sure," Sid said, and adjusted the knob on his guitar a quarter turn.

Felix leaned into the opening chords, pounding the Jackson, thinking about nothing but the music, putting a depth of rage and frustration into it he never knew he had. But he couldn't sustain it; the drummer was pounding out 2-and-4, oblivious to what Felix was playing, and Sid had cranked up again and was whaling away on his Gibson with the flat of his hand.

Felix jerked his strap loose and set the guitar back in its case.

"What's the matter?" Sid asked, the band grinding to a halt behind him.

"I just haven't got it today," Felix said. He wanted to break that pissant little toy Gibson across Sid's nose, and the strength of his hatred scared him. "I'm sorry," he said, clenching his teeth. "Maybe some other time."

"Sure," Sid said. "Listen, you're really good, but you need to learn some solos, you know?"

Felix burned rubber as he pulled away, skidding through a U-turn at the end of the street. He couldn't slow down. The car fishtailed when he rocketed out onto Rundberg and he nearly went into a light pole. Pounding the wheel with his fists, hot tears running down his face, he pushed the accelerator to the floor.

Karen was gone when Felix got home. He found a note on the refrigerator: "Sherry picked me up. Will call in a couple of days. Have a lot to think about. K."

He set up the Princeton and tried to play what he was feeling and it came out bullshit, a jerk-off reflex blues progression that didn't mean a thing. He leaned the guitar against the wall and went into his studio, shoving one tape after another into the decks, and every one of them sounded the same, another tired, simpleminded rehash of the obvious.

"I didn't ask for this!" he shouted at the empty house. "You hear me? This isn't what I asked for!"

But it was, and as soon as the words were out he knew he was lying to himself. Faster hands and a better ear weren't enough to make him play like Beck. He had to change inside to play that way, and he wasn't strong enough to handle it, to have every piece of music he'd ever loved turn sour, to need perfection so badly that it was easier to give it up than learn to live with the flaws.

He sat on the couch for a long time and then, finally, he picked up the guitar again. He found a clean rag and polished the body and neck and wiped each individual string. Then, when he had wiped all his fingerprints away, he put it back into the case, still holding it with the rag. He closed the latches and set it next to the amp, by the front door.

For the first time in two days he felt like he could breathe again. He turned out all the lights and opened the windows and sat down on the couch with his eyes closed. Gradually his hands became still and he could hear, very faintly, the fading music of the traffic and the crickets and the wind.

• • •

Lewis Shiner has played drums professionally on and off since the 1960s. He's written about music for *Crawdaddy!*, the *Village Voice*, *LA Weekly*, and others. His seven novels include *Say Goodbye*, which deals with the music business, and the World Fantasy Award-winning *Glimpses*. To quote Cory Doctorow: "It's a rare novel that can capture the raw energy of rock and roll, but *Glimpses* has this and a tense, thrilling story besides."

• • • •

" . . . How My Heart Breaks When I Sing this Song . . . "
Lucius Shepard

The summer I turned sixteen, rock 'n' roll came back to the fishing village of Daytona Beach for the first time since the Winnowing nearly a century before. The gypsies brought it in a horse-drawn cart, shrouded beneath a plastic tarpaulin (my cousin had a peek underneath and said it was locked in a metal coffin), and they off-loaded it inside the dancehall at the end of the wooden pier that sticks out from the Boardwalk just south of the Joyland Arcade. Then the lot of them—around thirty all told, crammed into four rickety wagons—drove up and down the beach, beating hide drums and shouting about the musical marvel they were going to put on display. My wife Darcy tells me now that not enough happened that night to make a story, and in a way she's right; but it seems to me that it was at least the end of a story, an important one, and as such ought to be written down.

There wasn't a prayer that Pa would have let me go to the pier. Not that he was like the Rickerds, who claimed that relics of the old days were Satan's handiwork and praised God for having delivered us. No, Pa's objections would have been more pragmatic. Hadn't I gone to the Casadaga fair last month? What did I think, that the world was made of weekends? And didn't I have nets to mend? But I wanted to go. The previous winter a peddler had come through Daytona and had played some rock 'n' roll on a dinged-up cassette recorder. Listening to it, I had felt dangerous and edgy and full of urgent desires. I'd liked that feeling. And so just after moonrise I stole from the house to meet Darcy—then my wife-to-be—at the ruin of the Maverick Motel, which stands at the junction of A1A and a nameless street that peters out into the jungle.

Drenched in the milk-and-silver light of a three-quarter moon, A1A was a spooky place, with its line of hurricane battered condos and motels stretching away like worn teeth in the jawbone of a leviathan; the humps of sand dunes glowed snowy white between them, and on the western side of the road, where once had stood shopping malls and restaurants and bungalows, now there was only a wall of palmetto scrub and palms, oaks and acacias. Darcy ran ahead of me over the tilted-up slabs of asphalt: a slim, sun-darkened girl with blond streaks in her chestnut hair, barefoot, wearing a flimsy dress that the wind plastered against her thighs. She was carrying a waterproof bag to keep our clothes in when we swam out to the pier. Every once in a while she'd stop and let me kiss her. Those kisses were playful at first, but they lasted longer and longer each time, until finally we would be locked together for two or three minutes, with land crabs scuttling around our feet like live pieces of a dirty-white skull. By the time we reached the ramp where we intended to turn down onto the beach, I was in so much pain from wanting her I could hardly walk, and I tried to convince her that it was foolish to wait another month. We loved each other, I said. Why didn't we hole up in one of the old motels instead of going to the pier? But she pried my hand loose from her hip and skipped off along the ramp, laughing at me.

"Goddammit, Darcy!" I shouted. "It hurts." I walked after her, exaggerating my limp.

"I heard it can be fatal," she said, smiling and darting away.

Combers were tossing up phosphorescent sprays, crunching on the shore. In the distance I could make out the spidery silhouettes of the canted Ferris wheel and the Tilt-A-Whirl rising from the darkened Boardwalk, and past them, the centipede-on-stilts shape of the pier; the lights on the dancehall at its seaward end were winking on and off, all colors, like a constellation gone haywire. That pier had been around for a couple of hundred years, surviving storms that had twisted newer piers into a spaghetti of iron girders. Ever since I'd been old enough, I'd climbed all over it, and early on I'd learned that if you could keep from being scraped against the barnacles by the surf, you could scale the pilings out near the end and sneak into the dancehall through a storeroom window with a busted latch and listen to whomever was playing: usually fiddlers and guitar players. Not having the price of admission, this was what Darcy and I had planned to do.

We had reached the beginning of the Boardwalk—stove-in arcades (except for Joyland, which was kept up and ran off the same generator as the dancehall) and fallen-down rides and wrecked miniature golf courses with Spanish bayonets sprouting from their rotted carpeting—when a shadow heaved up from the deeper shadow of the crumbling sea wall and called to us. Mason Bird. A loutish, pudgy kid, whom I didn't like one bit. His family had wanted to arrange a marriage between him and Darcy, and he had convinced himself that Darcy was marrying me against her will, doing it to please her parents and in reality pining away for him. He came shambling over, a sappy grin splitting his round face, and tried to make eye contact with her. "If you're goin' to the show tonight," he said, "you better have a fortune in your pocket."

"We're just walkin'," I said stiffly.

"Gonnabe quite a show," said Mason, his eyes glued to Darcy's chest. "This ol' gypsy girl was tellin' me 'bout it."

"Oh?" said Darcy, and I frowned at her: Mason didn't need any encouragement.

"Yeah," said Mason. "Seems they was pokin' 'round in New York City two, three years ago, and they found themselves an android. That's kinda like a man. Got blood and organs and all, but no personality. No mental stuff."

"Bullshit!" I said.

Mason acted as if he hadn't heard. "But them ol' scientists had a way of stickin' real people's memories inside its head, and they give it the memories of this famous musician. Fella named Roy John Harlow. Plays up a storm, I hear."

I took Darcy's arm. "So long, Mason," I said. We started walking, but he fell into step beside us.

"Reckon I'll wander along and see if there ain't some stray honey who wants to go," he said. "Me and Pa sold us a load of dried shrimp, and I got money to burn."

It occurred to me that Mason must have guessed we'd be coming down the beach and—knowing I never had any money—had staked himself out by the sea wall in hopes of persuading Darcy to ditch me. I was furious, and Darcy must have sensed it, because she squeezed my arm and gave me a look that seemed to be asking me to spare Mason's feelings. I clammed up, but it put me in a sulk; I could see how the night would go, with me and Darcy trying to slip away and Mason dogging our every move.

About a hundred feet further along, we ran into a group of people on the beach in front of the Joyland Arcade, and one of them—old man Rickerd, locks of his gray hair whipping like flames in the breeze—was shouting that we should stop the gypsies from bringing this evil into our midst. "Might as well feed your kids poison!" he said. "Know what they used to call rock 'n' roll? The Devil's music!" From where I was standing, the neon word JOYLAND was spelled out in an arc above his head, adding an incongruous caption to his evangelic witnessing, and inside the arcade, dark figures were hunched over the games: it looked strange, that one brightly lit place among all the shadowy ruin. "Roy John Harlow!" sneered Rickerd. "It's got a man's name, but you can't fool a fool for Christ! That's the Devil in there, sure as I'm born!"

Some people argued against Rickerd, but the majority were in agreement. That struck me as funny, because, while most of the adults in Daytona would say that the world was better off than it had been before the Winnowing, you could tell they didn't really believe it; the stories their grandparents had told had made them long for things they'd never seen, and their attitude was, in part, sour grapes. As for us kids, we had too much distance from the Winnowing, and we were merely curious about the past, not haunted by it. The argument heated up, and though everybody there knew that nothing was going to come of it, judging by all the yelling and fist-shaking, you'd have sworn that a lynch mob was forming. Mason chipped in his two-cents'-worth, no doubt trying to impress Darcy with his intellect; since he was the only kid involved in the argument, he soon became its central focus and was drawn into the middle of the group. Seizing the opportunity, Darcy and I sprinted off toward the pier, holding hands and laughing at our slick escape.

It was high tide, which was the only time you could manage the swim; when the tide was going out, there was a fierce undertow and you'd have to be an idiot to risk it. We let a wave carry us close to the pilings, grabbed a cross-piece, swung up, and before long we were crawling under the railing at the rear of the dancehall: a big two-story affair with peeling yellow paint. The music had already begun—shards of searing melody mixed in with the rush of wind and surf—and it was the music as much as my wetness that caused me to shiver. I pulled on my pants and caught a glimpse of Darcy shrugging into her dress. In the moonlight she looked like a woman of copper, and the sight of her small pointy breasts made me shiver even more. We cracked the storeroom window. Inside, the planking of the walls and floor was black and bubbled with creosote, shined to ebony by the glare of a dangling light bulb. Cobwebs spanned between a number of old packing crates, and next to the door that led to the stage was a coffinlike box of gray metal. You could hear the music fine. We clambered through the window and settled behind one of the crates, where nobody would see us. I put my arm around Darcy, and she snuggled close, enveloping me in her clean, briny scent. After that we just listened.

I wish I could say the things that music said to me, I wish I could write down the notes into words. Sometimes it sounded like metal animals having a fight (I imagined a cloud of dust with lightning jabbing out the sides), and other times it was eerie and full of spaces, with a gravelly voice floating between the guitar passages. But no matter what the mode, it maintained a grumbling bottom, and most of all it was loud. The loudness got inside you, jumped along your nerves and made you arch your back and throw back your head. Maybe Rickerd was right and it was the Devil's music, because while there were several instruments playing, it had the feel of a single fiery voice howling from a pit, the voice of a spirit, angry and despairing. Yet for all its anger and despair and loudness, it was still beautiful. Not a mental, thoughtful beauty, a beauty that's easy to recognize, but a beauty of muscle and blood and violent emotion. And I wondered if that might not be what the Devil really was: that kind of beauty misunderstood.

The crowd responded to each song with sparse applause. I pictured them ringing the stage, my friends and their parents dressed in threadbare hand-me-downs, applauding less for the music than for the diversion—a bit of glittering life caught in the dull nets of our lives—and confused by this monstrous noise and the odd creature who had produced it. Then Roy John Harlow would introduce the next song, saying once, "Here's a little tune I wrote 'bout a hunnerd 'n forty years ago," and giving a sarcastic laugh. Embodied in the laugh was the same powerful despair that moved in the music, and the longer he played, the more dominant that despair became. Finally, following an extended silence during which the crowd muttered and rustled, Roy John Harlow said, "I wanna do one more for you. Somethin' I finished a few days ago. It's probably gonna be the last tune I write, 'cause it says all I gotta say 'bout the way things are nowadays." The song had no music but was accompanied by echoing doubled handclaps that he inserted at the ends of lines and—now and again—in the middles. Though as with the other songs, many of the words were unfamiliar, there was no mistaking its meaning: he was evoking our common sadness, making us feel what we had tried not to for so long.

> "Once I had a lady, she moved like a river and looked like an
> angel in red,
> And I knew a guy name of Gordon, he could always sell you
> somethin' good for your head.
> There used to be a joint down on the corner where you could
> grab a beer or two . . .
> And sometimes I'd catch a jet plane to Paris and go dancin'
> on the Cote d'Azure . . .
> Dancin' on the Cote d'Azure

> "Once there were Cadillacs . . . Cadillacs!
> Once there were space shots and astronauts,

Bluejeans and silver screens,
Diamond rings and dyin' kings with computer hearts.
Once there was everything you wanted and too much to
    choose,
And once I felt like fallin' in love . . .
    Once I felt like fallin' in love."

Most of the song was like that: lists of names and things and places that—as I've said—were foreign to me. Looking at them now, I can't understand why they affected me so much; but at the time they seemed emblematic of something rare and alluring, and when Roy John Harlow sang the chorus, I'd feel an awful tightness in my chest and would have to lower my head and close my eyes.

"Hey, hey, baby! It feels so wrong!
Ain't no sense in keepin' on, keepin' on . . .
My head starts achin' when I think about it's all gone,
And how my heart breaks when I sing this song . . .
    How my heart breaks when I sing this song."

There was hardly any applause afterward, and it wasn't more than a second or two later that the storeroom door creaked open and footsteps scraped on the planking. Darcy and I kept dead still. We hadn't expected the performance to conclude so abruptly, and we had believed we'd have time to climb out the window.

"Don't put me back in there, man," said a, gravelly voice. "Lemme sit up tonight."

"I don't know," said a deeper voice. "I got . . . "

"C'mon, man! You gotta gimme some life once in a while. Just cuff me and lemme sit."

"All right," said the deep voice. "But I'm postin' a guard out front. Don't you think 'bout goin' nowhere."

"Where am I gonna go in this goddamn world?" said Roy John Harlow.

I heard a metallic snick.

"You wanna smoke?" asked the deep voice, and Roy John Harlow said, "Yeah." Then the door banged shut.

Until that moment I'd thought of him as a man, imagining him to be similar to the run of Daytona men—burly, bearded, tanned—only dressed fancier. But now I wondered what fearsome thing might be waiting on the other side of the crate. From beyond the door came a thump, voices fading and then sheared away by a second thump, and I realized that the gypsies had closed the dancehall. Soon they'd be shutting down the generator. I didn't want to be trapped in the dark with an unknown quantity, and so—screwing up my courage—I had a peek at Roy John' Harlow.

He was sitting on the gray metal box, his wrist cuffed to its handle, smoking a crookedy cigar and staring at the wall. In only one particular had my image of him been correct: he was wearing red leather trousers and a white silk shirt. His black hair had been molded into a pompadour that had more-or-less the shape of a rooster's comb, with a curl hanging down over his forehead. He was thin, and his long-jawed, hollowed face had an evil handsomeness; it was a face better suited to a sneer than a smile. Then he turned to me, stared straight at me, and I saw that instead of normal irises and pupils, the whites of his eyes were figured by two black hearts. I had the idea that—like the cherries and lemons on the windows of the slot machines in the Joyland Arcade—those hearts could be whirled away and other symbols would roll up in their place. Two spades, maybe, or two roses. He didn't seem surprised by my being there, just puffed his cigar and blew smoke. The fact that he didn't react eased my fears, and I understood how perfectly his appearance fitted his music. To my mind rock 'n' roll and Roy John Harlow were one and the same. He was the personification of that spirit-voice singing out from the flames of hell, and I guess that's the way he perceived himself: a lost soul trapped in a world that was the ashes of a fuller, brighter place.

"What's happenin'?" he said at last.

Darcy, who hadn't yet seen him, dug her nails into my arm. I stood, feeling innocent and foolish. "Nothin'," I said.

"You got that right," said Roy John Harlow. He jetted smoke from his nostrils and held up his manacled hand. "Don't s'pose you got a key?"

The handcuffs were rusty, frail-looking, and it would have been no trouble to pick the lock with my Swiss Army knife. But I was leery about doing it. Though he had—except for the eyes—the presence of a man, I couldn't escape the notion that he was property. And, too, even if I let him loose, the gypsies would hunt him down. They were a persevering bunch when it came to holding onto something they considered theirs, and nobody with Roy John Harlow's eyes would be able to hide from them. Then they'd be after me for having helped him. "No," I said.

Darcy stood, and he gave her the once over. "How'd you get in?" he asked. I told him about the swim, the window, and he said, "You better swim on back. They might change their minds 'bout lettin' me sit."

"Can't do nothin' 'til the tide turns." I explained about the undertow. "It'll drag you clear 'cross to Africa," I said.

"Africa," he said. "That's a helluva name for it."

I didn't understand what he meant.

"Why they keep you in that box?" asked Darcy.

He shifted his eyes toward her; the light struck full into them, and I saw that those heart-shaped pupils had narrow red borders around them, giving them the look of demonic valentines. "There's needles in the side that inject me with shit," he said. "Knock me out. They wake me up when they need me." He let out a dispirited laugh. "Parceled out like that, you could live ten thousand years in this fuckin' wasteland."

"World might be different in ten thousand years," said Darcy.

Again he laughed—it seemed that downhearted laughter was his reaction to most everything. "It'd just be worse," he said. "You shoulda seen where I come from. Machine sex, separate governments for different age groups, joykillers. That's why I let 'em do this to me. I was an old man, and I wanted to outlive that craziness. So when these guys come to me and say, 'Roy John, we wanna record you and preserve your vast experience,' it appealed to me, y'know? It was as close as I was gonna get to seein' the glorious future, and I was enough of a pervert to think these goddamn eyes were cool. Well, I got my wish, man, in a kinda shadowy way. I seen the glorious future. The world I grew up in wasn't much, but it sure as hell beat the world I was old in. And this world . . . shit!" He was silent for a bit, and I could hear the wind sighing, the tide sucking at the pilings below. "Tell me 'bout the Winnowing," he said finally. "No one seems to know nothin' 'bout it."

"Nobody does," I said.

"My pa told me that the earth passed through a comet's tail," said Darcy. "And most everybody just keeled over."

"Some folk'll tell you it was a kinda poison gas," I said. "And some'll tell you it was Jesus weedin' out the sinners. Government up in Atlanta's s'posed to know for sure."

"Why don't you ask 'em?" He glanced back and forth between us. "Don't you wanna know? Ain't you curious 'bout why six billion people died?"

"Government's just a buncha' crazies with a computer," said Darcy. "We don't like to have much to do with 'em."

He stared at us as if we were something pitiful, and that made me defensive. "Besides," I said, "the Winnowing was terrible, it's true. But now we got clean air and water, and plenty of room. Most people think it's an improvement."

"Yeah?" he said. "Then how come I just had five hundred of those people lookin' at me like dogs at a steak?"

I shrugged, having no answer, and after a moment Darcy asked, "How'd you get all those guitars and drums goin' at once?"

"Computer programs." He stubbed out his cigar and laid it on the metal box.

"It was really great music," said Darcy. I thought he was going to say something, but he merely shook his head, amused, and leaned back against the wall. Darcy wasn't to be put off, however. "It was so strong," she said. "I never heard nothin' that strong."

"You woulda loved it, wouldn't you?" he said nastily. "Little cooze like you, shakin' her butt, dyin' to go down on some asshole like me, who could make it thunder when he plucked a string."

If anybody else had talked to her in that tone, Darcy would have responded in kind; but all she did was flush and shift closer to me.

"Rock 'n' roll wasn't shit," said Roy John Harlow. "The music was okay, but music was 'bout two percent of it. Most of it was copin' with the stooges in your band, makin' sure they'd show up on time and be straight enough to play. Dealin' with brain-dead roadies and crooked promoters and crowds so stoned they couldn't unzip their flies." He laughed. "I remember one night I got to the bottom of all that."

The lights flickered and went out. For a moment the storeroom was pitch-dark, but then a red glow began to shine from Roy John Harlow's eyes. The heart-shaped borders around his pupils were blazing neon-bright, illuminating his cheekbones. It was an uncanny thing to see, and I took Darcy's hand.

"We were playin' a party in a VFW hall," said Roy John Harlow. " 'Bout a thousand people, wasted on beer and smoke and pills. Kids splashin' in puddles of spilled beer, barfin' in the shadows. One girl was dancin' in front of me, her eyes rolled back in her head, makin' these clawin' gestures at me. Weird! We were opening for a band called Mr. Right. They thought they were hot shit, but we could kick their butt and we were doin' it that night. Halfway through our set, this bearded guy with his arm in a cast crawls up onto the stage and while I'm singin' he starts unpluggin' my mike. I push him off with my foot and keep singin', but he tries to unplug me again. I push him off again, and that's how we finish the song, with this crazy dude goin' for the plug and me kickin' at him. After it's over I jump down and grab him and say, 'What the hell you think you doin?' And he says, 'Mr. Right wants to come on now,' and tries for the mike plug. I haul him back and say, 'Fuck Mr. Right!' I got the picture, you see. The dude's one of Mr. Right's roadies and they've told him to cut us off 'cause we're makin' 'em look bad. The rest of the band crowds around, and we tell the dude he better be cool or he's gonna wind up with somethin' else in a cast. But he won't listen. Later I found out they'd threatened to fire him if he didn't get rid of us. The next thing here's this fat son of a bitch waddlin' through the crowd. Mr. Right's manager. And he starts spoutin' off 'bout us bein' reasonable, compromisin'. One of my roadies leans in. His pupils are the size of train tunnels, and he's grinnin' like a maniac. 'Lemme handle him, Roy,' he says. 'Fore I can say anything, he hooks the manager in the gut and sets him down. Then all hell breaks loose. Here comes Mr. Right. Five guys wearin' glitter and swingin' mike stands and shit. A regular fuckin' Battle of the Bands. Somebody clips me on the forehead, and I go down for the count. When I wake up, it's all over and I guess we musta won 'cause my band's on stage, fillin' in with instrumentals."

Roy John Harlow closed his eyes, and the room went dark for several seconds. "After my head stops hurtin' enough so's I can stand, I head to the bathroom. There was blood on my face, and I wanted to wash it off. Inside the bathroom, it's even more of a hellhole than the hall. 'Bout an inch of piss and beer on the floor, garbage floatin' in it, and buzzin' fluorescent lights that are blindin' me. Sittin' in one of the stalls with her dress hiked up 'round her hips is this teenage girl, who's passed out. She's kinda pretty, but her mascara's run and her lipstick's smeared. Makes her look warped. I check out my head in the mirror. Nothin' serious, but blood is coverin' half my face and I'm thinkin', 'Here I've been beatin' my brains out in the business for seven goddamn years, and this is what it's come to—standin' in a bathroom, bleedin', wasted, and my audience passed out on the toilet.'

"I don't wanna go back out. I just lean against the sink and read the graffiti, which tells me what fun it is to be a lesbian and that Jesus sucks and how some cooze wants to lay everybody in my band. Reading it, I decide I've had it. Time for a new profession. 'Bout then, in walks two teenage boys. 'Hey!' says one. 'Terrific fight, man!' Then he notices the girl. He leans over to look at her, makes his hand into a pistol and shoots her 'tween the legs. 'Bang,' he says. The other kid starts gigglin'. 'Hey!' says the first kid. 'You wanna ball her, man?' And I tell him, 'No thanks.' He staggers over and says, 'C'mon, man! She won't mind. Big rock 'n' roll star like you. She won't even look at us, but she'd be fuckin' grateful to you.' I tell him to leave me the fuck alone, and he goes back over to his buddy. They hang out for a while, crackin' jokes 'bout the girl. It was weird, watchin' 'em in the mirror. Reminded me of those cartoons where Daffy Duck or somebody's got good and evil in a cloud over their head, tryin' to convince 'em what path to follow. Finally they're ready to go, and the first kid says, 'Hey, man! You guys got a really great sound.' He sticks his fist up in the air. 'Rock 'n' roll!' he says. 'Rock 'n' roll!' "

Roy John Harlow scratched a match on the metal box and relit his cigar; the coal wasn't as bright as his eyes. "The kid was right," he said. "That goddamn bathroom . . . that was rock 'n' roll."

"Why didn't you quit?" I asked.

"Two weeks later I landed a record contract. I thought maybe bein' on top would be different. But it was the same shit, only dressed up in money." He chuckled. "Maybe you're right 'bout this world bein' better off than mine. Maybe I just can't accept it." He waved his cigar at the window. "Open that up. Let's see what it's doin' outside."

I did what he wanted. A chute of moonlight spilled into the room; the surf of low tide was a seething hiss. Roy John Harlow lifted his head, as if he'd scented something new and strange. "Pretty night," he said, and then, with a touch of desperation in his voice, he added, "Jesus God! I wish I was out in it!"

Darcy nudged me; she knew about my Swiss Army knife.

"You couldn't get nowhere," I said. "Those gypsies, they can track an ant through jungle."

"He could head south," said Darcy, fixing me with a disapproving stare. "The Indians might take him in."

"He'd never make it," I wanted to let him go, but I was still afraid of what the gypsies would do.

"Where I'd go," said Roy John Harlow, "couldn't nobody track me."

"Where's that?" I asked.

"Africa."

"What do you mean?" I asked.

He studied me, and I had trouble meeting his eyes. "You know how to get me outta here, don't you?" he said; he yanked at the handcuff. "Damn it! Help me!"

I couldn't say anything.

"You know what it's like for me?" he said. "I feel wrong. Outta place. I'm not even sure what the fuck I am, but I'm sure I'm not Roy John Harlow. His ghost, maybe, or his shadow. That makes me crazy, sick at heart. I spend most of my time in this box"—he rapped it—"and once in a while those bastards wake me, stand me up in front of a buncha raggedy fuckers so I can play 'em a blast from the past. That makes me even sicker, seein' how puny and screwed-up everything's gotten. It's been like that for three years. Livin' on stage, and dyin' after each show." His voice dropped to an urgent whisper. "I don't want it anymore, man! You gotta way to turn me loose, do it!"

"Let him go," said Darcy.

I looked at her, alarmed. "Darcy!" I said. "I think he's gonna kill himself."

Her face grave, she was watching Roy John Harlow, who was half-illuminated by the moonlight, appearing part shadow, part real. "Let him go," she repeated. "It's his right."

"Maybe so," I said angrily. "But his right don't include my havin' to help him." That, I realized, was bothering me as much as my fear of the gypsies. The thought of helping someone die, even someone not quite alive or alive in a peculiar way, didn't sit well with me.

"You think this ain't death?" Roy John Harlow kicked the box. "And this?" He gave the handcuff a savage jerk. "And these"—he pointed to his eyes—"you think that's life? C'mon, man! Lemme loose."

How he said that last part reminded me of him asking the gypsy to let him sit instead of returning to the box. I was doing the same as the gypsy, acting like the landlord of his soul . . . if he had one. And at the moment I couldn't believe that he didn't. "All right," I said, and kneeled beside him. I held his wrist to keep it steady while I worked on the lock. His flesh was warm, his pulse strong . . . so warm and strong that I was repelled again by the idea of his killing himself, and I stopped.

"Please," said Darcy, touching my shoulder. "It's like with Tony. Remember?"

Tony had been her pet cat, and after some kids had tortured it, leaving it half-crushed and spitting blood, I'd put it out of its misery. I wasn't sure that Roy John Harlow was a sick critter who needed death, but Darcy had a sensitivity to people that I didn't and I bowed to her judgment. I went back to work, and before long the cuff sprang open.

The glowing valentines of Roy John Harlow's eyes seemed brighter, as if registering an intensified emotion. He rubbed his wrist where the cuff had bitten into it. Then he got to his feet, boosted himself onto the window ledge and sat with one leg in, one out. Then he eased the other leg out and walked away. We climbed through the window after him. He was leaning on the railing, gazing toward Africa. Clouds were fraying across the moon, and the sea had a dull shine all over, like a plain of polished jet.

"I thought it'd be easier," he said.

"Maybe Darcy's right 'bout the Indians," I said. "We could . . . "

He cut me off. "Make it easy for me," he said to Darcy. "C'mere a minute."

She looked beautiful, walking toward him, with her long hair tangling in the breeze, the fine bones of her face sharp under the moonlight, and I felt a pang of jealousy. But though I knew scarcely anything in those days, I understood that whatever was to happen between them was a compassionate formality, that it existed in a separate context from what was between her and me, and I held myself in check. They stood close together. He ran a finger along the curve of her cheek, lifted a strand of her hair. "Jesus," he said. "Back when I was in style, they didn't make 'em like you anymore." He nuzzled her cheek, kissed it, then kissed her mouth. She started to put her arms around him, but he pushed her, gently away. "Not too much," he said. "Too much and I'll wanna do more than remember." He sat down on the edge of the pier, grasping the lowest rung of the railing, dangling his legs off the side. Darcy moved away from him and took a stand beside me. He remained motionless for a long time, so long that I thought he must have changed his mind. I could feel my heart slugging in my chest, tension crawling along my nerves, and I wanted to run over and haul him back. At last he turned to us, his face pale and set, and I wondered what he was seeing: was it life, the good things that even the most meager of lives can hold, or was it just two ragged kids with the dark ruin of the Boardwalk and a darker world behind? Then, so quickly that it was hard to believe he'd ever been there, he slipped beneath the railing and was gone.

Though in the years to come I was to think of his suicide as simply that—a man drowning himself, a sorrowful occurrence but nothing momentous—at the time he seemed a fabulous presence, and I half-expected a sign of his passing to appear in the sky or some great moan to be dredged up from the sea. But there was only the wind and the surf as always, and neither Darcy nor I went to the edge to see if he had surfaced. We sat in the lee of the dancehall, sheltering from the wind, which had suddenly picked up. We didn't talk much, just things like, "You warm enough?" and such. The longer I sat, the worse I felt. Roy John Harlow had wanted death, had acted of his own will, but who was to say he had known what was best, and hadn't I—by helping him—exerted as much influence as I might have if I had refused? The ripples of his death spread through my thoughts, magnifying them, until the event took on a complexity and importance that wouldn't fit inside my head, and I was left numb and hollow-feeling. Soon the sky began to pink, crimson streaks fanned across the horizon, and the tide turned. We climbed down the pilings and jumped into the cold water; we caught a comber and body-surfed toward shore, barreling straight for the facade of the Joyland Arcade, with its sun-bleached image of a goofy clown melting up from the gray light. I scraped my knee on the coquina-shell bottom and was almost grateful for the pain.

We stood on the beach, dazed, not knowing what to do next. Going home didn't make any sense after the night we'd had. Darcy fingered the zipper of the waterproof bag; she pulled it open, then she dropped the bag and started to cry. I hugged her, trying to give her comfort; but the comforting soon evolved into a kiss, and I was cupping her breast, and she was grinding her hips against me. Pa had told me not to hope for too much my first time with Darcy, that our nervousness and inexperience might make it more problematic than pleasurable; but our need for each other was so powerful that our anxieties were washed away, and it was perfect between us. And afterward, lying with my arms around her, our bodies crusted with sand, I felt that I had gotten clear of whatever wrongness there had been, that our lovemaking had been a spell worked contrary to the intricate sadness of the night. I was entranced by the sight of Darcy's body, which though I'd seen it often, had acquired a heightened gloss, a freshly matured beauty.

Sunrise flamed higher, a towering city of clouds pierced by sharply defined rays and mounted against a banded backdrop of mauve and crimson and gold. It was such a vivid, burning sky, it didn't seem that anything as old and ordinary as day would follow, that those colors would only deepen and grow richer, and for a moment I think I believed that the day would not follow, that with the death of Roy John Harlow and his music, something had been freed, some last smoke of the gone world faded, some change come full, and what passed for day would from now on and forever be something else, something new and green and hopeful, with its own music to suit. Maybe I was wrong, but it didn't matter. I turned again to Darcy, and—as the sun began to warm my back and seagulls mewed, wheeling above the ancient pier and the dancehall, looking dilapidated in that brimstone light—I moved with her in a sweet hectic celebration of what we had lost, and what we loved, and what we did not understand.

• • •

Lucius Shepard earned his living as a rock musician in and around Detroit for almost a decade. Stories like this are informed by his journey through the outlying precincts of the music business, a time he now views as a kind of affliction. His fiction has been awarded many honors including the Hugo, Nebula, and World Fantasy Awards. Forthcoming is a new collection, *Five Autobiographies*, and a novel, *The End of Life as We Know It*.

• • • •

The Big Flash
Norman Spinrad

T minus 200 days . . . and counting . . .

They came on freaky for my taste—but that's the name of the game: freaky means a draw in the rock business. And if the Mandala was going to survive in LA, competing with a network-owned joint like The American Dream, I'd just have to hold my nose and out-freak the opposition. So after I had dug the Four Horsemen for about an hour, I took them into my office to talk turkey.

I sat down behind my Salvation Army desk (the Mandala is the world's most expensive shoestring operation) and the Horsemen sat down on the bridge chairs sequentially, establishing the group's pecking order.

First the head honcho, lead guitar and singer, Stony Clarke—blond shoulder-length hair, eyes like something in a morgue when he took off his steel-rimmed shades, a reputation as a heavy acid-head and the look of a speed-freak behind it. Then Hair, the drummer, dressed like a Hell's Angel, swastikas and all, a junkie, with fanatic eyes that were a little too close together, making me wonder whether he wore swastikas because he grooved behind the Angel thing or made like an Angel because it let him groove behind the swastika in public. Number three was a cat who called himself Super Spade and wasn't kidding—he wore earrings, natural hair, a Stokely Carmichael sweatshirt, and on a thong around his neck a shrunken head that had been whitened with liquid shoe polish. He was the utility infielder: sitar, bass, organ, flute, whatever. Number four, who called himself Mr. Jones, was about the creepiest cat I had ever seen in a rock group, and that is saying something. He was their visuals, synthesizer, and electronics man. He was at least forty, wore Early Hippy clothes that looked like they had been made by Sy Devore, and was rumored to be some kind of Rand Corporation dropout. There's no business like show business.

"Okay, boys," I said, "you're strange, but you're my kind of strange. Where you worked before?"

"We ain't, baby," Clarke said. "We're the New Thing. I've been dealing crystal and acid in the Haight. Hair was drummer for some plastic group in

New York. The Super Spade claims it's the reincarnation of Bird and it don't pay to argue. Mr. Jones, he don't talk too much. Maybe he's a Martian. We just started putting our thing together."

One thing about this business, the groups that don't have square managers, you can get cheap. They talk too much.

"Groovy," I said. "I'm happy to give you guys your start. Nobody knows you, but I think you got something going. So I'll take a chance and give you a week's booking. One a.m. to closing, which is two, Tuesday through Sunday, four hundred a week."

"Are you Jewish?" asked Hair.

"What?"

"Cool it," Clarke ordered. Hair cooled it. "What it means," Clarke told me, "is that four hundred sounds like pretty light bread."

"We don't sign if there's an option clause," Mr. Jones said.

"The Jones-thing has a good point," Clarke said. "We do the first week for four hundred, but after that it's a whole new scene, dig?"

I didn't feature that. If they hit it big, I could end up not being able to afford them. But on the other hand $400 was light bread, and I needed a cheap closing act pretty bad.

"Okay," I said. "But a verbal agreement that I get first crack at you when you finish the gig."

"Word of honor," said Stony Clarke.

That's this business—the word of honor of an ex-dealer and speed-freak.

T minus 199 days . . . and counting . . .

Being unconcerned with ends, the military mind can be easily manipulated, easily controlled, and easily confused. Ends are defined as those goals set by civilian authority. Ends are the conceded province of civilians; means are the province of the military, whose duty it is to achieve the ends set for it by the most advantageous application of the means at its command.

Thus the confusion over the war in Asia among my uniformed clients at the Pentagon. The end has been duly set: eradication of the guerrillas. But the civilians have overstepped their bounds and meddled in means. The Generals regard this as unfair, a breach of contract, as it were. The Generals (or the faction among them most inclined to paranoia) are beginning to see the conduct of the war, the political limitation on means, as a ploy of the civilians for performing a putsch against their time-honored prerogatives.

This aspect of the situation would bode ill for the country, were it not for the fact that the growing paranoia among the Generals has enabled me to manipulate them into presenting both my scenarios to the President. The President has authorized implementation of the major scenario, provided that the minor scenario is successful in properly molding public opinion.

My major scenario is simple and direct. Knowing that the poor flying weather makes our conventional airpower, with its dependency on relative accuracy, ineffectual, the enemy has fallen into the pattern of grouping his forces into larger units and launching punishing annual offensives during the monsoon season. However, these larger units are highly vulnerable to tactical nuclear weapons, which do not depend upon accuracy for effect. Secure in the knowledge that domestic political considerations preclude the use of nuclear weapons, the enemy will once again form into division-sized units or larger during the next monsoon season. A parsimonious use of tactical nuclear weapons, even as few as twenty 100 kiloton bombs, employed simultaneously and in an advantageous pattern, will destroy a minimum of 200,000 enemy troops, or nearly two-thirds of his total force, in a twenty-four hour period. The blow will be crushing.

The minor scenario, upon whose success the implementation of the major scenario depends, is far more sophisticated, due to its subtler goal: public acceptance of, or, optimally, even public clamor for, the use of tactical nuclear weapons. The task is difficult, but my scenario is quite sound, if somewhat exotic, and with the full, if to-some-extent-clandestine support of the upper military hierarchy, certain civil government circles and the decision-makers in key aerospace corporations, the means now at my command would seem adequate. The risks, while statistically significant, do not exceed an acceptable level.

T minus 189 days . . . and counting . . .
The way I see it, the network deserved the shafting I gave them. They shafted me, didn't they? Four successful series I produce for those bastards, and two bomb out after thirteen weeks and they send me to the salt mines! A discotheque, can you imagine they make me producer at a lousy discotheque! A remittance man they make me, those schlockmeisters. Oh, those schnorrers made The American Dream sound like a kosher deal—twenty percent of the net, they say. And you got access to all our sets and contract players, it'll make you a rich man, Herm. And like a yuk, I sign, being broke at the time, without reading the fine print. I should know they've set up The American Dream as a tax loss? I should know that I've *gotta* use their lousy sets and stiff contract players and have it written off against my gross? I should know their shtick is to run The American Dream at a loss and then do a network TV

show out of the joint from which I don't see a penny? So I end up running the place for them at a paper loss, living on salary, while the network rakes it in off the TV show that I end up paying for out of my end.

Don't bums like that deserve to be shafted? It isn't enough they use me as a tax loss patsy, they gotta tell me who to book! "Go sign the Four Horsemen, the group that's packing them in at the Mandala," they say. "We want them on *A Night With The American Dream*. They're hot."

"Yeah, they're hot," I say, "which means they'll cost a mint, I can't afford it."

They show me more fine print—next time I read the contract with a microscope. I *gotta* book whoever they tell me to and I gotta absorb the cost on my books! It's enough to make a Litvak turn anti-Semite.

So I had to go to the Mandala to sign up these hippies. I made sure I didn't get there till 12:30 so I wouldn't have to stay in that nuthouse any longer than necessary. Such a dive! What Bernstein did was take a bankrupt Hollywood club on the Strip, knock down all the interior walls and put up this monster tent inside the shell. Just thin white screening over two-by-fours. Real shlock. Outside the tent, he's got projectors, lights, speakers, all the electronic mumbo-jumbo, and inside is like being surrounded by movie screens. Just the tent and the bare floor, not even a real stage, just a platform on wheels they shlepp in and out of the tent when they change groups.

So you can imagine he doesn't draw exactly a class crowd. Not with The American Dream up the street being run as a network tax loss. What they get is the smelly hard-core hippies I don't let in the door and the kind of j.d. high-school kids that think it's smart to hang around putzes like that. A lot of dope-pushing goes on. The cops don't like the place and the rousts draw professional troublemakers.

A real den of iniquity—I felt like I was walking onto a Casbah set. The last group had gone off and the Horsemen hadn't come on yet, so what you had was this crazy tent filled with hippies, half of them on acid or pot or amphetamine or for all I know Ajax, high-school would-be hippies, also mostly stoned and getting ugly, and a few crazy schwartzers looking to fight cops. All of them standing around waiting for something to happen, and about ready to make it happen. I stood near the door, just in case. As they say: "The vibes were making me uptight."

All of a sudden the house lights go out and it's black as a network executive's heart. I hold my hand on my wallet—in this crowd, tell me there are no pickpockets. Just the pitch black and dead silence for what, ten beats, and then I start feeling something, I don't know, like something crawling along my bones, but I know it's some kind of subsonic effect and not my imagination, because all the hippies are standing still and you don't hear a sound.

Then from monster speakers so loud you feel it in your teeth, a heartbeat, but heavy, slow, half-time like maybe a whale's heart. The thing crawling along my bones seems to be synchronized with the heartbeat and I feel almost like I am that big dumb heart beating there in the darkness.

Then a dark red spot—so faint it's almost infrared—hits the stage which they have wheeled out. On the stage are four uglies in crazy black robes—you know, like the Grim Reaper wears—with that ugly red light all over them like blood. Creepy. Boom-ba-boom. Boom-ba-boom. The heartbeat still going, still that subsonic bone-crawl and the hippies are staring at the Four Horsemen like mesmerized chickens.

The bass player, a regular jungle-bunny, picks up the rhythm of the heartbeat. Dum-da-dum. Dum-da-dum, The drummer beats it out with earsplitting rim-shots. Then the electric guitar, tuned like a strangling cat, makes with horrible heavy chords. Whang-ka-whang. Whang-ka-whang.

It's just awful, I feel it in my guts, my bones; my eardrums are just like some great big throbbing vein.

Everybody is swaying to it, I'm swaying to it. Boom-ba-boom. Boom-ba-boom. Then the guitarist starts to chant in rhythm with the heartbeat, in a hoarse, shrill voice like somebody dying: "*The* big *flash* . . . *The* big *flash* . . . "

And the guy at the visuals console diddles around and rings of light start to climb the walls of the tent, blue at the bottom becoming green as they get higher, then yellow, orange and finally as they become a circle on the ceiling, eye-killing neon-red. Each circle takes exactly one heartbeat to climb the walls.

Boy, what an awful feeling! Like I was a tube of toothpaste being squeezed in rhythm till the top of my head felt like it was gonna squirt up with those circles of light through the ceiling. And then they start to speed it up gradually. The same heartbeat, the same rim-shots, same chords, same circles of light, same "*The* big *flash* . . . *The* big *flash* . . . " same bass, same subsonic bone-crawl, but just a little faster . . . Then faster! Faster!

Thought I would die! Knew I would die! Heart beating like a lunatic. Rim-shots like a machine gun.

Circles of light sucking me up the walls, into the red neon hole. Oh, incredible! Over and over faster faster till the voice was a scream and the heartbeat a boom and the rim-shots a whine and the guitar howled feedback and my bones were jumping out of my body—

Every spot in the place came on and I went blind from the sudden light—

An awful explosion—sound came over every speaker, so loud it rocked me on my feet—I felt myself squirting out of the top of my head and loved it.

Then:

The explosion became a rumble—

The light seemed to run together into a circle on the ceiling, leaving everything else black. And the circle became a fireball. The fireball became a slow-motion film of an atomic bomb cloud as the rumbling died away. Then the picture faded into a moment of total darkness and the house lights came on. What a number!

Gevalt, what an act!

So after the show, when I got them alone and found out they had no manager, not even an option to the Mandala, I thought faster than I ever had in my life.

To make a long story short and sweet, I gave the network the royal screw. I signed the Horsemen to a contract that made me their manager and gave me 20 percent of their take. Then I booked them into The American Dream at ten thousand a week, wrote a check as proprietor of The American Dream, handed the check to myself as manager of the Four Horsemen, then resigned as a network flunky, leaving them with a $10,000 bag and me with 20 percent of the hottest group since the Beatles.

What the hell, he who lives by the fine print shall perish by the fine print.

T minus 148 days . . . and counting . . .

"You haven't seen the tape yet, have you, B.D.?" Jake said. He was nervous as hell. When you reach my level in the network structure, you're used to making subordinates nervous, but Jake Pitkin was head of network continuity, not some office boy, and certainly should be used to dealing with executives at my level. Was the rumor really true?

We were alone in the screening room. It was doubtful that the projectionist could hear us.

"No, I haven't seen it yet," I said. "But I've heard some strange stories."

Jake looked positively deathly. "About the tape?" he said.

"About you, Jake," I said, deprecating the rumor with an easy smile. "That you don't want to air the show."

"It's true, B.D.," Jake said quietly.

"Do you realize what you're saying? Whatever our personal tastes—and I personally think there's something unhealthy about them—the Four Horsemen are the hottest thing in the country right now and that dirty little thief Herm Gellman held us up for a quarter of a million for an hour show. It cost another two hundred thousand to make it. We've spent another hundred thousand on promotion. We're getting top dollar from the sponsors. There's over a million dollars one way or the other riding on that show. That's how much we blow if we don't air it."

"I know that, B.D.," Jake said. "I also know this could cost me my job. Think about that. Because knowing all that, I'm still against airing the tape. I'm going to run the closing segment for you. I'm sure enough that you'll agree with me to stake my job on it."

I had a terrible feeling in my stomach. I have superiors too and The Word was that *A Trip With The Four Horsemen* would be aired, period. No matter what. Something funny was going on. The price we were getting for commercial time was a precedent and the sponsor was a big aerospace company which had never bought network time before. What really bothered me was that Jake Pitkin had no reputation for courage; yet here he was laying his job on the line. He must be pretty sure I would come around to his way of thinking or he wouldn't dare. And though I couldn't tell Jake, I had no choice in the matter whatsoever.

"Okay, roll it," Jake said into the intercom mike. "What you're going to see," he said as the screening room lights went out, "is the last number."

On the screen:

A shot of empty blue sky, with soft, lazy electric guitar chords behind it. The camera pans across a few clouds to an extremely long shot on the sun. As the sun, no more than a tiny circle of light, moves into the center of the screen, a sitar-drone comes in behind the guitar.

Very slowly, the camera begins to zoom in on the sun. As the image of the sun expands, the sitar gets louder and the guitar begins to fade and a drum starts to give the sitar a beat. The sitar gets louder, the beat gets more pronounced and begins to speed up as the sun continues to expand. Finally, the whole screen is filled with unbearably bright light behind which the sitar and drum are in a frenzy.

Then over this, drowning out the sitar and drum, a voice like a sick thing in heat: *"Brighter . . . than a thousand suns . . . "* The light dissolves into a close-up of a beautiful dark-haired girl with huge eyes and moist lips, and suddenly there is nothing on the sound track but soft guitar and voices crooning low: *"Brighter . . . Oh God, it's brighter . . . brighter . . . than a thousand suns . . . "*

The girl's face dissolves into a full shot of the Four Horsemen in their Grim Reaper robes and the same melody that had played behind the girl's face shifts into a minor key, picks up whining, reverberating electric guitar chords and a sitar-drone and becomes a dirge: *"Darker . . . the world grows darker . . . "*

And a series of cuts in time to the dirge:

A burning village in Asia strewn with bodies—

"Darker . . . the world grows darker . . . "

The corpse-heap at Auschwitz—

"Until it gets so dark . . . "

A gigantic auto graveyard with gaunt Negro children dwarfed in the foreground—*"I think I'll die . . . "*

A Washington ghetto in flames with the Capitol misty in the background—

" . . . before the daylight comes . . . "

A jump-cut to an extreme close-up on the lead singer of the Horsemen, his face twisted into a mask of desperation and ecstasy. And the sitar is playing double-time, the guitar is wailing and he is screaming at the top of his lungs: *"But before I die, let me make that trip before the nothing comes . . . "*

The girl's face again, but transparent, with a blinding yellow light shining through it. The sitar beat gets faster and faster with the guitar whining behind it and the voice is working itself up into a howling frenzy: *" . . . the last big flash to light my sky . . . "*

Nothing but the blinding light now—

" . . . and zap! The world is done . . . "

An utterly black screen for a beat that becomes black fading to blue at a horizon—

" . . . but before we die let's dig that high that frees us from our binds . . . that blows all cool that ego-drool and burns us from our mind . . . the last big flash, mankind's last gas, the trip we can't take twice . . . "

Suddenly, the music stops dead for half a beat. Then:

The screen is lit up by an enormous fireball—

A shattering rumble—

The fireball coalesces into a mushroom-pillar cloud as the roar goes on. As the roar begins to die out, fire is visible inside the monstrous nuclear cloud. And the girl's face is faintly visible superimposed over the cloud.

A soft voice, amplified over the roar, obscenely reverential now: *"Brighter . . . great God, it's brighter . . . brighter than a thousand suns . . . "*

And the screen went blank and the lights came on. I looked at Jake. Jake looked at me.

"That's sick," I said. "That's really sick."

"You don't want to run a thing like that, do you, B.D.?" Jake said softly.

I made some rapid mental calculations. The loathsome thing ran something under five minutes . . . it could be done . . .

"You're right, Jake," I said. "We won't run a thing like that. We'll cut it out of the tape and squeeze in another commercial at each break. That should cover the time."

"You don't understand," Jake said. "The contract Herm rammed down our throats doesn't allow us to edit. The show's a package—all or nothing. Besides, the whole show's like that."

"All like that? What do you mean, all like that?" Jake squirmed in his seat. "Those guys are . . . well, perverts, B.D.," he said.

"Perverts?"

"They're . . . well, they're in love with the atom bomb or something. Every number leads up to the same thing."

"You mean . . . they're *all* like that?"

"You got the picture, B. D.," Jake said. "We run an hour of *that* or we run nothing at all."

"Jesus." I knew what I wanted to say. Burn the tape and write off the million dollars. But I also knew it would cost me my job. And I knew that five minutes after I was out the door, they would have someone in my job who would see things their way. Even my superiors seemed to be just handing down The Word from higher up. I had no choice. There was no choice.

"I'm sorry, Jake," I said. "We run it."

"I resign," said Jake Pitkin, who had no reputation for courage.

T minus 10 days . . . and counting . . .
"It's a clear violation of the Test-Ban Treaty," I said.

The Under Secretary looked as dazed as I felt. "We'll call it a peaceful use of atomic energy, and let the Russians scream," he said.

"It's insane."

"Perhaps," the Under Secretary said. "But you have your orders, General Carson, and I have mine. From higher up. At exactly eight fifty-eight p.m. local time on July fourth, you will drop a fifty kiloton atomic bomb on the designated ground zero at Yucca Flats."

"But the people . . . the television crews . . . "

"Will be at least two miles outside the danger zone. Surely, SAC can manage that kind of accuracy under 'laboratory conditions.'"

I stiffened. "I do not question the competence of any bomber crew under my command to perform this mission," I said. "I question the reason for the mission. I question the sanity of the orders."

The Under Secretary shrugged, smiled wanly. "Welcome to the club."

"You mean you don't know what this is all about either?"

"All I know is what was transmitted to me by the Secretary of Defense, and I got the feeling he doesn't know everything, either. You know that the Pentagon has been screaming for the use of tactical nuclear weapons to end the war in Asia—you SAC boys have been screaming the loudest. Well, several months ago, the President conditionally approved a plan for the use of tactical nuclear weapons during the next monsoon season."

I whistled. The civilians were finally coming to their senses. Or were they?

"But what does that have to do with—?"

"Public opinion," the Under Secretary said. "It was conditional upon a drastic change in public opinion. At the time the plan was approved, the polls showed that seventy-eight point eight percent of the population opposed the use of tactical nuclear weapons, nine point eight percent favored their use and the rest were undecided or had no opinion. The President agreed to authorize the use of tactical nuclear weapons by a date, several months from now, which is still top secret, provided that by that date at least sixty-five percent of the population approved their use and no more than twenty percent actively opposed it."

"I see . . . Just a ploy to keep the Joint Chiefs quiet."

"General Carson," the Under Secretary said, "apparently you are out of touch with the national mood. After the first Four Horsemen show, the polls showed that twenty-five percent of the population approved the use of nuclear weapons. After the second show, the figure was forty-one percent. It is now forty-eight percent. Only thirty-two percent are now actively opposed."

"You're trying to tell me that a rock group—"

"A rock group and the cult around it, General. It's become a national hysteria. There are imitators. Haven't you seen those buttons?"

"The ones with a mushroom cloud on them that say 'Do it'?"

The Under Secretary nodded. "Your guess is as good as mine whether the National Security Council just decided that the Horsemen hysteria could be used to mold public opinion, or whether the Four Horsemen were their creatures to begin with. But the results are the same either way—the Horsemen and the cult around them have won over precisely that element of the population which was most adamantly opposed to nuclear weapons: hippies, students, dropouts, draft-age youth. Demonstrations against the war and against nuclear weapons have died down. We're pretty close to that sixty-five percent. Someone—perhaps the President himself—has decided that one more big Four Horsemen show will put us over the top."

"The President is behind this?"

"No one else can authorize the detonation of an atomic bomb, after all," the Under Secretary said. "We're letting them do the show live from Yucca Flats. It's being sponsored by an aerospace company heavily dependent on defense contracts. We're letting them truck in a live audience. Of course the government is behind it."

"And SAC drops an A-bomb as the show-stopper?"

"Exactly."

"I saw one of those shows," I said. "My kids were watching it. I got the strangest feeling . . . I almost wanted that red telephone to ring . . . "

"I know what you mean," the Under Secretary said. "Sometimes I get the feeling that whoever's behind this has gotten caught up in the hysteria themselves . . . that the Horsemen are now using whoever was using them . . . a closed circle. But I've been tired lately. The war's making us all so tired. If only we could get it all over with . . . "

"We'd all like to get it over with one way or the other," I said.

T minus 60 minutes . . . and counting . . .
I had orders to muster *Backfish*'s crew for the live satellite relay of *The Four Horsemen's Fourth.* Superficially, it might seem strange to order the whole Polaris fleet to watch a television show, but the morale factor involved was quite significant.

Polaris subs are frustrating duty. Only top sailors are chosen and a good sailor craves action. We spend most of our time honing skills that must never be used. Deterrence is a sound strategy but a terrible drain on the men of the deterrent forces—a drain exacerbated in the past by the negative attitude of our countrymen toward our mission. Men who, in the service of their country, polish their skills to a razor edge and then must refrain from exercising them have a right to resent being treated as pariahs.

Therefore the positive change in the public attitude toward us that seems to be associated with the Four Horsemen has made them mascots of a kind to the Polaris fleet. In their strange way they seem to speak for us and to us.

I chose to watch the show in the missile control center, where a full crew must always be ready to launch the missiles on five-minute notice. I have always felt a sense of communion with the duty watch in the missile control center that I cannot share with the other men under my command. Here we are not Captain and crew but mind and hand. Should the order come, the will to fire the missiles will be mine and the act will be theirs. At such a moment, it will be good not to feel alone.

All eyes were on the television set mounted above the main console as the show came on and . . .

The screen was filled with a whirling spiral pattern, metallic yellow on metallic blue. There was a droning sound that seemed part sitar and part electronic and I had the feeling that the sound was somehow coming from inside my head and the spiral seemed etched directly on my retinas. It hurt mildly, yet nothing in the world could have made me turn away.

Then two voices, chanting against each other:

"Let it all come in . . . "

"Let it all come out . . . "

"In . . . *out* . . . in . . . *out* . . . in . . . *out* . . . "

My head seemed to be pulsing—in-out, in-out, in-out—and the spiral pattern began to pulse color-changes with the words: yellow-on-blue (in) . . . green-on-red *(out)* . . . *in-out-in-out-in-out-in-out* . . .

In the screen . . . *out* my head . . . I seemed to be beating against some kind of invisible membrane between myself and the screen as if something were trying to embrace my mind and I were fighting it . . . But why was I fighting it?

The pulsing, the chanting, got faster and faster till *in* could not be told from *out* and negative spiral afterimages formed in my eyes faster than they could adjust to the changes, piled up on each other faster and faster till it seemed my head would explode—

The chanting and the droning broke and there were the Four Horsemen, in their robes, playing on some stage against a backdrop of clear blue sky. And a single voice, soothing now: "You are in . . . "

Then the view was directly above the Horsemen and I could see that they were on some kind of circular platform. The view moved slowly and smoothly up and away and I saw that the circular stage was atop a tall tower; around the tower and completely encircling it was a huge crowd seated on desert sands that stretched away to an empty infinity.

"And we are in and they are in . . . "

I was down among the crowd now; they seemed to melt and flow like plastic, pouring from the television screen to enfold me . . .

"And we are all in here together . . . "

A strange and beautiful feeling . . . the music got faster and wilder, ecstatic . . . the hull of the *Backfish* seemed unreal . . . the crowd was swaying to it around me . . . the distance between myself and the Crowd seemed to dissolve . . . I was there . . . they were here . . . We were transfixed . . .

"Oh yeah, we are all in here together . . . together . . . "

T minus 45 minutes . . . and counting . . .
Jeremy and I sat staring at the television screen, ignoring each other and everything around us. Even with the short watches and the short tours of duty, you can get to feeling pretty strange down here in a hole in the ground under tons of concrete, just you and the guy with the other key, with nothing to do but think dark thoughts and get on each other's nerves. We're all supposed to be as stable as men can be, or so they tell us, and they must be right because the world's still here. I mean, it wouldn't take much—just two guys on the same watch over the same three Minutemen flipping out at the same time, turning their keys in the dual lock, pressing the three buttons . . . Pow! World War III!

A bad thought, the kind we're not supposed to think or I'll start watching Jeremy and he'll start watching me and we'll get a paranoia feedback going . . . But that can't happen; we're too stable, too responsible. As long as we remember that it's healthy to feel a little spooky down here, we'll be all right.

But the television set is a good idea. It keeps us in contact with the outside world, keeps it real. It'd be too easy to start thinking that the missile control center down here is the only real world and that nothing that happens up there really matters . . . Bad thought!

The Four Horsemen . . . somehow these guys help you get it all out. I mean that feeling that it might be better to release all that tension, get it all over with. Watching The Four Horsemen, you're able to go with it without doing any harm, let it wash over you and then through you. I suppose they are crazy; they're all the human craziness in ourselves that we've got to keep very careful watch over down here. Letting it all come out watching the Horsemen makes it surer that none of it will come out down here. I guess that's why a lot of us have taken to wearing those "Do It" buttons off duty. The brass doesn't mind; they seem to understand that it's the kind of inside sick joke we need to keep us functioning.

Now that spiral thing they had started the show with—and the droning—came back on. Zap! I was right back in the screen again, as if the commercial hadn't happened.

"We are all in here together . . . "

And then a close-up of the lead singer, looking straight at me, as close as

Jeremy and somehow more real. A mean-looking guy with something behind his eyes that told me he knew where everything lousy and rotten was at.

A bass began to thrum behind him and some kind of electronic hum that set my teeth on edge. He began playing his guitar, mean and low-down. And singing in that kind of drop-dead tone of voice that starts brawls in bars:

"I stabbed my mother and I mugged my paw . . . "

A riff of heavy guitar-chords echoed the words mockingly as a huge swastika (red-on-black, black-on-red) pulsed like a naked vein on the screen—

The face of the Horseman, leering—

"Nailed my sister to the toilet door . . . "

Guitar behind the pulsing swastika—

"Drowned a puppy in a cement machine . . . Burned a kitten just to hear it scream . . . "

On the screen, just a big fire burning in slow motion, and the voice became a slow, shrill, agonized wail:

"Oh God, I've got this red-hot fire burning in the marrow of my brain . . .

"Oh yes, I got this fire burning . . . in the stinking marrow of my brain . . .

"Gotta get me a blowtorch . . . and set some naked flesh on flame . . . "

The fire dissolved into the face of a screaming Oriental woman, who ran through a burning village clawing at the napalm on her back.

"I got this message . . . boiling in the bubbles of my blood . . . A man ain't nothing but a fire burning . . . in a dirty glob of mud . . . "

A film-clip of a Nuremburg rally: a revolving swastika of marching men waving torches—

Then the leader of the Horsemen superimposed over the twisted flaming cross:

"Don't you hate me, baby, can't you feel somethin' screaming in your mind?

"Don't you hate me, baby, feel me drowning you in slime!"

Just the face of the Horseman howling hate.

"Oh yes, I'm a monster, mother . . . "

A long view of the crowd around the platform, on their feet, waving arms, screaming soundlessly. Then a quick zoom in and a kaleidoscope of faces, eyes feverish, mouths open and howling—

"Just call me—"

The face of the Horseman superimposed over the crazed faces of the crowd—

"Mankind!"

I looked at Jeremy. He was toying with the key on the chain around his neck. He was sweating. I suddenly realized that I was sweating too and that my own key was throbbing in my hand alive . . .

T minus 13 minutes . . . and counting . . .

A funny feeling, the Captain watching the Four Horsemen here in the *Backfish*'s missile control center with us. Sitting in front of my console watching the television set with the Captain kind of breathing down my neck . . . I got the feeling he knew what was going through me and I couldn't know what was going through him . . . and it gave the fire inside me a kind of greasy feel I didn't like . . .

Then the commercial was over and that spiral-thing came on again and whoosh! it sucked me right back into the television set and I stopped worrying about the Captain or anything like that . . .

Just the spiral going yellow-blue, red-green, and then starting to whirl and whirl, faster and faster, changing colors and whirling, whirling, whirling . . . And the sound of a kind of Coney Island carousel tinkling behind it, faster and faster and faster, whirling and whirling and whirling, flashing red-green, yellow-blue, and whirling, whirling, whirling . . .

And this big hum filling my body and whirling, whirling, whirling . . . My muscles relaxing, going limp, whirling, whirling, whirling, all whirling . . .

And in the center of the flashing spiraling colors, a bright dot of color-less light, right at the center, not moving, not changing, while the whole world went whirling and whirling in colors around it, and the humming was coming from the dot the way the carousel-music was coming from the spinning colors and the dot was humming its song to me . . .

The dot was a light way down at the end of a long, whirling, whirling tunnel. The humming started to get a little louder. The bright dot started to get a little bigger. I was drifting down the tunnel toward it, whirling, whirling, whirling . . .

T minus 11 minutes . . . and counting . . .

Whirling, whirling, whirling down a long, long tunnel of pulsing colors, whirling, whirling, toward the circle of light way down at the end of the tunnel . . . How nice it would be to finally get there and soak up the beautiful hum filling my body and then I could forget that I was down here in this hole in the ground with a hard brass key in my hand, just Duke and me, down here in a cave under the ground that was a spiral of flashing colors, whirling, whirling toward the friendly light at the end of the tunnel, whirling, whirling . . .

T minus 10 minutes . . . and counting . . .

The circle of light at the end of the whirling tunnel was getting bigger and bigger, and the humming was getting louder and louder and I was feeling better and better and the *Backfish*'s missile control center was getting dimmer and dimmer as the awful weight of command got lighter and lighter, whirling, whirling, and I felt so good I wanted to cry, whirling, whirling . . .

T minus 9 minutes . . . and counting . . .
Whirling, whirling . . . I was whirling, Jeremy was whirling, the hole in the ground was whirling, and the circle of light at the end of the tunnel whirled closer and closer and—I was through! A place filled with yellow light. Pale metal-yellow light. Then pale metallic blue. Yellow. Blue. Yellow. Blue. Yellow-blue-yellow-blue-yellow-blue-yellow . . .

Pure light pulsing . . . and pure sound droning. And just the *feeling* of letters I couldn't read between the pulses-not-yellow and not-blue-too quick and too faint to be visible, but important, very important . . .

And then a voice that seemed to be singing from inside my head, almost as if it were my own:

"Oh, oh, oh . . . don't I really wanna know . . . Oh, oh, oh, . . . don't I really wanna know . . . "

The world pulsing, flashing around those words I couldn't read, couldn't quite read, had to read, could almost read . . .

"Oh, oh, oh, . . . great God I really wanna know . . . "

Strange amorphous shapes clouding the blue-yellow-blue flickering universe, hiding the words I had to read . . . Dammit, why wouldn't they get out of the way so I could find out what I had to know!

"Tell me tell me tell me tell me tell me . . . Gotta know gotta know gotta know gotta know . . . "

T minus 7 minutes . . . and counting . . .
Couldn't read the words! Why wouldn't the Captain let me read the words?

And that voice inside me: *"Gotta know . . . gotta know . . . gotta know why it hurts me so . . . "* Why wouldn't it shut up and let me read the words? Why wouldn't the words hold still? Or just slow down a little? If they'd slow down a little, I could read them and then I'd know what I had to do . . .

T minus 6 minutes . . . and counting . . .
I felt the sweaty key in the palm of my hand . . . I saw Duke stroking his own key. Had to know!

Now—through the pulsing blue-yellow-blue light and the unreadable words that were building up an awful pressure in the back of my brain—I could see the Four Horsemen. They were on their knees, crying, looking up at something and begging: *"Tell me tell me tell me tell me . . . "*

Then soft billows of rich red-and-orange fire filled the world and a huge voice was trying to speak. But it couldn't form the words. It stuttered and moaned—the yellow-blue-yellow flashing around the words I couldn't read—the same words, I suddenly sensed, that the voice of the fire was trying so hard to form—and the Four Horsemen on their knees begging: *"Tell me tell me tell me . . . "*

The friendly warm fire trying so hard to speak—

"Tell me tell me tell me tell me . . . "

T minus 4 minutes . . . and counting . . .

What were the words? What was the order? I could sense my men silently imploring me to tell them.

After all, I was their captain, it was my duty to tell them. It was my duty to find out!

"Tell me tell me tell me . . . " the robed figures on their knees implored through the flickering pulse in my brain and I could almost make out the words . . . almost . . .

"Tell me tell me tell me . . . " I whispered to the warm orange fire that was trying so hard but couldn't quite form the words. The men were whispering it too: "Tell me tell me . . . "

T minus 3 minutes . . . and counting . . .

The question burning blue and yellow in my brain: WHAT WAS THE FIRE TRYING TO TELL ME? WHAT WERE THE WORDS I COULDN'T READ?

Had to unlock the words! Had to find the key!

A key . . . *The* key? THE KEY! And there was the lock that imprisoned the words, right in front of me! Put the key in the lock . . . I looked at Jeremy. Wasn't there some reason, long ago and far away, why Jeremy might try to stop me from putting the key in the lock?

But Jeremy didn't move as I fitted the key into the lock . . .

T minus 2 minutes . . . and counting . . .

Why wouldn't the Captain tell me what the order was? The fire knew, but it couldn't tell. My head ached from the pulsing, but I couldn't read the words. "Tell me tell me tell me . . . " I begged.

Then I realized that the Captain was asking too.

• • •

T minus 90 seconds . . . and counting . . .
"Tell me tell me tell me . . . " the Horsemen begged. And the words I couldn't read were a fire in my brain.

Duke's key was in the lock in front of us. From very far away, he said: "We have to do it together."

Of course . . . our keys . . . our keys would unlock the words! I put my key into the lock.

One, two, three, we turned our keys together. A lid on the console popped open. Under the lid were three red buttons. Three signs on the console lit up in red letters: ARMED.

T minus 60 seconds . . . and counting . . .
The men were waiting for me to give some order. I didn't know what the order was. A magnificent orange fire was trying to tell me but it couldn't get the words out . . . Robed figures were praying to the fire . . .

Then, through the yellow-blue flicker that hid the words I had to read, I saw a vast crowd encircling a tower. The crowd was on its feet begging silently—

The tower in the center of the crowd became the orange fire that was trying to tell me what the words were—

Became a great mushroom of billowing smoke and blinding orange-red glare . . .

T minus 30 seconds . . . and counting . . .
The huge pillar of fire was trying to tell Jeremy and me what the words were, what we had to do. The crowd was screaming at the cloud of flame. The yellow-blue flicker was getting faster and faster behind the mushroom cloud. I could almost read the words! I could see that there were two of them!

T minus 20 seconds . . . and counting . . .
Why didn't the Captain tell us? I could almost see the words!

Then I heard the crowd around the beautiful mushroom cloud shouting: "DO IT! DO IT! DO IT! DO IT! DO IT!"

What did they want me to do? Did Duke know?
9
The men were waiting! What was the order? They hunched over the firing controls, waiting . . . The firing controls . . . ?

"DO IT! DO IT! DO IT! DO IT! DO IT!"
8

"DO IT! DO IT! DO IT!" the crowd screaming.

"Jeremy!" I shouted. "I can read the words!"

7

My hands hovered over my bank of firing buttons . . .

"DO IT! DO IT! DO IT! DO IT!" the words said.

Didn't the captain understand?

6

"What do they want us to do, Jeremy?"

5

Why didn't the mushroom cloud give the order? My men were waiting! A good sailor craves action.

Then a great voice spoke from the pillar of fire: "DO IT . . . DO IT . . . DO IT . . ."

4

"There's only one thing we can do down here, Duke."

3

"The order, men! Action! Fire!"

2

Yes, yes, yes! Jeremy—

1

I reached for my bank of firing buttons. All along the console, the men reached for their buttons. But I was too fast for them! I would be first!

0

THE BIG FLASH

• • •

Norman Spinrad is the author of over twenty novels, including *Little Heroes*, a definitive rock/sf novel, and the latest to be published in the U.S., *He Walked Among Us*. He has a long history as a song writer and sometime performing and recording vocalist, having co-written about half the stuff on the Heldon album *Only Chaos Is Real*, recorded on the Heldon album *East/West* and the album *Home of the Page*, among others, performed live in Paris, New York, Bordeaux, the Transmusical Festival, etc. Other novels include *Bug Jack Barron*, *The Iron Dream*, *Child of Fortune*, *Pictures At 11*, *Greenhouse Summer*, *The Druid King*, and *Passing Through the Flame*, the title song for which he was recorded, as vocalist, by Schizotrope. It can be found on YouTube, along with the title song of *Only Chaos Is Real*.

• • • •

About the Editor

Rock On is Paula Guran's sixteenth anthology; her seventeenth, *Season of Wonder*, will be published about a month after this one. She serves as senior editor for Prime Books. A volume of her Year's Best Dark Fantasy and Horror series appears annually. She edited the Juno fantasy imprint for six years from its small press inception through its incarnation as an imprint of Simon & Schuster's Pocket Books.

She often leaves her biography out of anthologies altogether, and never says anything personal if she includes one. But this time, she is.

The idea for this anthology came out her love of rock and roll, science fiction, and fantasy. Guran's one of those editors who knows she doesn't have the imagination to write fiction, so she wisely avoids trying to. That only enhances her admiration of those who *do* write fiction. The same is true of musicians. She's hopelessly unmusical, never accomplished much with an instrument of any sort, and can't carry a tune in either a bucket or vocally.

Although she passed her love of music on to all four of her children, Erik, her youngest, was particularly talented. The beginning of the introduction to this anthology is a near-verbatim conversation with him.

But he didn't much like reading fiction. So, when his mother came up with the idea for this anthology, she thought she might finally produce something he might read.

Now it is done, but he won't be reading it.

Erik died in his sleep on June 9, 2012 at age twenty-two.

The editor really wishes you could have heard him sing.

••••

Acknowledgements

All stories are published with the permission of the authors.

"Hobnoblin Blues" by Elizabeth Bear © 2008 Elizabeth Bear. First publication: *Realms of Fantasy*, February 2008.

"Arise" by Poppy Z. Brite © 1998 Poppy Z. Brite. First Publication: *Are You Loathsome Tonight?* (Gauntlet Press).

"Stone" by Edward Bryant © 1978 Mercury Press Inc. First publication: *The Magazine of Fantasy & Science Fiction*, February 1978.

"Rock On" by Pat Cadigan © 1986 Pat Cadigan. First publication: *Light Years and Dark: Science Fiction and Fantasy Of and For Our Time*, ed. Michael Bishop (Berkley).

"Mercenary" by Lawrence C. Connolly © 2012 Lawrence C. Connolly. First publication, original to this volume.

"We Love Lydia Love" by Bradley Denton © 1994 Mercury Press Inc. First publication: *The Magazine of Fantasy & Science Fiction*, October-November 1994.

"The Erl-King" by Elizabeth Hand © 1993 Elizabeth Hand. First publication: *Full Spectrum 4*, eds. Lou Aronica, Betsy Mitchell & Amy Stout (Bantam Spectra).

"Mourningstar" by Del James © 2012 Del James. First publication, original to this volume.

"Last Rising Sun" by Graham Joyce © 1992 Graham Joyce. First publication: *In Dreams*, eds. Paul J. McAuley & Kim Newman (Gollancz).

"Paedomorphosis" by Caitlín R. Kiernan © 2000 Caitlín R. Kiernan. First publication: *Tales of Pain and Wonder* (Gauntlet Press).

• • • •